PRAISE FOR MARY ELLEN TAYLOR

After Paris

"*After Paris* by novelist Mary Ellen Taylor is impressively original, skillfully written, reader engaging, and a fully entertaining story from start to finish . . . The kind of tale that will linger in the mind and memory of the reader long after the book has been finished and set back upon the shelf . . . An extraordinary and highly recommended pick."

—Midwest Book Review

The Words We Whisper

"Taylor expertly employs the parallel timelines to highlight the impact of the past on the present, exploring the complexities of familial relationships while peeling back the layers of her flawed, realistic characters. Readers are sure to be swept away."

—*Publishers Weekly*

"A luscious interweaving of a spy thriller and a family saga."
—*Historical Novels Review*

Honeysuckle Season

"This memorable story is sure to tug at readers' heartstrings."
—*Publishers Weekly*

Spring House

Winter Cottage

The View from Prince Street

Sweet Expectations

"Absorbing characters, a hint of mystery, and touching self-discovery elevate this novel above many others in the genre."

—RT Book Reviews

"A charming and very engaging story about the nature of family and the meaning of love."

—Seattle Post-Intelligencer

The Union Street Bakery

"Taylor serves up a great mix of vivid setting, history, drama, and everyday life."

—The Herald-Sun (Durham, North Carolina)

THE SKY
BENEATH HER

OTHER TITLES BY MARY ELLEN TAYLOR

After Paris

The Promise of Tomorrow

When the Rain Ends

The Brighter the Light

The Words We Whisper

Honeysuckle Season

Spring House

Winter Cottage

The Alexandria Series

At the Corner of King Street

The View from Prince Street

The Union Street Bakery Series

The Union Street Bakery

Sweet Expectations

THE SKY BENEATH HER

A NOVEL

MARY ELLEN TAYLOR

Published by Montlake, Seattle

www.apub.com

Amazon, the Amazon logo, and Montlake are trademarks of Amazon.com, Inc., or its affiliates.

EU product safety contact:
Amazon Media EU S. à r.l.
38, avenue John F. Kennedy, L-1855 Luxembourg
amazonpublishing-gpsr@amazon.com

ISBN-13: 9781662530142 (paperback)
ISBN-13: 9781662530159 (digital)

Cover design by Mumtaz Mustafa
Cover image: © Gabriela Alejandra Rosell / ArcAngel Images; © Braden Call / Getty Images; © Jamiesmyname2024 / Shutterstock

Printed in the United States of America

THE SKY
BENEATH HER

PROLOGUE

Sunday, September 21, 1941, 2:00 a.m.
Vienna, Austria

This wasn't the first time I'd run for my life. But if this escape failed, it'd be my last.

The calm waters of the Danube River flowed gently past as I ran along its banks. It was a peaceful night. The skies were overcast. Encouraged, I hurried and ignored my body's pleas to stop. But there was no sign of the promised vessel that would carry me to safety. I was alone.

A dog barked. Soldiers' distant shouts echoed off the water. A gunshot rang out. Vienna had become a city of treachery, filled with neighbors who betrayed neighbors for honor, prestige, or fear.

No need to see my face to know it was red, my right eye swollen. Breathless, I ran and clutched my bundle tighter. I had hours before my absence would be noticed.

"Please be here," I whispered.

Finally, I reached a bend in the river, and my stomach cramped. I stopped and caught my breath.

Had I been deceived by the woman who'd floated in and out of my life over the years and promised me a chance to escape? Had she sent the boat she'd sworn to deliver?

The waters licked against the shore, splashing soft waves over pebbles. My mother used to say the Danube River dreamed in currents and hid mythical shape-shifting sea and river creatures.

My mother, Elke, had always sworn she'd found me on the banks of the Danube on a clear, cold spring day. Elke maintained she'd been strolling along the river, as she often did during her midday break from the bookshop. She said blistering winds had carried my wails as if I'd railed against the river gods who'd abandoned me to the land.

At first my howls frightened her. But she kept walking and searched the river's muddy edge. She said she'd found me lying in the grime, naked, dressed only in green algae and river silt. My pink face was scrunched, and my fists clenched as I cried.

Mama said she'd immediately scooped me up, wrapped me in her wool coat, and carried me back to the bookshop where she lived with her Uncle Eric. My great-uncle was shocked to see me, and he immediately closed the store early, something he never did. After some discussion, the duo decided to keep me. Uncle Eric suggested they call me Naida, a nod to his love of Greek studies and the river gods.

We three, along with the shop's petulant cat, Grimm, became an unconventional family. Grimm, who had no use for humans, took to cuddling next to me in my crib. Uncle Eric joked that Grimm was attracted to the lingering scents of sturgeon and carp clinging to my skin.

Most in the small Viennese neighborhood, filled with cramped town houses, were amused by the story, but none believed it. They suspected Elke had secretly married a young Roma man who'd left her to travel the river with his people. My father had promised to return, but never did. Elke, like many other young women who'd lost their husbands and lovers in the Great War, was left to carry on. I was seven when my mother died.

From that moment onward, I worked with Uncle Eric in the corner bookshop, just as my mother had. I grew up playing soccer with the other children until my dark Roma eyes and hair eventually became troublesome for some. I slowly retreated to the bookstore, devouring the classics and learning the literary likes and dislikes of all our neighbors.

When I was seventeen, the winds of war blew again, and the city filled with soldiers and strangers. Desperate neighborhood friends fled. Many who couldn't run, or who refused to leave their homes, simply vanished.

A few years before that, a young woman entered our shop. She was tall and lean, and her ink black hair set off vivid blue eyes. She somehow knew that Eric purchased the rare, special books many escaping citizens were forced to sell. He'd always become anxious whenever the woman arrived and was relieved whenever she left. Grimm, ancient and half blind by now, hissed and hid when she'd enter the shop.

"Stay away from that one," Uncle Eric had said one day. 'She's a selkie. Trouble."

My mother had told me stories of the selkies. The creatures lived in the waterways and often spied on humans. Some of these fabled beings, tricksters by nature, shed their skins and walked among people. If their skins remained hidden, they were free to return to the water. However, if a human found their casings, they were bound to that person.

As I was tucking newly purchased dusty tomes under the counter, I asked, "Then why do you buy from her?"

His stooped shoulders lifted in a shrug. "She knows sellers who need money. I know buyers. I help when I can."

"It's dangerous. And it must be illegal," I said. "Soldiers and police watch the store."

He shrugged. "So be it."

Now as the Danube's meandering waters rolled past, I prayed the selkie hadn't betrayed me.

CHAPTER ONE

Tula

Monday, June 8, 2026, 1:00 p.m.
Norfolk, Virginia

The computer cursor blinked, daring me to type the legal brief I'd been attempting to write for most of the morning. All my meticulous research was complete. But whenever I began to write, my well-organized notes turned liquid, and the facts and figures leaked away like water through clenched fingers.

My stomach grumbled, and my head ached. I'd written hundreds of briefs. That's what paralegals do. We write summations for attorneys. Projects like these should write themselves. Bing, bang, boom. Done. And I was one of the best in the firm.

I pressed my fingers to closed eyelids. If I could just wade through the project and make the words flow in order, then I could take a deep breath, go home, and get some sleep.

Lately, good sleep had become a thing of the past. Each night I'd tumble into bed about midnight, only to have my eyes pop open at 3:00 a.m. I'd roll onto my side. My stomach. Punch my pillow. Threw off blankets and then add more when I became cold. I needed sleep, but my brain kept firing on all pistons.

In these restless hours, the ghosts I'd kept at a distance for years stepped out of the shadows, circled, and taunted. They replayed all my mistakes.

Last night, despite the three melatonin gummies and two glasses of wine I'd consumed, the spirit of my recently failed marriage drifted close. My now ex-husband, Dave, had sent me a notice yesterday, via his lawyer, ordering me to vacate the house we'd shared. He owned the property and wanted me out so he could sell it. The message had been quick and to the point. It stated that I could buy the house or move out in two weeks. Buy the house. Right. The email ended with the complimentary close, "Best."

I didn't miss Dave or long for him. But he and his house had been my safe harbor for almost six years.

I'd finally risen at five and dressed for the gym. I drove a few miles to the facility and was on its doorstep at 5:30 a.m. I spent an hour swimming laps in the pool, cutting through the water until I was breathless and my arms ached. I went home, showered, and dressed for work. The plan had been to get a jump on the brief before my energy crashed.

"How's the brief coming?"

I looked up at Nan, my boss. She was dressed in her signature all-black. Her V-neck sweater curved over her breasts in a seductive but still professional way. Her blond hair was tied back in a ruthlessly smooth ponytail, and subtle makeup softened stern features.

"The research is done," I said. "Notes are right here."

She hovered over my cubicle. She was intense, but I liked her. "Don't worry about that. The boss wants to see you."

"Why?"

"I don't know. A special assignment."

"But this brief is due today."

"I'll give it to another paralegal. Mr. Brooks is waiting for you in his office."

Mr. Brooks. One of the three named partners in the firm. This felt a little like being summoned to the king's court. No struggling employee wanted a partner's attention. And here it went. I was getting fired. I'd dropped the ball too many times since my separation.

My cubicle was stark, decorated with a single silk plant, a "Girl Boss" mug from Dave, and the picture of Mom and me taken eight years ago in Greece. I'd never kept much on my desk. Seemed odd to make a workspace feel like a home when it wasn't.

Sweat dampened my armpits. "I know I've been distracted and a little slow, but I'm getting my work done. Did I screw something up?"

Faint hints of pity flickered in Nan's eyes. "I don't know why Mr. Brooks wants to see you."

Right. Fired. All I had to do was drop the picture in my purse. The plant and mug could stay for the next inhabitant.

When Nan left, I reached for a chocolate bar in my purse and took a large bite. The sugar and fat wouldn't remedy this, just as they hadn't fixed my marriage. But the chocolate tasted good, and I took pleasure wherever I could.

I adjusted the coin-crystal necklace into the hollow of my neck and rose. Dusting the chocolate bits from my skirt, I walked down the line of cubicles to the elevator. I pressed the top-floor button, and as the doors closed, I drew in a breath. I'd survived worse before. And I would do it again.

The elevator doors opened to plush gray carpet, a mahogany reception desk, and an expanse of tinted windows that overlooked the waters of the bay. It was a beautiful day. So, if I was to get fired, the weather was at least working in my favor.

As I walked up to the desk, a woman with sleek gray hair and an angled face looked up. "Miss Cassidy?"

"That's right." Never good to be expected.

"Mr. Brooks is waiting." She rose, and I followed to a closed office door. She knocked.

I looked presentable, but I was dressed more for cubicle brief-writing work. If I'd known I'd see the big boss, I'd have picked the newer dress that fit a little better.

As tempted as I was to ask, I didn't. If my late mother had taught me anything, it was to shove my feelings deep. Asking was a sign of weakness.

A man said, "Enter." The receptionist pushed open the door.

As I passed her and moved into the office, my gaze wasn't drawn to the sweeping views of the bay but to the man standing behind the large wooden desk outfitted with pedestal feet and carvings of sea creatures and waves. It was a ship captain's desk that must have dated back centuries. A polished surface caught and reflected the lights in the room. A single manila folder and envelope rested to his right.

Mr. Robert Brooks's age was hard to guess. Maybe late fifties. He wore black from head to toe, and his gray hair was swept back in a cut reminiscent of the 1940s. His face was bronzed, not from a bottle or tanning bed but from years in the sun. Everyone knew he loved to sail.

Mr. Brooks, beyond his expensive suit, wasn't impressive. In fact, he looked rather ordinary, like a favorite worn, albeit expensive, pair of jeans. If he were plainly dressed and passing me on the street, sipping coffee in a café, or raking leaves in a yard, I wouldn't have noticed him. He didn't have the bearing of a man who'd built a half-billion-dollar law firm that had global reach. I suspected Mr. Brooks's ordinariness was an advantage. While no one was watching him, he was surveilling and planning chess moves ten steps ahead.

Oil paintings of clipper ships and centuries-old coal-powered vessels graced the white walls. Like our firm, which specialized in maritime law, the entire Norfolk region revolved around the water.

The Brooks name was front and center on the firm's masthead, Tierney, Brooks, and Bainbridge. I'd never met any of the other named partners and assumed they were older than Mr. Brooks. Frankly, I was surprised either was still alive, let alone came into the office.

Mr. Brooks studied me as if searching for something. Perhaps he didn't see mid-level paralegals often and was just as curious about me as I him.

I cleared my throat. "Mr. Brooks. It's a pleasure to meet you. I'm Tula Cassidy."

"Tula. Welcome. Would you have a seat?" His accent was neutral and could be assigned to endless locations.

Twin leather chairs angled in front of his desk. This seemed like a lot of trouble for a firing, and he didn't have the look of a guy ready to make a sexual advance.

Still cautious, I smoothed my skirt and sat down. He sat in the leather chair behind his desk, which frankly felt more like a fortress.

Again, he studied me a beat before reaching for a pair of wire-rimmed glasses. Carefully he slid the manila folder to the center of his desk. "You've been with the firm almost seven years?"

"Yes. Nearly seven years, sir." The anniversary of my hiring was in September, but that didn't matter now.

"You're a paralegal?"

"I started in the mail room and worked my way up through the firm's apprentice program." Did this bit of ancient history matter? Men at his level didn't know where the mail room was located. And they sure didn't pay much attention to apprentices, first-year lawyers, or paralegals housed in endless cubicles.

He didn't open the file. "You've had stellar reviews until this last one."

I straightened. Getting the work done over the last year had been a struggle. Dave, the anchor in my life, had left. I might not have loved him, but at the time I'd met him, my life had felt like it was trapped in the outer bands of a hurricane. Dave was calm and steady and had promised a solid, stable life.

But that endless consistency had tightened around me like a noose. I began to resent Dave's so-predictable schedule and his ten-year plans for our lives. Dave wasn't stupid, and he'd come to dislike my lack of interest in us. He began drinking and spending more time away from home. And then, after a horrific fight, he took off for two weeks. He hadn't answered any of my calls.

During his hiatus, I became furious. My resentment grew, although it wasn't directed toward him but toward myself. I believed I couldn't make it without him. I drank. Worried. And when he'd finally texted and said we should talk, I'd wished for a different life.

As soon as Dave returned, I was slightly relieved. But as he poured a bourbon, he asked me for a divorce. Pride kept me from saying anything. I sat in silence as he pointed out that we wanted different lives. One day I would see that. He packed a bigger bag, moved out of the house (which he owned), and told me to get a lawyer.

I'd stayed in the house during the divorce, but now the limbo was ending. I had two weeks to find somewhere else to live. So far, finding an affordable place had been challenging. To make the numbers work, I'd have either a long commute or three roommates.

Mom had often said wishes are as slippery as eels and as unpredictable as the ocean. The line separating wishes from curses was thin, and it leaked.

So here I was, free of my marriage but on the verge of joblessness and homelessness.

"It's been a rough year. But I'm back on track." Personal excuses were only valid if the work was done well and on time.

"Good to hear." Mr. Brooks leaned back. "You're familiar with the Outer Banks in North Carolina?"

"Sure. I lived there for three months during my senior year of high school." The Outer Banks were the last stop Mom and I had made together.

The two of us had lived a nomad's life. We traveled the world, moving from one scuba diving spot to the next. Mom was a master diver and made her living as an instructor and guide. She'd done well enough, so we always had something to eat. But there were no extras, and anything that didn't fit in my suitcase was unnecessary baggage.

Still, it was a good life. We saw the world. I'd witnessed miracles most only dreamed of. Vacationers on Mom's diving expeditions envied us. To have no attachments. What a dream.

But we were rootless. We stayed on the move, never staying anywhere for long. And then, right before my eighteenth birthday, we returned to the Outer Banks. She'd enrolled me in high school and rented a place for the spring. She taught lessons and led more expeditions into waters dubbed the Graveyard of the Atlantic. Two months later, my mother dove a local wreck called the *Oceanus* and vanished.

"Your mother passed, from what I hear. Seven years ago, in a diving accident."

"That's right."

Mom and I were diving the *Oceanus*. When we'd set out, the weather was clear, with no signs of a storm. But her on-again, off-again dive buddy had not shown at the dock. So, we'd set off alone. I didn't think twice when I followed her under the water.

We drifted past the ship's hull, which had rested on the ocean floor for almost eighty years. Though I'd explored many sunken ships, this was the first time I'd seen the *Oceanus*. Instantly, I was uneasy. The water started churning more. I checked my dive computer and realized I was low on air. I signaled Mom to return to the dive boat. She nodded, held up five fingers, and then motioned for me to lead the way. The hand signal told me she'd be five minutes behind me. Fair. She knew how to manage her oxygen better than anyone, so I ascended, but when I looked over my shoulder, I saw her gliding a gloved hand along the large gash made by a German torpedo in 1942. Her dark hair floated around her tanned face. Her eyes looked so bright and blue behind the mask. She must have felt my attention because she waved and gave me a thumbs-up.

Confident she was minutes behind me, I rose and popped above the surface. I was surprised to see that the clouds had blackened and the water was still churning. Waves smacked against the boat. I hoisted myself onto the dive platform.

When Mom didn't surface, I readied myself to go back down. But a wave hit the boat and knocked me backward. I smacked against the deck. I struggled to my feet and scrambled to the boat's radio. I called in a Mayday. More and more minutes passed. And Mom didn't surface.

The waves kicked up higher, and it was hard to maintain my footing. When the coast guard helicopter arrived, the waves were washing over the side. A guardsman descended on a rope and ordered me to put on a harness. I tried to explain that Mom was still in the water. He insisted they would look for her. And I was pulled aboard the helicopter. From above, I stared at the rolling, angry waves. It was clear any search was too dangerous. Another guardsman promised me that they'd search once the storm had passed.

And hours later, they returned. But Mom was never found.

I returned to our rental house. We both traveled so light, there wasn't much more than a suitcase full of clothes that belonged to her. I held her T-shirt to my nose, inhaling the familiar scent of coconut suntan lotion.

In her suitcase, I'd found a two-hundred-year-old coin fashioned into a corded necklace. My mother had always worn it. The coin was as fixed to all my memories of my mother as her smile and vivid blue eyes.

Attached to the necklace was a note written on a grocery receipt. *For Tula.* No tender words. No warnings. No hints of her impending disappearance. The brief message was so Mom. I'd slid the coin on my sea-glass necklace chain.

I'd lingered on the Outer Banks for months, hoping Mom would be found. When our lease expired, I moved in with a friend from high school. I'd begged the ocean to give her back. I pointed out that Mom was too stubborn, too tough, too full of fight to stay lost. I believed the ocean would eject her and she would swim ashore, just as she'd done a million times before.

But the ocean had kept her.

The community rallied around me—*the girl whose mother was swallowed by the ocean.* That close to the Atlantic, stories of lost loved ones weren't uncommon. The deep sea had claimed fishermen daring rough waters, surfers who'd underestimated rip current warnings, or swimmers seduced by calm waters, only to venture out too far. Living on the barrier islands came with risk.

Still, our story caught headlines. Mother Lost at Sea. Teen Girl Rescued.

As days turned into weeks and Mom still didn't return, the locals set up a trust fund for me. It wasn't enough to make me rich, but it would bridge the distance between now and the next part of my life. At the end of the summer, I'd left the Outer Banks and returned to Norfolk.

When I married Dave, I thought I'd put my unsettled nomadic life behind me. But it always tugged at me. And then resentment festered for the too-stable guy and the cubicle that grew smaller and smaller every day.

"I'm not sure that has anything to do with my job performance," I said, pulling myself from my memories.

"It doesn't."

"Then why bring it up?"

He ignored the question. "My great-uncle built a house in the Southern Shores area on the Outer Banks in the late 1940s. I spent many vacations down there."

"It's a beautiful place." What else was I going to say?

"He passed about the time your mother died. I held on to the house, but I never use it anymore."

"Okay." If he was dropping a trail of breadcrumbs, I wasn't following them.

"My great-uncle died in 2019, but I've kept and maintained the house as it was when he lived there." He flipped through the pages in his file. "When I was in my great-uncle's home office a few months ago, I found a partial manuscript. It's about the *Oceanus*."

I'd avoided all articles and online videos featuring the wreck. It might have been a curiosity for history or dive buffs, but for me it represented loss. "I see."

"I want to give you the pages. I thought if there was anyone who might have an interest, it would be you." I was ready to refuse the offer, when he raised his hand. "There's no one else I know who cares as much about the vessel as you. And maybe reading about it will spark your interest in diving again."

His suggestion annoyed me. "How do you know I don't dive anymore?"

"News travels."

"It doesn't, because I don't share it."

He studied me as if coming to a decision. "I've heard you're not much of a gossip."

"I'm not. Again, why does this matter?"

My anger didn't seem to faze him. "I have a job for you."

"A job? I thought I had one."

"Think of this as an extension of what you do now. I need someone who doesn't gossip to close my great-uncle's house. It's remained untouched for seven years. There will be boxes of files to weed through and destroy, and all the contents need to be sold or donated."

"Do you want anything from the house?"

"No. But you're welcome to anything in the house."

"Seems like there are more efficient ways to close up a property."

"There are, but I would rather someone who has a connection to the firm and area tackle it."

A summer at the beach. Nice, but the rental prices were too high for me. Maybe I could bunk with my high school friend Kaitlin, who was still there.

And then, "You can stay at the house, but it's likely a dusty mess. Or, if you have friends, stay with them. I'd like the job done by mid-September. You'll receive your regular salary, benefits, and an allowance for food and gas."

He pushed the manila envelope toward me. "That's the first portion of the manuscript."

"Where's the rest?"

"In the house, I presume. I couldn't find it. I'm not sure why it was divided into sections."

"Have you read it?"

"No."

I didn't reach for the folder. "I haven't been back in seven years. It's not a good place for me."

"Don't prejudge. This might be the kind of project that launches you on a new start."

I'd wished for a change, and here it was. "Do you want weekly reports?"

"Not necessary." A smile teased the edges of his lips. "If this offer doesn't appeal, you can go back to writing briefs in your cubicle."

I'd longed to be untethered. To move on. And here was the chance. I pulled the folder toward me. It felt heavier than I'd imagined. This was the last outcome I'd imagined. Ever. The coin felt warm against my chest. And still, I said, "Okay. I'll do it. Thank you."

"Excellent." He rose, signaling this meeting was over. "Pick up the house key from my assistant."

I stood and extended a clammy hand, which he easily accepted. "You really don't want anything from the house?"

"It's served its purpose. Feel free to keep what you want."

"Okay." I turned and walked toward the door and then paused. This was all too out of the blue and odd for me not to question Mr. Brooks's motive. "Did you know my mother?"

Still standing, he stared at me. "Only by reputation. She was quite the diver, from what I hear."

"Yes." Diving and the ocean had been her life.

"But we never met."

"Okay."

"Best of luck to you, Tula."

"Thank you."

When I exited his office, the folder tucked under my arm, Mr. Brooks's assistant stood by her desk waiting for me. "Miss Cassidy. Will you be accepting the house key?"

"I will."

"Excellent." She moved to her desk and snatched up an old metal key. She handed it to me.

It felt heavy in my hands. "I'm surprised he doesn't have a digital lock."

"The locks are excellent, and the doors and windows are old but sound. Mr. Brooks saw no reason to change anything if it was working."

"Do I need to check in with you?"

"At the end of the summer. No need before then."

I'd lived on tight deadlines for nearly seven years. And now to have one that extended all summer felt freeing and unsettling. "Okay. I'll be in touch then."

She handed me a credit card. "This is to cover your incidentals."

"But I'm still getting my paycheck, right?"

"You will. But you never know with old houses. Expenses come up."

I hesitated. "Why me?"

"I'm sure Mr. Brooks explained."

"Kind of."

She smiled. "Mr. Brooks never says what he doesn't mean."

"He didn't say a lot."

"But enough."

"I suppose."

I left the woman and crossed to the elevator. I pressed the button. The doors opened. I stepped inside, gripping the key and envelope as the elevator closed on the executive suites.

The ride down seemed much faster, and before I knew it, I was in my cubicle. I grabbed my purse out of my bottom drawer. I reached past the fake plant and the "Girl Boss" mug to the picture of Mom and me.

Nan appeared. She didn't like drama. She liked clean, tidy breaks and airtight briefs delivered on time. Shipshape was kind of my superpower. Life on boats had required it.

And I'd faced enough real turmoil to put this moment in perspective. No tears or outraged tirades for a job or failed marriage. I picked up the photo and mug, and then I set the mug back down. "Okay."

Some of the tension faded from her face. "What about the mug and plant?"

"Keep them."

I fished my ID out of my wallet and handed it to her.

"I'm told you're to keep it. Your job will be waiting if you decide to return."

"Right. Thank you." I angled around Nan.

"Take care of yourself, Tula."

I left the building, suddenly feeling slightly panicked to leave it behind. Over time, even cages offer some comfort. I crossed the parking lot to my car, which I'd bought with the donation monies seven years ago.

Sliding into the hot front seat, I looked up at the impenetrable glass building, which reflected the morning light winking on the water behind me. I allowed the heat to sink into my bones and then reached for my phone. I knew only one person on the Outer Banks. Kaitlin Stewart. I'd met Kaitlin during my brief months attending First Flight High School. We'd become friends.

It was kind of a miracle that Kaitlin and her mother had taken me in after Mom vanished. My dad had never been in the picture, and Mom and I had no roots. A few times I'd made friends, but we were always gone soon after. Friendships didn't gel with a nomad's life. So, I'd stopped trying to get close to anyone. Mom had become my buddy. She'd started teaching me how to dive when I was five, and the undersea world became my home. In the water, I felt free of worldly dramas. In the silence of the ocean, the past and future compressed into the present.

Mom became obsessed with shipwrecks when I was about eight. The first wreck was a Spanish galleon that had gone down in a Caribbean hurricane in 1749. She taught lessons in the mornings, and during her off-hours, she researched wrecks. So that I could spend more time with her, I became her research assistant. We'd learn all we could about a downed ship, and then we'd lead expeditions to their remains. Wreck dives became her thing, and she started taking jobs near interesting ones.

I had no formal education, but when I arrived on the Outer Banks, my collection of homeschooling teachers, made up of sailors, dockmasters, and local tour guide historians, put me ahead of my fellow students.

Kaitlin had also been a senior at First Flight, and she was really into surfing. She was failing history, and our teacher paired us as study buddies. Our friendship took off.

We'd texted and called each other over the years, but I hadn't seen her since I'd left the Outer Banks. She was all I had, and I could use a friendly face. I typed.

Kaitlin: You r alive?
Me: I am.
Kaitlin: When's the last time you reached out to me first?
Me: Maybe never.
Kaitlin: LOL. What's up?
Me: Coming to OBX. Can I crash?

I wasn't ready to camp out in the Southern Shores house.

Kaitlin: Sure. Why are you coming here?
Me: Longish story.

My phone rang. It was Kaitlin. "The divorce must be final."
"It is."

"Are you crying?" she asked.

I sniffed. "No. Just not sleeping great."

When I'd lived with the Stewarts, I was plagued by terrible nightmares. I'd had a front-row seat when Mom had her diving accident, and it had left a mark.

"These days it's anxiety, mainly," I added.

I'd never spoken to anyone else about my panic attacks but my therapist and her. Somehow distance had not derailed my friendship with Kaitlin, mostly because she'd been great about writing, texting, and calling.

"You get fired?" Kaitlin asked.

"New assignment. Kind of."

"What's that mean?"

"I'll explain when I see you," I said. "But I'm there for the summer."

"If you're looking for cash, I could use the help."

Kaitlin ran MERmaids, a lucrative home-cleaning service on the Outer Banks. Among her clients were private homeowners as well as rental companies overseeing hundreds of vacation homes. I'd worked with Kaitlin and her mom cleaning that long summer seven years ago.

"Not glamorous," Kaitlin said. "But cleaning up other people's messes has always paid the bills. And you can stay above the surf shop for free."

"You have no help?"

"I have a few kids joining me, but it'll be a couple of weeks until they arrive."

I had no idea what the Southern Shores house required, but Kaitlin and her mother had taken me in when I was lost. The least I could do was help her for a couple of weeks. "Sure. I can help, but I have this house to clear out."

"You won't be the first person who balances a couple of jobs," Kaitlin said.

"I know." Scrubbing toilets had never been my jam. But the easy, predictable duties had helped me to cope. Whenever life felt out of control, I could count on freshly wiped countertops, crisp lines in vacuumed carpets, and fresh bedsheets.

"You going to take up diving again?" Kaitlin asked.

I pulled the manuscript pages out of the folder. "One step at a time."

"One step is better than no steps. Traffic isn't crazy on Tuesdays and Wednesdays. We can get a few drinks. We have another week before the tourists show up in droves and the bars are jam-packed."

I groaned. "Crowds."

"Who spend a lot of money down here. We like their tax dollars and the services they buy."

I knew hordes of tourists were great for business. But jam-packed roads and restaurants weren't ideal. "Okay."

"Okay, what?"

"I'm on my way, first thing in the morning."

"Terrific."

I ended the call, dropped the phone into my lap, and started the car. Warm air-conditioning blasted my skin. I looked at the yellowed, water-stained title page, which read only: *The Oceanus.*

Mom had always said, *A ship in port is safe, but if it remains too long, it will decay.* I put the car in drive. "Time to knock the barnacles off, Tula."

CHAPTER TWO

CHIEF MATE KEVIN RIGGS

Monday, April 20, 1942, 12:00 noon
Four days until the Oceanus *is torpedoed*
Port of Spain, Trinidad

Passage through the calm waters of the Gulf of Paria into Port of Spain had been smooth and uneventful. With no U-boats, no mines, no trouble, the *Oceanus* had arrived in port at sunset yesterday.

He had slept a few hours last night, falling into his bunk only when the ship reached the dock. He woke at 5:00 a.m. to shave and dress in a freshly pressed uniform that he reserved for the days when new passengers boarded. First impressions mattered. Passengers needed to feel that their captain's top enlisted man was up for the job.

He was born in Currituck County, North Carolina, in 1920. His father, a coast guardsman and fisherman, often joked that the boy's mother had plucked him from the Atlantic when he was seconds old. Covered in sand, seaweed, and brine, the infant child was said to be clutching a conch shell and wailing so loud the wild horses of Currituck County came to investigate the creature.

He often said he didn't know where the Atlantic Ocean ended and he began. The water had not only birthed him but nourished him.

Though he'd been up for hours, his passengers maintained a different schedule. Most who'd boarded in Cape Town, South Africa, were either still sleeping, dressing, or making their way to the dining hall for a late breakfast. Because they were in harbor, he'd allowed his passengers to go ashore last night to visit the cafés and restaurants. At sea, his passengers would have to maintain quiet, because sound attracted the U-boats like blood drew sharks. Though he'd been tempted to stroll dry land, he'd stayed on the *Oceanus*, given that they were now at war.

For those who'd stayed on board last night, festivities in the dining room had gone late. A young opera singer traveling from Cape Town had been in fine form, and her soprano voice had captivated those in the dining room. He'd wanted to end the festivities, but the captain had allowed them to continue. Once the ship was out of port, evening activities would be reduced to cards, games, and political talk of the war.

Until this past winter, Port of Spain had been untouched by the war raging in Europe. And then, two months ago, a U-boat had entered the harbor and sunk a half dozen ships. The midnight attack had sent flames soaring into the night sky, illuminating the lighthouse and harbormaster's tower. The waterfront danced with a demonic light as the U-boat evaporated back into the Caribbean.

As lovely as the singer's voice was, he'd worried the sound could attract another U-boat. So, he'd remained on deck, scanning for signs of ripple patterns in the water or U-boat periscopes.

As the singer glided into the high notes of *La traviata*, he thought of the vessels lost in the Atlantic in the last four weeks. The tanker *Dixie Arrow* had been sunk off the North Carolina coast by a German U-boat twenty-five days ago. Five days later, the same submarine had sunk a tanker called the *San Gerardo* southeast of New York City. He'd known men who'd served on both ships. They'd crossed paths in ports, and they'd drunk and laughed together. Nearly eighty vessels and twelve hundred souls had gone missing in the waters off the Outer Banks since January. And now he was about to sail into those same waters.

The once-untouched US coastline of his boyhood was now littered with shattered lifeboats, spewed oil, and human remains. Mariners had always been wary of the North Carolina coast because of its fickle, ever-changing shoals that routinely fooled impatient captains rushing through its shifting underwater channels.

Now berthed at Queen's Wharf, he enjoyed this tentative moment of safety as he stared out over Port of Spain's busy waterfront. Loud rattling cranes worked methodically along the docks, loading supplies destined for Allied forces. Nearby, warehouses buzzed with longshoremen moving crates of food, ammunition, and military equipment. Honking car horns blended with the metallic whir of an electric streetcar skimming along its tracks on Dock Road. Palm trees swayed in a warm breeze and carried the scent of diesel from the new fuel depots and the rain leaking from plumping dark clouds hovering over the mountains ringing the harbor.

The United States was arming the shipping convoys now vital to the survival of the Allies. US soldiers were encamped on the island's eastern shore in the newly constructed US naval base.

No part of this earth was immune to the war raging in Europe and the Pacific.

Today, the *Oceanus* would return to the perilous sea, infested with German U-boat subs, or wolf packs, prowling the waters. Most vessels now traveled in convoys, hoping their numbers would save them. The *Oceanus* had been delayed from Cape Town due to a storm off Africa, and they'd missed the last convoy. But in his mind, these slow-moving maritime caravans were sitting ducks. The *Oceanus* would use her fast engines to outrun any trouble.

Marine Square, the center of town, was a few blocks to his right. Palm trees, arched walkways, decorative wrought iron railings and stucco facades with shuttered windows hinted at the city's Spanish and Georgian roots. Shops, hotels, and bars served all manner of people— dark-skinned Trinidadians and uniformed US and British soldiers.

Life carried on here, even as blackout curtains lined tall windows and harbor patrol boats scanned for enemy activity.

As the chief mate, he oversaw all the daily duties required to keep the ship moving. The captain had given him a list of the twelve passengers who would be boarding soon. Like this city, they were a melting pot of nationalities. Some were European, two were from the United States, and the others were from South America. They'd pass through the customs warehouse before being allowed to board.

A flicker of sparking chrome caught his attention as a Ford Packard parked by the gangplank. The back door opened, and a man dressed in a white linen suit and a fedora emerged. He was tall and well proportioned, and he had the look of a man accustomed to travel. He reached into the back seat and took a lady's gloved hand. Seconds later a tall, slender woman appeared. She was wearing a sapphire-blue dress that hugged full breasts and gently rounded hips, and she rose out of the vehicle like a siren from the water. As she looked up toward the ship, he caught the long line of a pale neck. She moved easily in black high-heeled shoes that elongated slim legs.

The man was Mr. William Weller, a US industrialist, rumored to have helped arm the Nazis during the 1930s. With the United States now in the war, Mr. Weller was wise to have left Europe.

The woman, according to the manifest, was Sigrid Stein, an Austrian by birth. Her profession was listed as "actress" on the ship's passenger manifest. She wore diamond earrings that captured the sunlight. A half dozen ivory buttons trailed up each cuff and along the front of her jacket.

Weller had an attentive gaze as he took Miss Stein's elbow. He kept her close at hand. A few passing US sailors paused to admire her beauty. Mr. Weller escorted Miss Stein up the gangplank.

Adjusting his uniform, Chief Mate Riggs moved to the entryway so he could greet them. "Welcome aboard the *Oceanus*. Mr. Weller and Miss Stein, I presume."

"That's correct," Mr. Weller said.

Miss Stein stayed close to Weller, her shoulder touching his as if he were her anchor. This close, Chief Mate Riggs had to appreciate her beauty. Jet-black hair, smooth pale skin, blue eyes, and cherry red lips were hard to ignore. Like the mythic sirens he feared brought bad luck.

"I'll have a seaman escort you to your cabin." The ship had second-class and third-class suites. Weller's cabin was one of the largest the ship offered. And it was one of the last available.

"Excellent. And my bags and crates are being loaded?" Mr. Weller said.

"As we speak."

"Can I inspect them before we set sail?"

Riggs's weakness was impatience, but a stoic stare hid it. "It's not customary, but it can be arranged. Say in one hour?"

"That will suit," Mr. Weller said.

Miss Stein nodded graciously to Riggs. The couple followed the apprentice seaman below deck.

"Thank you." The chief mate watched other passengers approaching the gangplank. Most were neatly, if not modestly, dressed, and all had tight expressions pinched with worry and fear. He guessed their need to reach the United States outweighed any concerns about the dangerous, dark waters ahead. Europe meant certain death for many now. But there was a chance the U-boats patrolling the oceans would spare them all.

An older man dressed in a ship's officer's uniform approached. The man was Captain Joseph Stoddard. The captain had served with the US Navy in the North Atlantic when he was younger and had joined the shipping company a decade ago.

"Chief Mate Riggs," Stoddard said. "Lovely day."

"Captain." The seaman raised his face to the sun. "It's beautiful."

"How is Seaman Hanson?" the captain asked. "He still in clinic?"

"No, sent him back to his room this morning with extra aspirin. I suspect the headaches were caused by rum rather than an ailment."

"No time for that when we cross the Atlantic. I need all my men in top form."

"Understood."

Stoddard let the matter drop.

"The radios are quiet today. No sightings outside the harbor," Chief Mate Riggs commented.

"Good." A frown deepened the lines of Stoddard's sun-etched face.

"It's the trouble I don't see that always worries me," the chief mate replied.

"We'll be riding low in the water, and we're the kind of vessel a sea wolf likes to devour."

The *Oceanus* was a 452-foot-long passenger freighter now laden with South African chrome ore that was destined for the manufacturing of stainless steel, as well as wood, hides, and asbestos. On board were forty-four civilians and eighty-eight crew members. Riggs knew as well as the captain did that the Germans weren't hunting ships as much as tonnage. And sinking this vessel would earn a submarine captain eight thousand pounds of spoils.

"What about activity near the US coast?" the captain asked.

"Calm, but by the time we arrive, that information will be old news."

"Correct."

As he turned, a horse-drawn carriage arrived by the gangplank. In Trinidad, it was as common to see horse conveyances as automobiles. Left to its own devices, Trinidad would have remained trapped in the last century. But its prime coastal location had dragged it into modern warfare, no matter its slower pace.

The driver, a dark-skinned man wearing a worn suit, climbed down from the cart to help his passenger. She was a very pregnant woman, her rounded belly making the chief mate wonder if he could sail this vessel fast enough before she gave birth. She eased to the street and accepted a small suitcase from the driver.

"Better keep a close eye on that one," Captain Stoddard said. "I'm not anxious to become a nursemaid."

Riggs smiled, despite having similar concerns. "The manifest lists a doctor on board. A Dr. Brooks?"

"That's right. But he's a book dealer, isn't he?"

"He is."

"If it's all the same, I don't want that baby born on my ship."

"Should I issue an order to the child, sir?" Chief Mate Riggs asked.

Captain Stoddard stifled a grin. "Been my experience, women and babies have minds of their own."

"Fingers crossed that she'll make it to a proper hospital in New York."

CHAPTER THREE

GERTRUDE

Monday, April 20, 1942, 1:00 p.m.
Four days until the Oceanus *is torpedoed*
Port of Spain, Trinidad

The hot, humid weather in Trinidad was a stark contrast to Vienna, which had just emerged from its bitter winter. The moderate winds gave me hope that I would reach New York City and leave Vienna behind forever. But faith was dangerous. And I needed to keep my guard up and remain cautious. Though no other Austrians were likely on the ship, I could leave nothing to chance. The war had made the world a smaller place, and I didn't dare trust luck.

The local morning papers had few updates about the war in Europe, and the little I'd found was in the Spanish papers. I'd gleaned enough to know that the United States had joined the war in mid-December, and those from the United States who'd been in Nazi-controlled Europe had now either fled or been arrested. When I'd left Austria, many Austrians were being deported, gunned down, or imprisoned. The city I'd once loved so much was gone.

In Port of Spain, the news focused on the arrival of US troops and the U-boats now hunting ships loaded with supplies bound for Europe.

The Germans, once solely tethered to their ports in the Baltic Sea, now controlled France's western Atlantic coastline, putting these underwater vessels over a thousand nautical miles closer to the US East Coast. Hundreds of ships had been sunk in the Atlantic Ocean since January.

My German was excellent and my Spanish acceptable, but my English was lacking, so I'd spent my idle hours during this long journey studying English and preparing for the day I would be safely on US soil. Normally, I didn't speak much to anyone, but when I did, I carefully scrubbed any hints of my Austrian accent.

I'd reinvented myself several times since I left Vienna in September. In Vienna, I was the wife of an Austrian military industrialist whose career had been rising long before we'd wed three years ago. And when Germany annexed Austria, he'd gained more prominence, fame, and notoriety.

On the first leg of my journey, I was Ingrid Swenson, a woman of humble birth on her way to take a job with a family in Bucharest. By early November, I'd crossed the Mediterranean Sea into Spain and taken refuge in a small hotel room in the port town of Barcelona. I'd spent the next few months hiding, trying to forget Vienna. But there were times when I'd cried so hard, I'd made myself sick to my stomach. The tears dried, but my nausea didn't settle. I'd sought help from a local physician, who'd declared me with child. The news wasn't shocking, but it was deflating. The past now would follow me forever.

I remained vigilant, changing my name to Johanna Benson. I was careful to listen for anyone looking for a woman like me. I went to no restaurants or plays in Lisbon. I kept to myself until I was able to buy passage on the *Star*, which would take me only as far as Port of Spain. I'd been frustrated by the extra stop but had been assured that a direct crossing of the Atlantic was too dangerous. Securing passage to the United States as the newly minted Gertrude Werner had been difficult. I'd learned the Salvadoran embassy issued visas to Jews fleeing Europe, so I'd approached a sympathetic staff member. My purchased Salvadoran visa had cost me several generous bribes.

The nausea had long cleared, but my belly expanded, and the child, unmindful of the world, grew bigger, turning my slim figure pear shaped.

And now I would finish my journey to the United States before the weight of my impersonations crashed around me or the child was born.

The *Oceanus* had a black hull, the upper decks painted white. It had an open promenade deck for passengers, with railings, and with lifeboats mounted along the side. The large vessel had two smokestacks, and rows of portholes lined the lower deck. A chain of colorful flags stretched between the masts, fluttering in the soft breeze.

As I stepped out of the carriage, the ship loomed large as I hefted my bag and walked toward the gangplank. My wide-brimmed hat shadowed my face, already turning pink in the Caribbean sun. I gripped the leather handle of my satchel, wondering how it had become so heavy.

"May I be of assistance?"

The man's voice was directly behind me and startlingly close. I hadn't heard his approach. I stopped and faced a midsize man with broad shoulders, dressed in a linen suit. A fedora covered dark slicked-back hair, brown eyes, and a striking nose reminiscent of a Roman. It was difficult to judge his age, but I guessed early forties.

"Thank you," I said carefully. "I am fine."

He easily ate up the distance between us, moving with the posture of a confident man. "I cannot let a woman heavy with child carry her own bag."

I stood above most women, and this stranger wasn't much taller than me. "It's not so heavy," I insisted.

He stepped in front of me, forcing me to stop. "My name is Dr. Atticus Brooks. I am a book dealer. I am from the United States. *May* I carry your bag?"

My true valuables and my false papers were sewn into my dress, and if he was intent on stealing a lady's oversize dresses and a few old books, he was in luck. I held out the bag for him. "Very well. Thank you."

He accepted it, lightening my load immediately. "And may I ask your name?"

"Gertrude Werner." I'd practiced the name endlessly, making sure it rolled automatically off my tongue. Any hesitation would be a red flag signaling a spy or wanted refugee.

There was no flicker of recognition when he heard the name or studied my flushed face. "Do you have family in New York City?" he asked.

"Yes. A cousin." That was the story I'd given the administrator at the Salvadoran embassy in Lisbon when I'd handed him two gemstones from my cache.

He held out his hand, indicating he would follow. "And where are you from, Mrs. Werner?"

I traced the underside of my slim, now tight, gold wedding band with my thumb. "Innsbruck," I lied. I didn't offer that I was alone, but I assumed he'd already determined that.

"Frau Werner, do I hear hints of Vienna?" he asked.

"No, I have never had the pleasure." I focused on my accent. As a business titan's wife, I knew how to make meaningless conversation from the smallest details.

He seemed kind, but I didn't trust either my first impressions or his story. Many now lied easily. "What is the rarest book you have held?"

Carts ladened with fruits and vegetables rumbled past us. An army jeep honked. A sailor shouted orders to another. More nicely dressed passengers gathered at the gangplank. I scanned the crowds, searching for anyone who might be staring at me.

"A volume of Shakespeare. *The Tempest*. A Vienna broker brought it to my attention. I still get a thrill when I think of that robust volume."

I'd owned a similar volume once. Sweat pooled under my swollen breasts as I walked. "How old was it?"

An easy smile held no hints of bravado. "This was part of thirty-six plays published in 1623."

How many of those exact copies still existed? A couple of hundred? "America was a fledgling colony that year, and King James sat on the throne of England."

"And in your country, Leopold V was archduke of Austria."

Dr. Brooks had a way of easily ingratiating himself. A good salesman, I knew, had to be friendly. "You must be a student of history."

"It's a requirement of the job. Sounds as if you know our history too."

The distant past was filled with strangers and no emotional attachments. Recent history and current events were far more charged. "Yes."

I was slightly winded when we arrived at the base of the gangplank. My hand on the railing, I stared up at the narrow metal trail. This mountain would carry me away from Europe.

"May I assist?" Dr. Brooks asked.

Pride had me lifting my chin as I stepped off the dock onto the incline. "I am fine."

The ascent was slow but steady, and Dr. Brooks walked unhurriedly and patiently behind me. When we reached the deck, I paused to catch my breath and to glimpse my last view of Port of Spain's white one- or two-story buildings threaded along the water. Green mountains rolled along the horizon, reaching toward a vivid blue sky.

"A beautiful city, no?" I sounded breathless.

"It is. But you'll find New York City more to your liking."

"And why is that?"

"Vienna has more history, but New York City teems with energy and life. I suspect you don't mind a challenge."

"I couldn't compare your city to Vienna. I am from Innsbruck," I corrected.

"Ah, right. My mistake."

A crewman dressed in a dark uniform walked up to us. I removed my ticket and visa from my purse and handed them to him. He studied the papers and then me before offering both back to me. I met his gaze as I donned a not-too-expectant smile.

"Welcome aboard, Mrs. Werner. I am Chief Mate Riggs."

"A pleasure," I said.

Dr. Brooks plucked a slim black leather wallet from his breast pocket and presented his papers. Whereas I questioned and double-checked each decision, Dr. Brooks never hesitated, as if he expected the world to make space for him.

One glance at Dr. Brooks's face, and the chief mate's eyes lit with recognition. "Welcome aboard again, sir. Did you find any rare books in port?"

"Not last night," Dr. Brooks said easily. "The rare ones are hard to find." He nodded toward me. "May I introduce Frau Gertrude Werner? We made our first acquaintance on the docks moments ago."

My distended belly had stretched my once-trim body into a painfully awkward shape. When I took a step toward him, the swaying ship forced me to stagger. Dr. Brooks steadied me.

"Thank you." Nervous and tired, I felt my Central European roots sloshing between my words.

Since the Germans had taken over Austria in 1938, many Austrian Jews were fleeing to the United States. The Jews and Roma who denied the country's dark turn were either in hiding or being rounded up and transported to camps.

"Your husband isn't on the manifest," Chief Mate Riggs said.

"My husband died in Salzburg last year," I said carefully.

The story was very plausible and not easily challenged. Thousands of good Austrian men had died in the last few years.

He nodded his head. "I am sorry for your loss."

My cheeks warmed. "Thank you."

"We have another Austrian on board. I'll tell the captain to introduce you two at dinner tonight."

Another Austrian wasn't a surprise, but still I was wary. "Thank you."

Dr. Brooks shifted the weight of our cases, reestablishing his grip. "We were both lucky to get tickets for the voyage. I believe I purchased the last ticket."

"We're always willing to accommodate loyal customers," Chief Mate Riggs said.

"This might be my last trip for some time," Dr. Brooks said. "The war makes travel too dangerous."

"We all keep saying the war will be over by Christmas, now that the United States is in the fight," Chief Mate Riggs said.

"That would be excellent," Dr. Brooks said. "Best get our mother-to-be to her cabin."

I considered arguing but realized resistance could draw attention. "Thank you, Dr. Brooks. Chief Mate Riggs, it was a pleasure."

"Ma'am. Dr. Brooks," Chief Mate Riggs said. "Can I have someone escort you to your room?"

"I'm happy to see her to her cabin," Dr. Brooks said.

The doctor's kindness caused concern. I'd found few on my journey who helped without expecting something.

As I walked across the deck, the shifting water tossed my swollen belly off balance. Dr. Brooks was ready, taking my elbow in hand and steadying me. We stepped through a portal into a narrow hallway. Walking into the ship set my senses on edge. In this vessel I was trapped, and if we encountered trouble, I'd have nowhere to go.

"Accommodations aren't luxurious on ships like this one, but they're acceptable, especially in war," Dr. Brooks said.

"I'm used to simple."

He tossed me a sideways look. "I would argue that you have known luxury."

"Why do you say that?" I held on to a railing as I descended a set of stairs.

"The war has stripped away many things, but a good upbringing is hard to disguise."

Silent, I continued down a hallway, and I was relieved when Dr. Brooks announced we'd reached my cabin. He twisted the key dangling from the lock and opened the door for me. "Your new home, Frau Werner."

"Thank you for your assistance, Dr. Brooks."

"Very happy to help. Perhaps you can join me for dinner."

A question that sounded more like a directive. "I'm very tired. I'm not sure if I'll make it to dinner." I didn't know the man, and I was hesitant to take his kindness at face value.

"Of course. You must rest." He carried my bag into my room and set it on a small bunk.

The room was furnished with a tiny closet, a table with one chair, and an oval mirror over a washbasin. The room retained the port's heavy wet heat, making the air oppressive. I'd grown to dislike tiny rooms.

Dr. Brooks crossed to the twelve-inch porthole overlooking the harbor. Twisting the brass latch, he opened it. Thick, slightly cooler humid air rushed the room. Despite the heat, the fresh air was welcome.

"Perhaps I'll see you during the journey," Dr. Brooks said.

"Yes," I lied.

"I find the ocean invigorating," he said. "I hope you do too."

"I'm looking forward to the voyage," I lied.

He removed the key from the door lock and handed it to me. "Your cabin is number 110. I'm 120. On the same level, but at the far end."

"Excellent," I lied.

As he turned to leave, he paused. "The toilet is at the end of the hallway."

"You're very kind, Dr. Brooks."

"Not at all."

When he closed the door behind him, I released the breath I'd been holding. I tugged off my gloves and set them and my hat on the small table. I sat on the bunk and unlaced my shoes and wiggled my swollen toes. The short walk had taken its toll on my lower back, which had been aching for days. I unrolled my thin socks and laid them on the chair to air out. Sweat pooled at the base of my back and under my full breasts.

I'd had little activity over the last eight months. And the journey from the carriage had been more taxing than I'd imagined.

Very carefully, I lay back on the bunk and stared out the porthole. The baby kicked in my belly as the boat rocked gently in the harbor waters. I breathed in and out, trying to calm the energy surging in my body. I was certain I would never fall asleep. But slowly my eyes drifted closed.

CHAPTER FOUR

Tula

Tuesday, June 9, 2026, 9:15 a.m.
Norfolk, Virginia

I wanted to sleep in. I didn't want to face cleaning out vacation rentals or an old house or think about how I'd gotten here. A silent current had pulled me, like an untethered boat, out to sea, and now here I was, lost.

I'd slept like shit. I rolled over every hour, checking the red numbers on my ex-husband's digital clock. Everything about this room, from the heavy wood furniture to the dark walls, was Dave's. Beyond my clothes in the closet, there wasn't much of me in this house. There never had been. I'd woven myself into Dave's world and lost mine. But even after seven years on dry land, I could still stuff my worldly belongings into a large garbage bag.

Over the last year, it had been hard to wake up most days. My alarms would blare several times before I'd finally rouse myself and notice the empty side of the bed. At first, panic had swamped me, but now I felt nothing.

My mother had always been good about locking down her emotions. And my ex-husband had accused me many times of being cold and distant. I'd tried to assure him I was not like that. But now I realized, maybe I was. Good. I was done feeling anxious or needing a hero.

Out of bed, I stumbled into the bathroom. I turned on the shower tap and stepped inside. I stood under the water, letting it run over my face and body for a good half hour. Only when the hot water ran cold did I shut off the tap. I toweled off, coiled my damp hair into a bun, and dressed in a T-shirt and my largest shorts.

In the kitchen, I made a strong cup of coffee. Because I wasn't rushed, I scrambled the last few eggs in the fridge and toasted the only slice of bread. Breakfast was usually coffee to go and candy from the office vending machines, which had packed an extra ten pounds on me the last year. I set my dirty plate and mug in the sink. I reached for the dish soap and then decided Dave could wash his own plates.

I stuffed all my clothes and belongings into a trash bag and shoved it in the back of my car. I looked back at the town house, which I'd once seen as a safe harbor. Through no fault of its own or Dave's, this world had grown too tight. I tossed the keys inside onto the parquet floor and closed the front door behind me.

Behind the wheel, I backed out of the driveway and followed Lynnhaven Parkway toward I-64 south and finally took Route 168, which led me over the state line into North Carolina.

I hadn't been back here in seven years, but it was amazing how much most of it really hadn't changed. Sure, there were a few new housing developments, but the old fruit stands, dive restaurants, and water park remained.

Kaitlin had said there were more tourists and cars on the road, but as promised, the traffic on a Tuesday morning was light.

At the final bend, I caught sight of the Wright Memorial Bridge and the waters of Currituck Sound. The sky was a vivid blue, but the whitecapped waters were choppy.

Hesitation rushed my body. I eased up on the accelerator. Not a full-on stop. But for a second I was tempted to turn around. This long strip of land was the dividing line between my past and present.

Pressing on the gas, I focused on the bridge ahead of me. I didn't look at the water on my left or right. I gripped the wheel as the wind whipped sideways across the bridge. I crested the bridge's peak and locked my gaze on the land on the other side. When I rolled onto solid land, my hold on the steering wheel eased.

I passed the country club, fast-food shops, and the grocery store before I took a right toward the south on the bypass. Five miles later, I cut over on a small side street toward the beach road.

After a few blocks, I pulled into Kaitlin's surf shop parking lot. The building was a two-story cinder block building painted aqua with the silhouetted figure of a woman riding a surfboard. Kaitlin had opened the shop two years ago and now balanced a cleaning crew and the surf business. I wondered if she ever slept.

I sat in my car, absorbing the simple fact I was back on the Outer Banks.

Three women moved toward the surf shop's front door. All were young and fit and wore cutoff shorts and tank tops that hugged perfect bodies. Their long hair swished in ponytails as they laughed. I'd been that kind of girl in high school. Worries might have landed on my shoulders, but the slightest breeze brushed them aside. In those days, my size-four life was diving and surfing.

When I'd met Kaitlin in high school, she was a local surfing star. Her big plan had been to take the world surfing circuit by storm. And then, two months after I'd left, her mother died from a fast-growing cancer. Kaitlin put aside her dreams and took over the cleaning business so her mother's longtime employees would have work and she could pay her rent.

The surf shop had stayed slammed its first two summers, and in the falls, when the water turned cold, Kaitlin did whatever upgrades the shop needed. And then she'd returned to the international competition circuit. She'd yet to grab a major sponsor.

When I was landlocked, I'd often watch her videos on YouTube. Her body skimmed effortlessly along the massive waves as if she and the ocean were one. I was in awe. And jealous. Once, I'd had no fear of the ocean. The water and I had been simpatico. Mom had called me a mermaid.

Now I resembled a beached whale. The dry air had withered my lungs and turned me brittle.

I grabbed my purse, locked the car, and headed into the shop. Kaitlin was behind the counter, ringing up a set of fins for a young gal and her mother. A glance toward the door, and her smile shifted from *Hello!* to *Look what the cat finally dragged in.*

I waved and pretended to look at purple-and-yellow T-shirts sporting a surfboard cutting into a wave. I remembered when Kaitlin had sketched out the design for this logo. It was shortly before my mother died. I'd loved her business idea and had even pictured myself working with her. How could I live without the water? But I'd cobbled together another way. And now I could barely cross a bridge over the water without sweating.

The customers left, and Kaitlin came toward me. Her body remained as lean and tanned as it had been seven years ago. Her blond hair had been bleached white by the sun, and she'd plaited her long tresses into thick braids. She'd added a crescent-shaped tattoo to her right bicep. A few slight crow's-feet feathered from the corners of her eyes. We both wore our lives on our bodies. She looked free and satisfied with hers. I was rudderless and adrift.

Kaitlin wrapped her arms around me, swaddling me in strong arms and the scents of suntan lotion and CBD oil. "You made it. I wasn't so sure you'd cross the bridge."

My anxiety drained a fraction. "I can't believe it either. But I said I'd be here, so here I am."

She held me at arm's length, studying my pale skin and toneless muscles. "I'm glad you're out of that office. And that marriage. Neither was healthy. Both robbed your soul of energy."

Kaitlin was a big fan of life force theories. She was convinced if she was away from the ocean too long, she'd wither and die. I hadn't expired, but I felt as delicate as old paper. "I still have the job. The firm sent me down here to clean out the Brooks house. It's a flattop in Southern Shores."

"I know the house. It's been empty for years. Doesn't surprise me they're going to sell. The big clean is the first step toward letting go. Kind of like moving out after a divorce."

Kaitlin had never liked Dave. She'd met us once in a Norfolk bar. "Regarding the divorce," I said, "Dave was good for me for a long time. He helped me when I was lost. He wasn't bad or evil. I was just tired of him steering my ship. And he'd grown tired of my resentment."

"Resentment?"

"I blamed him for my choices."

She made a face. "Sounds like someone has had more therapy."

"I've been trying. So don't bust on Dave."

"Did I say anything bad about Dave?"

"'Land shark.' 'Land walker.' 'Predator on pavement.'"

She laughed. "That was a long time ago."

"We just weren't good for each other."

"Message received." She held up her hands in surrender. "Are you glad to be back? I could never work for someone else."

"The benefits are nice."

"Don't be sucked in by goodies like that. A healthy life and sunshine are our best defense."

"What about catastrophic injuries and illness?" Her mother's treatments had strained their insurance. And I'd become the worst-case-scenario disaster symbol after Mom died.

A brow rising, she grinned. "If it's that bad, money is the least of your worries."

Kaitlin had never worried. Life was easy and cool if you only relaxed. Law of attraction was her jam. I hadn't been around when her mother was ill, but I could imagine her always finding the positive in each day. If you can see it, it'll happen, according to Kaitlin.

But when her mother died, Kaitlin had been with her. She could visit her mother's grave.

"I'll keep that in mind," I said.

"I need more cleaning supplies, but I'll get more tomorrow. I've got to get to work."

"I'm here to help, as promised." She was letting me stay with her at her apartment upstairs from the surf shack, so I could at least help for the next two weeks.

She grinned. "I woke up yesterday morning asking the universe how I was going to get it all done. And then you texted."

"You have excellent karma."

She laughed. "That's how it works. Put good into the world, and it comes back."

"How many cleaning jobs today?" I asked.

"We have a big one this afternoon."

"I thought there weren't checkouts on Tuesdays."

"They are every day these days. With Airbnbs, people rent for a day, a night, and some still a week."

"Okay."

"Don't look so grim."

"And the surf shop? Who watches this place while you're cleaning?"

"I close for a few hours. No camps on Tuesdays. On Wednesdays and Thursdays, I clean in the mornings because of the afternoon surf camps."

"You must be doing pretty well."

She crossed her fingers. "Not quite breakeven, but it's getting there."

"Good. Nice to have a steady income."

After Mom died, I'd developed a fear of poverty. A counselor, Dr. Miller, had reminded me that—*news flash*—fear didn't stop us from dying or losing money. I'd pointed out that people starved to death and drowned daily. Beyond exercising reasonable caution, he'd warned, giving in to fear was unnecessary and indulgent. His no-nonsense advice had not helped initially, but it had slowly diluted some of my fears. Several months ago, Dr. Miller had questioned my inertia. I'd quit therapy.

"Money doesn't make you happy," Kaitlin said.

"It helps."

Kaitlin arched a brow. "You look like you just bit a lemon."

A smile broke over my face. "My resting sour face."

She laughed. "Surf and sun will fix that. Life is too short to worry, Tula."

But not too short to scrub toilets, push a vacuum, or wipe down kitchen counters.

"Want to see the van?"

"Van?"

"Our rolling cleaning machine."

"Sure."

We walked out the back door to the lot, which faced small rental homes and an old green van. Imprinted on the side was a magnetic sign that read **MERMAIDS**. More waves and fish tails splashed in the background.

"That's your mom's van," I said. "And it's the same color."

"Still runs great. More or less. She drips a little oil, so I carry extra. Had a friend repaint it for me."

"It's the same color."

"Fewer colors are cheaper." She combed fingers through her hair. "Hard to believe you're here."

"I don't believe it either. It wouldn't take much to talk me out of all this."

"But you won't, because you know I'd come after you."

"I did consider that."

"Smart woman."

"Where's our first job?"

"A duplex in Nags Head. It needs to be cleaned after a family reunion. The renter arrives this afternoon."

"Sounds like a lot of cleaning."

"Yeah, this one is chaos. But it's a surface clean. Basically, fresh linens, tidy up, and wipe down. No deep scrubbing required," she admitted. "I checked it out this morning." She looked me over. "You good to clean in those clothes?"

My shorts and athletic T-shirt weren't fancy, but they weren't exactly grunge. "I have other clothes for cleaning."

"Well, grab your bag from the car. We've got to get going."

"Like now?"

"Like five minutes ago."

I headed outside to my car and from the back seat opened my trash bag. I grabbed old cutoffs, a tank top, and worn sneakers. I vanished into the ladies' room. As I tied back my brown hair, the woman looking back from the mirror had a tight expression and eyes wide with fear. "What the hell am I doing here?"

When I emerged, Kaitlin had flipped the shop's OPEN sign to CLOSED and was already behind the wheel of her van. I tossed my travel clothes into my car and slid into the van's passenger seat.

"Just like the old days, right?" Kaitlin asked.

It was an uncomfortable full-circle moment. My mother had died, and I was staying with Kaitlin's family while I got myself together. Kaitlin's mom was too tired to work much, so I'd taken her place. I'd scrubbed toilets, wiped out refrigerators that smelled like death, mopped floors, and changed more bedsheets than I could count. "We cleaned our share of houses that last summer."

I'd hated every minute of it, but the job had given me time to shake off the shock of Mom's death. And at the end of each day, I'd had an odd sense of satisfaction. Cleaning was something I could control. Dirty. Clean. No gray areas. I'd left in late August, made a short detour to the mountains, and then fallen back to Norfolk and the job at Tierney, Brooks, and Bainbridge.

"Let's hope I remember your cleaning lessons," I said. "I don't want to slow you down."

"You'll pick it up quickly." She fumbled with her keys. "What's the deal with the Brooks house? Why are you dealing with it?"

"The former owner had an interest in the *Oceanus*. And my boss, his great-nephew, thought I might be interested."

"Seriously?"

"Mr. Brooks gave me a partial manuscript someone wrote about the ship. He said the rest might be in this house."

"Who wrote it?"

"Don't know. No name on it."

"And you want to know more about that wreck?"

Surprising myself, I said, "I think I do."

The van rumbled down the beach road. At milepost ten Kaitlin pulled onto a cracked concrete driveway that cut between larger, lightly colored homes built in the last few years.

The van's tires rattled over the driveway's ruts filled with weeds. The shrubs on either side were overgrown. "Is this the land that time forgot?"

The duplex looked as if it had been built in the seventies. It had a slightly pitched roof, faded green window shutters, and a porch that wrapped around the entire house. Amazing ocean views suggested that whoever stayed in this house wasn't interested in lingering inside.

"Just about," Kaitlin said. "The owner says he won't sell if he can keep renting. But rentals are slowing. He wasn't booked for June, and then it suddenly rented for the summer a few days ago."

Even rentals like this weren't affordable for locals on a long-term basis. "Lucky for Mr. Homeowner."

"The duplex is dated and rough, but the view from the back deck of the sunrises is stunning."

"Sunrises? You start that early?"

A nonchalant shrug lifted her shoulder. "I know the owner. We used to date. I stayed over a few times."

"Not dating anymore?" Kaitlin was always very private about her love life. Given that the Outer Banks felt like a small town on a long stretch of land, maintaining privacy was a challenge.

A beaded bracelet rattled as she smoothed her hand over her head. "No, but we're friends. And he always throws in a generous tip when he calls last minute."

"Like now?"

"Yeah. He wasn't expecting this rental and thought he could clean it himself, but he has work."

"Hence the emergency cleanup?"

"Yes."

"Let's hope this mess won't reach a level ten ick factor."

"I predict it's just untidy. A level three."

We'd rated the jobs in high school. A level ten was the stuff of nightmares. "Let's hope."

Kaitlin cut the engine, waiting as the motor rattled until it shut off. She got out of the van, and as I followed, she opened the back hatch and handed me a bucket and a mop. A warm breeze brushed strands of hair across my face.

She grabbed another box full of cleaning supplies, rags, and large plastic garbage bags. "Welcome to Team MERmaid."

"Do I get a T-shirt?" I quipped.

"You do. But it's at the office. Now on to the job."

I wrestled with the bucket, mop, and vacuum cleaner as I followed her up the stairs. She punched a code into the digital lock, and it opened. "Folks like us get a special code that works for all our clients."

"'Folks like us'?"

"Plumbers, electricians, any vendor that needs to get into a house."

"And they just give out the codes?"

"The codes get changed from time to time. It's a pain when they fail to notify me, but I have everyone's phone in my contacts."

"Are the busiest days still Saturday and Sunday?"

"And Friday. Friday check-ins and checkouts help with traffic."

The mop shifted and clunked me in the side of the head. "Do you get a lot of one-off jobs like today?"

"I never say no to any work."

She pushed open the door, and we stepped out of the heat into the cool, dark interior. Sandy grit ground under my athletic shoes. I flipped on the lights and was a little taken aback by the carnage. Beer cans, pizza boxes, wrappers, and other trash were spread throughout the house as if whoever was here just dropped whatever they didn't want and left. The couches had been pulled toward the sliding glass doors and were covered in sand. The couch legs and skirting were wet.

It appeared the renters had taken furniture on the beach. "It's a level eight."

"Yeah," she said with a frown. "But between the two of us, it'll go quickly." She snapped several pictures with her phone.

"For your memory book? Ten worst cleanup jobs? Before and After for the website?" I set down the bucket and vacuum cleaner. I reached into the supply bag, grabbed rubber gloves, and wiggled my fingers into the cool plastic.

"Good to document."

"Must have been some reunion." I picked up a pizza box filled with stale slices and shoved it into the garbage bag.

"I would say so."

We moved around the room, collecting bottles, cans, wadded-up sandwich wrappers, and stuff balled in tissues I didn't dare look at After we'd gathered all the debris and set the bags on the porch, I nodded toward the back bedrooms.

"I'll strip the sheets and bag them up," she said. "You tackle the kitchen."

"Right."

As Kaitlin moved to the bedrooms, I stepped into the kitchen. I loaded the dirty dishes into the dishwasher, filled the soap dispenser, and pressed start. Once the machine was humming, I filled the sink with hot soapy water and washed the large pots and platters.

"All the fast-food garbage, and they had time to trash the kitchen," I shouted.

Kaitlin paused, a bundle of sheets in her arms. "This won't be the worst you'll see in the next two weeks."

"Oh, I know. I'm already having flashbacks."

After another hour of picking up trash, making beds, and cleaning bathrooms, I finally had a clear path to run a vacuum and mop the floors. It took us a solid two hours to turn this disaster zone into a nice space.

"We better get going. The next renter will be here in an hour."

"Right. Any more places to clean today?"

"No, we have the evening to ourselves. How about we grab a beer at Arthur's and walk the beach after."

The sun wasn't too hot, and the crowds wouldn't be intense this week. But I'd have to build up to the beach. "Beer sounds good. But I'm not quite ready for the ocean." I'd avoided looking at the rental's views of breaking waves.

"It's not like you'll get in. We'll just sit on the sand. Terra firma. Nothing happens on the sand."

But the ocean churned up memories I'd spent seven years either burying or dragging kicking and screaming into the light with my therapist.

My mother, Mariah, had been an explorer. She'd traveled the world ever since she'd run away from Norfolk on her eighteenth birthday. She'd started as a crew member on whatever ship would take her to the best dive spots. Before I was born, she'd explored reefs and undersea life in all the most exotic locations.

And then, somewhere off the coast of Australia, she'd met a guy and gotten pregnant with me. They'd married a few months after I was born, and then they'd split. She had a few pictures of Dad and had only said nice things about him, but I'd never met him face-to-face. A week after I'd turned five, he was killed in a motorcycle accident in Indonesia. It had always been just Mom and me, so his loss didn't really land.

I didn't regret my childhood. It was magical in so many ways. I'd traveled to the Far East, the five oceans, and at least ten seas. By age ten, I could navigate by the stars or charts, sense when the weather was shifting, tie any kind of knot, and thrive in very small living spaces. I knew enough about backwater seaports to stay out of trouble. And I could size up brewing arguments on a ship and diffuse them. And once Mom's focus shifted to the wrecks, the metal boneyards became my playgrounds.

Mom had insisted I read at least twenty pages a day. Books, she'd said, were a sailor's best companion. I'd always had a pile by my bunk, and whenever we'd arrive in port, I'd find a store willing to swap my old titles for new ones. Oddly, I'd read very little in the last seven years.

It was a good life. I liked the freedom. And then, when we were in Greece, Mom had decided our next move would be the Outer Banks. She'd said it was time for a real school for at least a semester. I wasn't sure, but I was willing to give it a try.

The Outer Banks were rich with diving grounds. The water off the coast had earned the nickname "the Graveyard of the Atlantic" for good reason. Over the centuries, upward of three thousand ships had fallen prey to the area's shifting shoals, storms, or German U-boats. Mom was spoiled for choice.

While I hoisted my first school backpack onto my shoulder and headed off to high school, Mom became a regular at the history center in Manteo. She'd said she was hunting for treasure, and her focus quickly settled on the *Oceanus*, submerged in two hundred feet of water off the town of Southern Shores in the northern Outer Banks.

The *Oceanus* had been sunk by a German U-boat on April 24, 1942, when its torpedo had struck her broadside and hit her boilers and fuel tanks. The twelve-year-old passenger ship had been carrying 6,612 tons of chrome ore, wood, hides, and asbestos, along with 132 souls. Nineteen passengers or crew hadn't survived the attack.

What had caught Mom's attention was a passenger named William Weller. Born in New York City in 1900, he was an industrialist who had really made his money as a dealer of secrets and guns.

Mr. Weller had fled Vienna in December 1941, after the United States had declared war on Germany. Before he'd left Austria, he'd sold secrets to the Germans in exchange for gold bars. According to a cable sent the day of departure to his wife in New York City, he'd overseen the loading of his gold into the hull of the *Oceanus*.

I'd soon become well versed in the history of the *Oceanus*, and when Mom suggested we check out the location where she'd sunk, I'd been thrilled and anxious to get out of the classroom. On May 1, 2019, seventy-seven years after the *Oceanus* had sunk, we boated out to the site, less than three miles off the coast.

"You look lost," Kaitlin said as she opened the back of the van and loaded her supplies and bag of dirty linens.

"Remembering." I placed my supplies next to hers.

She closed the back hatch. "That's not a good thing, is it?"

"It didn't used to be. Too many broken hulls scattered in my past." I thought about the manuscript in my suitcase.

"I hate looking back," she said.

That was true. Kaitlin hated talking about last week, let alone seven or, worse, eighty years ago. "Nice to learn from old mistakes."

In the front seat, she started the engine. "What mistakes?" she asked.

"Don't marry a man you don't love."

Kaitlin put the van in reverse. "I thought you loved the land shark."

"I thought I did. And a part of me still cares. I wish the best for him."

"Seriously?"

"Yeah."

"You make it sound easy."

"It really is."

We drove down the beach road, but she took a quick left into a parking lot near the fishing pier. "Let's meet the beach now."

"No."

"Don't be a baby. Come on."

I drew in a breath. Too prideful to wimp out in front of her, I got out. We crossed the warm sand and stood by the pier's massive pilings.

"Take off your shoes," she said. "Only way to experience it.'

I removed my sneakers. The sand felt rough against my soft feet.

"Now, we step a little closer," Kaitlin said.

I watched her move with confidence toward the water. When I didn't follow, she clucked like a chicken. I followed.

As soon as I reached her side, a wave crashed against the shore and raced up to our feet. Cool water playfully ran between my toes and pulled the sand from under my feet as it slid back to the ocean.

"You mentioned mistakes earlier. Don't marry a man you don't love and . . ." Kaitlin let the statement dangle.

"The ocean will always be able to kill you."

"Only if you ignore her. Isn't that what you used to say? Listen to her, read her moods, notice the winds, and she won't let you down. I think about that all the time when I'm watching the waves. High peaks, sharp angles, or fast speeds, the water is always communicating."

"Sometimes she doesn't share every secret. She always has a trick or two up her sleeve." From the shore, the waves barreled up in an easy, timeless rhythm. Out on the water, it was less predictable. Sandbars shifted constantly, waves arrived in clusters, and rip currents tunneled out to sea with a gripping, swift force. This stretch of ocean was stunning, but its beauty didn't fool me. She could be dangerous.

"Do you miss it?" Kaitlin asked.

I'd grown up on the water, and being under or riding the waves had felt so natural. Now, it did not. "I miss feeling free."

"You are free," Kaitlin said softly.

I scooped up a handful of sand and let it drain through my fingers. "The *Oceanus* still haunts me."

"Then tackle it head on. Resharpen your diving skills and go see her again. Have a conversation with her. Tell her she's not welcome in your headspace anymore."

Mom had always said disasters weren't triggered by one big event. She'd said calamities erupted after a sequence of errors and failures. The first misstep for the *Oceanus* was the storm off Africa, which delayed her five days and cost her a spot with the convoy traveling to the United States. The second blunder belonged to Captain Stoddard, who thought his ship could outrun trouble. The next link in the tragic chain of events had been forged by the well-seasoned U-boat commander Korvettenkapitän Schulz. The German hadn't fulfilled his quota of sunken tonnage and refused to return to port with a torpedo still chambered. Schulz had taken a wild shot as the *Oceanus* turned. Miraculously the projectile had found its mark. When the torpedo struck, the damage would have been survivable if not for the last bit of bad luck. The explosion had ignited the ship's boilers and extra fuel.

I raised my phone and took several pictures. I texted them to my therapist. Look at me now. We hadn't spoken in months, but I felt as if I owed him something in the way of an apology.

"I'm sitting by the ocean," I said. "That's good enough for right now."

"It wasn't enough for the Tula I know."

"That Tula died seven years ago."

"No, she's sitting right here."

That Tula never would have married a controlling guy, taken a job in a cubicle, wedged her feet into sensible shoes, or collected Ann Taylor office wear on sale. That Tula had been like Kaitlin: tanned skin, sun-streaked hair, and shorts and flip-flops.

"And why did Mr. Brooks pick you?" she asked.

"My history isn't a secret, and I guess Mr. Brooks figured it would be of interest to me."

"Weird."

"Yeah."

"Have you started reading it?" When I didn't respond, she added, "It's a sign from the universe."

"A sign?"

"The ocean wants you to settle the past. Which you must do before you can move forward."

Kaitlin's phone dinged with a text. "Speaking of the past, you forgot to leave towels in the cottage."

That was a problem with an easy fix. "Give me the address. I'll drop them off."

Years of therapy faded as I thought about those yellowed pages. I'd been skimming the surface of my issues while sitting on the gray couch in my therapist's office. But I knew the undercurrents ran deeper than the day my mother had vanished.

CHAPTER FIVE

SIGRID

Monday, April 20, 1942, 3:00 p.m.
Four days until the Oceanus *is torpedoed*

William tucked in his shirt and then zipped up his pants. He fastened his belt and walked toward the long mirror and reached for one of the red ties he favored. He tied a tight knot and then shrugged on his jacket.

"I'm starving," he said.

I raised my gaze, avoiding eye contact with him as I climbed out of the bunk, naked and covered in his scent, and slid on a silk robe. "The lunch hour has ended, but I'm sure someone will feed you."

"Join me."

I sauntered toward him, the drape of my gown gaping open. "Darling, I'm not the least bit presentable."

He cupped my breast. I knew William better than he knew himself. He was wondering if it would be hard to let me go when we arrived in New York City. As much as he wanted to tuck me in an apartment, his wealthy wife would likely take offense. "You look fine. Put on one of your frocks."

"I need a bath and a few hours of quiet before I dress for dinner. I want to make you proud."

He touched my messy hair. He'd been gripping those strands fifteen minutes ago as he'd shoved inside me. His lovemaking was always hurried and vaguely unsatisfying, but that didn't stop me from moaning and faking an orgasm. "How hard can it be to fix a few flyaway hairs."

"Easier to start over than to repair." My practiced expression always conveyed ease.

"Suit yourself." He took in the round curve of my breasts bracketed by silk. "Stay in the room. It's not safe to move about the ship alone."

"I will."

He kissed me on the forehead, left the room, and locked the door with the one key. He'd done this routinely ever since we left Vienna. Safer for me to stay put, he'd always reasoned. But I knew he didn't trust me. I had contacts all over Europe, and if I turned against him . . .

He had also taken to securing his papers and telegrams in the room's safe. I could crack almost any lock and had many times. Save for removing my identity papers, I'd left his other items alone. He wouldn't rest easy until his gold in the ship's hull was safely unloaded and locked in his city town house's safe.

Ever since his last business deal in Vienna in late November, he'd grown more paranoid. Some had openly accused him of being a double spy, which I believed was true. William had no country allegiance and sold his services to the highest bidder.

I hadn't wanted to leave Vienna. In Vienna we'd lived like royalty. He'd traded secrets with my help and used my connections to enter the highest German and Austrian circles. I was as well known in the backstreets as I was the wealthiest ballrooms.

But I'd learned firsthand how the Germans treated suspected spies or independent women. I'd been arrested and held by the gestapo for five days in late November. The time was grueling and harsh.

But I had struck a deal with my interrogators that included leading William out of Vienna. I was practical enough to know I needed him right now. Not money, not jewels, but something far more personal. Still, despite my precarious position, I'd demanded a price of William.

We'd left Vienna with his gold last December on a boat owned by my distant cousin, who knew the waterways better than anyone. From Budapest, we'd sailed to Portugal, where we boarded another ship traveling to Port of Spain. William never questioned our route, grateful to be clear of the Germans and police.

I'd hated to leave my silk dresses, art, and jewelry behind, but in the end, I had no choice. Since my arrest, I had my own agenda, and if I didn't fulfill it, the gold and the United States wouldn't matter.

Our cabin wasn't generous by shipping standards and was a letdown from where I'd been. But it was the best the *Oceanus* had to offer, and it was only temporary.

Outside the door, I heard William pause as if listening to the sound of my feet padding around the room. Finally, his footsteps echoed down the hallway.

I rejected fear and her cousin desperation. Both were vicious sirens who always lurked close by, ready to lure me toward destruction. In the United States the war would be so far away, and soon, once I had what I needed from William, the war, the Germans, and the losses would fade like a dream.

CHAPTER SIX

GERTRUDE

Monday, April 20, 1942, 3:30 p.m.
Four days until the Oceanus **is torpedoed**

Land had fallen out of sight, and we were surrounded by endless choppy waters smacking against the ship. My stomach curled in knots.

The currents of the Danube River, bordered by muddy banks, might have felt trivial compared to the Atlantic's mighty rolling waves, but they were just as dangerous. Though I'd put miles between myself and Strauss's blue Danube, its waters flowed west to east, dumping into the Black Sea before trickling into the Aegean and Mediterranean Seas and finally the Atlantic Ocean. I imagined some of those waters now sliding past the *Oceanus*, circling the hull of the ship named for the Greek god who'd fathered the river creatures. Four years ago, I'd stood on the Danube's banks and struck a deal with those gods when I'd tossed my wedding coin into the sliding waters.

I drew in a breath. *You won't escape me.* The words whispered close to my ear.

A knock on my door had me turning. "Yes?"

"It's Chief Mate Riggs. Captain Stoddard asked me to check in on you and deliver you a lunch plate."

I unlatched the chain and opened the door. I'd barely noticed him when I'd boarded the ship, but now I had a clear view of his face. The seaman was a pleasant-looking man with thick dark hair that swept across his forehead. Crow's-feet radiated from brown eyes. And when he smiled, his sun-drenched skin set off even white teeth.

"How are you feeling?" he asked.

My rounded belly was hidden by the partially opened door.

"I am well, thank you."

He held up the tray. "The lunch hour passed, but the captain said you might want to eat. The baby must be hungry."

Baby. *I am not afraid,* I reminded myself. Early in my pregnancy, I'd ignored the baby's existence. I'd blamed the morning illness on poor food, stress, and dread until the physician had confirmed my fears. Whatever creature was inside always pulled at me now.

I am not afraid. The mantra, worn bare now, had lost most of its power as it was overshadowed by my growing belly. I fully opened the door and accepted the tray. "You are very kind."

"You'll get in touch if you need any help? The captain wants you to ask for any assistance."

I'd seen the astonished looks on the sailors' faces when they'd seen my large stomach. The men were terrified I'd deliver on the ship. "Of course."

He dropped his voice. "Are you really well?"

"Very well."

"If you're still hungry, the first dinner seating is at six. You will join us?"

"I hadn't planned on it." I braced against the door as the ocean swayed beneath the ship. I hadn't traveled by water for over two months, and my sea legs had abandoned me. The rolling water felt unnatural, and I craved solid ground.

His eyes brightened. "I'd be happy to escort you around the deck after dinner."

"Very kind, but I will manage."

Disappointment chipped at his smile. "Of course."

"I've been on the ship since Cape Town," he added. He'd missed my cue to leave. "The food is good, and you'll find the company acceptable. You've met Dr. Brooks. He's promised to entertain us with his cards and charms tonight."

"I don't have formal wear." I owned the frock I wore and two others. And unfortunately, the best of the three was tight around my waist.

"We don't stand on ceremony on the *Oceanus*."

My manner of dress was the very least of my fears or worries. What bothered me most was that I might become the topic of conversation among strangers. The human mind liked having neat facts, and if there were no answers to be found to questions, the brain filled the cracks with fiction and speculation. It didn't matter if their theories were right or wrong. They were as real to them as fact. I could not risk their gossip for the remaining five days.

"I will consider it."

"Excellent." He bowed slightly.

I closed and locked the door. I set the rattling tray on the table and lay down on my bunk. My body reverberated with fatigue. I wanted to pull the blankets over my head and sleep for the next year. In that year, the distance between the past and me would have widened, and perhaps the world would have changed for the better.

I rested knitted fingers across my chest. The cabin rocked back and forth, creaking and moaning as if trying to soothe me.

You are safe here now, the waters whispered.

"I'm not safe anywhere." My husband's reach was far, and he would not rest until he found me.

My fingers skimmed the rough skin just below my neckline. It was a crescent scar that mirrored the signet ring my husband had worn.

Alfred heated his metal signet ring in the fireplace and crossed to me. I was so naive. I didn't understand what he planned, but then he climbed on top of me and pinned my arms with his knees.

As the hot metal drew closer to me, I squirmed. "What are you doing?"

"This is for your own good."

The heat drew closer. "Alfred, please stop, I beg you."

And then the metal pressed hard against the skin above my breast. My flesh seared. Shock gave way to pain. I screamed.

When he pulled the ring away, I struggled to catch my breath. "What man does this to his new bride?"

"One who loves her more than life."

He climbed off me, and I rolled to my side. Tears streamed down my cheek.

He set the ring down and reached for a vial of ointment. Gently, he rolled me onto my back.

"Stop," I demanded. "Not again."

"Shh." His salve-dipped finger smoothed the wounded skin.

I winced. "Please, you're hurting me."

He continued to rub, and soon the pain eased. "You'll find that I'll always do what's best for you."

His touch was now so gentle. So soft.

"You understand, don't you?" he asked.

Back was the kind man who'd wooed me with rare books and treats for an old cat, protected our little bookshop from those who would burn it, and helped me bury my uncle.

When he kissed me on the lips, I tasted the champagne from our wedding toast. His face hovered inches from mine, and he said tenderly, "I love you so much. Tell me you understand."

I wanted to believe the monster was gone forever. But the worst monsters shifted shapes and never vanished completely.

"Yes. I do." But I would soon learn that Alfred enjoyed cruelty.

The warning signs were lost on me early in our marriage, and I paid dearly with more of his lessons in love. But I grew to watch his moods carefully, ready for a light mood to darken. Eyes to narrow. His voice to harden. A fist to rise. I quickly learned never to ignore harbingers of trouble. I'd lived on tenterhooks for three years.

Now, I stared at the ceiling of my cabin, watching the sun dim and cast shadows. Most nights, I never fell into a deep sleep. My mind always hovered somewhere below consciousness, as if I was ready for danger.

Shouts rang out from the hallway, and I sat up. My heart knocked against my ribs. Sweat dampened my upper lip and pooled at the base of my spine.

Swinging my legs over the bunk, I rose. The rolling floor caught me off balance, forcing two quick staggered steps until my unwieldy frame steadied.

And then the clock chimed six. Somehow, I'd fallen into a deep sleep.

Footsteps thumped past my doorway. I had become skilled at listening for signs that Alfred was outside my door. Now, I heard only the rattle of keys and the tones of conversations. Whoever was passing by my cabin sounded relaxed, slightly joyful. A deep voice mentioned beef tips and sorbet.

I looked toward the tray of food. Safer to eat here and keep to myself. But I didn't want to remain in this cramped room alone with my darkest memories.

I walked toward the washbasin and filled it with water. I splashed cold water on my face and pressed fingertips to puffy eyes. I didn't dare gaze in the mirror as I turned from the stand and dried my face. These days I didn't recognize myself, and the near stranger staring back reminded me of my own stupidity. I brushed my dark hair, noting more strands clinging to the bristles. I secured my hair in a twist with the few pins I still had and brushed the wrinkles from my dress.

Lowering myself into the tufted chair, I slid on my shoes and grunted slightly as I leaned over to tie the laces. In five days, I would be in the United States. I would deliver this child in a hospital, and then I would leave the infant behind in the care of people better suited than me. Though I hated what this child represented, I prayed my small act of mercy would allow me to one day forgive myself.

CHAPTER SEVEN

Tula

Tuesday, June 9, 2026, 7:15 p.m.
Outer Banks, North Carolina

I arrived at the rental condo, carrying a basket of folded, freshly cleaned towels and hand cloths. The scent of pine drifted around me as I waited for the renter to answer the door.

The door opened to a tall guy with tanned skin and dark hair that skimmed his wide shoulders. I was smiling even before I raised my gaze because that was business 101. You mess up, you be nice.

My gaze rose over flip-flops, board shorts, and a black T-shirt. His dark hair was tinged with strands of silver, and even the curiosity darkening his eyes didn't register. Time, context, whatever, wasn't syncing. And then the past drew back like the tide, and I saw familiarity in blue eyes that even seven years hadn't changed.

"Nathan." I clutched the towels, holding on to them as if they were armor. "Wow. How are you?"

Nathan Rogan had interned with my mother when we were in Greece, and he'd followed us to the United States to dive the *Oceanus*. He was an excellent diver and was a wizard with maps that charted the ocean surface and bottom. He'd mapped the entire area around the

Oceanus for Mom. Because of him, Mom knew where the large hole had punctured the vessel's hull. She knew the boat lay on its port side, and one of its two smokestacks had cracked and drifted two hundred yards south. The plan had been for Nathan to dive with Mom that last day. He was going to be her eyes and ears and the lone voice of reason Mom would accept.

But that day, Nathan had broken his arm somehow. He'd called Mom from the emergency room and told her he couldn't come and to wait. But Mom was impatient to see the wreck that day, so she drafted me as her dive buddy, allowing me to skip school. I was thrilled. We'd dived hundreds of times before, and neither of us worried about the last-minute switch. That was another small link in a string of missteps that would matter a great deal later.

"I'm great." His voice was deeper than I remembered, with hints of gravel. "I didn't know you were back."

"Just arrived today. I'm working with Kaitlin." I held up my bundle as proof. "I'm here to bring you towels."

My face warmed as he stared at me. Shit. When we'd met, I was sixteen and he was twenty-two. God, I had such an intense crush on him. But he always kept things so professional. He might joke or kid around, but he never reacted to my awkward flirting.

Back then, I was tanned, fit, and so confident. And now here I stood. No makeup. Covered in sweat. And sporting an extra ten, maybe fifteen pounds that had settled on my ass. *How far the mighty have fallen.* It was the lone Bible verse my mom would quote when someone—mostly me—got a little too full of herself.

I handed him the towels. "Good to see you."

"And you. You here for good?"

"No. Just for the summer." *Here* could never be home. I hadn't forgiven this place for taking Mom. "Helping Kaitlin and cleaning and clearing out a house in Southern Shores for my company. And then, who knows?"

He grimaced. "Back to the city and a cubicle and the husband?"

His teasing shifted me to defense. "Maybe to the cubicle. Divorced the husband."

Nathan's grin widened. "I never pictured you in an office."

No more mention of Dave, which was just as well. I said sarcastically, "And yet, I make my living in an office." I was a coward. I'd traded the ocean I loved for the land. "Again, sorry about the towels."

As I turned, Nathan said, "Hey, I'm glad I saw you. I want you to hear this from me first."

The last person who had said those words to me had been a coworker who'd reported she'd seen my soon-to-be ex-husband sucking face with his new administrative assistant in a darkened restaurant booth. I heaved the edges of my lips into a smile and faced him. "What's that?"

"I'm going to be diving the *Oceanus*."

The ground shifted as if I were on the deck of a rolling ship. "Really?"

"I hated the way it ended. I want to spend time with her and see if she has any more secrets."

The *Oceanus* had more to her story, but I still hadn't decided whether I wanted to know it. Annoyance long buried deep swam to the surface. "How it ended? An understatement, I think."

He stabbed long fingers through his hair. "It always bothered me that I didn't dive with Mariah that day. I would've dragged her to the surface."

Nathan was right. Mom would've listened to him. But hearing it from him felt like salt water on a wound. "I get it. She didn't listen to me. I should've tried harder."

"You had a soft spot for her. And she could talk you into all kinds of crazy adventures. That's natural. She was your mother, and she loved you. But I'd have grabbed her by the arm and dragged her to the surface. No one survives without air or in a storm like the one that swept up the coast that day."

Weather forecasters had eventually classified that storm as a nor'easter. Arriving in May, it was late for the season, but its tardiness didn't weaken its impact. Winds had reached forty miles an hour. Mom was so convinced the storm wouldn't materialize.

The seas were still relatively smooth as we motored north. Mom was moody but optimistic. She was never happier than when she was preparing to dive a wreck. And her enthusiasm was measured. She'd always been blessed when it came to the water, and reliance on luck was the first major mistake.

We'd dropped anchor at the wreck's coordinates. I kept glancing at the few clouds gathering to the north. She told me not to worry. And then we jumped into the water, and the ocean pulled us under.

The final mistake was mine. I'd assumed Mom would follow me when I'd signaled her to rise. I believed she'd have the sense to leave the wreck, knowing we'd return another day.

After, Nathan had called me several times, but I let it all go to voicemail. He'd left the Outer Banks by July, and that was that.

I cleared my throat. "Why dive here now?" I asked.

"I applied for a grant to explore the *Oceanus* and received it."

Imagine that we'd end up here at the same time.

"I tried to write you a dozen times, but I never knew what to say," he said.

"Not much you could say."

"You're wearing her coin," he said.

"I found it in my mother's suitcase after. She left it for me."

"Why did she leave it?"

"I don't know. Why do you want to dive the *Oceanus* again? She's cursed, as far as I'm concerned."

"Cursed? You sound like a true sailor."

"Still think the gold is there?"

A frown deepened the lines bracketing his mouth. "It was never about the gold for me."

"It was for Mom. She said it could be her big payday."

"Do you really believe that? She'd never dived for treasure before."

Mom's shift toward money was an odd change, but I hadn't questioned her. "She was then."

"Not me. I just want to see the wreck. It'll help me make peace with it all. And I'm making a film."

He had a YouTube channel with over a million followers. His videos received hundreds of thousands of views, proof that people liked his adventures. Monetization of the channel had to pay a few bills. I'd watched his channel over the years when I'd had too much to drink or was feeling nostalgic.

"You found a way to drive up those clicks?"

"No one is going to get rich off these dives."

I shook my head, wondering why I was getting into this with him. "Mom was so far in debt when she died. She thought the gold would solve all her problems." I was a minor, so no one had told me how deep the debt ran until after she'd died. I wasn't held responsible for her bills, but she'd left nothing behind of value.

Absently, I fingered the coin and sea-glass necklace. "All I inherited from Mom was PTSD and an irrational fear of the ocean."

"You used to love it. I'm sorry."

"Don't be. It was great until it wasn't. Life goes on." I took a step back. I thought I could return to the beach and clean out that house without any emotional consequences. But I found myself swimming in deep waters. No amount of steady breathing or meditation would fix what was churning inside me.

"I didn't mean to blindside you," Nathan said. "But I'm glad you heard about the dives from me."

"I appreciate that." The muscles in my chest pulled, making a deep breath hard. It had been a while since I'd had a full-blown panic attack. And I didn't want to have one in front of Nathan. *Please, just give me a little dignity. Let me walk away without breaking down.* "Call Kaitlin if you need any supplies or are having trouble with the house."

"Everything is great." He held up the towels slightly as if to prove his statement.

"Terrific."

I turned and walked toward my car. I didn't look back, because I knew his expression remained a mixture of sadness and expectation.

With each step, my muscles twisted tighter. My breathing grew more deliberate. Being this close to the ocean and now Nathan was testing all my therapist's positive mantras.

Breathe in. Breathe out.

Behind the wheel of the car, I started the engine and backed out of the driveway toward the beach road. A horn blared and a car zoomed past me. I slammed on the brakes and gripped the wheel, triple-checked the road, and pulled out. My vision was narrow, and tension rippled over my body. I drove to the surf shop at thirty miles an hour, fearful I'd implode.

When I pulled into the parking lot, the building was dark. Good. Everyone was gone. I hefted my suitcase and climbed the back staircase.

The evening air was warm and the breeze gentle. When I reached the second floor, I could see over the cottages to the beach road by the ocean. My stomach tumbled. The damn water was everywhere.

Kaitlin's apartment upstairs had two bedrooms, with a central living room and kitchen. The couch was long, its olive green tweed obscured by several brightly colored quilts. The coffee table was a reclaimed door, filled with shells covered in a polymer. Surfing magazines were strewn across the table. Four colorful, scratched, and well-used surfboards hung from hooks on the walls. Kaitlin adored surfing.

My purse dropped to the grass-colored carpet, and I sat on the sofa. Dipping my head back, I stared at the ceiling, painted with waves. I drew in a partial breath. And then another and another. Finally, the pressure eased. My muscles still ached, but they no longer cramped.

I fished my phone from my pocket and found the few images I had of Mom and me. In all the pictures, we were standing by a body of water. The South Pacific. The Mediterranean Sea. The Black Sea. Tanned bodies. Swimsuits. Scuba gear.

There were no baby pictures of me. Mom had said she'd taken a few with an old camera but had lost track of them over our many moves. The reality was she'd been working long hours when I was little, and collecting memories was an afterthought.

The first picture of me was on my sixth birthday. It was taken in Fiji. Mom and I were diving an Australian freighter wreck called the *David J. Magnus*. Mom had just argued with another dive instructor over air tanks, and tension edged her smile. The next image was taken five years later. We were off the coast of Italy. Mom was a paid guide, and we were diving a Roman ship that had sunk two thousand years ago. By eleven I was working on the dive boat, helping the customers with their gear. And the last photo was here on the Outer Banks. We hadn't dived the *Oceanus* yet, but we'd boated out to the dive spot. The water was calm and the sky a crystal blue. Mom had slung her arm around me, and we were laughing. Nathan had taken the picture.

Our years together boiled down to a few captured moments, my necklace, and the ocean. Why hadn't either Mom or I tried harder to record our lives more?

"We were a sad little duo, you and I."

Maybe Mom's detachment had been what had driven Dad off. My talent for distance had tanked my marriage.

The door opened to Kaitlin with a couple of bags of groceries. "How did it go?"

"Towels dropped off." I closed the phone and rose. "Did you know the guy renting was Nathan Rogan?"

She set the bags on the narrow aqua counter. "Maybe."

"And you didn't think to give me a heads-up?"

As she shrugged, a strand of hair fell forward. "Either way, the towels needed to be delivered."

"And I would've done the job either way."

She pulled out a bag of apples and a jar of almond butter from the refrigerator. "Would you?"

"I would have."

Her brow rose. "Tell me the truth."

"Okay. I'd have dropped them on his porch, rung the bell, and run."

"What are you afraid of?"

"What aren't I afraid of?"

She tilted her head to the side. "One way or another, you needed to bite the bullet and talk to him. Now you have seen him, so it'll be fine. If you run into him, it won't be as weird."

"I almost had a panic attack on the way home."

"Almost? That's positive, right?"

"It wasn't great, but it wasn't terrible."

She fished bread from the bag. "Do you admit it was a little progress?"

"It's not saying much when I can brag about not screaming and falling into the fetal position."

"I disagree. Being here is good for you."

"He's diving the *Oceanus*. He received a grant kind of out of the blue."

Kaitlin drew in a breath. "I know."

"How did you know this?"

"We've traded texts over the years."

"He's filming this trip."

"Good. It could help."

"It's ridiculous."

"Is it? You took the job to clean out the house of a guy who might be an *Oceanus* buff." She sliced an apple into quarters. "Maybe this is your chance to make peace with the shipwreck that ruined your life."

CHAPTER EIGHT

Tula

Wednesday, June 10, 2026, 6:15 a.m.

I'd lain in bed last night at first staring at the waves painted on the ceiling. Sleeping under the ocean might be dreamy for some, but for me it was overpowering. I'd finally closed my eyes, and conjured fields of wheat and rolling mountains filled with clean, crisp air. Living in the mountains had always been on the top of my bucket list, but I'd lasted two weeks in the Blue Ridge Mountains before moving back to Norfolk. Like it or not, I remained chained to the coast. Couldn't live with it or without it.

Finally, at about 2:00 a.m., I'd turned on a light and dug the partial manuscript out of my bag. I'd run my fingers over the type. The letters *a* and *l* were deeper than the others, suggesting the typewriter's or typist's uneven strikes. When the clock crept past two thirty, I read a couple of dozen pages until the day's fatigue caught up. Finally, I'd fallen asleep close to 3:00 a.m.

When my alarm went off, I woke to the steady beat of crashing waves and the smell of coffee. I blinked. The coffee made sense, but not the waves. In my nightmares, the surf was always louder and angrier.

But these breakers were soft and steady, as if to say they'd been here a long time and would remain well after we'd all passed.

I closed my eyes and convinced myself that I wasn't at the beach. Dave and I were still good, and solid predictable days were what I wanted. We were planning to build our mountain cabin. I wasn't unsettled or yearning for something that remained out of reach

And then my brain cleared. And I remembered.

Groaning, I sat up and swung my feet over the side of the twin bed.

I found the small restroom, which had a sink, toilet, vanity, and shower all within centimeters of each other. The closet-sized bathroom triggered a few flashbacks. How many times had I blown the breakers on a sailing ship with my hair dryer or tripped over the toilet coming out of the shower? Living on a boat sounded like a dream for many, but it came with challenges.

I showered quickly in the small space. Shaving my legs was a balancing act, with one foot planted on the plastic wall and my butt shoved against the other side of the narrow stall.

The floor was wet when I stepped out and reached for a dark blue towel. I dried my hair and returned to my room so I'd have the space to dress. I chose cutoff jeans, a blue T-shirt, and flip-flops.

I moved through the small apartment toward the kitchen. I found Kaitlin standing at the counter, sipping coffee as she stared out the back window. Without a word, I grabbed an "OBX" mug and the carafe from a beige Mr. Coffee that had been in her mother's kitchen. I envied this relic. I had only a necklace and a few pictures to connect me to my mother.

"What's on the docket for today?" I asked.

She remained still for a moment, and I thought she hadn't heard me. Then she turned. "Chaos. But that's par for the course."

"Define 'chaos.'"

"Six Airbnbs need to be flipped by three. Mini-camp at six this evening."

"I'm not helping with the surf camp, correct?"

"No, but as soon as you finish that coffee, we ride. We need to grab cleaning supplies and then hit the first property at nine a.m."

"Where?"

"They're all north of Duck."

"We get ahead of the traffic." The two-lane road that wound through Duck spent most of the summer in a state of gridlock. I added, "After we're finished, I want to stop by the house in Southern Shores. I can drive if you don't have the time to stop."

"No, I should have a little time. It's on the way back to Nags Head."

"Can I take my coffee with me?"

"Sure. You hungry?"

"Not really."

"You didn't eat much."

"I'll grab a candy bar or chips at some point."

She cringed. "That kind of eating is going to kill you."

"Dave said that a lot. And I'm still standing." And ten or, realistically, twenty pounds heavier.

She grabbed a granola bar and handed it to me. "What's the land shark up to these days?"

"I believe he's prepping for an ultramarathon in Wisconsin. Maybe an IRONMAN, I think. Whatever, it's a ridiculous amount of time running." Dave was addicted to working out. There wasn't a moment when he wasn't either preparing for a ride, racing, or recovering from an injury or muscle strain. I'd been his support team for several years. I never liked the races, but he loved them, and I was on Team Dave.

"I never said I'm sorry about the divorce. I know you wanted the marriage to work."

"Lesson learned. No one can be your anchor, no matter how hard you wish it." I'd thought living with a land lover who worshiped solid ground would provide the distance I needed from the ocean. But the longer I stayed away, the more miserable I became. And still, I hadn't quit the cubicle job, because I was afraid to be totally untethered.

"We've all had lessons like that."

I summoned a bright smile. "Can we focus on scrubbing toilets? I'm kind of jazzed about that."

Kaitlin laughed. "Your wish is my desire."

Cross-body purse slung over my shoulder and coffee in hand, I followed her through the dimly lit living room. "How did you find this place?"

"The former owner ran a bait-and-tackle shop. I heard he was retiring, and I came to see him. We hit it off immediately, and he priced this place so I could afford it."

"That was nice."

"Beyond kind. He loved the idea that I surfed."

"How's it working for you?"

"Location's great and the monthly payment manageable, but being a property owner is more of a commitment than I realized."

Whitewashed beams, blond wood floors, and light blue walls gave the space a magical feeling. The secondhand cargo furniture found on the side of the road had been painted all shades of blues and whites, along with the coffee table, covered in shells and polyurethane coating. The surfing art covered walls in need of a paint job. Air-conditioning strained against the late-spring heat, and the windows looked like they couldn't stand up to a nor'easter's winds and rain.

This building promised years of evening and weekend work. It could be cool—one day. But I didn't plan to be here that long.

"There are times I want to sell," Kaitlin said. "I have this desire to travel the world with my board. A free spirit, you know? I've always been stuck here."

"Why don't you sell? There's nothing really holding you here."

"I've worked hard to build all this. And my mother would roll over in her grave if I gave up the cleaning business."

"Honey, your mother has passed. You got to live your own life."

"I envy you sometimes. You've always been able to distance yourself. You never get too attached emotionally, if you know what I mean."

"Not exactly a superpower."

"I wish I was more like the old you."

I did too sometimes. "Be careful what you wish for."

Kaitlin sighed. "Right. I'm sorry."

"Don't apologize." There was a slight hitch in my throat when I spoke. "I read some of the manuscript last night. Slow going. Some of the type has faded."

"And?"

"Talk of spirits and magical coins among the passengers. Dr. Brooks mentioned he wished for a long life. He got it."

"Never underestimate magic. This is a magical place. Some say we live on the edge separating the living and dead."

"Mom used to toss some of her coffee into the ocean each morning before she dove. She said it was for the ocean gods."

I couldn't remember if Mom had poured any coffee into the water that last day.

"She also wore that coin on a cord around her neck, like you do now."

"She left it behind that final dive."

"I remember." She hesitated, not voicing what I'd feared. That Mom knew she wasn't coming back. "Where did she get it?"

"She said her dad gave it to her." All I knew about my grandfather was that he served in the merchant marines and was at sea for most of his life.

"Do you ever take it off?"

I fingered the coin and crystal. Dave had often asked me to take off the necklace when we had a formal event for his work, but I never did. "No."

"A good luck talisman."

"Maybe."

Outside, we crossed to the van. I slid into the front, clicked my seat belt. The morning heat had already warmed the seats. The pine scent of cleaning supplies wafted around the cab. I rolled down my window, hoping not to asphyxiate in the next thirty minutes.

As the van rolled over the bridge, Kaitlin mused, "Amazing what you learn about people when you clean up after them." Her van window was open, too, and a cool breeze wafted through the cab.

We were driving across the bridge to the mainland to pick up supplies at Currituck Cleaners. Many of the people who made daily life possible—plumbers, electricians, police, even teachers—didn't live on the Outer Banks. Housing on OBX was tricky. The houses were either too expensive or in need of so much repair that it would take a decade and hundreds of thousands of dollars to bring them into this century. Kaitlin had gotten lucky when she'd bought the former bait store.

I gripped the armrest on the van's door and arrowed my gaze forward, avoiding the sight of the sound's choppy waters. High winds made the bridge sway slightly, and I was certain the waters mocked me.

"You haven't asked me about the secrets I've discovered while cleaning houses," Kaitlin said.

"Not interested."

"Everyone wants to hear a little dirt."

She was trying to distract me from the lapping sound beneath the bridge. "You gossip about your clients?"

"Never. But now I have you."

"I'm not sure I need more dirt in my life." We crested the top of the bridge and glided down toward the mainland road.

Her sunglasses tossed back my reflection when she looked back at me. "Are you sure?"

"My dysfunctional life is at capacity. I'm not sure how much more I can handle."

"Your life is tame compared to some."

Did that make me feel better? Misery always craved a little company. "I really don't want to know."

"Excellent. You just passed a test." She shifted in her seat and tightened her grip on the steering wheel. "I never share what I see in any of these homes, but a few employees of mine have. I fired them. You're going to see some stuff. And I'll stay in business longer if you only tell me what you see."

"People talked about me when I lived here, and it wasn't fun to be the girl whose mother was lost at sea. The long lingering stares and whispers weren't fun. No matter how hard I worked at being normal, I was always That Girl."

"That wasn't your fault."

"Maybe, but people still love a tragic tale. It makes them feel better about their lives."

Mariah Cassidy had become larger than life after her disappearance. She became super smart, well traveled, funny, kind, and brave.

Everyone, including me, edited out the bad stuff: dangling questions, run-on flaws, and meandering choices that had led nowhere. I stopped thinking about the times she'd drunk too much or taken off for days, leaving me to fend for my ten-year-old self with the ship's cook, a salty sailor named Madge, or hotel staff. There were times when we packed our suitcases and left at night because she didn't have rent money.

Dying dramatically had cleaned up a lot of issues. And these days, I only pictured the woman with a fit body, muscled arms, and a laugh that always lightened my mood. And it was kind of a relief. Ever since my separation from Dave, I'd caught myself asking Mom for advice. And sometimes I thought maybe she'd reached from the beyond and offered me sage counsel. *Don't open another bottle of wine, and avoid the local dive bar for a hookup.*

My therapist said that Mom and I were a lot alike. We both were prone to emotional distance. And Mom could no sooner let go of her wrecks than I could abandon my sixty-hour workweeks. We clung to what helped us avoid the messy moments families or loved ones required of us. Fixation was our hiding place, but it chipped at our tethers to the real world.

Kaitlin crossed onto the mainland, and my fingers eased on the armrest. I flexed the stiff joints. "You're not a tragic tale," she said. "Be positive."

A misshapen smile strained my facial muscles.

She cringed. "Stop, you're scaring me."

"I'm trying to be positive. Smiles are optimistic, right?"

Wind flicked the edges of her blond hair around her face. "Oh, they are, but that smirk reminds me of the Joker or Loki."

For the first time in months, maybe years, something broke loose inside me. Ice cracked and floated down a frozen river. "It's not that bad."

My tone had softened, and she knew she had breached the armor. "A cartoon evil mastermind would be jealous."

"Fine. It was a little forced." Coiled anxiety unfurled a bit more, and a genuine grin flickered.

"But now it's not. And that's progress. You're going to find living at the beach to be good for you."

"Or it's going to kill me."

"Maybe. But you'll survive."

"Survive dying?"

"You know what I mean."

Five more miles down the road, Kaitlin pulled into the parking lot of a one-story warehouse building that appeared to house several businesses. Pool supplies in A-1, lawn service in B-2, and cleaning supplies in C-3.

In C-3, we were greeted by a heavy pine scent that conjured up images of bottles of liquid gold. The floor glistened, and the countertops were wiped clean. Behind the counter was a slim woman with dark hair. She wore wire-rimmed glasses and a sober expression.

"Hey, Lynn," Kaitlin said. "Ready to pick up my order."

Lynn's expression tightened. "We just finished boxing up a partial order. You ready for the season?"

That question got asked a lot this time of year. "The season" meant higher prices, more traffic on the roads, and crowded beaches and stores. The prime twelve weeks of summer were the gold rush for most down here. This was the make-or-break time, because as soon as the tourists left, life and revenue reduced to a crawl.

"I'm ready," Kaitlin said. "We have a packed schedule, which is a good thing. Last two years have been great."

"Good and bad, I guess. Can't enjoy warm empty beaches if you don't have money."

Kaitlin jabbed a thumb toward me. "This is my friend Tula Cassidy. She's back on OBX and is helping me clean for a couple of weeks."

"Your friend?" Lynn hesitated as she mentally flipped through memories. "That's right. Tula used to live here. Your mother was lost at sea."

In high school, this bold mention of my mother's death would have sent me scrambling from the room. I would have refused to cry, but bottled emotions would have festered and stewed until late at night, when tears finally fell. Now the old wound was covered in scar tissue.

"That's me," I said.

"I'm very sorry for your loss," Lynn said. "We all felt so bad for you."

My story had been a cautionary tale for everyone on the Outer Banks. You could live close to the ocean, and though it was stunningly breathtaking at times, it could also consume you or someone you loved. I reminded everyone of that dark fact. After Mom vanished, and before she became a saint, many questioned her judgment regarding currents, the potentially looming storm, and Mother Nature's wrath.

Even as volunteers searched for her body, many whispered that Mariah Cassidy thought her long-standing relationship with the ocean exempted her from danger. They righteously stated that the ocean did not care about backstories, reasons, or excuses. It did its thing. It was up to us to heed the warnings.

Her loss had reignited interest in the *Oceanus*. Some divers hoped to find the mythic gold. And even years later, others wondered morbidly if they could find Mariah Cassidy's body. A few posted videos on YouTube about their adventures. I'd watched one, and it had triggered a full-blown panic attack. I hadn't seen an *Oceanus* video in over six years.

Thankfully, no one had found Mom or the gold. The ocean had decided to keep them both.

"Thank you," I said to Lynn, returning to the present.

"Are you here all summer?" she asked.

"I'm cleaning out a house for the owners. Been in the family for decades. I'm not sure how long it will take."

"Where's the house?"

"Southern Shores."

Lynn nodded. "Must be the Brooks house."

Small-town living. "That's right."

"It's been empty for several years," Lynn said. "You think they'll sell?"

"No idea. My job is to clean it out."

"If you need supplies, you know where to find me," Lynn said.

"Will do."

"Being back here doesn't bother you?" she asked.

I had to hand it to Lynn. She served her questions right to my face. "Check back in a few weeks. I'll let you know."

Lynn nodded and waved us behind the counter. "Come get your supplies."

She led us through a maze of boxes and bottles of all kinds of containers filled with pink and blue cleaning solutions. She stopped at two marked "Kaitlin."

"Help yourself, ladies. Your order is light, but come back later in the week for more."

Kaitlin nodded thoughtfully before lifting the bigger of the two boxes. "Okay. Text me when it arrives."

Lynn handed Kaitlin an invoice.

Kaitlin didn't scan the bill. "I'll take care of this right away."

"Good," Lynn said.

I hefted one of the containers, straining a little as I adjusted my grip. Back muscles tensing, I followed Kaitlin, who easily balanced her box on a hiked knee and opened the door. She held it for me. I followed.

She raised the van's back hatch and dumped her box next to a vacuum cleaner and several mops. She took mine. I shook out my fingers, recharging the circulation.

"When did you get so strong?" I asked.

"When did you get so weak?" she countered.

I swam laps a few times a week, but lately I'd found reasons not to go. I didn't think the lack of exercise had caught up. "It's been a slow and sloppy slide down the hill."

She laughed. "Time to climb back to the mountaintop." Inside the car, the engine rumbled. "Now we need to stop by the repair shop. Otto is fixing two of my vacuum cleaners."

Of course, the prep work made sense. But I had pictured just showing up with a mop, a bucket, and a vacuum cleaner. "A bigger production than grabbing a few cleaning items at the grocery store."

"You'd be amazed what happens before that. And then there's the paperwork. Billing. Taxes. Insurance."

We stopped at another warehouse office three miles east of Lynn's. We grabbed the two vacuums and another invoice. By the time we headed back across the bridge, the wind had kicked up more. The clouds had grown plump with rain. I blinked and drew in a breath. As my therapist advised, I imagined standing in a large field surrounded by solid mountains. Grass. Hard dirt. Clear skies.

As I reached for tranquility, a crack of thunder yanked it further away. *Breathe in. Breathe out.*

The strain banding my body didn't ease, so I switched to my therapist's plan B. Face the demon head on.

I grabbed the first question that came to mind. "Has anyone dived the *Oceanus* recently?"

Kaitlin looked surprised. "Why do you ask that?"

"Just wondering." My heart beat faster, and sweat dampened my palms.

"There is the occasional recreational diver who talks about the *Oceanus*, but it's not a regular spot. A few wrecks are closer to shore." She tapped the steering wheel with a ringed finger. "I dove the *Oceanus* a few years ago."

"Why?"

"Curious. I thought I might see something that I could share with you."

"Like Mom floating around?" My fear voiced itself without me thinking it sounded angry.

She shook her head. "That was my biggest fear. I thought maybe I'd find a few trinkets or something tangible to give you."

"Did you find anything?"

The car rolled over the bridge and onto the Outer Banks. A few fat raindrops hit the windshield. "A few things."

"Like what?"

"An ivory comb. A coin. And a wineglass that never broke."

I touched the coin around my neck. "And you never told me."

"You didn't want anything to do with this place. And you seemed happy. No reason to stir up the past."

The past's silty bottom never settled so the waters could clear.

"Do you still have those items?"

"I never took them. The *Oceanus* is within three miles of shore, so it's illegal."

"Did you take pictures?"

"I did. They're on my computer. I'll show you when we get back to my place."

"You look nervous."

"Not like I saw a ghost or anything. But I did get a bad feeling when I picked up the coin." Nervous laughter bubbled.

"It was like that the day when I approached the *Oceanus*. Felt as if we were swimming into a graveyard and the spirits weren't happy to be disturbed. I'd feared a life force would attach to me and follow me home. Maybe one did. Mystics in other cultures believe spirits can travel via water."

Kaitlin looked a little paler. "Don't say that. I don't need a ghost. Got enough on my plate."

I shrugged. "Open ocean water freaks me out. But ghosts don't move the needle on my fear meter."

"Seriously?"

"I mean, they're dead. What can they do? Throw a vase or creak across a floor? Make a spooky sound?" I grinned. "Heard any weird sounds lately?"

"Don't say that!"

My smile broadened. Since the first day she'd welcomed me to her lunch table in high school, we'd teased each other a lot. "They can do a lot of damage. Never underestimate them."

"Shut up!"

I laughed. "Come and get us, ghosts!"

CHAPTER NINE

Sigrid

Monday, April 20, 1942, 6:30 p.m.
Four days until the Oceanus *is torpedoed*

My hand was tucked in the crook of William's arm as we entered the dining room for the dinner service. I was glad to be out of our cabin and around the company of others. I drew my energy from people and attention. My beauty was an asset that I'd used since I was a child. William had been no exception, although he soon realized that sharing me with others was tiring. He preferred my attention on him and not distracted with others, especially men. But I liked to flirt and enjoyed how it made his face red with jealousy. If he released me, maybe I'd stop. Maybe not. The hum of chatter drifted down the hallway.

The *Oceanus* was clear of Port of Spain, and now we were in open waters. No one was talking about the dangers of travel, but we were all aware this voyage was not without risks. There'd be no bands or loud parties. We were to remain quiet, our porthole curtains drawn so as not to attract the attention of a U-boat captain.

My dress was not overly formal. It was made of a light blue silk with billowy sleeves that gathered at my wrists. The dress's collar was trimmed in white lace, and the neckline plunged to a modest depth.

He wore his customary dark suit, polished shoes, and a blue tie that matched my dress.

"You look lovely, my dear," William said.

I beamed, tracing my naked hand over his. "It's important I make my husband proud."

"Shh. That is our secret."

I mimicked a coquettish pout. "When ours becomes a truly legal union, I will shout it out loud."

"Soon enough."

I'd told myself a hundred times the journey would be flawless, that I would accomplish what I needed to do, but as we passed several large portholes, I caught myself staring at the horizon. The stars shone bright in the dark sky, but the waxing moon didn't drip much light on the water. I'd never feared the water and instead found it invigorating.

As the steward escorted us to the captain's table, I scanned the dining room. There was no one here I recognized, but it was still early in the voyage.

At our table, we were greeted by three other people. There were Mr. and Mrs. DuPont. From what William had told me, they were from old New England money. The DuPont family had made their fortune in shipping, and since the war, Mr. DuPont had shifted his efforts toward supplying Britain. He and his wife were returning from Cape Town and had been on the *Oceanus* for weeks.

DuPont was a midsize man with a thick mustache. His belly was round, his skin blotched as if sensitive to the sun. His wife wasn't much older than William, but she had a dour demeanor that aged her a decade. Her dark hair was ruthlessly pinned back, and her starched collar was so high my throat itched at the thought. She greeted me with cool eyes and a pleasant expression, as many women did.

Our places were marked with our names, and to my delight, couples were not seated next to each other. I was happy to have distance from William, though I could see he wasn't thrilled to have me out of his control. He knew I liked to drink and strike up conversations with anyone. One never knew what other bits of information others had, but he always feared I'd overshare.

Despite William's frown, he was careful to not make a fuss in a crowd.

Dr. Brooks, the book dealer, seated to my left, stood immediately. He was a medium-size man who didn't look extraordinary in any way. He was the first to extend his hand, and he struck me as a little overeager. "Atticus Brooks of New York."

I shook Dr. Brooks's hand, nodding as my fingers tightened. I'd heard from several at the hotel that Dr. Brooks was quite the world traveler. He, too, had boarded this ship in Cape Town after having traveled the whole of Africa this past year. A purveyor of books, charms, and art, he'd gone into Port of Spain last night to see what treasures he could find. He'd boarded with a very pregnant woman on his arm. She was tall with delicate bones, but her hat had hidden her face from the sun and me.

Dr. Brooks reminded me of men I'd crossed paths with in Vienna. They worked in the shadows and went unnoticed by most. But as I searched my memory, I couldn't place him.

To my right sat Mrs. DuPont. She smelled like the lavender soap I favored. Dr. Brooks and Mr. DuPont waited until I'd sat.

"I'm William Weller. It's good to meet you," William said to Mrs. DuPont. "And my companion is Miss Sigrid Stein."

Mrs. DuPont's smile was tepid. "I hear you've traveled extensively across the European continent."

He nodded, careful to keep the details vague. "I've had the great pleasure of visiting the biggest cities in Europe."

"And Miss Stein, tell me about yourself," Mrs. DuPont said.

"I am from Vienna," I answered.

"Ah, a lovely city. I haven't been there in years. I've heard it's taken a dark turn."

"Yes," I said, softening my voice. "Many changes."

"Dr. Brooks has also crossed Europe multiple times," Mrs. DuPont said.

The steward showed William a wine list. He wasn't much for wine, but a good whiskey was always welcome.

"Dr. Brooks, when was the last time you were in Europe?" I asked.

"My last trips were to Germany and Austria." His confident tone was reminiscent of generals ready for battle. "Vienna is a stunning city. I was there in 1938."

"What was your favorite part of the city?" I asked.

"The Danube River is stunning, especially by moonlight."

"It's a stunning river," I said. I'd spent my younger years traveling from country to country on the river. Once it had had gentle curves and turns. But over the centuries, industrious men had found a way to straighten its bends, enabling faster river travel. A shame.

William, who knew my heritage, frowned. "Heavily patrolled these days."

"There's very little of the world not shadowed by the war now," Dr. Brooks said.

"So true," William said. "But it won't last forever."

"Dr. Brooks, what kind of trinkets did you gather on this trip?" Mrs. DuPont asked.

"I have many items that might be of interest," he said. However, like a good salesman, he teased us with his silence.

A steward presented Dr. Brooks with two bottles of wine. "I hope you don't mind. I ordered a couple of reds for the table," Dr. Brooks said. The steward filled his glass, and he swirled the burgundy, sipped, and nodded. As the steward presented the bottle to the others at the table, Dr. Brooks added, "Join me if it's to your tastes."

Everyone accepted a glass, and when I sipped the wine, I found the oaky flavors exquisite. Dr. Brooks knew his wines. William took a sip, but I could see he didn't love it.

Mrs. DuPont's tight expression eased as she drank. "Doctor, I hear you collect items that are supernatural in nature."

In Europe, the wealthy were fascinated by the occult, which I'd used to my advantage many times in the salons. Even those highest in the German and Austrian governments were fascinated by the spiritual activities of the past, present, and future. However, those who traded in these arts were careful to keep their messages positive.

Dr. Brooks reached in his coat pocket and pulled out two coins with rough edges. Embossed on the metal were long faces with large eyes. They looked primitive and very old.

"I got these from a dealer in a small shop in Madagascar."

"Where is that?" I asked.

"Nearly three hundred miles due east of Mozambique," Dr. Brooks said. When my confusion was clear, he added, "The southern edge of Africa, on the east coast."

"Ah. But why would anyone want to be there?"

"It's a lovely island. Dry deserts. Mountains. Beautiful beaches with white sand. Ancient trees. And all kinds of wildlife creatures. Lovely natives."

"And what do those coins signify?" Mrs. DuPont asked.

Dr. Brooks's smile was slight—the expression of a man ready to lure his quarry. A good salesman never answered a question immediately when there was a story to tell. "The natives of the island are very spiritual. They believe in *ody*, or magical charms or talismans. I was fortunate enough to speak to a Malagasy elder who believed in Zazavavindrano, or water spirits. I held one of these magical coins from the sea and wished for a long life."

"Do you believe your wish will be granted?" Mrs. DuPont asked.

"Who knows? These magical realms and their creatures can be as dangerous as they are helpful. I suppose it comes down to how the winds are blowing that day."

"You don't really believe these stories, do you?" I asked.

"For so many stories to persist all over the world, I can't but wonder if there's merit to them."

He handed one coin to Mrs. DuPont and one to me. "Their beliefs aren't far from the Gullah traditions."

"Gullah?" William asked.

"Descendants from Africa who live in the Carolinas and Florida now. Some of their peoples have a water goddess named Yemaja. She's the mother of all river and ocean creatures."

"And here we are on the *Oceanus*," I said. "Namesake of a Greek Titan and the father of the Oceanids, or river gods."

Dr. Brooks raised his glass in appreciation of the detail. "Ah, Miss Stein, you're a Greek scholar."

"Not really." My tone softened with a sigh. I was charmed.

"How does one find a water creature?" Mrs. DuPont asked.

Dr. Brooks's eyes brightened as he sipped his wine. "I've heard the natives leave gifts on the bank of a river or lake. If they appreciate your gift, then you might be blessed."

"How so?"

"The ocean is a dangerous place. Never hurts to have help just in case."

"But you said they can also be dangerous," I said.

Dr. Brooks nodded. "I would think these gods wouldn't appreciate humans sailing their waters."

"Very true." The stories of river creatures were ingrained deeply in me. "It's quite taboo to swim in such waters while the gods are close by. Don't want to make the creatures angry."

"Are these creatures in the Atlantic?" Mrs. DuPont asked.

Absently Dr. Brooks turned another coin over his fingers like a well-practiced magic trick. "That I cannot say, but it would stand to reason. Yemaja is a mother goddess. Oceanus is a father. Very protective parents." He leaned forward a fraction. "I suspect one followed me from Madagascar to Cape Town, and then to Port of Spain."

"How could you know such a thing?" Mrs. DuPont asked.

"Every vessel I've traveled has been cursed with some malady."

"There's a war, Dr. Brooks," Mrs. DuPont said.

"What better way to annoy the gods?" he asked.

I inspected the coin closely. It had an energy, and I couldn't determine whether it was either good or evil. "Could I buy this from you?"

"No. These coins are a gift from me to you ladies. Just as this coin will grant me a long life, it will keep you safe while we're on the water."

My fingers curled around the metal. I never said no to good luck. "And where did you say you got this?"

"From a man who practices magic. Took me hours to find him. Found myself in the most remote village. Well off the beaten path. Hot as Hades. But I refused to quit my search. I heard he had some of the most powerful charms."

Mrs. DuPont was enthralled. "Were you in fear for your safety?"

Dr. Brooks leaned forward and half whispered, "I'm always armed and ready for anyone who wishes to cause me mischief."

The dealer had a self-deprecating charm that I suspected had most underestimating him. William was clearly not interested in his story.

I raised the glass to my lips, but as I sipped, I noticed sweat glistening on William's upper lip. He dabbed his lips with his napkin as I tried to focus on Mrs. DuPont's comments about nonsense and fairy tales.

Sensing the coin between my fingers was a charm, I said, "It feels odd."

"It's quite powerful," Dr. Brooks said. "Not only will it keep you safe, but if you grip it hard and make a wish, it will be granted. But the man who sold it to me reminded me to be very careful what I wished for. Wishes that come true aren't always what we expect."

I'd had many wishes come true. And I wasn't always better for it. I was traveling to the United States, but I'd made a deal with a devil to be here. I mouthed a small prayer. Finally, as if remembering I wasn't alone, I smiled.

"What would you wish for, Miss Stein?" Dr. Brooks asked.

To save those I loved. To be free. For a long life in the United States. To become a new person. "I've made too many wishes, and they always come with a twist." My candor surprised me.

"Sounds ominous," Dr. Brooks said.

"The world is in a tenuous place now, and it doesn't need me dictating what should come next," I said.

"You sell yourself short," Mr. DuPont said. "I would bet you have very good instincts."

"Are you superstitious, Mr. Weller?" Dr. Brooks asked.

"Not at all. I don't believe in such things." He raised the wineglass to his lips, but this time he didn't sip, as if the taste had soured his stomach.

Dr. Brooks chuckled. "Mr. Weller, you aren't afraid to take risks."

"Never." More sweat dampened his shirt. A look toward Mrs. DuPont suggested he was anxious to shift Dr. Brooks's attention back to her. "What would you wish for, Mrs. DuPont?"

She relaxed as if grateful to be pulled into the conversation. "Peace," she said. "We need this war to stop."

Dr. Brooks nodded. "Very wise wish."

I questioned Mrs. DuPont's real desire. Many people were profiting greatly from this war. I assumed Mr. DuPont was one of them.

"I suspect, by your accent, you're from the northeast of the United States," Dr. Brooks said.

Mr. DuPont nodded. "New Hampshire. Our family has been there for two hundred years."

As they chatted about the towns of New England, I marveled at the doctor's talent for drawing people into his sphere. "And you, Miss Stein, what did you do in Vienna?"

"I was an actress," I said.

"Ah, a woman of the arts."

I grinned. "Some would say that."

"I hear hints of southern Germany when you speak," Dr. Brooks said.

"I have traveled through many cities. You have an ear for accents."

He nodded. "An odd little talent. But it makes for good dinner conversation. It's been a decade since I was in Munich."

"For me as well."

"Beyond the river, my favorite area in Vienna is the Hotel Imperial, near the opera. And the Hofburg Palace. Stunning in the spring. And the theater is magnificent."

My face brightened. "It's the world's best, in my opinion."

"You're so far from home. Most young women never stray far from their village."

"As I said, I grew up traveling." My parents never stayed long in any one city. We would dock our boat and wait for the locals to find us and ask us for whatever their neighbors might frown upon. But it wouldn't be long before our presence angered others, and so we moved on. I was fourteen when I'd decided Vienna would be my home.

William cleared his throat. He was frowning. My guard rose.

William's cheeks were flushed now. "The wine is an excellent choice, Dr. Brooks. Thank you."

Some of Dr. Brooks's good humor faded. "I'm glad you like it."

At the rate William was going, I suspected he was unwell. He met my gaze. "Sigrid, I'm going to retire early. All the travel has caught up to me."

I set my wineglass down. "Would you mind if I have my dinner?" I was enjoying the company and being out of the small cabin.

"You can have a tray sent to the room." William stood and wobbled slightly.

Wine hadn't been his first choice, but he'd never had trouble with it. I laid my napkin beside my plate, ready to rise.

"Let Miss Stein enjoy her meal with us," Mrs. DuPont said. "We've only just touched on myths and magical creatures."

William frowned, swayed a fraction.

"Mrs. DuPont and I will look after Miss Stein," Dr. Brooks said. "Isn't that right, Mrs. DuPont?"

"But of course," Mrs. DuPont said.

"Sigrid," William said.

The warning was clear. One day I wouldn't care about his opinions, but for now I needed him happy. I rose from the table and moved to his side. "Thank you all for a lovely evening."

Dr. Brooks waved over a steward. "Can you help Mr. Weller back to his cabin? The poor man is exhausted."

The steward took William's arm. His body tensed, and he'd have pulled away, but the extra support was clearly now welcome. "See you all in the morning."

I moved slowly and carefully out of the room and followed behind William and the steward. As we climbed the stairs, the very pregnant woman I'd seen earlier was at the bottom step. She stood to the side and ducked her head as we passed. Whatever curiosity I had for her vanished when William doubled over.

CHAPTER TEN

GERTRUDE

Monday, April 20, 1942, 7:00 p.m.
Four days until the Oceanus *is torpedoed*

A couple passed by me. The woman was attending to a man who didn't appear well. The first day at sea could be unsettling for some.

As I climbed the stairs, a well-honed talent for seeing danger had me turning. I watched the steward and the man round a corner. The woman's back was to me, but an uncomfortable sense of familiarity washed over me. Her dark hair, full figure, and straight shoulders that spoke of confidence all reminded me of Vienna.

She prompted me to think of the black market book broker I'd first met in my great-uncle's shop years ago. She'd become a regular visitor by 1938, always with a rare book to sell. She'd saunter into the shop, wary but full of confidence. She'd carefully look at the titles first to make sure we were alone.

The woman wasn't like our normal customers. Though her dark dress was subdued, she favored bright lipstick, and her ringed fingers suggested she lived anything but a restrained life. The Germans didn't approve of ostentatious women who didn't fit their idea of chasteness.

On one occasion, she'd moved toward the counter, meeting my gaze with sharp blue eyes. "Is your uncle here?"

"No. Not today." My uncle was unwell, and he'd said many times now that he was grateful Alfred had asked for my hand and I'd agreed to marry him.

When she grinned at me, I was immediately cautious. My uncle had called her a selkie, but I worried more about the German spies who'd infested the city.

"Good morning," I added. "It's been a while."

"I've been on the go. I hear congratulations are in order. You're to be married," she said.

My engagement wasn't a secret, but still I was surprised she knew. "Yes."

"When is the wedding?"

"Two weeks." Alfred had insisted I visit an exclusive dressmaker in Vienna. She'd created a wedding dress fit for a princess, made of silk that was as modest as it was extravagant. There'd also been fittings for dresses and gowns for entertaining. It had been a whirlwind courtship, and I still hadn't processed my good fortune.

"I hear the weather is going to be lovely the following week, when you wed," she said.

"How do you know that?"

A shrug. "Magic."

When I'd last seen Alfred a few days earlier, he'd been tense and worried about his business. "I can only hope."

"Trust me." And then, in the wake of my silence, she asked, "Would you be interested in buying a rare book?"

Uncle Eric had bought many of the books she'd brought to us, but as the wedding grew closer, his health had also taken a bad turn, and he wasn't in the shop often. Alfred had allowed me to stay there, but I sensed that after our marriage, I would have to leave the bookshop behind. I expected a German soldier or the local police to be waiting outside. But she appeared to be alone.

"We are very careful about what we can buy now."

She reached into a small sack and removed a thin volume. Its old leather cover was embossed with gold flowers. "I think you'll find what I have of great value. And the price will be hard for anyone to resist."

Despite the dangers, I nodded. She set the book on the counter, and I realized immediately that what she was offering was quite rare—a First Folio of William Shakespeare's works. "Where did you get this?"

She shrugged. "A client."

Many of the wealthy citizens who'd used her as a broker had long fled the city, been transported, or died. I carefully opened the cover and studied the bold ink. The book had been published in the 1620s. Still fearing a trap, I asked, "Who is the owner?"

"I cannot say. But I can assure you it's genuine."

She wasn't lying. I'd handled enough books to know just from the binding which volumes were genuine and which ones were forgeries. I had special clients who still collected and could sell this if the price was right. "How much?"

Her smile widened. When she named her price, I was hesitant. She'd greatly undervalued the book.

"I am no German or police spy," she said. "I'm simply a woman looking to make a deal that would help us both."

Many in the city were struggling now. Food was scarce, the best saved for the Germans and Austrian officials.

"I could really use the money," she added. "I have never steered you wrong, have I?"

"No. But my uncle likes to make these deals."

"Then get him. I will wait."

I suspected she knew my uncle was bedridden. "I'm afraid that I will have to pass."

"Are you sure? This is a very rare opportunity."

"Yes."

"Very well."

When she'd left the store and vanished around the corner, I'd expected never to see her again. But three years later, she'd found me by the river. My body was bruised and my head ached. I'd never questioned how she'd found me. On that day, we'd struck a different deal, and I hadn't seen her since I'd left Vienna.

Was I now losing my mind? Was I so worried about Vienna that I was turning strangers into past ghosts?

I climbed the stairs and was slightly breathless when I reached the dining room floor. Following the sound of conversation and clinking silverware, I found a steward standing by the dining room entrance.

"I am late for my seating," I said.

His gaze bobbed between my face and belly. Whatever practiced rejection he had prepared for tardy diners never materialized. "A seat just opened. Let me clear the place, and I'll seat you."

The steward angled his hand toward the dining room. I recognized Dr. Brooks. He and the other man at the table stood.

"Frau Werner, what a lovely surprise. Are you our new dinner companion?"

"I must be." The steward pulled out my chair, and I sat.

"May I introduce the DuPonts. They're from New Hampshire."

"Good evening," I said.

Both greeted me as I accepted a fresh napkin from the steward. I unfolded it and spread it over my swollen belly.

"Just in time for the first course," Dr. Brooks said.

The waiters placed bowls of beef consommé in front of us.

"Frau Werner, do you like to play games?" Dr. Brooks asked.

My polished smile was careful, cautious. "Who does not?"

"Excellent. But first, you must eat," he said.

As we sipped soup from our silver spoons, we exchanged pleasantries. My story was as well practiced as my new name. I was from Innsbruck. My husband had passed in the war. I had a cousin in New York.

The next course was beef tips with a side of rice and green beans. The food was delicious, and it had been some time since I'd eaten in a formal setting. It was oddly comforting and reminded me of dinners with my uncle.

The three discussed their travels, the state of the war, and books. The locations weren't all familiar to me, but I'd seen and read enough to know the war was far from finished. Books were my forte, and I was familiar with all of them, especially the ones now banned in Austria. When we finished the main course of roasted chicken and then the sorbet, Dr. Brooks took the conversation toward a lighter topic.

"Is everyone ready for a little magic?" he asked.

"Magic?" Mrs. DuPont looked delighted and a bit terrified. "More magical than your wish coins?"

I found the older woman's childish delight amusing. For all her money and world travels, I suspected Mrs. DuPont had lived a cloistered life in a rarified world.

"Ah, there are all kinds of magic," Dr. Brooks said. "I would say we are always surrounded by it."

"Magic? Is that truly real?" Mrs. DuPont asked. "One thing for primitive natives to believe, but we're educated people."

Dr. Brooks looked delighted by her curiosity. "I'm here to tell you it's very real. And it's very powerful. Do you want to know your future?"

It was a question many had contemplated of late. I had dared not look more than a day or two into the future. Each day brought potential challenges that could end it all for me.

Dr. Brooks shuffled a deck of cards and then divided them into three even piles. "Restack the cards, Mrs. DuPont."

She carefully lifted the middle pile and set it on the first. The last became the top.

The steward brought the others after-dinner drinks and for me a cup of tea.

Dr. Brooks set three cards face down on the table. Mrs. DuPont shifted closer in her seat. He flipped the first card. It was the Death card.

The older woman paled, and for all that I'd experienced, I felt a chill. Ghosts of the past swirled around. We were crossing waters infested by wolf packs ready to devour us.

"Not to worry," Dr. Brooks said. "This card simply means change. Your life is about to change."

The next card was a tower being hit by a thunderbolt. More change, he insisted. The final card was the final word. It was the Sun. "Prosperity."

Air whooshed from Mrs. DuPont as she sat back. She sipped her drink as if she needed fortification and then, lowering her voice, said, "I hope it means my husband's ships to England make it there intact. He's invested everything in them."

Dr. Brooks tapped the last card, a gold, gleaming sun, before calling the steward over to refill wineglasses. After the steward had filled the DuPonts' glasses, Dr. Brooks said, "His shipments will be just fine."

She looked relieved. "Excellent. The food will help those poor, starving people."

Mr. DuPont looked slightly embarrassed by his wife's oversharing. "My dear, no one wants to hear our boring news."

Unrebuked, Mrs. DuPont sipped more wine as she picked up the Sun card. "How do you know the cards have magic?"

"I bought them from an elder in a Roma encampment who insisted they were very accurate."

"That doesn't mean anything," Mrs. DuPont said. "Those tribes can spin all kinds of lies."

I thought about the kind Roma who sailed the Danube River, and my mother's love of her family.

Dr. Brooks nodded. "I've read the cards for myself dozens of times. They're always right."

"And what do they say for you?" I asked.

Dr. Brooks chuckled. "They confirm my greatest wish—that I grow old and fat in a small house by the ocean."

"And me?" Mrs. DuPont said.

"You have a very bright future," he insisted. "Wealth beyond your dreams."

The woman's tight features relaxed.

The man was charming. A deceiver and a con artist, no doubt, but delightful. For so long, I'd been on guard, weighing all my words and actions.

When Dr. Brooks laid out three stacks of cards face down and asked me to restack the deck, my lightheartedness shattered. The idea that anyone could peer beyond the false life I'd created into my real one was too dangerous. All my protests slid behind a waterfall of reserve.

He slowly turned the first card over. It was a woman standing by water. The next was the Sun again. And the final one was the Moon. "Very interesting, Frau Werner."

"How so?" I asked.

"Water has always been a part of your life."

"We're surrounded by it now," I said.

"But your connection goes back much further than this voyage. I would say a long, ancient river has flowed through your life."

"Many live near rivers in Europe."

"Yes, but few are as influenced by it."

His comments were just vague enough to mean many things and nothing.

"Ah."

"You don't believe me?"

I did. But any true facts of my past were too perilous to toy with. "It's very entertaining."

Dr. Brooks laughed. "But I feel your hesitation."

"She's a wise woman," Mr. DuPont said. "Better to take all of this with a grain of salt."

"Perhaps," Dr. Brooks said as he scooped up the cards. "And I can see you aren't convinced."

"I am not," Mr. DuPont said.

Unruffled, Dr. Brooks carefully stacked his cards. "I insist we all have dinner again tomorrow night. I'll convince everyone that this magic is real."

"I would be delighted," Mrs. DuPont said. "Perhaps you have other games, Dr. Brooks."

He bowed slightly. "I have many."

Her cheeks warmed with a girlish hue. "I have no doubt."

I shifted in my seat. The baby pressed against my bladder, reminding me of its presence. As much as I reached for a new life, the old one lingered. Suddenly, I was in no mood for games. It was time for me to rise. "If you all will excuse me. I must stand and walk."

"I remember the last days before my children were born," Mrs. DuPont said. "I understand."

Dr. Brooks rose and pushed in his chair. He offered his arm to me, and because it would be rude not to take it, I did. "Let me escort you to the deck. The seas are getting rougher, and you should not be walking around alone."

"Thank you."

He ushered me out of the dining room, and soon we were in the windy fresh air on the top deck. The crescent moon dangled in the starry night. The fresh ocean breeze wrapped around me.

"Are you chilly?" he asked.

"The air is bracing and welcome."

He shrugged off his jacket and laid it on my shoulders. The warmth enveloped me. "And what will you do in New York City?"

The idea lifted my mood again. "I haven't charted my voyage that far. But the war is very far from New York. And I want to be away from the war."

"A wise choice." His voice had a calming effect on me.

"Tell me about New York."

"It's full of lights, cars, people, and ships in the harbor. There are theaters and restaurants. The city never really sleeps."

I couldn't picture New York, but I was familiar with chaos where one could get lost.

As we strolled, Dr. Brooks chatted easily about the specifications of the *Oceanus*. "She was built in 1930."

"And the ship's namesake was a Titan."

He looked pleased by my response. "Son of Uranus and Gaia. Heaven and earth. An interesting fellow, as Greek gods go. He married his sister, who gave him numerous sons, or river gods. His daughters were naiads. They oversee ponds, marshes, and lakes."

I thought about the Danube River's swirling waters. Had one of these creatures been staring at me as I lingered on the banks? "You have an excellent command of facts."

"'A brain full of trivialities,' as my great-uncle used to say. A casualty of reading so many books." He slid his hand into his pocket.

"Books are their own form of magic," I said. "I've been a voracious reader since I was a child."

"I knew I liked you the instant we met. What have you read lately?"

"I'm rereading *The Tempest.*"

"Is it as old as my volume?"

I'd learned to downplay assets for fear of theft. "No, it's less than fifty years old."

"This Shakespeare classic is a bold choice while crossing the Atlantic." He guided me toward the cabins. "Don't you worry about a great storm also blowing us off course?"

"All ends well in this story."

"You're an optimist, Frau Werner."

"I have to be."

As we approached my hallway, he slowed his pace. "I hope to see you again, Frau Werner. This has been a delightful evening."

"I truly appreciated the distraction. It's been a while since I enjoyed myself like this."

"If you find yourself in need of an escort tomorrow, knock on my door. I'm free to walk again and discuss books."

It had been some time since a man was kind to me. Not to be trusted, but nice. "Thank you for the escort. Good evening."

He bowed slightly. "Madam."

When I entered the cabin, I heard the agitated voices of the couple in the room next to mine. The man sounded angry and the woman conciliatory.

The sounds conjured more dark memories from my marriage. I closed the door quietly and crossed to my bunk. Around Alfred, I always tiptoed as if the floor were covered with shattered glass.

I unlaced my shoes and rubbed the stiffness from my swollen feet. As delightful as Dr. Brooks had been, he'd admitted he had connections all over the world. And then there was the lady who had conjured memories of the woman who knew me too well.

I couldn't risk any of these people being connected to Alfred.

CHAPTER ELEVEN

Tula

Wednesday, June 10, 2026, 8:15 a.m.

The traffic was still light as we drove down the beach road, but that would change in the next hour as vacationers headed to the breakfast dives, beach, the shopping centers, or trinket stores. Today, like yesterday, was supposed to be clear, so the chances were good the crowds wouldn't be terrible. Tomorrow's weather predicted overcast skies and a little rain. Then the ripe-red bodies would flock from the sand and surf toward the attractions.

The Airbnb was a small third-floor condo just south of Duck. Located on the ocean side of the road, it embraced the mauves and grays of the early 1990s. The living room had a puffy couch, a few side chairs, and a bamboo coffee table. The deck looked out over the ocean.

But before this place could be rentable again, we'd have to clear out the explosion of trash scattered over every square inch.

"Did a bomb go off?" I asked.

Kaitlin shook her head. "Looks like it."

"I thought these were easy cleans?"

"They usually are." Kaitlin looked annoyed but not surprised.

The trash cans were overflowing, the refrigerator was full of half-eaten takeout, pizza boxes littered the place, and sand had been tracked over every square inch of floor.

"On a scale of one to ten . . ." I asked.

She regarded the first bathroom. "Eight. Maybe a nine. But no serious damage beyond the trash. Grab a garbage bag, start cleaning out the kitchen, and pick up anything that looks like it doesn't belong."

"What's the deal with people?"

"They're on vacation. Some just think that cleaning isn't part of the package."

I pulled on plastic gloves, half wishing I had a hazmat suit. "I can't imagine a ten."

"Because you're a neatnik and control freak when it comes to organization." When I looked up, she smiled. "And I love, love when people like you check out of one of my properties."

"Cleaner than when they moved in, right?"

"Exactly. Amazing."

"I left my dirty dishes in Dave's sink before I left."

She laughed. "Aren't you the little rule breaker."

"It kind of bothers me."

"Let the land shark wash his own dishes."

I dumped several pizza boxes into the bag. "Pizza is the cuisine of choice."

"The seafood leftovers are generally in the refrigerator. At least I hope they are."

"What's the worst thing you've ever found?"

"A handgun on the kitchen counter. Vibrators in a nightstand. Fish in the bathtub."

"Were the fish alive?"

"At one time, but not by the time I found them."

I refused to remind myself that I'd taken top honors in the paralegal program. Several instructors had suggested I consider law school.

Tierney, Brooks, and Bainbridge had been my first job offer. They liked that I worked hard in the mail room, and when they discovered I could write, the powers that be decided to train me in paralegal work. I'd been so grateful for the work that I didn't realize that writing summaries and legal briefs didn't energize me.

I filled three large green bags and hauled them outside to the dumpster. My next mountain to climb was the refrigerator. The renters had been here two weeks, and I bet they'd saved every bit of takeout since their arrival. Several of the meals and the milk had developed a real odor.

Doing my best not to gag, I dumped it all into the bag. Several whole fish lay in the icy freezer. Wide glossy eyes stared at me as if asking why anyone had bothered to catch them.

I used a blunt kitchen knife to pry the fish off the freezer bottom. "I hope they lose their security deposit."

"They will." Kaitlin appeared with three bags stuffed with clean linens.

After all the clutter had been collected, I wiped all the surfaces while Kaitlin tackled the sheets and bathroom. Within the hour, two vacuum cleaners were sucking up sand and debris.

The condo was still old and worn, but it was now immaculate and smelled of pine. Oddly, I felt a real sense of satisfaction. This was only two weeks' worth of trash. Who knew what waited at the Southern Shores house, filled with a lifetime of stuff.

After we'd cleaned the next five condos, which thankfully were in good shape, we headed south. I asked, "Do we still have time to stop at the Brooks house?"

Kaitlin loaded her mops and the vacuum cleaners into the back of her van. "Sure. It's on the way."

When we pulled up in front of the old cottage, it was nearly three. The "flattop house" was one level and made of cinder blocks covered with sun-washed stucco. White hurricane shutters covered the windows facing Route 12. Cinder block homes like these had earned the "flattop house" name because the roofs were, well, flat. The horizontal roofs and large overhangs protected the originally un-air-conditioned interiors from sun and wind while blending with the landscape.

Many houses around this cottage had added a second floor or painted the exterior a bright color, but not this one. It looked as if it hadn't changed since it was built in the 1940s. These homes had a mid-century modern vibe, and most had been renovated. Few remained in their original form, like this one.

Out of the car, I tipped my face toward the sun. "I have no idea why I accepted this job. It makes no sense."

"The firm must trust you. Cleaning out the home of a founding partner's great-uncle is important to them."

A ripped, faded awning dangled over a window. "This place is going to need more than a broom."

"Have you been inside yet?" Kaitlin asked.

"No. This is my maiden voyage."

I pulled the old key from my purse and shoved it into the lock. This close to the ocean, anything metal rusted, and the lock resisted as I twisted the key. I wiggled it until it finally gave way, and the dead bolt opened. Turning the knob, I pushed open the front door.

Warm, musty air rushed out, and the interior was shrouded in shadows. I flipped on a switch that looked original to the house. A small bulb dangling from a ceiling fan spit out enough light for me to cross the room and push back dusty curtains covering a salt-streaked window. Beyond was a small patio abutting a retaining wall that held back the sand. Stairs led to a platform on top of the dunes. I coaxed the second door open and stepped outside into sunshine. Beyond the sandbank, waves tumbled onto the beach.

"Houses today can't be built this close to the dunes," Kaitlin said. "This is a true throwback to the 1940s. The Wright Memorial Bridge was only two lanes and kind of rickety. It was a bit like the Wild West here then."

"I wonder why Dr. Brooks picked this spot?"

"If he wanted to cut off the world and commune with the ocean, this was the place to do it. What do you know about the senior Dr. Brooks?"

"Nothing. I only met his great-nephew once, two days ago."

"You know your *Oceanus* wreck is almost three miles due east of here."

"I know." I'd always approached the dive spot via boat, and I'd never paid attention to the distant beach.

"Someone wants you to face the *Oceanus*."

"My therapist." Who had still not acknowledged my text.

"Would he orchestrate all this?"

"No. He's a fan of nonintervention." There'd been times when I'd wished he'd just tell me how to feel. Now I was glad he'd left me to figure me out. "Let's have a look inside."

The walls were covered in wood paneling and images of ships and the North Carolina coastline before many homes had been built. The rattan furniture with fabric cushions sporting wide palm leaves had a nautical vibe. There was a soot-stained fireplace with black andirons, a raw-edge wood mantel displaying two vintage brass lanterns, and a large basket filled with yellowed newspapers.

In the galley kitchen, brown paneling, a double oven, white metal cabinets, and a white speckled Formica countertop were reminiscent of a 1950s sitcom. The Frigidaire freezer/refrigerator was also vintage, as were the stove and the farmhouse sink.

I opened the fridge. It was small but clean and cold. The freezer needed defrosting, but otherwise, it was spotless. This old place was dusty but basically tidy.

"The house has a good vibe," Kaitlin said.

This house wasn't designed for lounging. It had been built with the beach in mind. No lingering on the couch watching TV or scrolling. It wanted its occupants outside by the ocean.

One of the three bedrooms was furnished with a white four-poster bed, and one of the others had twins. The art had a nautical theme, and the windows were small. The third room was the largest and served as an office, dominated by a desk that had a ship's captain vibe, much like the one Mr. Brooks had in Norfolk. The room had ten filing cabinets, all covered with stacked files on top. Shelves, crammed with books, lined all the walls.

"Where do you start?" Kaitlin asked.

"A basic cleaning of the kitchen, a bedroom, and bathroom. I'll tackle the rest bit by bit. Mr. Brooks said I could stay here while I worked."

"You're welcome to bunk with me."

"Thank you. But this place has real beds, and your twin bed . . ."

"Lumpy, hard, short?"

"Yeah. But I'll still cover the two weeks of work I promised you. I'll just get up a little earlier and meet you at the surf shop."

Kaitlin dragged a finger over the dusty counter, leaving a trail. "It's got quite the history."

I walked into the office, flipped on the light, and walked toward boxes stacked in the corner. I lifted the lid and found manila folders stuffed with yellowing papers and a few photographs. "The man never met a piece of paper he didn't love." That was one of the odd things I'd appreciated about my job at first. Printed pages felt solid, and after a lifetime of traveling, they signaled a safe harbor.

"From what I've heard, Dr. Brooks became a super-volunteer when he retired. Everyone at the rec center, library, and animal shelter knew of him."

"Really?"

"He never was out front at an event, but he was the organizational brains behind some big fundraisers. He passed seven years ago, shortly after your mom vanished. He was well over one hundred years old."

"Wow." I smoothed my hand over the dusty desk and wondered what it would be like to live such a long life. "Even I can see this is a nice place. Has a lot of character."

"And it'll sell for a good price, despite all the reno work that needs to be done."

"I hope the new owners don't change too much. Maybe whitewash the wood paneling and add a bright color outside."

Kaitlin laughed. "I've never known you to get attached to anything down here."

I shrugged. "Don't get used to it. I'm only here for the summer."

"I'll help you deep-clean a bedroom and bathroom. Then you'll have a clean start."

"You don't have to do that."

She wiggled her fingers. "Many hands make light the work."

"Thanks. I appreciate the help."

We opted to divide and conquer the housework, as we had before. I stripped the bedding on the double bed and shoved it into an old washer. "No dryer."

"There's a clothesline outside," Kaitlin said. "You wanted vintage, and you got it. There's laundry soap in the van."

At the van, she grabbed a mop bucket while I unloaded soaps and rags.

Inside the house, I opened the windows, the wooden hurricane shutters, and the front and back doors. Fresh air immediately tunneled through the house as if it had just taken a full breath.

Kaitlin flipped on the breakers and then cleaned the bathroom, which was in decent shape, while I wiped down the bedroom. I mopped the floor in the bedroom and quickly washed the kitchen counters. Soon, wet sheets draped over the clothesline and flapped in an ocean breeze. The hot sun and wind would dry them out within hours.

It was nearly five when we'd finished our tasks. I closed up the house and locked the front door.

The sharp anger always directed at Mom, the Outer Banks, and the *Oceanus* had faded to a dull ache. I no longer saw all my mom's faults, but I recognized the good she'd done. She'd shown me the world, given me life skills few kids had, and taught me how to be independent. She hadn't been perfect, but neither was I.

We both crossed to the van. Kaitlin started the engine, which rattled to life. The air-conditioning felt good against my sweaty skin. I lifted my shirt and leaned in to the vent. I didn't know anyone who'd known Mom when we were here, beyond a few sailors we'd spoken to in passing. But there had to be someone who'd known her.

"The dinner crowds will hit soon. Want to grab a quick burger and celebrate your first full day?"

"You have time before camp?"

"I do."

"Sounds amazing."

"Arthur's has great burgers. And it's on the sound side of the beach road."

"Perfect. Shouldn't we shower?"

"We can wash our hands and faces in the diner's ladies' room. This place is the spot for local contractors. Everyone is wearing their day's grime. Not many tourists until later."

"Sounds good."

We parked in front of a two-story wood building with upstairs and downstairs porch seating. The tables and chairs were painted in aqua and white, and colorful strips of fabric dangled from the porch roof.

"What's with the fabric?" I followed her up the stairs.

"Supposed to catch bad spirits," she said.

"Seriously?"

"Yep."

Inside, the cool air brushed my salty skin. Kaitlin and I made a beeline for the restroom. Kaitlin peed, washed her hands quickly, and was reaching for the door while I was still splashing cool water on my face. By the time I'd dried my face and hands, combed my fingers through my hair, and secured it back in a ponytail, Kaitlin had already gotten a table and two beers.

"I see a friend," Kaitlin said. "Let me say hi quickly."

"Will do." I saddled up on a stool and took a long sip of beer. The salty barley flavor was about the best I'd ever tasted. I huffed out a breath and relaxed. This place wasn't my home or my permanent anything, but it felt good to be here.

"Tula."

The deep voice drew me to Nathan, standing there with a cold soda. He was wearing a dark blue T-shirt, board shorts, and flip-flops. His sun-streaked brown hair was wet and brushed off his face. "What brings you here?"

"Taking a break after work. Kaitlin will be right here."

He sat on the barstool next to me as if we hadn't missed a beat in the last seven years. He looked me over. "Rough day?"

I guess I really should have stopped at the apartment and taken that shower. "Kaitlin says our projects averaged a five on a scale of one to ten."

His smile was dazzling. And there was an edge of humor in his deep tones. "I'd hate to see you after a ten."

My chin lifted. "Me too."

"Far cry from office work?" he asked.

I sipped my beer. "Very different. My back might have more comments to make tomorrow. But all in all, better than moving papers from one end of the desk to the other."

"You'll get used to the manual work. Give your body a chance to adapt."

Once I had been very strong, so I knew he was right. "You look like you've been in the water."

Hair curled against the nape of his neck. "I took a group of tourists out to dive."

"I thought you were here for the *Oceanus*."

"I am, but as you know, bills don't care about dreams."

I laughed. "That's very true."

Many guys at the law firm wouldn't admit they didn't have money. Most were spread thin and relied on credit cards for their expensive watches and suits.

But not Nathan. He had never lived large or beyond his financial means. His reputation as a diver was more important to him. I remembered him saying once that life was what it was. Good times came with leaner ones. No sense pretending otherwise.

Kaitlin walked up to the table and sat across from Nathan. "I thought we might see you here. How did the dive go?"

"All the students had some experience, so it wasn't bad. Didn't lose anyone. No injuries. So, all good."

"How do you find your students?" I asked.

"Just like your mom used to. I let the local hotels know I'm coming and offer to partner with them. I also let everyone know I'm giving wreck tours. Not everyone says yes to my services, but enough do so I can pay the bills and fund the real interesting dives."

"You sound like Mom," I said. "She never worried. Said 'Brink's trucks don't follow hearses.'"

Again, that easy, cool smile. "She was a wise woman in many ways."

And in others, not so smart. She'd had a temper, and when someone questioned her diving skills, she always stood her ground, ready to burn bridges to make a point.

"So, you're a traveling teacher and documentary filmmaker?" I asked.

"That about sums it up."

"Weren't you in the Caribbean?" Kaitlin asked.

"Over the winter."

"You look thinner in person," she said.

He was so fit, it made me feel five pounds heavier than this morning.

Nathan laughed. "I get my share of comments online about my weight. Too many holiday desserts and someone comments."

"They do not," I said.

"The cyber-world is harsh, Tula," he said.

Kaitlin set her beer down. "When do you dive the *Oceanus?*"

"First dive is this Friday morning. You both are invited to come. I can always use the extra hand with the divers."

"I've got paperwork," Kaitlin said.

"And I have an old house to clear out," I said.

"Come on, Tula, you should come," he coaxed. "You can reacquaint yourself with the ocean."

My palms sweat a little. "I don't think so."

"Your fears can't be that bad," he said easily.

"Believe me, they are."

"We could work on that. Practice makes perfect." The words sounded genuine, inviting.

I pictured the murky waters offshore and the shadows of a wreck coming into view. A dull dread, always with me, sharpened. "Right."

CHAPTER TWELVE

Tula

Wednesday, June 10, 2026, 7:15 p.m.

While Kaitlin taught her mini-camp, I packed up the few items I'd taken out of my bag last night and loaded it into my car. I stopped at a local grocery store and picked up eggs, bread, cheese, tea, coffee, and peanut butter. I also grabbed toilet paper, jasmine soap, and shampoo.

The drive to the flattop house took thirty minutes because traffic was heavy. The tourists who'd dined at the southern end of the Outer Banks were headed north back to their rentals.

I parked on the aggregate driveway in front of the house and sat in my car staring at the low roof, the fading color, and the neatly trimmed shrubs surrounded by a bed of small rocks. With no aqua lawn chairs, bright planters, or flags, this house, though neat and in good shape, could easily have been missed by a passerby. This house wasn't looking for attention.

Juggling my suitcase and grocery bags, I walked to the front door. The old key slid into the lock and easily turned this time.

Inside the house, I flipped on the lights and locked the front door behind me. The sounds of crashing waves drifted through closed doors and windows. The ocean never settled, and it always made its presence known.

I'm still here.

I set my groceries on the kitchen counter, then put the cold items in the small refrigerator and the staples in the cabinet. Unable to resist, I walked out the back door and climbed the stairs to the sandbank's perch. Plumes of sea oats on the dunes wafted back and forth. A few people still lingered on the beach, walking along the waterline as the waves rolled in and out. The air was warm but not oppressively hot, and the sky was a vivid blue. My sheets, dried by the salt air, snapped on the clothesline. This really was one of the prettiest places on the planet.

"Stop being so beautiful," I grumbled. "I'm never going to love you again."

As I turned back toward the house, I imagined laughter rumbling under the waves. *You will love me again.*

I unpacked my bag, placing my clothes in the simple dresser I'd wiped out earlier. I returned to the clothesline and retrieved the clean sheets and towels, now dry and crisp. I pressed the sheets to my face, inhaling the sunshine.

After remaking the bed, I stocked my soaps in the small bathroom, outfitted with a tub and shower, and placed the toilet paper on the roll. Twisting a stainless handle, I turned on the hot spray.

I stripped and stepped inside. The water pulsed against my upturned face, flooding my body and washing away the day's salt, grime, and stress. The scent of jasmine floated around me. When the water turned cool, I shut off the tap and toweled off. I dressed in clean shorts and an oversize T-shirt.

I rinsed out a pot and filled it with water before setting it on the stove. Soon the burner warmed. I dropped a tea bag into the water and rustled up a mug from the cabinet. I washed it, and when the tea had darkened to a rich brown, I filled a cup and walked into Dr. Brooks's office.

When I turned on the light, I sensed I was intruding into a space that wasn't quite sure it wanted me here. "This wasn't my idea. I'm operating on orders above my pay grade."

Settling behind the desk, I set my mug on a pile of papers. I swiveled to the left, and the springs groaned as if dusting off years of lack of use. I grabbed one of the boxes stacked behind the desk. I leaned forward and tossed off the lid.

The papers inside were organized in bent, yellowed file folders. Bold handwriting marked each file tab. Utilities. Rent. Billing. All typical business records for any homeowner.

I opened the utilities file and noted that electricity had cost $7.20 a month in July of 1955. A fraction of what it was now. Nothing earth shattering. Prices had gone up.

Dust kicked up as I thumbed through more files that were just as routine as the first. My eyes watered as my allergies kicked in. I'd never had trouble with allergies when Mom and I had been traveling, but they'd exploded once I'd moved inland.

I set the top box aside and dug into the second container. This carton was filled with old newspaper clippings and black-and-white photos from the 1940s and 1950s. The first was of a man standing in front of the *Oceanus* on a tropical dock, likely Port of Spain. He wore a light suit and a panama-style hat. Had to be Dr. Atticus Brooks. He had a slight build and looked, well, ordinary, like his great-nephew, Mr. Brooks.

The family resemblance was striking. Both men wore similar glasses, and both dressed in suits with a white handkerchief in the right breast pocket.

Several of the other photos featured Dr. Brooks on the Outer Banks in front of this house, with a petite brunette with rounded sexy curves. A small time stamp on the side of the photos read *June 1946*. The barren yard had no plantings, and the driveway was rough crushed seashells and sand.

The woman had an ample bosom, full lips, and a sharp jawline. She appeared to be wearing a vivid lipstick. Her dress was a light color, and her shoes dark with a slight heel. She leaned into Dr. Brooks, and he wrapped his arm around her waist. His body language suggested he was relaxed and happy.

I flipped the pictures over, but there was no note identifying the woman. In all the images, while Dr. Brooks stared directly at the camera lens, the woman looked down or away from the camera. I couldn't tell if she was camera shy or it was just bad luck that her face was never fully captured.

Mr. Brooks had implied his great-uncle had left no heirs. If this woman was his wife, they had no surviving children.

The clippings moved through the decades, but there were no more pictures of the couple. I did find an article that covered a high-profile local hit-and-run case. A man vacationing here had been struck by a car. A local doctor had treated the unidentified man, who'd died at the scene.

The next articles featured a local couple who'd purchased a large tract of land in Kitty Hawk. In the upper-right-hand corner, someone had scribbled "client." Dr. Brooks wasn't quoted directly, but a line was attributed to a "local doctor": "We are glad to have the Millers investing in the community."

I found more articles like this one. Dr. Brooks was never mentioned by name, but he appeared to be tracking articles mentioning the unnamed doctor.

As I flipped through the yellowing newsprint, I came across an article highlighting a woman in her late teens. She had broad tanned shoulders, dark hair, and a wide grin. She wore scuba gear on her back and had a mask perched on her head.

I sat back on my heels. "Mom."

Her smiling eyes jumped out at me. Mom could light up a room. The date was 1995, six years before I was born. The article had appeared in the local Outer Banks newspaper, and there was a similar version in *The Virginian-Pilot*, which covered Norfolk and Virginia Beach news.

The headline read, Local Teen Dreams of Finding Nazi Gold.

The article detailed Mom's desire to find a shipwreck off the Outer Banks. She didn't divulge the name of the ship or where it had gone down exactly, but she was on the hunt for a vessel that had sunk in 1942. It had to be the *Oceanus*. The ship's name wasn't common knowledge in those days. Most residents had long forgotten the sunken ships that had gone down in the spring of 1942.

Another piece written days later had another picture featuring Mom and another young woman and man. The headline read, Teen Surfing Star Wins Local Competition. The other woman wore cutoffs, a halter top, and long hair drifting over her shoulders. The man looked like Kaitlin. The woman bore a resemblance to Kaitlin's mom, and she'd won a surfing award.

Kaitlin's parents?

I'd never realized they'd all been friends. It made sense, of course—the Outer Banks community was even smaller then, and it wasn't a surprise that many young people ran in the same circles. I snapped pictures of the black-and-white images.

The doctor's files followed Mom's around-the-world adventures that had made it into newspapers. I found pictures of her in Bermuda, Greece, and Hawaii. One image was snapped in the Florida Keys, and that one captured a five-year-old version of me in the background. I remembered that trip. We'd stayed in a pink house, and the woman who looked after me, Cookie, spoke Spanish and made me cheese quesadillas.

On that trip, Mom had been hired by several well-off men to dive a Spanish galleon that had sunk in a storm off Key Largo in 1700. I remembered Mom explaining to the divers that the wreck had been explored often for the last fifty years, and the chances of finding anything of value were small. But the men had wanted to dive, and Mom, never one to miss an opportunity, took them down to the wreck. Cookie's husband, Bert, laughed at my scowling face when I grumbled that I'd wanted to dive. He told me stories of his navy days and cautioned me about spending too much time in the sun. His sun-weathered skin, etched with wrinkles, was covered in tattoos, and I'd worried about tattoos appearing on me if I stayed in the sun too long.

The next article was from 2019, and it was about Mom and me. Her bright smile contrasted to my moody teenage grimace. **Local Returns to Find Gold.** We'd been in town a couple of weeks when the reporter, Mr. Lex Green, had tracked us down on the boat dock in Wanchese.

I wondered if this was one of the last articles Dr. Brooks clipped before he died in 2019. He would have been close to 118, and I still couldn't imagine anyone living to be that old.

Why would Dr. Brooks care about Mom's career? She wasn't from the Outer Banks, and though she was known in diving circles, she'd never had a national or international reputation. Maybe Dr. Brooks had been a sort of fan of a good treasure hunter and someone else had shared his interest. Many of the people on Mom's dive expeditions were lawyers, accountants, and real estate agents. All shuffled paper behind a desk, and all longed for a grand adventure.

The next series of articles were far more sobering. They headlined basically the same news: **Local Diver Lost at Sea.**

I hadn't read any of these pieces when they'd first appeared, but I'd heard the kids at school talk about them. That was the spring of whispers, long stares, and a few snide remarks about Mom and about my failure to save her.

High school. If God really wanted to punish me, he'd send me back to high school.

I read the first article, printed in 2019. It detailed Mom's life, her adventures around the world, and her fixation on the *Oceanus*. The reporter, who'd interviewed Mom just before the last dive, noted that Mom had said the only reason she'd returned to the Outer Banks was for the *Oceanus*.

The next piece detailed the accident again and was a rinse and repeat of Mom's background. The last line mentioned that Mariah Cassidy had left behind a daughter, Tula. The website for my trust page was listed.

I checked the author's byline. Again, it was Lex Green. I grabbed my phone and searched his name. He was still living in the area but had retired to the town of Manteo on Roanoke Island. He was the author of several books about Outer Banks history, but nothing more about Mom or the *Oceanus*.

Suddenly very tired, I closed the box. I sipped my cooling tea and leaned back in the chair. I pressed the mug to my temple, trying to cut off an emerging headache.

Rising, I shut off the lights, left the office, and crawled into the double bed. The mattress was firm and the bed frame solid, saving me a night of endless squeaking. I pulled the sun-soaked sheets up to my chin and rolled into a ball.

The Outer Banks were a long, thin strip of land. Nothing was close to anything, and a forty-five-minute drive for groceries or supplies wasn't unheard of. But the population was small. And though full-time residents could be spread over a hundred miles, gossip, if it wasn't buried deep, traveled fast.

This fascination with Mom appeared to be one of those bits of information no one spoke about. Dr. Brooks and Mom might have both lived briefly on the Outer Banks at the same time, but she had never mentioned him.

My eyes drifted closed. Despite my exhaustion, my mind buzzed. I wanted nothing more than to sleep and forget about the doctor, his lawyer great-nephew, the flattop house, Mom's death, and Nathan's offer to dive the *Oceanus*.

Even as questions prattled in my head, sleep floated around me. Images appeared of me struggling against a dark current as I swam away from the *Oceanus* and toward my last dive boat.

My hand slipped once off the dive platform's handrail, but I regripped it and hauled myself up. I'd stared at the choppy waters, searching for Mom. She didn't surface.

I wiped the water from my eyes and adjusted my mask. I clamped my teeth around my mouthpiece and sucked in a breath. I still had enough air to get down and back to the surface. In what couldn't have been more than seconds, the sea's churning sped up, and the boat rocked violently.

"Mom!"

More choppy waters splashed my face.

"Come on, Mom."

Then the waves grew higher. Even if I reached Mom, then what? The boat might not survive the rising waves. I scooted back onto the boat and wrestled off my tanks. I shrugged on a life jacket and stumbled to the wheel and radio. I called in a distress message to the coast guard. Mom wouldn't like me calling for help. She'd always gotten herself out of dangerous situations before. But at that point I was too terrified to care.

"Mayday, Mayday."

And then, just like that, I jostled awake. I was back in Dr. Brooks's bed and sucking in a lungful of air.

I'd known coming back here was going to be hard. And it was.

CHAPTER THIRTEEN

GERTRUDE

Tuesday, April 21, 1942, 9:30 a.m.
Three days until the Oceanus *is torpedoed*

The Germans had entered Austria in 1938, shortly after my husband and I had married. Many, like my husband, had rejoiced. They welcomed the Germans as saviors. Others, like me, feared what would come next.

As the spring of 1938 turned to summer, I'd questioned Alfred about Germany's annexation of Austria. He was impatient when he said, "Don't ask so many questions. Let me worry about such things."

By fall, many of the Jewish shops had been smashed or burned during Kristallnacht, the Night of Broken Glass. Others of the faith were forced to scrub the streets. Ration allotments were reduced. Children had to leave school. I had seen nothing good after the arrival of the Germans. But I was too consumed with surviving the dark waters of my marriage.

After I'd lost my first pregnancy, I was very ill with a fever for days. But even in my delirium, I'd been so grateful. Fearing Alfred would want more children, I realized I most likely couldn't have more. When I finally recovered, I packed a bag and took a taxi to the train station. I was in my train compartment, counting the seconds to departure.

And then Alfred walked onto the car. He was calm, smiling. Without a word, he took my arm and hauled me out of my seat. He pressed his lips close to my ear.

"Don't make a scene," he said easily.

"I don't want to go home." My words were awash with fear.

"You're upset over the loss of our child," he said. "I'll forgive you this lapse. But don't test me."

No one in the car stood or spoke out. Vienna had been gripped with fear and tension ever since the failed civil war in 1934. We'd all learned to avoid trouble, attention, and the police.

Alfred pulled me from the car, through the train station, and toward a gleaming black Mercedes. Inside the car, I met the driver's gaze in the rearview mirror. His gaze registered my panic and then shifted to the bustling road ahead.

"The next time I catch you running, I will break your feet." Alfred lifted an imaginary thread from my shoulder. "Soon we'll make another child. Soon you'll give me a son."

The thought of children in this marriage terrified me.

The driver didn't drive us directly home, but we detoured through a small neighborhood filled with small, modest town houses. Next, we passed my uncle's shop.

The windows had been smashed, and amid the shattered glass on the sidewalk lay burned books that still smoldered from the fire. My one refuge was gone.

"Such a shame," Alfred whispered.

Oddly, after that day, Alfred was kind and attentive. He bought me a one-of-a-kind ruby bracelet, which he'd proudly looped around my wrist at a candlelit dinner. The stones and gold carried the weight of a manacle.

From then on, I walked on eggshells. Under the tentative peace with Alfred swirled a temper as violent as the undercurrents of the lower Danube's Iron Gate gorge. It was only a matter of time before he destroyed me.

I'd begun to plan and think how I'd escape. I had no allies in Alfred's circle, but there was the woman who'd come into the bookshop to sell her rare books. She had connections in every corner of the underworld.

The *Oceanus'* upper deck horn screamed. I woke up, fists clenched, cringing as I lunged forward in my bunk. The sudden move crimped my swollen belly, forcing me back. I looked around my cabin, anchoring myself in the familiar.

My breathing calmed, and I rose and pushed back the curtain. The sun was high in the sky. I had slept the night away. A first since Vienna. The ocean had rocked me gently to sleep and held me there all night as the ship took me farther away from Vienna. Soon, I would not be confined, and the vast world would open to me.

The hallways were quiet, giving me a chance to hurry to the toilet down the hall and use the facilities. Back in my room, I washed my face in the basin and took time to comb my hair. My stomach grumbled, and as much as I wanted to avoid people, hunger got the better of me. I dressed in a simple navy blue dress and my brown shoes.

As I walked toward the stairs, I heard the fading sounds of a laughing couple. At the dining level, the chatter of conversations and the clink of dishes greeted me.

The steward looked up at me, frustration etched in the lines of his face. I was tardy again for another meal.

"I only have one seat available now," he said. "And you'll have to share the table."

I considered who this person might be. I thought about the DuPonts and the woman who reminded me of Vienna. If I wanted to eat, I had no choice but to share. "Of course."

He escorted me around the side of the room toward a small table near the kitchen doors. Thankfully, most everyone was so busy eating or looking out at the ocean that no one noticed me.

My breakfast companion had laid his or her napkin by the plate, a sign they would return. I took my seat and accepted a menu from the waiter. As he poured coffee from a silver pot, I ordered eggs, toast, and whatever fruit was available.

I stared out the porthole. The vast waves rolled, turning in on themselves. There was no end in sight.

In Vienna, I could stand at the shore of the Danube and stare at the other side. But the Atlantic was so vast, but not too large for the submarines to find the *Oceanus*.

Submarines ran more efficiently on the surface using diesel engines. But once they submerged to pursue a target, those engines became useless. Underwater, they relied on electric power, which cut their speed in half.

The *Oceanus* was a desirable target. She might carry 132 souls aboard, but I suspected her cargo hold was packed with precious raw materials like uranium, manganese, and chromium, all favorites in military manufacturing circles.

Large guns positioned at the bow of the ship were manned by young soldiers with gazes trained on the horizon.

I'd come so far. Hunger, humiliation, and so many lies. I'd done it all to reach the United States. And now to think I could be so close to freedom, only to have it ripped away by an unseen team of men I could have been acquainted with in Vienna.

A flicker of movement caught my attention. Dr. Brooks approached me. "Frau Werner?"

I raised my gaze to him. "Good morning."

His gaze scanned over me. "You look nervous."

I painted over the worry with a grin. "You aren't worried? So much water. So many endless waves."

Dr. Brooks took his seat, spreading his napkin over his lap. "I work better with water under my feet. This great vastness is beautiful, no? Did you know water covers two-thirds of the world? We can't survive without it."

The waves smacked against the bow, jostling me. Stoneware dishes and glasses rattled. "It's also frightening."

A smile teased his lips. "You'll arrive in New York City, and you and your baby will live a fine life." His words were awash with such certainty.

His comforting words grazed their mark. "Tell me about New York."

"So much to say. I grew up in a brownstone in Brooklyn." When my brow rose, he added, "A town house on the east side of New York City. But I now spend most of my time in the port city of Norfolk, Virginia."

Before the war, I'd read US novels and magazines that described cities with tall buildings, solid roads, and so many people. Since Germany's annexation of Austria, Austrian newspapers only reported low US morale, a failing society, and weak soldiers. But the Lisbon papers spoke of the United States as a strong, vast country ready to supply the Allied war effort. "What do you like best about New York?"

"The food. The plays. The Hudson River."

"Water again. You sound like you're a creature of the water."

"I am." The definitive statement suggested a literal truth.

"What else do you love about the city?"

Hints of regret darkened his gaze. "The theater. The symphony. Central Park is in the center of the city. It's over eight hundred acres of trees, grass, lakes, and pathways. Nothing prettier on a warm spring day. It reminds me of the Volksgarten in Vienna."

"The People's Garden," I said easily.

"So, you have been to Vienna?"

I paused. "I've read about it."

"Ah. The Volksgarten is a stunning park. Very lovely. It was once an imperial garden. And of course, many rare books in all those narrow side street shops. I hear the books have been a casualty of the war in Vienna."

Even this far from Austria, I hesitated to speak out. One more slip, and I could reveal too much. "So I have heard." I rearranged my napkin. "How is Norfolk different from New York City?"

"Smaller. A large port city. Smaller shops. Families. Kids. By now, the city must be awash with soldiers and sailors ready to set sail for Europe and fight."

Many young men in Austria had already died on the battlefield. "I pray for them all."

As if he understood that fear dominated my calculations, he removed a card from his vest pocket. It read, **DR. ATTICUS T. BROOKS, BOOK DEALER**. There was no address under the name, but he removed a pen from his pocket and scribbled a phone number. "If you find yourself in need of assistance, you can send word."

I flicked the edge of the card with my gloved finger. "Thank you, but it would be too much to ask."

"Nonsense. Now that international crossings are precarious. I'll be staying stateside for the time being. I would consider it an honor if you contacted me. I can always use help in the Norfolk bookshop."

A bookshop was tantalizing. I wondered if his shop was like my uncle's store. I tucked the card deep in the pocket of my skirt. "Thank you."

I liked Dr. Brooks. He wasn't as physically impressive as Alfred. But he had intelligent eyes that missed little. "What was your favorite discovery on this trip?"

"You shift the topic very smoothly, Frau Werner."

My lips softened. "I would say you're better at it than me."

He grinned. "Guilty as charged." He leaned forward a fraction, straightening the untouched spoon by his plate. "I'd say the coins I found in North Africa. They date back to Roman times."

"Roman. Over a thousand years old."

"Older," he said. He reached into his pocket and removed a handful of silver pieces. He placed several in my palm.

Several were perfectly round and engraved with the profile of a Roman emperor sporting a laurel wreath. As I shuffled the bits of metal around my palm, I found one that caught my attention. It was identical to the coin I'd tossed into the Danube River four years ago.

When I looked up, Dr. Brooks regarded me closely. "You have found the outlier."

"Where did you get this one?"

"I don't remember." When I tried to return the silver pieces, he added, "Keep that one. It'll remind you of home and me."

I didn't want to remember home or him, but I didn't know how to refuse. "Thank you."

He sipped his coffee, motioned for the waiter, and ordered fresh coffee. "Tell me about your United States family," he said. "You said you have a cousin there?"

I'd learned to keep my stories and lies simple. "My late husband has a distant cousin in New York who has agreed to sponsor me. But I don't know very much about her."

"Very lucky that you have a sponsor. And that you were able to get out of Austria. Many are now scrambling. If you'd delayed much longer, it might not have been possible."

I'd witnessed the changes as the barge had floated out of Vienna along the Danube and down a canal toward the city of Constanța, on the Black Sea. Sunken ships, armored boats equipped with guns, soldiers lining the shoreline.

When military vessels approached the barge one time, I was shown below deck to a small compartment under the stairs. I'd remained hidden until weeks later, when the old sailor who'd carried me the length of the river had guided me to another boat. He told me, "In Lisbon, the Salvadoran embassy officer can help you with papers."

After spending months in Barcelona, I'd obtained identity papers in exchange for a diamond from one of my bracelets. I visited the Lisbon docks daily to buy passage, but no seats were available. And as I waited, I heard more news of bombings, deportations, troop movement. Yet I only worried that Alfred would find me. Finally, I was able to secure a small cabin. When I presented my papers, the guard fixed his gaze on mine as he studied them. I kept my stare steady as I slipped him 5,000 Portuguese escudos. Finally, he stamped my papers so hard I jolted. When I reached Port of Spain and saw the US soldiers, I'd taken some comfort. I was almost free.

"I was arrested in Vienna in 1938," Dr. Brooks said as if sharing a daring secret. "I had been in Austria on and off since 1935, and suddenly the local officials decided I was a spy. Cost me a fortune to bribe my way out of that country."

"I'm sorry to hear that." Many had vanished into those dark cells and never been seen again. "You're lucky to be free."

"Indeed. It's a shame such a lovely city has grown so dark. But we're both far from any troubles in Austria."

I didn't believe that. The troubles were spreading now like a plague. "Yes."

He left his meal untouched. "You said your husband passed."

He was a curious man, but I couldn't tell what he was after. Was he making conversation or digging for something deeper? My guard rose. "Yes. But if you don't mind, I'd rather not talk about him."

"Of course. I understand. Painful memories."

Dr. Brooks's gaze pried at the lid of my Pandora's box. "How far along are you, if you don't mind me asking?"

The waiter delivered my breakfast, and when I reached for my fork, Dr. Brooks buttered a piece of his toast. "The baby is due in June." The baby had been conceived on September 21, 1941.

"It'll be quite a joyous moment in such dark times."

"Yes." I set down my fork, drawing in a deep breath. The past hovered so close.

"You must eat," Dr. Brooks said.

I looked up, realizing he was still watching me closely. "My appetite comes and goes."

"The baby needs to eat. So, you must eat."

I was well trained to take orders and without thinking picked up a sliver of dry toast and took a bite. The bread was soft. As I ate, he made light conversation about the *Oceanus* and its history.

When I'd cleared my plate, he looked pleased. "That baby is hungry."

"Yes."

"Would you like to join me for a walk on the deck?" he asked. "It's a pleasant morning. In a day or two, when we're farther north, the weather will grow colder."

In the months I'd been in Port of Spain, I'd savored the heat. "Yes, I would like the fresh air."

He rose and came behind my chair, offering his hand. I took it and stood, feeling the weight of the baby bearing down on me.

"All right?"

"Yes," I said. "I'm just a bit awkward these days."

"That's normal."

He escorted me out of the dining room and up a flight of stairs. Soon we were stepping out on the windswept top deck. The morning sky was clear and the sun very bright. I inhaled the salt air, finding it more refreshing than city air, which always carried a stench.

We walked to the railing, and I stared out over the waves, which rolled under the sun's glare. Easy to fall prey to the vast ocean, ready to swallow ships like this whole. As much as I savored the fresh air, my nerves tightened, and I felt oddly claustrophobic.

"The ocean really makes you nervous," Dr. Brooks said.

"Yes." My honesty surprised me. "Rivers I know; oceans are a different creature."

"They're one and the same. The rivers feed into the ocean eventually. And the ocean isn't good or evil, but she's to be respected. She doesn't care much about either you or me."

Hints of bitterness washed over his words. "Have you been at sea for a long time?" I asked.

"I've voyaged across water more than most. A ship I was on, the *Valiant*, was sunk off the coast of Africa." He paused, and as the silence stretched, I wondered if he'd say anything else. "I don't wish to frighten you."

"Stories are just stories. They don't scare me."

A beam of sunlight washed out his face, making it tough to read his expression. "You're not one who heeds warnings?"

"I have enough to worry about." Dr. Brooks and I stood side by side at the railing, staring out over the rolling waves.

"Why do you still go to sea?" I asked.

"It's how I make my living." A smile nudged the corners of his lips. "I don't hate the water. But I respect her power. And I've accepted she can take me at any moment, as a thousand other things can."

"Death isn't the worst fate."

"Very true indeed." He shook his head. "Have you practiced putting on your life jacket?"

"No." I'd seen it hanging in the small closet.

"Practice. And take time to note where all the lifeboats are located. Do this several times a day, because when we panic, we forget what's not drilled deep into our memories."

Having a plan calmed some of my worries. "Better to be prepared."

"Exactly."

"Very wise, Dr. Brooks."

He grinned. "You strike me as a woman who's prepared to succeed."

"I am."

"Then you will be just fine."

The sailors manning the three large navy guns sounded an alarm. One sailor shouted orders as the two others angled their guns toward the north. Dr. Brooks followed the line of the gun barrels and studied the rising and falling ocean waters.

I could see nothing but lurching waves. "What do they see?"

"Hard to say. They're looking for any sign of a submarine."

A chill skimmed over my body. If the ship went down, would we all survive the explosions or make it to a lifeboat? The odds felt against us.

"What if we are hit?" I asked.

Dr. Brooks studied the waters. "Chaos will break out. Most will panic and run in circles. If the ship is sinking, you must get to your cabin if you can. Put your life jacket on as fast as you are able. Don't worry about your belongings. Then rush toward a lifeboat. Stay focused and keep moving, and you'll be fine."

An older couple walked arm in arm past us. It seemed impossible they'd lose control, but I'd seen how ruthless humans could be to one another. I gripped the coin tighter. "I will."

We both stood in silence for several minutes until one of the sailors announced an all clear. My breath remained trapped in my chest until Dr. Brooks's shoulders eased, and he faced me. The ruthless intensity melted. "See? Nothing to worry about. These moments are nerve racking, but they're common on voyages like this. We'll have more."

He couldn't make that kind of promise, but hearing it was a comfort. "I've enjoyed our conversation, Dr. Brooks."

"Always a delight, Frau Werner. Will I see you at dinner?"

"I'm not sure."

"I'll have more charms and stories to share."

"Always closing a sale?"

"Of course."

"How can I resist?"

He saluted. "I'll be looking for you."

"Thank you."

The lifeboats were large and looked as if they could hold a dozen passengers each. The baby stirred inside me.

"This has been lovely, but I must retire," I said.

"Of course. I will walk you to your cabin."

I'd journeyed across endless rivers, seas, and now the ocean, alone. "I can find my way."

"That may be true. But I feel it's my duty to walk you to your cabin."

My skin bristled at the order, but I kept my expression neutral. "Thank you."

We crossed the teak deck, went through the portal, and walked down the interior halls and stairs. When I reached my cabin, I was slightly winded, but a little less worried. I fished a key from my pocket and opened my door. "Thank you, Dr. Brooks."

"If you need anything, please let me know."

"I should be fine. Thank you."

Inside my cabin, I closed the door. I sensed Dr. Brooks standing outside. I held my breath until I heard his footsteps echo down the hallway. He was charming. But Alfred had been pleasant once.

CHAPTER FOURTEEN

Tula

Thursday, June 11, 2026, 7:15 a.m.

Kaitlin handed me a coffee. Neither of us had had much to say since I'd arrived at the surf shop and watched the coffeepot gurgle out the magic stuff. I looked as rough as I felt, and she didn't appear much better.

"I know I slept badly," I said. "What's your story?"

"The usual."

"Which is?"

"Life. The business."

"Did the camp go well?"

"It was good."

"So, what's up with the business?"

"Nothing. It's great."

"But?"

She threaded fingers through her hair, and as she secured the golden strands into a bun, she said, "You know I've been cleaning houses since I was thirteen."

"I know."

"I'm really good at it, and MERmaids has more business than I can handle."

She handed me a cup, and I pressed the warm stoneware against my temple, willing the headache to ease. "I'm not hearing the 'why you can't sleep' part."

Kaitlin frowned at me. "Do you think that I'll be cleaning houses for the rest of my life?"

"I don't know. Do you want to?"

"The money is good, it's necessary to keep the surf shop afloat, but . . ."

"You're wondering if there's more to life than money, Kaitlin. It's always the question of the day in the law office where I work. The work there pays well, but it's not always satisfying. A lot of people quit the legal field to find their bliss."

"And?"

I shrugged. "One guy left to hike part of the Appalachian Trail and then discovered he really liked sleeping in a real bed. He came back to the law firm, but he now works fewer hours. Another gal wanted to drive across the country. Car troubles forced her to get work as a waitress. She's still in Kansas City doing that but texted a few coworkers that she wants to return."

"You're saying there's no gold at the end of the rainbow?"

"I grew up with a treasure hunter. I know it all looks great when you see the five-minute montage on YouTube. But hunting treasure across the world is like all things in life. A few days are terrific. But just as many days, we were fighting wind and hard rain. There's always good and bad."

Kaitlin poured herself a cup of coffee and took several sips. "You're crushing my fantasy."

"I don't mean to do that. I'm just saying if you choose to go on a great adventure, it's never going to be perfect. Try to have a plan B. I should've followed my own advice when I moved into Dave's house. I thought I had a great plan, but I didn't insist on being added to the mortgage."

"What happened to jumping without a parachute?"

I paused before I took my next sip. "It's fun, at first. And then the ground"—I winced—"hits hard. I wouldn't advise leaving a parachute behind."

"I know it was rough for you after your mom died. Mom always worried that you'd never recover."

"I found a picture of our mothers and your dad together. They were teenagers, and they looked so happy." I pulled up the images on my phone.

She studied the one picture closely, enlarging her mother's face. "Where did you find the pictures?"

"They were in an article I found in the Southern Shores house."

She frowned. "That doesn't make sense. Why would Dr. Brooks save articles like that?"

"I don't know. I guess he knew both Mom and Carol."

"I never met him."

"Hopefully I'll find more information when I dig deeper."

"Yeah, keep me posted." She handed me back my phone.

I cleared the hitch in my throat. "I will. Your mom was always kind to me. I should've noticed how sick she was. I wish I'd paid more attention. I should've stayed longer so I could have helped."

"She was glad you didn't. She realized this place wasn't good for you after your mom vanished."

After the Atlantic swallowed Mom, I was so consumed that I didn't see that Kaitlin and her mother were also sinking. I'd always thought she was lucky because her mother had died of cancer. She was able to speak to her at the end. She had a funeral for her and knew where she was buried. But she'd also lost her mother. Pain was pain.

And here she was helping me again. I could at least help her for as long as I could.

"Let's get going," I said. "The work awaits."

"You're right. Those toilets won't clean themselves."

Kaitlin had always been able to put one foot in front of the other. She was double-timing the work and chasing a dream, while I'd stayed frozen in place.

We grabbed our coffees and a few energy bars and left the apartment. The van rolled down the beach road toward a collection of condos on the ocean. She pulled into the parking lot and put the van in park.

"What else did you find in the flattop?" Kaitlin asked.

"Pictures of Dr. Brooks and a lovely brunette in front of the house shortly after it was built. And several articles about Mom."

"Your mom was a big deal seven years ago. A lot of people lived vicariously through her adventures. Her death tossed cold water on their fantasies. Some Gen Xers still talk about her on the anniversary."

"They do?"

"If Mariah Cassidy could die, then anyone could."

"Is that why people tended to avoid me?"

Kaitlin sighed. "You were the living proof of their fears. And let's face it, dying at sea is sexier than cancer."

"Did people avoid you after your mother died?"

"No. I had more casseroles than I could eat. But life goes on, and the casseroles stopped."

Kaitlin hadn't had a trust fund. No articles about her mother, beyond an old surf competition and an obituary that I'd read in the Norfolk paper.

"Who was the reporter who wrote about your mom?" she asked.

"Lex Green."

"Lives in Manteo."

"That's right."

"You should track him down."

The house had brought me here, but I was back on the Outer Banks for a bigger reason. "I will."

Cleaning the condos this morning wasn't traumatic. The fifteen used condoms in unit number three weren't great, but they were in a lined trash can. And I was using plastic gloves and holding my breath. "A sex fiend rented this place."

"Jealous?" A grinning Kaitlin loaded up the last of the cleaning supplies into the van.

"Maybe. It's been a while."

"Have you had a date since the divorce?"

"No. I thought about it. Even got dressed up and stopped by a local bar. But my bra and heels were cutting off my circulation, and several attempts at conversation were painful. I'll give it another go soon, but not right now."

"Never say never."

"Are you dating?"

"Kinda. As soon as he grows up, he'll be a great guy."

"How old is he?"

"Thirty-one. Men tend to grow up a little slower in these parts."

"Ouch."

"I'm not knocking the guys. They're living their best life. You're not the only one who's jealous. I've always had to be grown up."

My mind tripped to Nathan. He was living a nomad's life, but he'd never been frivolous or immature. "An old soul," as Mom used to say. But he'd also not settled for less than what he wanted.

We pulled into the parking lot of the rec center. Kaitlin had to circle a few times to find a parking space. I had no idea it would be hopping like this.

"Let's see if Doug is here," Kaitlin said. "Maybe he'll have something to say about your Dr. Brooks."

I was still curious not only about why Dr. Brooks lived directly across from the *Oceanus* wreck but also about why his house held links to Mom. "Sure, why not?"

Inside the center, we found Doug standing by the reception desk. He was a tall, lean man with slightly hunched shoulders, white hair, and deeply tanned skin. Smiling, he was talking to a woman in her sixties. If I hadn't lost my touch, I'd have said he was flirting a little.

"Doug," Kaitlin said.

He turned, and that smile brightened when he saw her. He moved toward us at a slow and halting pace. He took Kaitlin's hands in his gnarled fingers. "How are you doing? Haven't seen you in a while."

"Working. Lost a few employees, and the new ones don't arrive for two weeks."

He turned over her hands and stared at her calloused palms. "Making bank, I hope."

"Can't complain. Doug, this is Tula."

His attention shifted to me, and recognition flickered. "Tula Cassidy, right?"

I braced for the uncomfortable moment people would always have back in the day when they met me. "Yes."

"I didn't realize you were back." Curiosity swam in his green gaze.

"I arrived two days ago. Here for the summer." The commitment had felt like forever when I'd made it, but now that same clock was ticking faster.

Doug grinned. "Good to have you back."

"Thanks."

He arched a brow "I know you two didn't show up to talk to an old man like me."

Kaitlin laughed softly. "Tula's agreed to do a move-out clean in Southern Shores. You knew Atticus Brooks."

"I was wondering when someone would clean the house out. It's worth a small fortune now. Atticus was a fixture around here. Died in 2019 at the age of one hundred and eighteen. That must have set a world record. Hell of a guy."

"What was Dr. Brooks like?" I asked.

"I didn't spend much time with him, but I got to know him a little. Quiet. He organized a lot of activities and schedules. Liked to work behind the scenes. We tried to present him with a Volunteer of the Year award in 2018, but he refused it. He didn't like attention."

That fit with the man I'd read about so far. "Someone wrote a partial manuscript about the *Oceanus*. Do you think it was him?"

Doug shook his head. "He was smart enough to write anything. So was his great-nephew, who is a lawyer in Norfolk. But Dr. Brooks never talked about the wreck."

"Why would the family hold on to the house so long?" I asked.

"The great-nephew came down here a lot, from what I heard."

"I found a box of articles about the ship." He'd never been mentioned in any piece. "He also collected news clippings about my mother."

"Dr. Brooks never mentioned her. But from what I heard about him, he always played his cards close to his vest. Maybe your mother's adventures reminded him of his younger days during World War II."

"What did he do during the war?" I asked.

"He said he traveled around the world, buying and selling rare books. But I never believed that."

"What do you think Dr. Brooks did?" I asked.

Doug shrugged. "This is just a guess, but I think he was a spy."

"Seriously?"

"He never said that. But again, I've pieced together stories I've heard about him. I mean, what kind of guy travels around the world during a major war?"

"But he never said 'spy.'"

"He was very tight lipped about the war. As a lot of those guys who served were. We had an autistic child go missing in the 1980s. He offered his service to the local police. They knew of him, and everyone here respected him, so they let him listen in on the briefing. Took him a few hours, but he pieced together the evidence and found the child huddled in a shed. No one knew how he figured it out. Sometimes the sheriff's office privately consulted with him on a few cases."

"He looked so ordinary," I said.

Doug winked. "The best spies do. But that man had a mind that never lost a fact. The police had nothing but respect for him."

"He lived in Norfolk as well."

"He did. He liked being close to an airport and still was on the move well into his early eighties. He spent his last years in Norfolk."

"And he was on the *Oceanus* when it sank?" I asked.

"He was. But he never talked about it."

I thought about the stack of yellowed manuscript pages I'd read. The people I'd read about so far had been well drawn, but they still felt so distant and removed. Maybe the book was an academic exercise, a way of remembering.

"How did he die?"

"He had a stroke while he was in Norfolk. He was here one day and gone the next. Just like he lived."

"Anything else you can tell me about him?"

Doug seemed to think before he shook his head. "Not really."

I thought about all the books, stacks of papers, and boxes. But Dr. Brooks remained a mystery. "Thanks, Doug."

"Sure thing. Give me a shout-out if you find whatever he was working on. Good to have you back, Tula."

"Thanks. Hey, if I had a house of furniture to sell, who would I reach out to?" I asked.

"Morrison's Auction House. Ask for Sharon."

"Thank you again."

We left the rec center. In the front seat of Kaitlin's van, I leaned my head back and closed my eyes. She slid behind the wheel.

Seven years had put a little distance between me and the wreck. "I wish I could have talked to Dr. Brooks. He might have been able to explain why Mom was so obsessed. She'd have ended any other dive when her oxygen was so low. But that day, she didn't. It wasn't like her."

Humor flickered on the edges of Kaitlin's lips. "You sound like your mom. She was always curious. Couldn't leave a question unanswered."

"I do not sound like Mom," I groaned.

A shrug lifted her shoulders. "There's a lot of your mom in you."

"Hopefully all I'll do is investigate, and I don't end up so obsessed that I dive with little oxygen."

"What about Nathan? Are you going to tell him about the book?"

I wasn't ready to talk to him about the ship yet. "All I have is fifty pages. For all I know, this all goes nowhere."

CHAPTER FIFTEEN

Tula

Thursday, June 11, 2026, 3:15 p.m.

I spent several hours at the Brooks house cleaning out the closets. All were organized but full of blankets, sheets, and more boxes of paper. The man hadn't met a clipping, document, or bill he hadn't loved and saved. I began organizing all the items in piles in the living room. Bedding in one heap. Paper in another. And books in another.

The bedding was older, worn but in good shape. All needed a good washing, and I wasn't sure if I should line everything up in an assembly line near the washing machine. It would take days to clean it all. I checked my weather app and saw we had a 20 percent chance of rain this afternoon, and it was clear skies for the rest of the week. Washing and line drying commenced. I'd clean what I could and drape it over the clotheslines.

As the washing machine chugged with the first load, I shifted my attention to the boxes of paper. They were heavy, each packed to maximum capacity, and they weighed at least thirty pounds each. These items would also need to be sorted. Shredding and disposal would be the main objective. I knew enough about Dr. Brooks to know he wouldn't want his papers shared. And then the books. So many books.

There were as many novels as there were nonfiction books, and the copyright dates spanned decades. A quick look, and I saw that some had copyright dates from the 1920s. I wasn't sure who would want these books. Donation centers and libraries preferred novels, not discussions on geopolitics and war. Still, just tossing them didn't feel right either. A tag sale would be the most profitable way to dispense of all these items, but I couldn't imagine Dr. Brooks wanting people milling around in his house.

I called Morrison's Auction House. I got a voicemail recording, and I left a message for Sharon to contact me.

My phone dinged with a text from Kaitlin. What are you doing?

Sorting. I scanned the piles around me. Less is definitely more in life.

Kaitlin: I hear ya. Want to meet for dinner? Surf camp ends at seven.

It was past six, and a peanut butter sandwich didn't feel so appealing. Sure.

Kaitlin: Arthur's. See you right after seven.
Me: Will do.

I walked to the bathroom, stripped, showered, and brushed my hair. And then, for whatever reason, I grabbed my mascara and lipstick and applied both. It wasn't like Kaitlin had said Nathan was going to be at dinner. And I sure wasn't expecting him, exactly. Still, it didn't hurt to look presentable.

❦

By the time I arrived at Arthur's, it was buzzing with customers. I saw contractors I'd noticed last night and now a few sunburned tourists.

I was ready to be around people. My back ached and my fingers felt swollen as I settled on the same barstool at the same round cocktail table, next to Kaitlin.

"Is this going to be our table?" I asked.

"Routine is your thing, right?"

I traced the laminated top. My stool wobbled a little, but I liked the familiarity.

"I remember how you lined up your hairbrushes, combs, and clips on your dresser," Kaitlin said.

"You kept rearranging them."

She smiled. "It was kind of mean. If I'd thought about it, I would have left your stuff alone."

The waitress we'd met last night brought us both a beer. "Burgers?" she asked.

"Yes," I said. "Just like yesterday."

The waitress winked. "I like a customer who doesn't hem and haw."

I took a long sip of my beer. As the cool beverage slid through my body, the front door opened, and Nathan entered the bar. Like me, he was a creature of habit. One of us might need to find a new routine.

He waved to us, grabbed a beer at the bar, and moved straight toward the seat beside me. "I knew you'd be here."

"I'm that predictable?" Seven years ago, we'd talked about having normal lives. Neither of us wanted one, but we both needed to manage the chaos. I'd created my own little bubble of certainty.

"You are. But so am I."

That coaxed a smile. His daily routine had been as quirky as mine.

"Tula had an interesting find," Kaitlin said. "Her boss gave her a partial manuscript about the *Oceanus*. She's cleaning out a house this summer, and the guy who once owned it might be the author."

"Really?" Nathan shifted his attention to me.

I could've reached across the table and strangled Kaitlin, but that wouldn't have ended well for any of us. I wasn't ready to go public with a story that felt so connected to me. "All true."

Kaitlin kindly updated Nathan on what we knew about Dr. Atticus Brooks.

"The name Atticus Brooks is familiar." He leaned forward a fraction, and I caught the scents of sunshine, seawater, and sweat. "When I was diving with your mother, I remember him. He was the oldest guy I'd ever met. He was often waiting by the dive boat each time we pulled into the dock. He always had questions for your mother and me about the dive."

I'd been in school most diving days. And neither Mom nor Nathan had mentioned Dr. Brooks's visits.

"Why didn't you tell me?" I asked.

"Didn't think about it," he said.

"What was he like?"

"Much older, but always pulled together and very sharp. He knew more about the *Oceanus* than either of us," Nathan said. "He and your mom had coffee several times."

"He was on the wreck when it sank," I said.

"Seriously? He never mentioned it. But he had a way of deflecting the conversation away from himself and back to us."

The waitress brought three burger plates. I didn't have to look to know Nathan's burger had extra onions and double fries.

"You going to share this manuscript with me?" Nathan's voice dropped a notch, as if we were now co-conspirators. But when it came to the *Oceanus*, I was territorial. The wreck had claimed nineteen people in 1942 and my mother in 2019. "There's not much to it. The rest of the manuscript might not exist."

"But even having a partial is exciting," Nathan said.

"It's just random insights into a few of the passengers."

He pretended to pout. "Tula. You don't believe that, do you?"

"Maybe."

He pointed a french fry at me. "I'll trade. I'll share the *Oceanus* footage if you show me your pages."

"You were going to do that anyway," I said.

He shrugged. "I can also guide you down there, if that's what you want. Still going tomorrow."

My stomach clenched. "I'm not diving."

He shook his head as if I'd spouted nonsense. "When you build up your nerve, and you will, I'll take you. You'll be too curious to resist. In the meantime, you can let me read those pages."

I imagined my mother in the murky waters, skimming her gloved hand along the barnacle-covered hull. "Not interested in diving."

"I don't believe you," he said. "You wouldn't have come back to the Outer Banks if you weren't curious."

"I'm curious about anything to do with my mom. Beyond that, I don't care."

I couldn't tell if I saw annoyance, hurt, or curiosity.

"But she was really into this shipwreck. And forever linked to it. Don't you want to know why she made the choices she did that day?"

"A dive won't tell me that."

"You never know."

I bit into my burger, savoring the feeling of energy and the flavors hitting my body. After seven years of vending machine foods, I was so glad for the change. My therapist had told me the candy and chips were papering over sadness and boredom. Duh.

"Tomorrow is your day to find out," Nathan said.

"Sounds like a great idea," Kaitlin said. "I bet Tula would go in a nondiving capacity."

"Friday is a big cleaning day," I said.

"You can join me after the dive," Kaitlin said.

Nathan shifted his gaze toward me, his brow raised. "She's too scared."

I was afraid. In fact, my palms were sweating now. I stuffed two french fries into my mouth. But if anyone other than Nathan had thrown down like this, I'd have laughed, skipped the trip, and stopped for ice cream on the way home. But there was something about Nathan that had always been under my skin. If I called my therapist, his answer would have been quick. *Of course you need to go.* His words rang in my brain. *Run toward fear.*

But I'd done such a great job of running away from it for seven years.

"She's not scared," Kaitlin said. "If she were, she wouldn't be on the Outer Banks now."

I checked the dessert menu, ready to order chocolate cake. But the waitress was busy taking a large order at another table.

"We're on land." He grabbed a fry. "Not a drop of water in sight. She won't take the risk of being on a boat."

"There's plenty of water around us," I said. "I could see it from the second floor of this place."

"How many times have you been to the beach since you arrived, Tula?" He drew out my name as if we were both middle schoolers.

"Once. No, twice."

Everyone had cut me so much slack after Mom died. I'd felt like crystal, knowing I might crack at the slightest hit. At the time, I wasn't worried about my lingering doubts. I was certain I'd have shaken them by that first Christmas. And then I was sure that I'd be myself by Easter and then the next summer break. And then Dave. But the more time passed, and the longer I followed Dave across solid ground, the more ingrained my anxieties became.

And now here I was. Still afraid. "Okay, I'll go on the dive boat. But I'm not diving."

For a split second, I thought I hadn't said the words out loud. But they both looked up at me, their faces mirroring their surprised pleasure.

"Really?" Nathan asked.

"Yeah. What time?" My stomach clenched, and I immediately regretted the words.

"Seven a.m. tomorrow. I can pick you up at Kaitlin's."

"I'm staying at the house in Southern Shores." I threw out the bit of information as if adding ten miles to the distance between us would protect me. "I can meet you at the dock."

"And give you the chance to chicken out?" Nathan asked. "No way. I'll pick you up in Southern Shores. Text me the address."

"I'm not backing out." But I was already running scenarios that would provide reasons to cancel and still save face. There were none.

Kaitlin texted. "There's the address."

Nathan's phone chimed, and he looked at the address. "Good. I'll be at the Brooks house at six a.m. tomorrow."

"Great," I ground out. "Can't wait."

"You can tell me about the manuscript, and I'll show you a few videos. You show me yours, and I'll show you mine."

Was that sexual innuendo, or did I just want it to be? I'd been thinking about sex ever since we'd cleaned the Love Shack. Color warmed my cheeks. I drank more beer, which made my head spin. "I'll look, but I can't promise there's anything valuable."

Kaitlin grinned. "This is going to be great. Nathan and Tula, the dynamic duo back in action again."

"We aren't a duo," I said. "It's a ride on a boat."

"We made a good team back in the day," Nathan said.

In Greece and that last spring, we'd both helped Mom and worked well together. Both of us knew our way around the boat and scuba gear. We were both fearless. And both of us were passionate about exploring the *Oceanus*. Nathan had stayed an avid fan, but I wasn't that intrepid girl anymore. Somewhere along the way, I'd stopped chasing everything and had become consumed with holding on as tightly as I could.

The old me had lived a life that was completely free and unafraid. And all that bravado was now foreign to me. I needed an infusion of the old Tula's naive fierceness. She might have been reckless, but she was so cool.

And I kind of missed old Tula. A lot. And I wanted her back. But standing between us were thousands of miles of choppy, shark-infested waters.

CHAPTER SIXTEEN

Tula

Thursday, June 11, 2026, 8:00 p.m.

Nathan's gaze lingered on me over our empty plates. Kaitlin was at the bar, talking to a bartender with blond hair that skimmed broad shoulders and an "Arthur's" T-shirt.

"You really should dive again," he said. "Maybe not the _Oceanus_, but the Atlantic."

"Why? I'll watch your videos of the wreck when you bring them back."

"Not quite enough, though, right?"

"That's a tad harsh." Why hadn't my therapist texted and told me how proud he was of my progress?

He shrugged. "It's true."

"My mother drowned in the Atlantic, and its waters also swallowed me whole."

"There's no safer person to dive with than me."

If I had any common sense, I'd give him the manuscript and rush back toward solid ground. There were plenty of landlocked jobs I could get. I didn't need the roar of the ocean. "No such thing as safe in the ocean."

He shook his head. "You always were stubborn."

My willfulness that had kept me going after Mom's death had been transformed into a very heavy set of armor. "Yeah, back at you."

"It's not easy being back here for me either."

"Why is it so hard for you?"

"You're not the only one who lost when your mom died. I thought the world of her. I should've been on the dive boat that day. I wonder how different the world would be if I had been there."

In all these years, I'd never thought about Nathan's loss. Only mine. Nathan and Mom had gotten along so well, as if they'd always known each other. "Many times, when you and Mom talked about a dive, I kind of resented you because I felt like the third wheel."

"That was never the intention."

Mom had trusted Nathan almost instantly when they'd met in Greece, and he'd joined our motley duo for several months. She'd never second-guessed him, and she listened to his opinions about currents and winds. Mom had had lovers over the years, some a little bit older than Nathan, and when they started day trips to Athens, I'd thought Mom and Nathan might have started sleeping together. "Were you and Mom lovers?"

The question caught him off guard. "Jesus, no."

"Mom confided in you."

He drew in a breath as if drawing back a secret. "I thought of her like a big sister. She was a great friend."

"You treated me like a kid sister."

He shrugged. "You were a kid. What else was I to do?"

I should've pressed him about those times my mother had been speaking to him, only to grow silent when I arrived. I should have pressed, but I didn't. "You never talked about your family."

"There wasn't much to tell. I never knew them. Both my parents drowned in a boating accident. I was raised by an uncle and the ocean."

I'd never known that. "So, you know what we face."

He shrugged. "I was nearly taken out by a car on land. Anything can kill you."

Kaitlin returned to the table, a bag of leftovers in hand. "Okay, you two. Back to your own corners."

I realized his frown mirrored the same expression tightening my face. "We're fine. Just having a chat."

"Yeah," Nathan said. "We were catching up."

"Right." The three of us left the restaurant and stood in the parking lot by Kaitlin's van. "Are you staying with me or headed to Southern Shores, Tula?"

"Going back to Southern Shores. It's been a long day."

"Right." She grimaced at Nathan. "Don't look so glum, pal. Life will pick up."

"My life is fine," he said.

Kaitlin laughed. "Okay, whatever you say."

He shoved hands in his pockets and shook his head. "See you in the morning, Tula."

Shit. "I'll be ready."

CHAPTER SEVENTEEN

Tula

Thursday, June 11, 2026, 10:15 p.m.

At the Brooks house, I changed into an oversize T-shirt and sat on the double bed. I removed the partial manuscript from its folder and thumbed through the sheets. I reread the first few pages, reacquainting myself with the ship's specifications, as told by Captain Stoddard and Chief Mate Riggs.

The writer profiled several other members of the crew. As I searched the names on my phone, I discovered most had birth and death dates. Some had died when the *Oceanus* sank. All the gunmen who'd been firing the ship's .50 caliber guns at the U-boat after the torpedo hit died after a secondary explosion. A few other sailors who'd survived served on military vessels for the remainder of the war and died at sea. A few made it to a ripe old age.

I could only guess that the author of this book had interviewed survivors, because many of the details were too personal to be secondhand.

Dr. Brooks had struck up a friendship with Gertrude Werner, a woman fleeing Austria. I searched her name on my phone but couldn't find a reference to her in Vienna or Innsbruck. But she'd said she'd changed her name several times since her escape. I did find a short biography of an Alfred Gruber. There was no mention of him, but I wondered if the name was real.

When I searched "Dr. Atticus Brooks," I found one picture taken forty years ago, but the image was in profile and grainy. I didn't see any older pictures of him except the ones I'd found in his private collection.

As I turned through the fragile pages, memories eased out of the shadows. I stared at a single picture of Dr. Brooks, and an old memory floated to the surface. Shortly after Mom and I had returned to the Outer Banks, we'd driven to the town of Duck and parked on the ocean side in a one-story shopping center woven around a grove of live oak trees. When we'd parked in the gravel lot, I was excited to shop. But shopping centers weren't Mom's vibe, so I was suspicious.

As we got out of the car, Mom pulled two rumpled twenty-dollar bills from her jeans pocket. "Tula, go buy yourself something."

A little surprised, I studied the money. "You never just give me money."

"I am today."

"Why?"

Her expression looked strained. "Just because, honey."

Honey. *She never called me* honey. *"What're you going to do?"*

"I'm meeting someone for coffee at the café."

"Who?"

"Someone about the dive."

"A diver?"

"He's interested in what I'm doing. It won't take long. Find me in the next hour."

It wasn't like her to give vague answers, so I assumed she might be meeting a guy she liked. Naturally inquisitive, I asked, "Is this person a sponsor or a diver?"

"No one you know. It'll be boring, and I know how you hate the business side of what I do."

I rolled my eyes. "You don't like business either."

A smile didn't soften the intensity in her gaze. "Fair point. But sometimes, I must take care of it." She laid her hand on my shoulder. "Just shop and have fun, okay?"

"Is this my birthday present?"

A blank look in her gaze came and went quickly. "It sure is."

"My birthday is in June, Mom."

"So, I'm a little early for once." She'd never been great about remembering special days, but I was used to her wishing me a happy birthday a week late. She was doing something nice now, and that was what counted, right? "Okay, I'll find you."

"Take your time."

I watched her vanish down the boardwalk toward the café. I was tempted to follow and see who she was meeting, but the idea of shopping was too exciting. I was rarely in a town large enough for malls or shops. Most towns where we stayed were small, and the only shopping consisted of T-shirts, beads, or sarongs.

As I wandered past the shops with sandals, trinkets, and candy, I ducked into a dress shop. I realized quickly the forty bucks would only go so far.

I took time to try on dresses, but as much as I liked them, I couldn't afford the new seasonal prices. I moved to a jewelry shop filled with necklaces made of glass beads, shells, and random bits of metal. These weren't like the ones I'd seen on the islands.

I was drawn to the display case filled with the better necklaces, which contained silver, nicer crystals, and a little gold. In the center of the case was a necklace made with a silver chain and a small shard of sea glass.

"Can I look at that one?" I asked.

The older woman had gray hair that brushed the shoulders of her tie-dyed T-shirt. Bangles circled her neck and wrists. "Sure."

She unlocked the case and lifted the sea-glass necklace off the velvet base. The rectangular white, smooth glass was less than a half inch long and arrowed into a point. I unhooked the silver clasp and secured it around my neck. The glass felt cool against my skin.

"It looks great on you," the clerk said.

I fingered the price tag, almost afraid to look. When I flipped it over and leaned toward a mirror, I noticed the paper tag was empty. "How much is this necklace?"

She leaned forward, squinted, and searched for a price. When she saw none, she shrugged. "Thirty bucks."

"Who made this?"

"We've got a local guy who scans the beaches with his metal detector for coins and anything that he thinks might look good on a necklace. He also collects a lot of sea glass. It must be one of his finds."

I smoothed my finger over the silver chain. I wasn't a jewelry person. I'd never had luck with trinkets like these. When I'd save up the bits of tip money I'd received from divers, I'd buy the cheapest ones I could find in beach huts. Inevitability, I'd lose the necklace or bracelet on a dive or see the strand break and the beads scatter around me. But I liked this necklace, even though the cost would eat up most of my newfound wealth.

"The color looks good against your skin," she said.

I gently tugged the chain, testing it. It held and didn't give. Still, thirty bucks. And I had several more shops to see. The sea glass caught the light. The rumpled bills had been in my pocket barely an hour before I was smoothing them out on the counter and sliding them across to the clerk.

She made change, and as I pocketed it, she found a small pair of scissors and clipped off the tag. "You down here for spring break?"

It was early May, and the beaches were full of college kids willing to lie out in cool weather to catch a few sunrays. "No, my mom is working here this spring." Many seasonal workers were flooding into the barrier islands.

"What does she do?"

"She's going to dive a shipwreck. The Oceanus.*"*

"We have so many shipwrecks around here. Where is it?"

"Close to here." I studied the necklace in the mirror. The glass winked in the sunlight and reflected off the case. "Less than three miles offshore."

"Sounds pretty fun."

A wreck dive was now mundane to me. "It's what she's always done."

"You going to dive the wreck?"

"I'm in school now. Maybe on the weekend."

When I left the shop, I had enough money for a large ice cream, which I enjoyed licking as I walked along the shops. Finally, I reached the café in the mall's interior, where I found a collection of tables and chairs nestled close.

At the center table sat Mom, talking to two men I didn't recognize. One of them got up and left.

The man still at the table had thick gray hair and stooped shoulders. When she shifted her attention to him, she bowed her head close, as if she didn't want anyone to hear what they were saying. Mom's face was tight with tension and worry. I'd seen her mad and sometimes happy, but rarely upset like this.

I was ready to call out when my ice cream tilted, and I was forced to lick it quickly before it fell to the ground.

By the time I'd triaged the cone and cleaned my hands, the second man was gone, and Mom was sitting alone. A frown creased her face, making her look twenty years older. She looked lost, angry, and sad all at once.

As if she felt my stare, she looked up and grinned. I came toward her. "Everything okay?"

She sat up straighter. "Never better. You going to give me a lick of that ice cream?"

I'd suddenly lost my appetite for the vanilla-and-chocolate swirl and handed it over. "All yours."

"Great."

I searched the boardwalks and exits. "Who were those guys?"

She took several bites before she pressed her fingers to her temple. "Ice cream headache."

"Who were they?"

She finally said, "Locals. No one I'll see again."

I sat across from her. "You look upset."

She laughed. "My blood sugar was low. Now I'm all fixed, courtesy of Dr. Vanilla Chocolate Swirl."

I didn't buy her explanation. She was always honest with me. If we were low on money, a client had bailed, or her equipment broke, she told me. When I had my first period, she was matter of fact and fed me necessary details. When I had my first crush, she had a frank conversation about men and babies. "You don't have low blood sugar."

"Well, I did today. Pretty sure I skipped breakfast."

"Was he asking about the Oceanus?*"*

"We talked about it. Everyone is a little curious." She nodded toward the necklace but didn't really study it. "That your newest purchase?"

I touched the sea glass, which now felt warm. "Yeah. Kind of different."

"It suits you. Whenever you see it, you'll remember it was my birthday gift to you."

"Mom, you're scaring me."

She laughed. "How?"

"You never do sentimental. Are you dying or something?"

Mom cocked her brow. "That's a bit dramatic, Tula."

"You're just acting weird."

"When am I not a little odd?" She licked the ice cream down to the cone and took a bite.

The moment faded as my fingers skimmed coin and glass. The necklace had survived seven years, and I wore it because Mom had given them both to me.

Now I realized one of the men was Dr. Brooks. I wondered why she had wanted to keep me busy while she'd met with Dr. Brooks and the other man. Had their conversation been about the *Oceanus*, or was it something more important? I'd watched her walk away from dozens of wrecks because they were too dangerous or the weather wasn't right. But she'd refused to leave the wreck that last day we'd dived.

"Why did you care so much about the *Oceanus*, Mom?"

It was almost midnight. I stacked the papers and put them back in the folder. "If the rest of this book is here, help me find it." I shut off the light.

CHAPTER EIGHTEEN

GERTRUDE

Wednesday, April 22, 1942, 6:30 a.m.
Two days until the Oceanus *is torpedoed*

Survival. Dr. Brooks was right. People did impossible things to live. I'd taken incredible risks. And I would be wise to remember them.

I'd spent the night dreaming about Vienna and the woman who'd visited the bookshop with her rare finds. I wasn't sure why she reminded me of the other passenger I'd glimpsed, but she did. There was no way the Viennese woman could have found me, right?

The hallways were quiet, as was the cabin next to mine. I slipped on my coat and opened my door. There was no one in sight. The ship was asleep.

I climbed the stairs to the dining room and found the steward already at his post. The dining room doors were closed, but I could hear the clink of glasses as the crew set up the breakfast service.

I moved toward the steward, who looked at me with a mixture of annoyance and concern. "Ma'am, we don't open for another hour, but I can get you toast if you're hungry."

"That's not necessary. I had a question for you."

"Yes, ma'am."

"I met a woman Monday evening," I lied. "A lovely brunette with a tall man who didn't appear well. She told me her name, but I've already forgotten it. We're to be seated together at breakfast, and I would feel the fool if I didn't know it."

The steward didn't have to think long. "The man is Mr. Weller, and his companion is Miss Sigrid Stein."

Sigrid. I didn't recognize the name, but I was also using a false name. "You have an excellent memory for names."

Pride flared in his eyes. "It's my job."

"She is from Vienna?" I asked.

"Yes, from what I understand. An actress."

I digested the information. Two women from Vienna. What were the chances we would know each other? "Thank you. I truly appreciate your help."

He seemed relieved to know he'd helped me and would also be rid of me. "Glad to be of help."

I climbed the stairs to the top deck and stepped outside into the bracing wind. Storm clouds rumbled on the horizon, and ocean waves arched and rolled toward the ship. The dark water surrounded us, flexing its powers.

I can crush you, but I won't, the water whispered.

I slipped my hand into my pocket and removed the coin Dr. Brooks had given me. Had the coin found me after all this time?

My mother often spoke of ancient gods playing tricks on humans and making them believe in coincidence. If the coin had found me, could others?

I strolled toward the bow, promising myself I'd only be outside a moment or two. I should have sensed trouble, but I didn't.

As I rounded a corner, I saw the woman standing by the railing. Her dark hair was pulled back into a neat twist. She wore a dark suit that didn't complement her pale skin. A breeze caught hints of her expensive perfume.

The scent conjured memories of the woman in the bookshop. As tempted as I was to turn and run, where would I go? We were trapped on this ship for three more days. I stepped toward her.

As if she sensed my approach, she turned and looked at me. "Good morning, Naida. I do love the moments before the sun rises, don't you?"

Hearing my true name from the woman I'd met so long ago was chilling. I didn't speak.

She continued to look out toward the water. "Funny that we would find ourselves on the same ship sailing to the United States."

"You act as if you know me," I lied.

Her grin widened. "So now we play pretend? I've done that many times and always enjoy the game."

I'd thought about her from time to time since I'd escaped Vienna, but it had never occurred to me I'd see her again. The last time I'd seen her, we'd been sitting on a bench by the Danube River. Alfred was in Berlin, and I had a few days of peace to myself.

She'd sat beside me on the weathered bench as if finding me by the river was no surprise.

"What are you doing here?" I asked.

"I've been watching you. I know you stroll down here whenever you can."

"Why're you watching me?"

"I think we could be of assistance to each other."

"You can't help me."

"Don't be so sure." From her purse she pulled out a small book. "I have a gift for you."

I wondered who else might be watching. Alfred had ensured the household staff tracked my movements. "I need no gifts."

"All ladies like presents, no?"

I rose. "It's not safe for us to be together."

She captured my hand. "No one will see us here. And Alfred is in Germany, no?"

I stilled.

"Stay. I mean you no trouble." She looked around. "Sit before someone notices us."

I slowly sat. "I can't be seen with anyone. Alfred doesn't like it."

"Alfred. Not such a hero, is he?"

I'd been alone and isolated for several years. Emotions buried deep churned, and I wanted so much to trust someone. But she was not that person.

She laid a slim volume in my lap. It was Shakespeare's First Folio that I'd refused to buy three years ago.

"I no longer have money of my own to buy anything."

"As I said, it's a gift."

Bitterness swept me. "I've never known you to give away anything for free."

She shrugged. "That's very true most days. But today I feel generous."

"Why?" I smoothed my hand over the book. My uncle would have been thrilled to see this.

"I would ask one small favor of you in exchange for the book."

I set the book between us. "I have no ability to grant favors."

"Ah, but you do." A breeze from the river pestered the strands around her face. "You're having a party next week, from what I hear."

I didn't question how she knew. She'd always seemed privy to information and unique items. She was right, of course. At Alfred's command, I was planning a large party for his associates.

"I would like an invitation for a friend and myself."

"The guest list has already been selected. I have no control over it."

"I think the hostess could find a way to sneak in two more people."

"It's all tightly guarded."

She didn't reach for the book. "Yes, big important men will be there. My friend would like to meet them. Meetings are hard to get these days. Everyone is so nervous. And my friend is American and finds he's less welcome than he once was in Vienna."

If Alfred were to find out about this conversation, I'd pay dearly. She rubbed my forearm where the flesh still bore the bruises from his tight grip. "I can't help you."

"What is it you want?"

"Freedom." The word escaped my lips before I could think.

"If you help me, I can help you escape."

The waters drifted past, peaceful and slow. "I don't see how."

"It's very simple. I know people who could get you out of the city. If you could get to the river again, there would be a boat waiting for you."

The idea of sailing away from Vienna was tantalizing. And the thought alone was dangerous.

"I cannot."

"Just two invitations to the party, and I'll help you escape."

"He would kill me."

"Alfred is a dangerous man. He has a reputation for violence. If you stay with him, it's a matter of time before he kills you. The way I see it, you have nothing to lose."

Raising my chin, I stared at the water. "This is a trick. Alfred has sent you."

She shook her head slowly. "He did not. I'm here because you can help me."

I said nothing.

"Take the book. Slip the two invitations between the pages and return it to this bench. I'll be here tomorrow night. If you do that, I'll find you safe passage out of the city. You can sail the Danube River to the Black Sea and disappear. The chaos of the party will be the perfect time to escape."

There would be hundreds of guests and staff in the house for the party. It would be chaos. And Alfred would be distracted with his guests.

She stared at the waters, her face calm and relaxed. "Can you acquire a maid's uniform? No one watches the maids when they're leaving."

The uniforms had been ordered. It was important that the staff all look the same so they could go as unnoticed as possible. My stomach churned at the idea.

"Get me those invitations, and there will be a boat waiting." She rose and faced me. "Think about it. This might be your only opportunity to escape."

I never responded, but I took the book and left. The next day, I slipped into Alfred's office and took two handwritten invitations. That night I returned to the river with the volume and the invitations. She wasn't there. And for several seconds, I expected to see Alfred. This had been another trick, another reason to punish me. But when the night remained silent and no one appeared, I set the book on the bench and left.

Now as we stood on the deck of the *Oceanus*, I watched her manicured fingers tapping the railing.

"I didn't think you'd make it this far," she said. "You are cleverer than I'd imagined. I'm told you barely made it to the boat in time."

Her familiarity was unsettling.

My past crashed in around me, and I could feel the air leaving my lungs as the ship rolled under my feet. Knowing I'd been recognized left me nauseous. A door opened, and a steward with an armload of towels passed us.

My mind raced.

"I hear Alfred was in rage when you vanished. He had all the train stations searched, alerted local police, and notified the army. He told everyone that you weren't in your right mind. I know he's still looking for you."

My husband would search to the end of his days to find me. Not out of love, but because of the wish I'd made. "What do you want?"

"Several weeks after the party, he sent police to question me. I spent a week in a prison cell until he came to see me."

If that was all he'd done to her, then she was lucky.

She flexed the stiff, gloved fingers. "He struck a deal with me. Find you and report back to him."

"Why would you do it? You're free now."

"He has a great hold over me."

"What?"

She sighed. "Perhaps I'm a selkie, and he has taken my skin hostage."

"This isn't a fairy tale," I said.

"No, it's not. Either way, I have no choice but to fulfill his request."

My mind shouted caution even as I asked, "How did you find me?"

"I followed the rivers and the oceans and spoke to the people I knew along the way. Remembering a quiet, bruised, and battered woman of means was not difficult."

"What do you want? I have no money."

"I want freedom too." She studied my rounded belly. "Did you know about the baby when you left?"

I had not. "Alfred must never know about the child."

"He would move heaven and earth for you and his child."

"Leave me in peace. There's nothing I can give you."

"Peace isn't in my future or yours. We're both trapped."

"We don't have to be."

She sighed. "I have a proposal for you. I will trade your freedom again if you give me the child."

I gripped my belly. "No."

"Alfred wants me to deliver you to him, or he'll find me and kill me."

"He wouldn't let you go. He'll kill you."

"Perhaps, but I have family and friends who have been taken to a camp. They will only be released if I return with you."

Alfred would think nothing of taking a family, especially with Roma roots, to get what he wanted. Though the explanation sounded plausible, I couldn't believe she wasn't lying. "And you believe him?"

Her eyes darkened. "I have no choice."

My fingers curled into a fist. "I'm not going back."

"Your husband would accept your child in your place. I could tell him you died giving birth. The child would settle my debt to him."

"He won't release your family. Or you. You have struck a devil's bargain."

She stared out over the water, her gaze growing distant before she leveled it back on me. "The man I'm traveling with also made a bargain with Alfred to escape Austria. And he can attest that Alfred's reach is far."

My inability to love this child did not mean I would treat it so cruelly. "I'm not giving you this child. I couldn't condemn anyone to that life."

"Consider my offer," she said. "You were willing to make deals within the bookshop and at the river. This exchange is no different. I suspect now that you've had a taste of freedom, you would hate to give it up."

CHAPTER NINETEEN

Tula

Friday, June 12, 2026, 5:45 a.m.

I slept badly again last night. I dreamed of fighting through water up toward the surface, where the sun glistened. The ocean was all around me, clawing at my limbs, pulling me back down to the bottom.

Stay with me, the waters whispered. *Stay with me forever.*

I kicked and flailed and, finally, I burst through choppy waves. My chest heaved as I sucked in air.

Slowly the fear passed, and I realized I was on dry land. I was safe. The drip-drip of water in the bathroom sink echoed in the house. The pipes would require a plumber, but that was a problem for the next homeowner. The ordinary thought was oddly grounding.

Out of the bed, I grabbed my phone and walked to the kitchen, my oversize T-shirt brushing my thighs. At the sink, I rested my face in my hands, then turned on the coffee percolator. Today was the day. Today I'd go out on the boat with Nathan.

My phone dinged with a text from Kaitlin. How u doing?

She knew I was an early riser. If I could back out, I would.

Kaitlin: 😊 You're an adult. You can go or not go. If you want to back out, then do it.

The ocean roared beyond the dunes. It was teasing me. Daring me to quit.

Me: No.
Kaitlin: Stubborn.
Me: Greatest asset. And weakness.
Kaitlin: You can change anything.

The percolator hissed as it heated, and I flexed stiff fingers.

Me: I need to do this.
Kaitlin: I know I've been pressing you, but you got nothing to prove.
Me: I do.
Kaitlin: That's the old Tula.

I was glad I didn't have to look her in the eye. She'd see the fear in my gaze.

Me: The Oceanus is just a lump of scrap metal in water. And the ocean can't stalk me forever. Neither has power.
Kaitlin: The power is in you.

No, it was lurking off the coast.

Me: Right. Stay tuned. I've got to get dressed.

The percolator was painfully slow, so I dashed to my bedroom and rooted through drawers, searching for my swimsuit. Finally, I found it under jeans, and I dressed in a swimsuit, board shorts, and a T-shirt. My flip-flops weren't by the front door, which cost me five more minutes. They were under the sofa. "Are you hiding my stuff?" I asked the house.

I grabbed my backpack and packed snacks, a towel, and a change of clothes.

As the sun rose over the ocean, I poured my first cup of coffee. Cradling the mug, I stepped outside to the patio and climbed to the deck on the dunes. The sky was a vivid blue, the air warm and thick with humidity.

I walked down the stairs over the dunes. On the beach, the sand sank between my toes as I walked toward the surf. A wave rushed toward me, stopping five inches short. I tipped my face toward the sun. "So beautiful. So dangerous."

I drank my coffee, watching as more waves crashed. Finally, I turned back toward the dunes and the house. As I closed and locked the back door, a truck engine rumbled in the driveway. Through the window, I saw Nathan's truck.

He slid out of the truck with ease. He wore shorts, a dark blue T-shirt, and flip-flops. I doubted the man had ever worn a suit. He knocked on the front door.

I opened it, realizing I was slightly excited to see him. "You've come all this way. Would you like the grand tour?"

"Yes, and if that's coffee I smell, I'll take a cup."

"Sure."

He stepped inside, his gaze scanning the small time capsule home. The linens, books, and boxes of papers remained stacked in the center. "How goes the clean-out process?"

"It's getting there." I walked toward the kitchen, retrieved a stoneware mug, filled it with coffee, and brought it to him. "As you can see, I've got a lot to sort through."

He picked up a hardback book and studied the spine before looking at the collection. "Dr. Brooks was a history buff. Half is medieval; the rest is World War II."

"I think he was an everything buff," I said. "These books cover subjects from history to science to philosophy."

"Can I see out the back?"

"Sure." I led him to the back door, across the patio, and to the perch. He sipped his coffee. "Stunning view."

"I know. I remind myself how many people would love to enjoy this view."

He nodded. "Hard to go back to a cubicle after this?"

The office felt like a lifetime ago. "The ocean is very seductive."

He drew in a deep breath. "It has my heart."

That was true. I wasn't sure if there was anything he'd love more than the water. My mother had been like that.

"Ready to get to the boat?" he asked.

"Super excited." My dull tone belied my words.

The wind teased his dark hair as he grinned. "It'll be fun."

I locked the back door and grabbed my backpack as he took a gulp of coffee. "Keep it," I said.

"Thanks. Really good coffee."

I unplugged the percolator. "Ancient brewing method. Great if you've got the time."

"The wait was worth it."

Outside, I locked the door and pocketed the keys. I tossed my backpack into the back of his truck and climbed into the passenger seat.

How many times had we been in this spot? An early call, headed out to dive a wreck off Greece. Oddly, we'd never dived the *Oceanus* together.

"Such a full-circle moment," I said.

"I was thinking the same. If your mom was here, it would be perfect."

"I'm sure she has a hand in this. I think I can feel her staring at us."

"She was always watching us." He pulled out onto the beach road and headed south. "Never fully trusted me."

"Ha! And you were always a gentleman."

"Because your mom would have skinned me alive if I wasn't. All the men on the boats we sailed feared your mom."

As we drove south, I looked left toward the rising sun over the ocean. How many peaceful moments like this had I missed in the last seven years?

"Did my mom ever talk about living in this area before I was born?" I asked.

"She never said anything to me."

"I found a picture with Mom and Kaitlin's parents. It dates to a few years before I was born. Kaitlin doesn't know anything, and her mother never said a word to me when I lived with them."

"Why the big secret?"

"I'm not sure why Carol never mentioned it."

"You ever ask your mother about her family?"

"A few times. She insisted it was just the two of us. Said her father had died a long time ago. I do know he was a merchant marine and sailed out of Norfolk."

"Really?"

"The ocean had a hook in all of us."

The truck rumbled through Southern Shores and then to the bypass. "I read the first fifty pages of the manuscript. It really personalizes some of the passengers and crew."

He ran his fingers through his hair. "That's good. The passengers tend to get forgotten. Keep me posted."

"For the film?"

"Yeah. And I want to figure what hold that ship had on your mother."

"She was so determined to see it."

Silent, he nodded.

After a half hour of driving south on the bypass and chatting about his latest dive spots, we veered west toward the small village of Wanchese and pulled into the parking lot next to a pier with a dozen boat docks.

"How many people are diving today?" I asked.

"Four. All have had some dive experience. The day is perfect and the ocean calm."

But he didn't say there was nothing to worry about. That was bad luck. Like any good man who made his living on the waters, he didn't tempt the ocean's goodwill.

Four people were gathered near the walkway.

Nathan got out of the van and strode toward them. "This the crew for the *Oceanus*?"

Everyone nodded. As I walked toward the group, Nathan pulled out a list from his back pocket and called out the names of the people gathered around. He shook hands and checked IDs. The ages of the group ranged from mid-thirties to early sixties. Judging by their suntans (and burns), I guessed this was the last day of vacation for many. This dive would be the finale of their beach getaway.

Mom and I had taken out groups like this. She didn't have much patience with newbies, but newbies paid the bills. So, she'd left the sweet-talking and smiling to me. She was all technique, while I listened to expectations and fears. Mom's newbie outings always began with a dive in a local pool, and once she was sure everyone could really operate the equipment, we'd head to the ocean. On land, most didn't reach out to fifteen-year-old Tula for tech support. But once we'd dropped anchor, I'd field many last-minute queries. By the end of our outings, no one thought twice about asking me questions.

Nathan came up to me. "Help me with the gear. You take the cooler, and I'll bring the tanks."

"Sure."

I grabbed the handle of the white cooler and tipped it onto its back wheels. I pulled, thinking it would be easy, but I quickly realized the weight was far heftier than cleaning supplies and boxes of files. Gritting my teeth, I dragged the cooler over the gravel to the pier gate. Nathan set down two tanks, unlocked the gate padlock, and swung the door open.

"Can you lead the group to the white boat at the end of the dock?" Nathan asked. "It's the *Intrepid*."

"Sure."

"Thanks." He jogged back to the truck and grabbed two more tanks.

"Everyone, follow me," I said.

The divers were quiet as they followed me and the cooler down the pier. The *Intrepid* was a midsize boat outfitted with a small cabin and a dive platform. She looked sturdy. If Nathan handled his dives like Mom had, this was a short-term rental.

"Load your gear on the boat," I said.

I looked at the cooler, too heavy for me to lift.

"You need a hand?" The question came from a tall guy with dark hair. "Tony Spagnolo."

"Tula Cassidy. If you could put the cooler on the boat, that would be great. I'll grab the tanks."

"Will do."

I jogged back to the gate and hefted two tanks. Several times, I paused and readjusted my grip. I half walked and half waddled down the dock toward the *Intrepid* as the other divers assembled on the boat. When I arrived, I was winded, my arm muscles strained.

A couple of the divers frowned at me, and I sensed my weak arms and very pale skin didn't foster much confidence.

Nathan easily set two tanks beside me. He leaned closer and whispered, "There was a time when two tanks would've been nothing for you."

And I'd have been wearing a bikini and tank top. My skin would have been as tan as my muscles were toned. "Older and fatter."

"Not fatter." His gaze lingered over my body. "The curves are very nice."

A touch of heat warmed my face. "Thanks, I guess."

Nathan easily loaded the tanks before jogging back to grab the remaining gear.

I braced one foot on the dock and the other on the boat. The ocean slipped and rolled. It had been seven years since I'd been on the water. The ocean splashed my ankles. I was trapped between land and sea.

I drew in a breath and hauled my second leg onto the boat. I took several giant steps, struggling to stay balanced.

Steady hands grabbed my shoulders. I turned to see Tony's even white teeth flash. "Okay there?"

"Yeah," I said. "Getting my sea legs back."

A half smile tugged his lips. "You know how to dive?"

I tugged the hem of my T-shirt down. "I used to back in the day. Just helping on the boat today." I turned toward the dock as Nathan set down the last two tanks and several bags of gear. My back strained as I lifted the tanks and wobbled them to the corner of the boat.

It was going to be a long day.

Nathan jumped on the boat, his feet firm in the spot where they'd landed. He introduced me as his first mate and encouraged anyone with questions to ask me if they couldn't get him. I wanted to correct him but kept quiet. He had everyone in the group introduce themselves.

Beyond Tony, a tall Italian guy from New Jersey, there was Jeff, a lean, late-fifties guy who was a contractor from Virginia Beach. Another diver, Rick, was tall and slim and had red skin that looked a little burned. He was a lawyer from Northern Virginia. And finally, Martha, mid-thirties, a super-fit teacher, also from Northern Virginia.

Minutes later, Nathan started up the boat and backed it out of the slot. The boat veered out of the harbor, past a collection of leisure and fishing boats toward the Atlantic.

The *Oceanus* was less than three miles due east of the Brooks house, and it wasn't in deep water. It had been struck by the torpedo near the Virginia–North Carolina border, near Carova Beach. The ship had listed badly and taken on water after the strike and boiler explosion. But she hadn't sunk right away. After the vessel had been abandoned, it drifted for a day, burning and smoking. Residents called it the "ghost ship" at the time. Finally, the vessel lodged on a sandbar, where a storm and large waves washed over her and filled the rest of her hull with water. She'd finally sunk in the spot where she'd rested for almost eighty years.

As the boat skimmed along the ocean, I tugged on a ball cap and wiped sunscreen on my skin. It had been so long since I'd been in the sun, and I was guaranteed to be lobster red within an hour.

Martha already had streaks of zinc oxide lotion on her face. Tony looked jazzed, Jeff and Rick slightly reserved.

"Head count four," I said. "Five with you."

"That's correct," Nathan confirmed.

I moved to the side of the boat and watched as we headed northeast. Toward the west, the Outer Banks were little more than a very distant thin strip of sand. Finally, the land vanished. When we arrived at the dive site, Nathan dropped anchor and cut the engines.

The waters lapped against the boat's hull as the four divers began to haul on their gear. Nathan suited up quickly, his movements sharp and crisp.

Staring into the calm waters, I couldn't see the wreck, but I knew she lay quietly on her side below us. I remembered that one of her stacks had cracked and fallen into the silt, and her side still bore the gaping circular gash. Anticipation and worry rushed me.

Nathan walked from diver to diver and asked each to check their air and gauges. "I know you all have dived before, but the safety lecture is a must."

As he ran through the instructions, some divers listened more closely than others. Generally, the newest to diving were often the best students. Those who had experience under their belts could be the most reckless. As the saying went, a little bit of knowledge was dangerous.

"Feel free to shoot questions to Tula," Nathan said. "She'll be manning the boat while we're down under."

The divers still seemed skeptical of the pale creature struggling to regrow her sea legs. I tried to appear stoic and confident, but no one looked convinced.

Nathan was the first in the water. He cleared his mask and resettled it on his face. The divers moved to the side of the boat. One by one they tipped backward into the water.

The last guy on the dive platform, Tony, sat facing backward. When he hesitated, I moved beside him. "Take a few deep breaths."

Nodding, he filled his lungs.

"Put your hand on your mask," I said. "Just tip right back into the water."

"I've done this before." An apology wove around the words. "It shouldn't be a big deal."

"I get it." I could sniff out fear with the best of them. "If you don't want to dive, you don't have to."

He looked at me, his jaw setting. "I can do this."

"I know you can." According to my therapist, our brains responded well to confident statements. I still wasn't sure about that, but it cost nothing to think good thoughts.

Tony nodded and drew in a breath. He leaned back and toppled. He hit the water hard. His arms flailed for a moment. My heart pounded. I had no idea what it would take to jump in and pull him out. He could very well drag me under. My vision narrowed to a thin tunnel. I toed off my shoes.

The waters lapped and splashed against the boat, a reminder it could close the distance between us in a blink.

I edged toward the lip of the dive platform. Water splattered.

Before I could jump in, Nathan was at Tony's side and grabbed Tony's tanks. He easily righted him. Tony stopped fighting, produced a thumbs-up, and dove under the water.

Nathan looked up at me. "You okay?"

I jabbed up my thumb. "Terrific."

And in the next instant, he vanished below the surface.

CHAPTER TWENTY

Tula

Friday, June 12, 2026, 8:15 a.m.

I clung to the edge of the boat and watched the waters churn around me. Below the surface, I saw the faint outline of the divers before they vanished completely into the dark. When Mom and I had dived in the Pacific and the Caribbean, the waters were crystal clear and the visibility sharp. But in the Atlantic, visibility was lower, and a few feet below the surface, a person simply vanished.

The last time I'd seen Mom, we were right here, below the surface at the *Oceanus* site. I'd been nervous those last few minutes. There was no Nathan, and Mom was über focused on the ship's hull. She'd looked so calm as she studied the jagged torn metal where the torpedo had ripped into the hull.

I checked my dive computer, watching my oxygen dip. Mom burned through oxygen faster than me, so her gauge had to be much lower. Our window to rise was closing fast. Mom had insisted this would be a quick trip.

I tapped Mom on the shoulder, and she looked at me with a mixture of annoyance and curiosity. She'd told me time and again on the surface that she never wanted me entering any wreck. And yet here she was, ready to vanish into the twisted gash.

I held up my dive watch, indicating my air was running low. She held up five fingers, a sign she was five minutes behind me. I didn't want to leave her but deferred to her judgment. And so, I swam to the choppy surface.

The waves were hitting the side of the rocking boat hard. A wave knocked me off the ladder, forcing me to regrip the cool metal and pull myself up. It took all my strength to pull myself onto the boat. When I dropped my tanks, I stumbled to the side of the boat and searched for signs of Mom. I checked my watch. She had two more minutes. I strapped on my life vest.

Two minutes turned to five and then to ten. Mom would be furious if I called in a Mayday, but I didn't care. I reached for the radio.

"This is Tula Cassidy. I'm on the boat Voyager, *and I'm almost three miles due east of Southern Shores above the* Oceanus *wreck."*

"Voyager, confirm your location."

I repeated my location.

"Ten-four. A helicopter has been dispatched."

The coast guard was in Elizabeth City, North Carolina, which was at least an hour drive. By helicopter, I estimated the trip would take twenty minutes.

I ran on the rolling deck and clung to the side. I really expected to see Mom surfacing and pulling herself back onto the boat. She always cut it close, but she didn't know the weather had turned. Getting to shore before the storm would be tight, but we'd make it.

Fat raindrops fell. At first the drips were slow and steady, but they quickly picked up their pace. Mother Nature had turned on the tap and opened the sky.

Seven years later, anxiety still scratched my insides as I watched the calm waters. The weather bureau wasn't predicting rain. But Mother Nature laughed when humans tried to predict her moods.

I do what I want, the waters whispered.

Now waves rolled against the side of the *Intrepid.* With each passing second, old fears grew stronger. The ocean had large monster muscles and was always ready to flex them. A wave crashed hard against the side of the boat, and I stumbled.

I blinked and shook off the memory.

A head bobbed to the surface. Tony swam toward the boat's dive platform. He grabbed the metal, and I could see the stress tightening his face.

I checked my watch. He'd been under the water twenty minutes. I leaned down and unhooked his harness, and the tanks slid off. I dragged them onto the dive platform. Lighter, Tony climbed onto the boat.

"Everything okay?" I asked.

He ripped off his mask and wiped the water from his face. "Yeah, fine."

I'd seen fear in other divers' faces before. No one was immune from close calls. "You don't look fine."

He drew in a breath, filling his lungs with air. "I'm not usually so claustrophobic."

"It's okay. Each dive is different. Did you tell Nathan you were coming up?"

"No. I didn't think to find him."

He'd panicked. I looked out over the smooth waters, expecting Nathan to appear any moment. "How deep did you dive?"

"One hundred and fifty feet."

"Did you take safety stops on the way up?"

"One."

He'd risen too quickly. He should have ascended at thirty feet per minute. "Have a seat. Let me get you a water."

"I'm fine."

"If you were fine, you'd be below the surface." I fished a water bottle from the cooler and shoved it at him. "Sit and drink the water."

He sat and with a trembling hand raised the bottle to his mouth.

"It's happened to me," I said. "The ocean is powerful, and we just don't realize it until we're under it."

"It wasn't the water," he insisted. "I've dived a hundred times before."

"What happened? Did something spook you?"

"The wreck."

"Have you dived wrecks before?"

He sniffed and stared out over the water as if he expected to see something. "In the Caribbean. But it was a small boat."

"The waters are darker here, and this wreck is huge."

He looked at me as if he were really seeing me for the first time since he'd returned to the boat. "You've seen it?"

"Yeah, once. My mom was kind of an expert on the *Oceanus*." I left out the end of Mom's story.

Dark lashes shadowed his eyes. He was silent for a moment, and then: "Has anyone ever said the *Oceanus* is haunted?" He looked embarrassed to ask the question. I supposed because it was just the two of us, he thought he could.

My first thought was Mom, not the other lost souls. Was Mom still lingering around the *Oceanus*? *You still at that wreck, Mom?*

He gulped down more water. "When's the last time you were there?"

"Seven years."

Another head popped to the surface. "Hey!"

I rushed to the side of the boat. It was Nathan, and he looked pissed. He'd shot that look at me before when a diver broke ranks.

Small waves lapped and struck the side of the boat. "Tony is fine. He's here with me."

He gave me a thumbs-up, and without a word, he put his regulator back into his mouth and dove under the surface.

"Next time, let your dive instructor know you're leaving. Kind of freaks them out when you don't," I said.

"Yeah. I should've told him. But I had kind of a panic attack."

"It happens."

"What do you know about the wreck?" Tony asked.

More than I wanted to. "Too much."

"Can you give me the one-minute pitch?"

I filled him in on the ship's voyage from Cape Town to Port of Spain and then to right here, where she'd sunk.

"How many people died here?" he asked.

"Nineteen when the ship was torpedoed," I said. Twenty total souls lost if you counted Mom.

"That's a lot of bodies."

"That's why no one goes into the wreck. It's a final resting place."

He took another swig of water. "I had no intention of going inside. Well, I did, but I never made it that far. I wasn't ever close when I saw it."

The sun winked on the ocean's smooth waters. "Saw what?"

"It could have been a fish. I don't know. But it was something large and floating above the wreck. It looked like it was coming toward me."

Lots of schools of random fish, sharks, and skates were in these waters. "Can you describe it better?"

"I'm not sure. Big, white, floaty. Like a ghost."

"Or like a fish?"

"I don't think so. Reminded me of a cloud."

Again, I thought of Mom's eternal soul and the nineteen souls guarding the wreck.

"I know, it sounds crazy," Tony said. "Do you believe me?"

"I believe there are all kinds of things under the water we can't explain. But you're here. And you're safe. Take the win."

"Did you see anything when you dove the wreck?"

"No. I was running out of air. And I was worried about getting back to the boat. But that doesn't mean you didn't see something."

He shook his head. "You think I'm nuts."

"Not at all. Just upset. You saw something that spooked you. So, chill. Breathe deep. The others will be back up soon."

He crushed the plastic water bottle in his fist. "Don't tell them, okay? I'll look like a pussy."

"I won't say a word."

I moved back to the edge of the boat and checked my watch. I sat on the side, watching the ocean.

My watch buzzed, and I checked the time. Nathan and the others had been down for forty minutes now. The divers were scheduled to surface in twenty minutes.

Minutes later, another diver cracked the surface. It was Jeff, the contractor from Virginia Beach. He swam toward the dive platform and hoisted himself up easily. He shrugged off his tanks, and I lifted them onto the boat. He removed his mask and climbed aboard.

I handed him a water bottle. "How did it go?"

He twisted off the top. "It was amazing. Hell of a sight."

"What part of the ship did you explore?" Tony asked.

"I started at the bow and swam toward the intact midsection. I was interested in seeing the .50 caliber guns on the deck. They must've delivered a hell of a punch back in the day."

"They did," I said.

"They were all angled upward."

It would take centuries for the ocean to totally reclaim the vessel, but eventually, centuries would pass, and she would. "She's trying to hold strong."

"The hull was covered in barnacles, corals, and sponges, seven years ago like it is now. Pretty amazing."

"Yeah, Mother Nature puts those wrecks to good use. It's home now to tons of fish, eels, and crabs."

Jeff took a long swig. "I saw glass bottles, plates, and military supplies. They were scattered on the ocean floor."

"You didn't take anything, did you?" I asked.

"No."

"Good. Bad karma, and the wreck is within three miles of the coast, so salvage is illegal."

"I'm more worried about karma than the laws," Jeff said.

I was satisfied that he hadn't swiped any trinkets, and I decided not to argue.

Another diver popped to the surface. It was Martha, the schoolteacher. I helped her onto the platform.

"Fantastic," Martha said.

"Glad you enjoyed it." I set her tanks aside and handed her a bottle. Then Rick appeared and climbed aboard.

The familiar strain fisted in my chest. Back in the day, I'd never have worried about Nathan. I'd once believed the ocean could never take a guy like him. Or my mom. But people died all the time.

Drawing in a deep breath, I leaned over the edge. And then I saw the waters swirling, and seconds later, Nathan broke through the surface. He kicked toward the boat and climbed onto the platform with ease. He shrugged off his tanks as if they were a light summer jacket.

I handed him a water bottle and took his tanks.

"Thanks. Everyone okay?" He shoved back a lock of wet hair.

"All present and accounted for," I said.

He dropped his voice. "What was the deal with Tony?"

"The ocean just got the better of him."

Nathan nodded slowly as if he sensed I was covering for Tony. He'd seen unnerved divers before, but it was always unsettling when a member of your party vanished. "I thought for a second I'd lost him."

"He feels bad about it."

"Good." A frown furrowed his brow. "He should've told me."

"Go easy on him."

Nathan drank more water as if swallowing his anger. "I will."

"Did you see anything?"

"I wouldn't be surprised if her hull finally cracks in two one day."

"I'm amazed she's made it this far." Life went on, but she'd barely changed, from what I was hearing.

"A stubborn old gal."

The morning air was warm, and once in the sun, the divers stripped off their wet suits.

"So, we head back to shore?" Martha asked.

"Yeah. We'll debrief at the dock."

Nathan spoke to each diver, clapped Tony on the shoulder, his touch easy and forgiving. He pressed a button and the anchor rose. Once we were untethered, he moved to the wheel and started the engine. Soon we were headed back to port.

Slowly, relief eased the stiffness in my shoulders. I hadn't seen the *Oceanus* today, but I'd come close to her. Not a huge win, but I'd checked a few boxes I never thought I ever would. I wasn't sure how many more boxes had to be marked off before I was my old self, but I had to be a little closer.

I raised my phone and took a selfie. I texted my therapist, Guess where I am?

No response, but I supposed he was still letting me figure myself out.

The boat engines revved, and we started moving south. The farther away we got from the site, the harder the *Oceanus* and ocean pulled. One of the two, or both, wanted me to linger.

A good chunk of my life was now attached to that wreck. And no matter how far I ran inland, it would follow.

We arrived at the Wanchese dock forty-five minutes later. Nathan easily angled the boat into its slip. I tied off the rope to the dock as he cut off the engine.

He moved to the center of the deck. "I hope everyone had fun today."

Everyone, even Tony, was nodding.

"It's not an easy thing to dive a wreck like that," Nathan said. "You never know what you'll find. I bet each of you has a different story to tell."

Heads bobbed.

"Can we ever go inside the hull?" Jeff asked.

Nathan shook his head. "I'll never take you in there. Don't ever forget that twenty people died on that wreck."

"I thought nineteen souls died there," Tony said.

"We lost a diver to the wreck about seven years ago."

Tony tossed side-eye my way, but he didn't say anything.

Nathan's answer satisfied some, but others looked a little frustrated. I knew how the lure of exploration nullified potential dangers and laws against possible desecration. I could tell the idea of danger excited a few.

Tony helped Nathan carry the cooler to his truck. I waited by the boat for Nathan's return.

Nathan had zipped his wet suit down to his waist, revealing dark hair covering a firm chest. The hair slicked off his face drew attention to his blue eyes and high cheekbones. He could never be described as pretty, but he was striking.

"You did a good job today," he said.

"I didn't do much."

"You helped Tony on the boat and kept him calm. I'd have suspended the dive if not for you."

"Did you know he was going to panic?"

"He was doing fine, and then suddenly he froze. I was following the others down when I realized he wasn't with us."

I dropped my voice. "He thinks he saw something."

"Like?"

I shrugged. "A white misty cloud. He thinks a kind of spirit."

He didn't laugh. "I didn't see anything, but I've heard my share of tales about haunted ships. Superstition and the ocean go hand in hand. You're an experienced diver. What do you think he might have seen?"

"I don't know. I've don't have the best record when it comes to this wreck."

"You were great today."

"I wasn't in the water."

"Did you see yourself this close to water a month ago?" he asked.

"I did not."

"One step at a time, Tula." He hefted tanks in each hand.

He loaded his tanks in the truck bed. His back to me, he grabbed a towel and dried off before unzipping the suit the rest of the way and peeling it off. I marveled at the expanse of his tanned, muscled back. I was kind of sorry he'd been such a gentleman when we'd dived together, but looking back, I was glad he'd kept his distance.

I slid into the truck, shifting against the heat of the front seat. Nathan was seconds behind me, and he turned on the engine and the AC. After it blew out hot air for a few seconds, cool air drifted over my heated skin.

"I'm going to take out another group next week. Want to come?"

"I'll have to check with Kaitlin and see when I'm scheduled for work. If I'm free, I'll go." I wasn't sure why I wanted to go back to the site. I had nothing to prove to anyone. "I'll text."

He grinned and nodded. "I was expecting a fast no."

"It could end up a no. But like you said, small steps."

"You going to keep me up to date on that manuscript?"

"I will. There are two women from Austria that are interesting. I think Dr. Brooks was a spy."

"Why is that?"

"It's a theory floated by a local. The theory makes sense. It was a world war. Dr. Brooks was visiting all kinds of places in Africa and Europe. He had to be doing more than collecting books."

Nathan shifted into reverse. The cooling AC skimmed over my skin, sending a chill into my bones. "I did see something down there."

"What?"

He drew in a breath. "There's another wreck close to the *Oceanus*. It's a small boat, and much older."

"I never saw it the first time."

"Last year's storms likely uncovered it."

"What kind of wreck?" I asked.

"A schooner, maybe. A wooden hull. It's falling apart."

I combed my memory. I'd had time to search the area when I was down there. "I never saw it."

"Like I said, the storms have been intense since then. Sands down there shift all the time. And there are a lot of wrecks off the Outer Banks."

"These waters are a mini Bermuda Triangle," I quipped. "Did you see a name?"

"No name."

The beaches here had so many secrets. And I wasn't sure it was such a good idea to dig too deep.

CHAPTER TWENTY-ONE

GERTRUDE

Thursday, April 23, 1942, 6:30 a.m.
One day before the Oceanus ***is torpedoed***

The couple next door had been up most of the night. The man, William, spoke in a low, growling voice filled with menace. The woman, Sigrid, spoke in soft, soothing, and sometimes desperate tones. She was trying to calm the beast who likely was ready to take my child.

Glass shattered, and I imagined the man hurling a crystal glass toward the cabin wall. Next came the violent sounds of rough grunts, met by her silence. I didn't need to see to know what was happening.

Finally, the room fell still, and I supposed he'd fallen asleep. I pictured her in his arms, staring stiff and wide eyed at the ceiling or looking toward the curtains covering the porthole and imagining the ocean's dark waters. How many times had a similar story played out with Alfred and me?

Rising, I checked my watch. The sun would soon rise, but there was no one on deck. The ship would be quiet.

Feeling the heavy weight of the walls and the past, I dressed, struggling with the buttons at the base of my spine. My belly pressed against the wool fabric. I had forgotten what it felt like to move with ease, to see my feet and sleep through the night.

I exited the cabin and found my way to the dining room. It wasn't open yet, but a coffee service had been set up outside the double doors. A steward dressed in a white jacket asked me if I wanted to sit.

"I'd like to sit on the deck. How's the weather?"

"Warmer, but there's still a chill in the air. I'd be happy to bring you a coffee."

"Thank you."

I climbed the stairs and exited via the doorway and found an empty chair. The wooden lounge chairs looked inviting. I eased into a chair, tipped my face to the emerging sun, and drew in a deep breath. The salt air was a balm to my scattered nerves.

The steward appeared with my coffee, a porcelain cup on a silver tray with sugar, cream, and several biscuits. "Can I get you a blanket?"

"Thank you, I'm fine. You have been very kind."

"Of course."

I leaned back and raised the cup to my lips. The warm coffee and soft breeze created the first pleasant moments I'd had in years. I could feel my guard dropping.

"Good morning."

The rising sun backlit the figure of a large man. As I shielded my eyes, anxiety set my senses back on a tightrope. It was Chief Mate Riggs.

Tall, he had the narrow waist of a young, fit man. Thick black hair resisted the cream he'd used to tame it. His angled face could have been sharp, if not for the curiosity warming his brown eyes. He had a book tucked under his arm.

"Please don't rise," he said. He stepped within striking distance.

"How are you?" I resettled into my seat, but I remained vigilant. Those who lowered their guard died.

"I am well. But I'm more interested in you." He pointed to the chair beside mine, and when I nodded, he sat. "How are you feeling?"

"Well."

"And the baby?"

"It moves often." Each time it kicked, darkness crept closer.

"That's good. The child is healthy."

"Yes."

"You're certain the baby will arrive in June?"

"Yes. I have at least another month. Plenty of time to arrive in New York. No need to worry."

"Worry is part of my job. If you have any issues during the voyage, please find me. I'll find you a medical professional. And when we reach port, I can also assist you."

"Thank you." There was a time when I could converse with anyone, but I'd kept to myself for so long, my conversation skills had rusted. "What are you reading, Chief Mate?" I asked.

"*A Farewell to Arms*, by Ernest Hemingway."

"Ah, the hero Lieutenant Frederic Henry."

Chief Mate Riggs didn't hide his amazement. "You've read it? I'm surprised it's still available in Austria."

"My uncle secretly stocked many English titles after the Germans arrived."

After I married Alfred, I'd kept several books in English hidden. Rebellion within their pages. I often sneaked them from their hiding place in my dresser and reread them, seeking comfort and disobedience. "I appreciated the hero's determination."

He nodded solemnly. "Did you like it?"

"I found it stressful."

He grinned. "But that's good, isn't it?"

"I suppose."

"It distracts me through long nights and months at sea."

I cleared my throat. "And where are you from in the United States? I think it's far vaster than I realized." I was counting on endless lands where anyone could get lost.

"North Carolina."

I was familiar with the large cities like New York and Washington, DC. But beyond, the country was a blur. "Where is that?"

"On the East Coast. Biggest city nearby is Norfolk, and beyond that, Washington, DC."

Dr. Brooks was from Norfolk. "I've heard of the city."

He removed a pen and an old telegram from his pocket and turned it face down. Resting it on his palm, he sketched out what looked like the East Coast of the United States. He drew a long ribbon of land that was close to the mainland but separate. He drew three dots. He pointed to the northernmost mark. "This is New York City, the second spot is Norfolk, and the last is the Outer Banks."

"What's the distance between the points?"

"Four hundred miles between New York and Norfolk, and then another hundred miles to the Outer Banks."

The map was a helpful reference. "Four hundred miles seems very far."

"The distance between New York and Norfolk is a day's train ride between the cities. After that, it's a short car ride to the Outer Banks."

"And the roads are in good shape?"

"Very good. We haven't been bombed like Europe."

"Good." A land without war and Germans was so encouraging. The red spring sky leaked through the canopy of clouds. "How did you get here?" I asked.

"I grew up on the water. Made sense when all this started, I'd join the navy."

The chief mate's easy manner teased some of the strain tightening my nerves. "How long have you served?"

"Since 1940."

"The war drew you?"

"I'd always planned to go to sea. My folks wanted me to wait until I finished college, and I would have if not for the war. I've promised my mother that I'll return once the fighting ends."

He was approximately twenty-two, very close to my age, yet I felt ancient compared to him. "Was that wise?"

"I don't know how a degree will make me happy. Maybe one day it will. It sure would make my ma happy."

University had always been out of the question for me, but I'd longed to go. My marriage to Alfred had been my uncle's greatest dream for me. "I'm sure they have great plans for you."

"I suppose you're right." He glanced at my belly, and then his cheeks reddened a fraction, as if he'd seen something indecent. "I guess you would know."

"Because . . ."

"You almost being a mother and all."

"I don't have any idea what I'm doing, Chief Mate. I don't know how to be a mother. For most of my life, it was just my uncle and me." I swallowed as I thought back to the coin I'd tossed into the river when I made my wish.

He eyed me as if he'd picked up a sorrow buried under the words. "Where are you going?"

"New York City." I spoke with surprising confidence. "A distant cousin is waiting." Again, I turned the conversation in a different heading. "Are you on duty?"

"Soon, but not yet. I was just killing a little time before returning to duty. You go ahead and drink your coffee before it gets cold."

"Thank you." I sipped. "What does a chief mate do?"

"I oversee all the operations on the ship. I'm in charge of the men who run the engines, maintain lifeboats, and service the big guns."

"I saw the guns when I boarded."

"They are .50 calibers. They are a force, and if any sub thinks it's going to get one over on us, we'll have a few words with them."

He sounded so brash. So sure. Young. "Have you fought the subs before?"

"I've seen them. We cracked off a few rounds in January when a periscope was spotted, but we didn't sink one. They're sneaky bastards." He blushed. "Excuse my language."

I waved away his concern. "Do you think we're in danger?"

"I'd be lying if I said we weren't. The subs have destroyed their fair share of ships near the United States' East Coast."

"I've seen nothing in the papers."

"Not much has been written about the sinking ships near the US coast. But we all know the North Carolina shoreline is a graveyard." As if catching himself, he added, "It's always been tricky sailing off that coast, but Captain Stoddard is experienced and won't be fooled by the U-boats or the shoals."

"Shoals?"

He drew a faint line off the Outer Banks where it elbowed into the ocean. "Sandbars under the water's surface. They shift often, and if a sailor isn't watching, he can get his ship caught up in one."

"How many ships have been sunk by U-boats?"

"I don't have an exact number. But my pa writes me from time to time. He can see ships burning on the water from the beach. Says there are nights when the skyline is all lit up. Government wants it kept quiet, so he doesn't say too much about it beyond me and my brothers."

"Why is this war such a secret in the United States?" It had been unavoidable in Austria and as I crossed Europe.

He carefully folded the map and placed the paper and pen back in his pocket. His gaze traveled toward the ocean and grew wistful. "Uncle Sam doesn't want anyone knowing the Krauts are that close to US soil."

"Uncle Sam?"

"The US government. They know if we can see the German subs, they sure can see us."

My heart accelerated with unease.

Again, as if he realized what he'd said, he amended himself. "Don't worry, Mrs. Werner. The *Oceanus* is sailing at top speed, and we're a hard target to hit. We'll be in New York City by the weekend."

Time was tricky. Seconds could fly by one day and drag painfully on the next. I held up my coffee cup. "Cheers to outrunning the Germans."

He nodded. "I second that."

"Where will you go after this trip?"

"It's back to Norfolk, Virginia. Normally, I don't serve on the *Oceanus*, but she was shorthanded, so I was ordered to serve as chief mate on this trip."

"And then?"

"I'll have a few weeks' leave to see my parents, and then I'll be reassigned to a new vessel."

My mother was a distant memory, and our time together felt more like a dream than part of my life. But I missed my uncle, who had smelled of tobacco and old books. "It'll be good to see your parents."

"Sure. I miss them something awful."

I was glad my uncle wasn't alive to see the war or the results of the marriage he'd put so much hope into.

"So, it's just you and the baby?" Chief Mate Riggs said.

I never thought about a future with the baby. In my mind, I was alone. But since I'd seen Sigrid again, I'd felt an overwhelmingly protective urge for the child. I couldn't love it, but I could keep it safe and away from Alfred. "And the distant cousin."

"That's rough."

"As I said, I'll be fine. I'm tougher than I look."

"I'd say you're tough. Takes a lot of pluck to get this far alone."

Desperation had required a lot of me. Dr. Brooks had been right. Survival forced people to make unnatural choices. I hesitated and then dared to ask: "There's another Austrian sailing with us."

"Yes. Miss Sigrid Stein. Do you know her?" My question had piqued his interest. And then, "She's with a man from the United States.

He's from New York. Very successful, from what I hear." He let the statements dangle, hoping I'd add onto them.

"They are in the cabin next to mine, but I haven't met him."

My simmering stress seemed to catch his attention. "I see things most don't, and I suggest you steer clear of him."

"Why is that?"

"I ask myself what he was doing in Germany and Austria until recently. He says he's a businessman, but I always have questions."

"Be careful what you say."

"This isn't Austria, Mrs. Werner. We can speak our minds here without worrying about a neighbor betraying us."

There'd always been people watching the bookshop. Books were dangerous, and coupled with the gossip that my uncle was raising a Roma, they always spawned whispered rumors.

"That's good to know."

He leaned his large frame forward a fraction. "I can't get into details. But best you avoid him."

"I'll do that." I thought about the chief mate's offer from earlier "Perhaps I'll take you up on your offer to escort me off the docks.' Sigrid would be hard pressed to get past a man as large as the chief mate.

He straightened his shoulders. "I would be pleased to do that."

"Excellent."

The ship's bell's clock chimed, indicating it was 7:00 a.m. "That's my cue. I've got to get back to duty, Mrs. Werner."

"Please call me Gertrude."

He blushed slightly. "Gertrude. Call me Kevin. No one calls me 'chief mate' off the ship. Always feels a little formal."

I doubted that. I could see he was very proud to have obtained the position. "I'll remember that."

He gripped the book in his large fist. "It was a real pleasure, Gertrude. Maybe I'll see you again before New York."

"I'm not hard to miss."

"Yes, ma'am." He studied the book. "Would you like to read this?"

"I can't take your book."

"I've got a lot of work between now and New York. I'll get it back from you as we depart the ship."

I accepted the book, noting the worn binding. "Thank you."

"I'll get you safely off the docks."

"I'm counting on it." When he left, it was a relief to be alone. As kind as Kevin seemed, I didn't dare trust him or anyone too much. The dark-haired woman, Sigrid, was proof that the past lurked close.

After the chief mate left, I lingered on the deck. I liked the open air and the steady breeze that teased away memories. When I finally rose, my legs were stiff and my lower back ached.

"I was pregnant. The last months are very uncomfortable."

I turned to see Sigrid staring at me. Her face was pleasant and soothing in some ways. But I'd never seen her worried or flustered.

Not a surprise she had a child, but I couldn't picture her cradling a baby. She'd never struck me as tender, but rather cold and calculating about her latest deal.

She stood in front of me, blocking my view of the ocean. "Is it exciting? Or do you dread the child?"

I didn't answer.

Her attention shifted to the rolling waters. "I think the rivers and the ocean brought us together. The waters know that, like you, I'm also willing to do what I need to survive."

Alfred's hold remained as tight as a vise. "I'm not giving you the child."

"You'll see the wisdom of the trade I offer, because I think you're very much like me."

We both shared Roma roots, but that was where the similarities ended. "We aren't alike."

"I was like you once. Young, idealistic. And then I learned life always forces very hard choices that can leave us on the losing side either way."

CHAPTER TWENTY-TWO

Tula

Saturday, June 13, 2026, 7:15 a.m.

I found Kaitlin at the condo properties in unit 2B. I ran fingers through my hair as I refashioned my ponytail and joined her in the living room. I'd been up until after midnight, going through more boxes at Dr. Brooks's house. I was combing through his papers, shredding what wasn't necessary, all the while searching for the rest of the manuscript.

We worked throughout the morning, cleaning a total of five condos, and by the time we were finished, I was exhausted. We grabbed burgers at a drive-through, neither of us up for talking. She had bookkeeping to complete and then a surf class to teach, and I had Dr. Brooks's manuscript to find and read.

It was after four in the afternoon when I opened the next dusty file box. I must have sifted through a dozen by now, and I wasn't feeling very hopeful that I'd find anything other than more legal papers, utility bills, or meeting notes from the town of Southern Shores' planning commission.

But as soon as I opened the box, I recognized the faded type of the yellowing manuscript pages. The first page read, "Chapter Six, page 51."

A rush of adrenaline surged. I lifted the sheets, bound with a large rubber band, and retreated to my bed.

The type was dense, and as before, the writer told me more about maritime shipping dangers during World War II than I'd ever expected to know. As tempted as I was to skim the pages and rush forward in the story, I didn't. Now that I was only miles from the wreck, its last voyage was resonating stronger with me, and I didn't want to miss a detail.

The author opened the sixth chapter by describing an incident Captain Stoddard had weathered as he'd sailed south off the Outer Banks shores in late December 1941. The freighter was fifty miles from shore when one of his men spotted a German U-boat. The ship's guns fired a barrage of shells, striking the water near the submarine. For whatever reason, the enemy vessel didn't take a shot and allowed the ship to pass. Captain Stoddard assumed that the U-boat was out of torpedoes and had headed back to its French port to restock.

Captain Stoddard reported the danger to his officers, who all agreed to keep the incident a secret. The supplies these vessels were carrying now were too vital to the Allied war effort. Risks had to be taken. Regardless of the dangers, once he was assigned to the *Oceanus*, he swore to do all he could to ensure the ship reached Cape Town to drop off its passengers and then load its hull with a load of raw materials and munitions.

I was growing tired, and if I wanted to keep reading, that would mean coffee, which would mean waiting on the percolator and then no sleep tonight. And sleep, as I'd learned, kept my anxiety at bay.

After flipping through the pages to the end, I found passenger and crew lists. The names were alphabetical and listed the passengers' home cities. I scanned the lists. The youngest crew member was seventeen; he was a navy sailor and would be over a hundred years old today. No doubt all these people were dead by now.

Chief Mate Riggs, born in 1920, was twenty-two at the time of the sailing. I did a quick search of his name, and his obituary appeared. He'd died in 1990 in a Norfolk hospital at the age of seventy. The obituary described a decorated sailor who loved the water and who had sailed it for nearly fifty years. The obit mentioned a wife, Margaret, who had died in 1978, and a son who'd been a merchant marine.

My phone rang, and when I saw Nathan's name, I almost laughed. "Do you have radar?" I asked.

"I know you. You never were a good sleeper. Have you found the rest of the manuscript?"

"I did."

"And?"

"Lots of intel on U-boats. Captain Stoddard was the focus in the latest pages. Weird to be reading about dead people when they were in their prime."

"I can't wait to read it."

"Soon."

After a moment's hesitation, he said, "Hey, you did a good job yesterday."

I rubbed the nape of my neck. "You didn't notice my terror?"

"We're all scared at one time or another. The point is you were there."

"Any reviews from your travelers?"

"A few texted. They liked the trip, and they all appreciated your help."

I laughed. "I can hand out water bottles with the best of them."

"Tony gave you a glowing review. I think he's in love with you."

"We fear-bonded. The ocean scared him, and it still terrifies me."

He chuckled. "Did you ask Kaitlin about the next trip?"

I was so tempted to tell him work demanded me, but it didn't. "She said I was free to go. But she wasn't crazy about it. In trade for the time off, I'm handling the supply run on Monday afternoon so she can have the time to prep for her surf camp."

"Supply run?"

"Cleaning supplies, linens, and towels."

"Exciting stuff. Think you can handle it?"

I chuckled. "What can I say? I live dangerously."

He cleared his throat. "I was wearing my camera yesterday. I have new footage of the *Oceanus* if you want to see it."

The idea of seeing the ship again was both thrilling and terrifying. My nerves had never really calloused when it came to that ship. "Yesterday was a warm-up, I suppose," I said. "You never serious-dive with customers."

On his own, he'd have taken more risks and explored the wreck more closely. "Exactly. I can't focus too much on the ship with the other divers going in all directions."

"What's the weather look like for your Monday dive?"

"It's clear in the morning. Possible chance of afternoon showers."

I drew in a breath. "And you're still going?"

"You know how it is down here on the Outer Banks. Rain predictions can mean it showers twenty miles north or south of you."

"That's what Mom used to say. She said if the rain wasn't hitting her face, she didn't believe it."

Nathan was silent for a moment. "I know I've said this before, but I think a lot about that last day and how different it would have been if I'd been there."

It was good we were talking on the phone. I didn't think I could look at him and not burst into tears. "You broke your arm. That wasn't your fault."

"You never asked how I broke it."

"Sorry. That detail got lost in the chaos."

"I was in a car accident. A tourist in a rush to pick up morning bagels ran a red light and T-boned me."

I remembered his arm in a sling and the bruise on his cheek. But I hadn't cared how badly he was hurt. I'd wanted him on that boat when Mom wasn't surfacing. I was convinced he could have saved her. I'd felt so alone and scared.

After Mom went missing, Nathan managed to join the search for her, even with a broken arm. I'd hoped he'd known her well enough to find her. And when she was never located, I blamed him for not finding her. For weeks, I kept thinking Mom would be found. I refused to hold a memorial service or to speak to Nathan. Finally, he'd left the Outer Banks and moved on to a new dive job, and everyone stopped asking me when there'd be a memorial service.

"It wasn't your fault," I said.

"I'd accept that if you could as well," he said quietly.

"I don't blame you anymore. I got tired of being angry. That day was Mom's fault and mine."

"How was your mother's choice your fault?"

"I was the last person to see Mom. I knew she didn't always listen to me."

"Your mother could be stubborn."

"I should've pulled her to the surface or stayed at her side." But I'd been running out of air, and Mom had always been adamant that we surface before the gauge dropped below five hundred pounds of pressure. I was so certain she'd follow her own rule as I swam to the boat.

"Do you think you could've really made her surface?"

"I wish I'd tried harder." Suddenly, the weight of the past settled on my shoulders.

"What are you doing tomorrow?"

"Cleaning Sunday-morning move-outs and then the Brooks house."

"And after?"

"Wishing every muscle in my body didn't ache."

He chuckled. "Let me take you out on the boat. No diving. Just a sunset ride. Clear skies. Calm waters."

I was charmed, I think. "The master diver does sunset rides?"

"Not as a general rule, but I make exceptions sometimes."

"Are these adventures your signature moves with the ladies now?"

He laughed. "Not as often as you might think."

Stood to reason there had been women. He was good looking, fit, and smart. Was I jealous? Even if I was a little, who was I to judge? I'd picked up and discarded a husband along the way. "Okay. I'll go."

"Great. I'll pick you up about five."

That was a few hours before sunset, but it would take time to get to the harbor in traffic and out to the sound. "I'll be ready."

When I hung up, I shifted my attention back to the passenger and crew lists. So many vibrant people with full and active lives. And they were all dead. Just like Gertrude, Sigrid, William, Kevin, Dr. Brooks . . . Mom. And one day, Kaitlin, Nathan, and I would be gone. That was the way.

I reached for my phone and texted Kaitlin.

Me: Are you up?

Kaitlin: Barely.

Me: Thinking about the last dive with Mom. I dropped a barrier around that time, and I couldn't break through it for a long time.

Kaitlin: And now? Ready to face it?

Me: I don't know. But the farther I run from it, the more messed up my life gets.

Kaitlin: Then swim toward it.

Me: I am. Kind of. Maybe, dogpaddling toward the past.

Kaitlin: Just keep moving. If you don't reach the other side, you'll drown.

I looked around the old place. The roaring ocean beyond the dunes was becoming kind of soothing. I was falling for the ocean again. After this house was clean, where would I go next? The cubicle in Norfolk wasn't so appealing anymore.

Me: I know.

CHAPTER TWENTY-THREE

Tula

Sunday, June 14, 2026, 5:00 p.m.

I'd jumped in the shower and done my best to scrub the scents of disinfectant from my hair and skin.

I'd been tempted to dress super casual, as if to reiterate that Nathan and I were just buddies. I pulled on a new T-shirt and white shorts, which no longer grabbed my ass as tightly as they had a few days ago. I'd taken a few extra minutes with my hair, even using a hair dryer, and applied a little makeup. And then at the last minute, I changed into a casual blue sundress and sandals.

Nathan arrived right on time. He got out of his truck and walked to the front door as if it were a proper date. I opened the door seconds after he'd knocked. His damp hair was brushed off his tanned face, making his blue eyes pop. He wore a V-neck shirt, shorts, and docksiders. He didn't need to do much to look amazing.

"Hey," I said. "Want to come in?"

"We better get going if we're going to catch the sunset."

The days were the longest this time of year, but June meant vacationers were checking in this time of day, and traffic was going to be thick. "Sure."

I grabbed my cross-body and closed and locked the door behind me. "Are we leaving out of Wanchese?"

"No, I'm borrowing a boat from a guy who docks in Colington." The neighborhood was located on the west side of the barrier island and faced Albemarle Sound and the sunsets.

"Do you have boat connections all over the Outer Banks?"

"Boat people run in similar circles," he joked.

He reached the truck first and opened my door.

"Wow, I don't ever remember you opening a door for me."

"I've evolved."

I climbed in and hooked my seat belt. The crumbs on the seat and floor mat were gone. My God, did he vacuum for me?

"So why the sunset ride?" I asked.

"It's beautiful. And we could both use a little beauty."

After a fifteen-minute drive, he turned onto Colington Road. We wove past an eclectic mix of small homes, trailers, and some larger houses. We crossed a small bridge that connected to Colington Island, where the yacht club was located.

"You have serious connections," I said.

"Jeff keeps a house and a boat down here."

"Jeff from Virginia Beach and the last dive?"

"One and the same."

We parked in the lot, and he grabbed a small cooler. I followed him to a docked pontoon boat. It had a flat bottom, perfect for the sound's shallow waters. He climbed aboard and held out his hand for me. I took it, liking the calloused warmth of his fingers around mine.

He set the cooler down and unknotted the ropes attached to the dock. From under the driver's seat cushion, he removed a key that fit the ignition.

The sun had dipped lower, and the air wasn't as hot as it had been. I took the seat beside his. "Any destination?"

"Thought we'd ride north."

That meant under the Wright Memorial Bridge and along the coast, past the towns of Southern Shores and Duck. I wondered if we could meet up without talking about or being in the proximity of the *Oceanus*.

He nodded to the cooler. "Drinks if you want one."

I opened the cooler and selected a light beer. He took a soda. For as long as I'd known Nathan, I'd never seen him drink on the boat.

The boat rumbled along the calm waters. The breeze was soft, and the evening sun had softened. This was nice. I'd forgotten how beautiful this area was.

"Anyone special in your life?" I asked.

He looked amused. "What brought that up?"

"Just curious. There's a seven-year gap in my knowledge of Nathan."

"I've dated. Once it was serious. I thought she was the one."

"Who?"

The sunlight reflected off his hat, shadowing his features. "Doesn't matter. We weren't right for each other."

"Why wasn't she the one?"

"I travel. I keep on the move. She wanted a house and the white picket fence."

Made me think about my ex. "Do you regret breaking up with her?"

He hesitated. "She's married now and expecting her first child. Happy ending."

"For her or you?"

"Both of us." He regarded me. "What about you?"

"My ex-husband wanted the house and the yard, and I thought I did. I moved into his place. Got all settled. Decorated a little. But we just drifted. He ended up moving out and filed for divorce."

"You got the house?"

"No. I'm now officially evicted."

"What drew you to him?" He kept his tone neutral, but I sensed a keen interest.

"Dave was as solid and unwavering as a mountain. It was good at first. But it began to feel restricting, like a straitjacket. He figured out that he didn't make me happy. And he stopped trying."

"Where's Dave now?"

"He found a sweet little thing that has no hang-ups. I expect a wedding announcement on social media soon."

"You follow him?"

"I did. I haven't checked lately."

"You miss him?"

"No. My therapist said I'm emotionally unavailable."

"I don't get that vibe from you. If anything, you're overloaded with emotions."

I'd never thought about it that way. There was so much boiling inside me that I had to keep my distance to survive.

I stared out over the calm waters of the sound as he angled the boat under the bridge that joined the mainland to the Outer Banks. The air was soft, and the sound waters smooth as glass. Something about this moment felt right. "I thought I was like Mom. She could be distant."

"She wasn't an easy person."

"Neither am I."

"I wouldn't say that. I always got along with you great."

"Really? We fought a lot."

A smile teased his lips. "Not about anything big. Always small stuff."

All our fights had felt huge to me, but I'd been a teenager. And now I could see he'd been right.

"I'm not sure I'll go back to the city." The admission surprised me. "I think cleaning houses suits me."

"You should find a way to work diving into that life plan. You're one of the best."

"Not as good as Mom."

"Better. She took risks that I didn't like." He drew in a breath. "I loved her like family, but she was hardheaded."

"She knew what she wanted."

"She did." Another pause. "But you aren't her. You don't have to live her life to be a success."

"I've been chasing my mother all my life."

"You don't have to. Do you know all the divers had something nice to say about you? All they saw was kindness and potential."

"Did they notice that I'm still uptight about getting under the water?"

"We all should be. The ocean isn't kind to anyone who underestimates its power."

"Still freaks me out a lot."

"Give it time. You're a natural. I'd bet once you get in the water, you'll realize that you've arrived home. You ready to dive tomorrow?"

The boat cut through smooth waters. "Will the dreams of me drowning go away?"

He frowned. "You get those?"

"Not as often anymore. But yes, I still have nightmares."

My attention drifted to the shore and the docks and houses on the sound. "I couldn't get in a pool until two years ago. Water terrified me. But I slowly started to miss it. So, I began swimming laps at the gym pool."

"Respect the water, and you'll be fine."

"That's what I keep saying."

"You need to dive."

No wiggle room to back out. "I will."

"Good." He maneuvered the boat up to a spot in the center of the Currituck Sound and cut the engines. "Ready for dinner?"

Bracketed by the mainland and Outer Banks, we weren't close to any dock. "Here?"

"Sure. Thought it would be fun."

"Is this a date?"

His sunglasses reflected my comical expression and hid his eyes. "What do you think?"

"Honestly, I'm not really sure."

He opened the cooler and pulled out a couple of wrapped sandwiches. "Me either."

It was good for now. But he would move on when this project was finished. And I had no desire to chase anyone around the world again. But I liked where I was in this moment. "Are there fries in that cooler?"

"No, but there are bags of chips."

I beamed. "You had me at 'chips.'"

CHAPTER TWENTY-FOUR

Gertrude

Thursday, April 23, 1942, 8:30 a.m.
One day until the Oceanus *is torpedoed*

I woke from a brief morning nap to terrible stomach cramps. My entire body twisted into a knot that strangled the breath out of me. Breathing in and out, I rose from my bunk and tried to straighten. My stomach convulsed. I gripped the side of the bunk and kept breathing in and out. Finally, the cramp passed, and I was able to uncurl and inhale deeply.

I checked my gown and was relieved I wasn't bleeding and that my water hadn't broken. I said a prayer of thanks. It wasn't time for the baby. I had at least another month.

"You cannot come now. You must wait. It's not safe yet."

The baby went very still suddenly, and I wondered for a brief second if something had happened to the child. I waited, and when the child kicked, I relaxed.

I carefully removed my gown, poured water into a pitcher, and dabbed a clean cloth into the water. I wiped the cloth over my distended belly, which looked as ripe as a fresh peach. I washed the sweat from my body. I stepped into underwear and then a skirt with a drawstring that rested above where my waist had been.

I wasn't the prettiest girl in Vienna, but there was a time when I'd taken great pride in my appearance. There weren't many young men in my district, so I'd been a little surprised when Alfred entered the bookshop on a cold Thursday in October. Alfred carried himself with a bearing few men possessed. He didn't approach the counter but stood back, examining a novel.

"May I help you?" I asked.

He didn't look up. "Have you read this novel?"

"Yes. But I think it might be too romantic for your tastes."

He lifted his gaze and then slid the book back onto the shelf. Without looking up, he asked, "And who are you?"

"Naida."

"An unusual name."

"I'm named after a Greek river god. My uncle is fond of the classics."

He met my gaze and studied me closely. "It's lovely."

I was flattered. He was one of the most beautiful men.

Uncle Eric came out of the back room and introduced himself. "Can I assist you, Herr Gruber?"

I was surprised my uncle knew his name.

"I've heard you carry rare books," he said.

"From time to time we have a few," Uncle Eric said. "May I ask how you found us?"

"Word travels. Show me what you have."

My uncle hesitated and then moved behind the counter and reached to the shelf underneath. He presented the German author Johann Wolfgang von Goethe's title The Sorrows of Young Werther, *originally published in 1774. Sigrid had sold him the book days before.*

"Have you read it?" Alfred asked my uncle.

"No, but my niece has."

Alfred looked at me. "Do you think I would like it?"

"It's a serious book, but I think you're up for the challenge."

A smile flickered before he refocused on my uncle. "How much?"

Despite my uncle's customary caution, he named his price. The markup was sizable, but our rent was due, and the stove needed to be repaired.

Alfred's brow rose. "Is it worth the price?" he asked me.

"It's a rare and valuable book. It would be welcome in any well-stocked library."

"Ah, then I must buy it." He reached into his wallet and counted out the required number of schillings.

I wrapped the book in paper and handed it to Alfred. "Thank you, Herr Gruber."

"Pleasure to meet you, Naida," he said.

My cheeks had warmed with a tingling glow. Young boys and old men had often flirted and talked to me, but never had a man as seemingly important as Herr Gruber shown interest. "And you, sir."

Alfred tucked the book under his arm and left the shop and climbed into the back seat of a gleaming black car.

"How did you know his name?" I asked.

As Uncle Eric counted his money, he said, "Herr Gruber is a very powerful man and well liked by the Germans."

"How do you know he's not a spy?"

"I don't. That's why I sold him a German book."

"Who told him about us?"

"I would guess the selkie. She has many connections."

Herr Gruber didn't return for two weeks, and when he did, he brought me a book of sonnets and fish scraps for Grimm. I was enchanted. The next time he entered the shop, he brought me Mozartkugel, a chocolate confection. I was convinced of his affection. So, I found the good luck coin my mother had given me. She'd always imagined I would carry it on my wedding day. I took to wearing it in my shoe.

Herr Gruber soon invited me to dinner, and over the weeks, he took me to several fancy restaurants. I felt like a princess. He sent me flowers, in early winter no less. At a dinner in November, another woman, dressed in a dark silk dress, approached our table. She carried herself like a queen and barely glanced in my direction when she spoke to Alfred. He stood and kissed her on the cheek, and after he introduced me, he'd immediately turned to her. The two had talked for several minutes. I felt invisible.

That night when I returned to the bookshop, I found my uncle waiting up in his worn chair, a book in hand. Grimm slept on his lap. "Is he all that you hoped for?"

"More than I could have dreamed of."

He pulled off his reading glasses. "But you look worried."

I thought about the stunning woman in black. "My father left my mother. Did it break her heart?"

His brow furrowed. "It was a terrible blow. Why do you ask?"

"I don't want Alfred to leave me."

"I don't think he would do that. He's enamored with you."

"But I'm not like Alfred and the people in his world."

"Perhaps that's why you're so special to him."

The snows fell in November. The city grew more tense, and many businesses closed, but my uncle refused to leave. But Herr Gruber didn't return in November or December. With the coin always pressing against my skin, I waited, watched, and imagined him with the lovely blond.

Uncle Eric knew I was disappointed, but neither of us spoke about Alfred Gruber.

With each passing day, I grew more determined to win him over. On a cold January evening, I walked to the Danube's riverbanks. I thought of the river gods my mother had once told me about. The Roma revered them, but they had great powers and could be tricksters. So, I removed my mother's coin from my shoe. The current was choppy and fast, and the fish jumping.

I clenched the coin in my fist, and, ignoring her warning, I made a wish. "Bring Alfred back to me. Make him love me forever."

I gripped the old coin. The current churned, swirling faster near the shore and splashing droplets on my shoes.

Wishes are dangerous, *the river whispered.*

"I know what I want."

Be careful what you demand, *the water whispered back.*

"Alfred is different. He must love me forever," I said. "I don't want to lose him to another woman."

The water teased the shore, rolling in and out. You don't know him.

"I do. I do."

And then I tossed the coin into the water. A cloud passed in front of the full moon, shrouding me in shadows.

Alfred returned to the shop two days later, carrying a lavish bouquet of roses. He asked my uncle for my hand. My uncle agreed. My wish had been granted. Alfred was bound to me forever.

Now as I lay in my ship's bunk, I realized the river had been right. I'd known nothing about the darkness lurking inside Alfred.

I skimmed my fingers over the brand above my breast. My mother's and the river's warnings haunted me. My wish had become a curse.

My belly tightened, but this time the sensation came and went quickly. I lay very still, smoothing my hand over my belly. The baby wanted to come, but it would have to wait a little longer.

In the room next door, I heard the deep timbre of William's voice and Sigrid's melodic responses. Sigrid had brought Alfred to me. And she'd followed me to this ship. The threat was so close and present now. Alfred's hold on me remained.

An hour passed, and I heard them leave the room. All our lives now rotated around the meals. More passengers left their rooms and walked toward the dining room.

When the hallway grew very silent, I rose and finished dressing. I left my room and hurried to the toilet. When my bladder was empty, I rearranged my clothes and washed my hands.

As I stepped into the hallway, Dr. Brooks was walking away from his room toward mine. He had a pipe in his mouth and was trying to ignite his lighter. When he couldn't turn spark into flame, he cursed.

He looked at me sheepishly. "I've never had much luck with fire."

I took the lighter and shook it as I'd done countless times for my uncle so he could light his pipe. I rolled my thumb over the flint. It sparked, and a flame danced to life.

"Ah, you're a miracle worker," Dr. Brooks said.

"Men strike too hard. It takes a softer touch to tease the flame to life."

Dr. Brooks accepted the lighter back. However, he closed the lid, extinguishing the flame.

I shifted my stance, the weight of the baby feeling heavy against my bladder.

"Are you feeling all right?" Dr. Brooks asked.

I walked toward the stairs, mindful that Sigrid might be listening. "Uncomfortable. But I'll be fine." When concern deepened the lines on his face, I shifted the topic. "What trick or game will you bring to dinner tonight?"

"I was thinking about a spirit board."

"What is that?"

"According to legend, it's a way to contact the other world."

Alfred would have been appalled by such talk. "That sounds very dangerous."

"Depends. Are you afraid of the dead?"

"The living concern me more."

He chuckled. "Very wise. I'm not afraid of meeting anyone who has crossed over. After all, what can they do?"

"Then why contact them?"

"There are many in the living world who are very curious and believe all the answers in this world can be answered in the next."

"The dead have seen more than the living."

"True." And then, a roguish grin. "Amazing what you can learn. People tend to talk about intimate issues that they never would otherwise, over a spirit board or a deck of cards."

I smoothed my hand over my tight belly, willing it to loosen. "What's the most scandalous thing you've learned?"

He smiled. "A woman told me her husband was worried about the ghost of a man he'd murdered."

"Oh, my. What happened to him?"

"I heard later that he was arrested."

"Ah."

"Join me for breakfast, and I'll share more stories from the cards and board."

"That's very kind." I slowly climbed the stairs.

"I'm being selfish." He gripped my elbow. "I'm now terrified that your baby is going to fall out and hit the floor if you do not sit down."

Even as my lower back ached, I said, "The baby is staying in place."

His hold tightened. Maybe it was the pipe or his gentle voice, but he reminded me of my uncle. I didn't pull away, realizing I needed human contact. I spent so much time in my own thoughts.

He carefully guided me to the dining room and toward a table by the window. He pulled out my chair, and before I realized it, I was sipping coffee, with toast and eggs on the way.

"Are you always this charming?" I asked. "You're good at getting your way."

He pulled a deck of cards from his pocket. "I am very good at that."

After we had eaten and our dishes were cleared away, Dr. Brooks carefully shuffled the cards and then set them in front of me. "Cut the cards."

I halved the deck and then rebuilt it. "This is a different deck."

"I purchased this deck in Port of Spain from a woman who claims to be a witch and a seer."

I watched as he laid three cards face down. His answers were always smooth and at the ready. "Is this game supposed to be fun, or are you looking for more secrets?"

"You're nervous."

My mother's warning about the river gods surfaced. *Be careful what you wish for.* "I am perfectly calm."

"I suspect you're nothing but. You're a woman willing to take dangerous chances."

"I don't look very dangerous."

"Which is why you are." His smile softened the charge.

He flipped over very ornate cards, all featuring aquatic scenes—waves, open water, lakes, and rivers. The first was a large wave crashing on a man. The second was a river splashing over jagged rocks. The third was a sun rising over the ocean.

"You've been through a great deal," he said.

"You could say that about anyone on this ship. In Europe. The world."

"Very true." He tapped the River card. "You've known heartbreak."

"Again, like everyone else on this ship."

"But your past nearly broke you in two. And you fear its return."

I stilled. I was careful that I didn't show any of my feelings to him.

"I'm not your enemy, Frau Werner."

Frau. I wouldn't use the very German-sounding form of address when I arrived in the United States. I threaded my fingers. "I didn't say you were."

"But you look at me and everyone on this ship as if you're worried."

"Worried about strangers? Not so uncommon for a woman alone."

"You're careful to keep your counsel, and the only people I've seen you speak to are me and the young US sailor."

And Sigrid. "He joined me on the deck."

"And you were comfortable with him because he was likely very unaware of your past."

I rested my knitted fingers on the table. "My past isn't perfect but hardly noteworthy. And it's over."

"Is it?" He shook his head, his eyes sharpening with a cunning that I hadn't seen before. "Who is chasing you, Frau Werner? Why do you always look so afraid?"

"I'm a widow traveling to the United States. I want to escape the war." I leaned forward. "Why would a book dealer care about me? I am nothing. Why are you so curious?"

He grinned. "I'm inquisitive by nature."

At that moment, Sigrid and William entered the dining hall. Both were well dressed and looked perfectly polished. My gaze dipped, but I watched them closely under hooded eyes.

"Do you know them?" Dr. Brooks asked.

"Their room is next to mine."

"Ah. So, you have heard the fights."

I stilled. "Excuse me?"

"They aren't a happy couple. I've seen the way he controls her interactions."

"You're quite in the know, Dr. Brooks."

There was that grin. "Again, details matter in the book-trading business. And I do enjoy watching people."

"And who else on this ship have you been watching?"

"I watch everyone. All the time."

"That makes you sound like a spy." There were many spies in Vienna. Ever since the civil war a decade ago, neighbors had often turned against neighbors. Everyone watched their words because the most traitorous could look the most innocent.

He laughed. "Now who would want a simple man like me as a spy?"

"Isn't that the point? It's important to blend in." Could Alfred have more spies on this ship? I didn't know Dr. Brooks and needed to remember he was not my friend.

The amusement from his face never faded. "I have underestimated you."

CHAPTER TWENTY-FIVE

TULA

Sunday, June 14, 2026, 9:30 p.m.

Nathan had not tried to kiss me, and when he dropped me off at the Brooks house, I hesitated. We sat in the silence before I said, "Thank you."

"Anytime."

I wasn't sure what the date had meant. "I haven't had such a good time in years."

"Same."

Out of the vehicle, I fished the heavy key from my pocket, hurried to the front door, and unlocked it. Flipping on the light, I looked back at Nathan's truck. He waved and then backed out onto the road. The truck soon vanished around a curve.

I closed the door behind me and stood in the silence. The dust danced and swirled in the light leaking through gaps between the blinds and windows.

I unlocked the back door and walked out onto the deck and moved toward the dune stairs. The ocean breeze was still warm and the stars burned bright in the night sky. I inhaled, listening as the ocean rolled up onto the sand. In the spray and sliding waters, a faint whisper rose above the churn.

How could you not love me?

The waters on the horizon were smooth and the air soft. Days like this convinced almost anyone that beach living was the way to go. On days like this, the ocean was benevolent. It spoke so softly no one saw the big stick clutched behind its back.

Anxiety should have been tightening my chest. I should have been afraid. But I wasn't. The pull of this kind version of the monster was seductive.

I turned back toward the house. I stepped out of the fading light into the house, which was now catching moonlight.

Next week would be my last helping Kaitlin, and though I enjoyed her company, I was ready to move on to something else. I didn't know what that was, but I was headed in the right direction.

As tempted as I was to return to the manuscript, I felt an obligation to give this house my time. After changing out of my dress, I spent a good hour boxing up the books in the middle of the living room. Once they were sealed and the sheets and towels in large trash bags, I turned my attention back to Dr. Brooks's papers.

I hefted a box onto the large desk in the office and found several images of Dr. Brooks. In the first, he was on the back porch of this house, smiling up from a newspaper as if he was happy to humor the photographer. In many of the pictures he was surrounded by books, magazines, and newspapers. A man of letters. A doctor of sorts who had been based in Norfolk, but who'd escaped to this house whenever he could. I wondered who'd taken the pictures. Maybe the woman in the photographs?

I pulled the yellowed newspaper clipping that covered a local hit-and-run accident that had occurred on the beach road in Nags Head in the sixties. A driver had struck and killed a man who'd been trying to cross the busy road on a moonless night. The driver had not stopped, and at the time of the reporting, the crime wasn't solved.

I smoothed out the article and dug through the layers of images. As I excavated deeper, I found more pictures from the fifties and sixties of the doctor and the lovely woman. She smiled in all the pictures, but her face was always slightly turned and her gaze glancing away from the lens.

I put all the pictures in a "keep" box and went about cleaning. I moved to the kitchen and began packing the cabinets, filled with stoneware dishes. Like the man, the dishes were simple, functional, and easily forgotten. I wrapped them all in paper and boxed them up. Next the drawers. Again, all carefully organized. There was no clutter, no disorganization.

My cell rang. I didn't recognize the number, but the area code was local. "This is Tula."

"This is Lex Green. I know I'm calling late. But I heard from Doug tonight that you were asking about me. I'd have called sooner, but I left my cell at home."

Communication in small towns was efficient. "Mr. Green. Thanks for calling. I was planning to contact you. You know I'm Mariah Cassidy's daughter, right?"

"I do. Are you up in Southern Shores?" His voice had the scruffy edge of an older man.

"I am. Hard at work cleaning out the Brooks house."

"How did you get that job?"

"My firm sent me down here to get it cleaned out so it could be sold."

"Great property. So much history."

Questions bubbled. "Would you have time to meet for coffee? You wrote several articles about my mother, and it would be nice to talk to someone who knew her."

"Sure. But I didn't know her that well. We only met a few times before she dove the *Oceanus*. I liked your mother."

Piecing together why Mom had wanted to return here and dive the wreck was becoming all important to me. "Where would you like to meet?"

"I'm in Manteo. I don't get up to Southern Shores that much anymore. My eyes aren't great, so I stay close to home."

"I'm happy to come to you. What time works for you?"

"Tuesday?"

"Sure." I mentally ran through that morning's cleaning schedule. "Middle of the day?"

"Let's say noon."

"Perfect."

He rattled off his address as I scribbled it on a piece of paper. "I'll unpack my notes and see if there's anything that might be of interest."

"That would be great."

"Anything in particular you want to know?"

"Why did the *Oceanus* spark Mom's interest?"

"That's easy. Her grandmother, your great-grandmother, Margaret, was on the ship."

CHAPTER TWENTY-SIX

Tula

Monday, June 15, 2026, 6:00 a.m.

When I'd texted Kaitlin about my dive with Nathan, she'd told me to go with her blessings. The work schedule was light on Mondays. She'd asked me to grab her cleaning supplies in Currituck. I'd agreed, even as I'd half hoped she'd declare she needed me, but I was free.

So, I arrived at the Wanchese dock as the sun rose. I parked next to Nathan's truck and grabbed a small cooler with my lunch. I also brought a small waterproof bag with a towel, a dry set of clothes, and extra sunscreen.

I walked down the pier and found Nathan loading a massive cooler onto the boat. The guy had always been as strong as an ox, and that hadn't changed. I'd been a little turned on by that when I was a teenager. And I still was. He was hot. I wasn't looking for promises or a house with a permanent address. But I realized I still wanted Nathan.

"Hey there." I grabbed a few of his bags and handed them to him. His gaze slid quickly over me. "You're here bright and early."

"I remember the dives always went better if I had time to check everything twice. Mom left many details like air in the tanks or gas in the boat up to me."

"She wasn't always as cautious about her equipment."

"I wish she'd worried more. She could be so reckless."

"Holding on to life too hard can crush the life out of it."

Maybe that's why I hadn't thrived the last few years. I was gripping so tight my fingers ached. "When did you get to be such a philosopher?"

He offered his hand to me, and I took it before climbing onto the boat. "I always have been. You just never noticed."

That was probably true. When I looked at him now, I felt like a teenager with hormones flooding my body. They were still raging, but life had taught me to slow down. I'd been riding the brake too long, and it was time to press the accelerator.

"Who's on the dive list today?" I asked.

"Tony is back, plus three others. I'll introduce you as they arrive."

"Tony is back? I thought he'd never dive again."

"Called me late last night. Apparently, he wants another crack at the *Oceanus*. He'll be glad to see you here."

"Tula, the emotional support boat crew member," I quipped.

"Are you getting in the water?" Nathan asked.

"No. But I'm less freaked out. Still adjusting to being surrounded by water again. But it's much better. The ocean and I are trying to become friends again."

"Best feeling in the world."

"Until you need a full breath and you realize there are two hundred feet of water between you and air."

His brow knotted. "This fear really is a thing with you."

"Sadly, yes. I'm not proud of it. I used to love the water, and now I see everything that can go wrong."

"Hey, you're here. That counts for a lot. Like you said, maybe the ocean is slowly seducing you."

The water had a lure. Even with the dangers, it drew me. "We'll see."

His half grin reminded me of someone who'd scored a winning shot. "Don't underestimate the waters. Very powerful magic."

"I know."

"Have you read more of the manuscript?"

Water lapped against the side of the boat. "I didn't get to it last night. But from what I do know, the torpedo hasn't hit the ship yet. The writer is very focused on a woman named Gertrude. She's on the run."

"From?"

"An abusive husband. A Nazi sympathizer. And there's a woman on the ship named Sigrid. She wants to take Gertrude's child. And Dr. Brooks is featured in the story. He's a rare book dealer."

"Do you think Gertrude survived?"

"I don't know. There's no Gertrude Werner on the survivors list."

"A mystery."

"The more I read about these people, the more invested I get. On Tuesday, I'm meeting with a reporter who met with Mom. He said I had a great-grandmother on the ship."

"Who?"

"My great-grandmother's name apparently was Margaret. But there was no Margaret listed on the passenger list."

"Interesting."

"Before, I only saw twisted metal covered in barnacles. Now I see people other than my mother. I want to know more about my family's connection to it. She must've survived, or I wouldn't be here."

He considered what I'd said. "The torpedo hit right after the second lunch bell rang on the fifth day at sea, about one fifteen," he said.

Several cars pulled into the lot, which was still mostly empty. Four people walked down the plank toward us, while others peeled off with fishing rods toward other boats.

An emerging blue sky, perfect for summer vacations, promised no rain or heavy winds. Mother Nature had planned another charmed day.

As the passengers boarded, a fit, tanned middle-aged guy moved toward the boat with bags of what must have been camera equipment.

Nathan climbed onto the dock and greeted him. "Welcome, Bob."

Bob's salt-and-pepper hair brushed his shoulders. "Thanks for thinking of me."

"Tula, this is Bob," Nathan said. "He's doing the underwater filming today. Bob, Tula."

My name caught Bob's attention, but all he said was "Nice to meet you." His hands were full of equipment, bags, and a cooler.

"Can I take one of those bags for you?" I asked.

"Thank you." He handed me the smaller bag and passed the bigger ones to Nathan. He climbed aboard. "Visibility is good?"

"Should be excellent," Nathan said. "Ready?"

"You bet."

I still hadn't watched Nathan's other footage, but my curiosity was growing. I was beginning to wonder if video footage would be enough.

Once all the divers (Bob, Tony, Chris, and Sara) and their equipment were aboard, Nathan gave his classic welcome and safety speech. He moved behind the helm and started the engines. In minutes, we were out of the harbor and headed north along the coastline.

Tony smiled. "Second time is the charm, right?"

"Absolutely," I said.

As Tony struck up a conversation with Sara, a slim blond in her mid-forties, Bob turned to me as he unzipped a scuba bag. "You dive with Nathan much?"

"I did back in the day," I said. "I don't dive anymore."

"Why not?"

"Diving accident. I've been spooked."

"Ah, Tula." Bob said my name as if tumblers had finally fallen into place. "Your mom was a diving explorer. Your mother loved the water. You were practically born in the ocean."

"You met my mother?"

He hesitated. "We crossed paths a few times. Mariah was a spitfire. Loved the water. Loved you."

She'd always been so tough on me, although I could see now that that was her way of preparing me for the world. It didn't seem fair at the time, but I realized it had been necessary. Still, the younger Tula couldn't forget how it had all ended. "And she left me."

Bob drew in a breath. "She died. She didn't leave you."

But she'd taken a terrible gamble that last day. "Did she say anything to you about the *Oceanus*?"

"No, that wasn't on her radar when we met." He shook his head. "What have you been up to the last few years?"

"Been a little landlocked."

He pretended to shudder. "Can't imagine. But now you're back at sea?" The simple question raised a bigger one.

"I'm on a boat. I'm not freaking out. So not 'at sea' like you and Nathan, but closer."

"Best thing you can do is dive," Bob said. "Face that fear. You'll remember all the old skills."

I smiled. "You sound like my therapist."

Bob's cheeks dimpled when he grinned, and his sun-bleached hair made him look younger. "I've been called worse."

"Ready to dive?" Nathan stopped the boat and dropped anchor.

An affirmative rumbled over the group.

"I can't hear you," Nathan said.

The group responded with a louder yes. Nathan and Bob suited up in their scuba gear.

"I'll get you some awesome footage, Tula," Bob said. "It'll be so good you'll think you're at the wreck."

I could feel the sunken ship's pull. "Thanks."

"Let me know over the radio if there's trouble on top," Nathan said.

"Will do." Clear sky dipped to smooth waters. "Looks perfect again. You have the luck of the Irish, Nathan."

"Here's hoping." The divers moved to the platform. Bob had a camera resting on his shoulder. Nathan jumped in, and the rest soon followed.

They vanished below the surface.

I lingered around the edge of the boat, watching the waters lap against the sides. I leaned over and dipped my hand into the water, letting its cool touch wrap around my fingers. A rolling wave bumped the side of the boat, nearly knocking me off balance and into the water. Cold, salty droplets splattered my face and shirt.

Heart pumping in my chest, I grabbed a bracket on the side of the boat and willed my body to straighten and steady. The waves rose close to my face, teasing my cheek, before I pulled myself upright.

"What the hell," I said. "Not playing fair."

The waters rolled gently as if smiling an apology.

"You aren't sorry."

Water slapped the side of the boat.

The divers were under the water for forty-five minutes.

And when they returned to the surface, Bob pulled off his mask. He looked pale and slightly shaken.

CHAPTER TWENTY-SEVEN

Tula

Monday, June 15, 2026, 9:00 a.m.

Bob's video footage started wide, capturing the hazy waters of the Atlantic. Schools of fish swam past the camera, fanning around the screen as if putting on a show for the rare camera. Nathan swam into view and led the way deeper into the water toward the ocean floor, where the visibility was dimmer and murkier.

It wasn't long before the other divers and Nathan reached the smooth sandy bottom, covered in trails of small, flat shells. I remembered slipping my fingers along that silty bottom on my last dive with Mom. The undisturbed floor had puffed into clouds as I swirled my fingers through the sandy muck. I'd felt oddly nervous, as if I was trespassing.

Pressure formed in my chest as I watched Nathan glide along the ocean bottom. The sea had never made a secret of its dangers. Never. Humans were tentative guests in the undersea world, and we entered at our own peril. And maybe that was the appeal. We were entering the forbidden.

"We approached the *Oceanus* from her stern," Nathan said. He stood close behind me. I could feel the cool ocean's damp waters still clinging to his bare chest.

I'd forgotten he was standing behind me. Certain he'd warn me if there was something I shouldn't see, I didn't speak as my gaze remained locked on the screen.

And then the vessel's debris field appeared. The *Oceanus* had drifted from Carova Beach to the spot where she finally sank and had deposited trinkets and items along the way. Many items had been found by weekend divers. When it was still legal to harvest their finds, many had donated their discoveries to local museums, and some had not.

The debris field grew heavier, and I could envision the dying ship listing badly in the choppy waters as waves jostled her guts onto the ocean floor.

The first crumbs in the debris trail were small pieces of jagged and torn metal that looked as thin as paper. Next a tangle of twisted metal, and beside it an uncorked wine bottle that had never broken, snarled chains, and a soldier's helmet. Portions of a mast covered in barnacles lay quietly in the silt.

These markers pointed toward a familiar trail that I'd swum past seven years ago. To see the debris field untouched felt odd. Life on the surface continued and changed, but down here, the world was locked in its own time capsule.

Up next would be the stern. The blunted edge was intact, as it had been seven years ago. Thicker layers of barnacles covered her metal hull. The faded word *Oceanus* came into focus. My heartbeat quickened.

I thought about the image I'd seen of Dr. Brooks standing in front of the *Oceanus* in Port of Spain. The ship stood proud and muscular, and the doctor wore a mild expression. His ordinariness had made him almost unforgettable by anyone passing by.

The vessel's bow nosed toward the north, marking the original path of the *Oceanus*' final days. After her engines had stopped working, the southward prevailing winds and current had pushed her south, carrying her farther away from New York City. When the ship finally sank to the ocean bottom, she was 300 nautical miles from New York City.

The camera hovered over the raw jagged hole on the upward-facing starboard side. Bent metal twisted inward, marking the path of the single torpedo. The strike hit below the waterline, and the explosion had destroyed one of the lifeboats.

The ship's .50 caliber guns that Jeff had seen, and Chief Mate Kevin Riggs had bragged about, remained pointing upward, as if, given a chance, they could fire again. I thought about the young officer who'd overseen the ship's day-to-day operations. He'd survived but was long dead, and I was sorry I couldn't talk to him.

The *Oceanus* had been a powerful, fast ship, captained by a seasoned sailor convinced he could outrun the Germans without the protection of a convoy.

"Time always moves on, but it stops down there," Nathan said.

"It's super weird." I kept my gaze on the screen, watching for signs of my mother. A tank, a flipper, or even her remains. But there was no evidence that Mom had ever been here.

"We didn't see signs of her," Nathan said softly. "I'm always on the lookout when I dive the wreck. But I saw nothing."

I wished I'd known that those last moments when I'd looked back at her would be the last. If I'd known our time was slipping away, I'd have dragged her back.

A forgotten memory fluttered forward. Nathan was one of several rescue volunteer divers who were in the water as soon as the storm ended. I'd been told to stay away from the docks, but I was unable to sit and wait at the rental house I'd shared with Mom. I'd driven there and sat and waited for six hours until the first boats returned. Nathan, still in pain from the car accident, emerged from the water. Water dripped from his dark hair and the arm cast, wrapped in plastic and duct tape. The water had leaked and seeped past the temporary barrier and soaked his cast.

When Nathan walked toward me, his steps were quick and determined, even as he cradled his arm.

Exhausted and angry, he argued with the lead rescue diver and asked to return, but he'd reached his dive limit. When his gaze met mine, he suddenly looked lost. He shook his head slowly, and I knew Mom was gone forever.

Without a word, I'd turned and walked off the pier. He didn't chase after me or call out to me. Later, he'd tried to call, and I'd ignored it. When I'd reached dry land, a barrier had sunk between the water and me.

"I didn't have a chance to get a good look at her the other day, but now, I took my time."

I shoved down the memory. "Did you notice anything new?"

"She's looking more fragile," Bob said. "The crack in her hull runs almost across her midsection. She'll eventually break in two one day."

"She's not as stable as I'd thought," Nathan said.

Torpedoes had sunk nearly four hundred vessels along the entire East Coast of the US. Over eighty of these ships went down off the Outer Banks, where the shifting sandbars near Hatteras had allowed Germany's U-boats to hide in deep waters. Sometimes storms unearthed these vessels, pushing fragments toward the shore, only for the tides to bury them in the sand. But most sunken remains were like the *Oceanus*, forever buried from sight.

"We think we're so powerful, but images like this remind me of how fragile it all is," I said.

"Are you doing okay?" Nathan asked.

Seven years of waiting and wondering, and I wanted to let it all go, although I still had a small kernel of hope that Mom was still alive, diving and living her best life. But if that fantasy were true, then she'd have swum away and left me to fend for myself.

"I'm a survivor," I said. "I'll be fine."

Nathan leaned forward as if he wanted to hug me. And for a moment, I was tempted to lean back and prop myself against his chest

But I was aware of the other divers encircled around us, so I kept my shoulders ramrod straight. I prayed he wouldn't touch me. He was the closest I had to anyone on this planet who'd suffered this wreck like I had, but I knew if I touched him, I'd dissolve.

The others were drinking water and eating snacks as if this were just an evening in front of the television.

When the film ended, Bob shut off the camera. "Nathan must have gotten good footage of the starboard side," he said. He sniffed and brushed back his wet hair as he walked toward me.

I thrust back any emotions welling inside. I wasn't sure how much I wanted to see. "What did you see?"

"It's kind of weird." There was no hint of humor as Nathan moved toward me.

"Weird how?" I asked.

"I don't know if the camera caught it or not." He hit fast-forward.

I leaned closer, bracing myself as I kept my gaze locked on the screen. He hit play.

These images were farther along the debris trail, and then they cut left. The camera skimmed along the partly upended section of the *Oceanus'* hull. The barnacle-coated underside was home now to small sea creatures who dwelled in cracks and crevices. Nothing out of the ordinary.

But as he swam toward the bow, a white cloud gurgled around the ship. Whatever it was, it wasn't marine life or shifting sands.

"What's that?" I asked.

"Good question," Bob said.

Nathan stepped closer. His body warmed some of the chill seeping into my bones.

"That's what I saw," Tony said. "I thought it was a ghost."

"I don't know about ghosts," Bob said. "But it was weird."

Nathan drew in a breath.

"It came around the bow, hovered, and then receded back to the starboard side. Did you see it?" Bob asked.

Nathan nodded. "I did."

"After dives, Mom liked to drink with the old sailors, and many had stories about sightings they couldn't explain. They'd say the barrier islands are full of restless spirits."

"There could be a dozen logical explanations," Nathan said. "Most likely one of the divers churned up the sea bottom as we all came around the other side."

Bob studied the screen. "Very logical. But whatever it was, it was gone when I rounded the bow."

"Nineteen people died suddenly when the *Oceanus* sank, and then Mom vanished," I said. "These are troubled waters filled with spirits."

"Did anyone else see it today?" Nathan looked at the divers.

They all shook their heads no.

Tony shrugged. "I saw it last week, but not today."

"Why the random appearances?" A chill slid over me. "Is it trying to tell us something?"

"When did you become so superstitious?" Nathan countered.

I shrugged. "Anyone who makes their living on the water is."

Nathan fixed his gaze on my necklace. "That coin you're wearing brought your mother good luck."

My brow knotted. "When did she tell you that?"

"Seven years ago. I teased her about it being lucky, but she was insistent."

"And she left the coin for me before the last dive."

"And now you wear it with the sea glass," Nathan said.

Seven years ago, when Nathan had noticed my new "fancy" sea-glass necklace, I thought I'd finally broken through his reserve. I thought he was flirting. But beyond the quip, he'd said nothing else, and never made a move on me. I was counting the days to my eighteenth birthday, hoping that's what he was waiting for.

The boat rocked from side to side as I moved to the edge and looked over the side. The wreck was too deep to see, but I still combed the waters, hoping for something more.

The other divers chatted about the wreck as Nathan's engines fired, and soon the boat was moving south toward the harbor. Water splashed up the sides. Several fistfuls of water hit me, cooling off my skin, now overheated by hours in the morning sun.

I didn't move away from the edge. I watched the bow cut through the water as the waves playfully splashed. I dropped my hand over the side so my fingers felt the cool wetness spattering up. Energy pulsed against my skin.

I'd accomplished more in the last week than I had in seven years of therapy. I was beginning to glimpse the girl who had lived in and loved the water.

The idea of diving in these waters terrified me. But I knew now I had to dive. I had to see the *Oceanus* one last time.

CHAPTER TWENTY-EIGHT

GERTRUDE

Thursday, April 23, 1942, 9:30 p.m.
Less than twenty-four hours until the Oceanus ***is torpedoed***

I strolled the quiet deck, unmindful of the chilling winds. Tightening my shawl, I gazed up at the clear night sky. The cool air felt good, a welcome break from the heat in Port of Spain. Sleep was becoming impossible.

The baby kicked and moved often, and each time, I remembered Alfred and our last, furious night together. It was after the party I'd worked so hard to host and the one Sigrid had wanted an invitation to. When I spotted Sigrid at the party, dressed in blue silk and flirting with a German colonel, I'd thought the plan might work. I quietly slipped away to my room and was on the verge of unpacking the maid's uniform I'd wear once I slipped out of the house with the extra crews.

I'd thought about the river and the boat Sigrid had said would be waiting for me. I prayed I could sail out of Vienna and disappear. But

Alfred had come into my room. He was agitated, wine on his breath, his gaze dark and dangerous. I'd seen this look before and knew what would follow.

What happened next was a blur of violence and pain. I lost consciousness, and when I finally woke, the room was shrouded in shadows. I was alone, and when I stood, I was unsteady on my feet. But I dressed in the dark maid's uniform, my hands trembling as I fastened the white buttons. I grabbed a knife I'd stolen from the kitchen days ago and wedged open my door lock. He'd kill me if I left. Or he'd eventually murder me if I stayed.

Footsteps jolted me back to the present. I tensed, drawing in on myself. A lighter flicked, and then the acrid smell of smoke drifted toward me on the breeze. I turned away from the shadowed person. I resented having to leave the fresh air, but until I reached New York City, I needed to be cautious.

"Frau Gruber, does my smoking bother you?"

The sound of my name was jarring. I looked toward the glow of the cigarette tip and searched the shadows. I recognized the man. Sigrid's lover. William.

"My name is Werner." I deliberately softened my accent, molding the vowels so they weren't so sharp. "It is late."

"A woman in your condition must be careful," he said, facing me. "Children are so precious."

I didn't speak.

He stared at the glowing tip of his cigarette. "How far along are you, Frau Gruber, if you don't mind me asking?"

His question felt oddly invasive. And again, I couldn't speak.

His gaze roamed over my rounded belly. "I would say sooner rather than later."

Smoke swirled around his head. "We haven't been formally introduced, but I remember you from the September party you and your husband hosted. Thank you again for the invitation."

My heart skipped for a second as I mustered a lie. "I don't know what you're talking about."

"Sigrid knows you very well. She has connections all over the city. Which enabled her to sell her books to your great-uncle."

How long had Sigrid and William been together? I stood silent. He was toying with me. Sigrid had told him about me, or maybe he'd always known?

"Alfred would never have found your tiny bookshop if I hadn't told him about it." When I didn't respond, he added, "German and Austrian officers are a very efficient group of men, though some have rather harsh methods. They don't tolerate resistance or disloyalty from their soldiers or their women."

Panic tightened harder, like Alfred's fingers around my neck. William was enjoying my fear, just as Alfred had.

"I found your husband a calculating bastard, but he could be very charming."

I met his gaze but remained silent. I didn't remember him from the party. So much had happened that night, and I barely recalled the hundreds of lost faces.

"When you vanished after the party, the poor man was beside himself. He'll move heaven and earth to find you."

Heat warmed my face.

"That night at the party, you played the piano. Many of the officers liked watching you. Many wondered aloud what you could do with those delicate hands."

I wasn't so naive that I hadn't heard such whispered comments. "This isn't a proper conversation."

"I'm sorry." He drew on the end of his cigarette and allowed the smoke to trickle out his mouth and nose. "I shouldn't be so bold with Alfred's wife. He would skin me alive."

"My husband died in the war. I've never been to Vienna. I'm not who you think I am."

"You're exactly who I think you are. You call yourself Gertrude now, but we both know your real name is Naida."

Naida. She was weak and always afraid. I'd left Naida behind in Vienna. "I must go."

He blocked my path. "Where are you going, Gertrude? We're trapped on this ship until New York. There's nowhere you can run that I cannot find you."

"Leave me alone."

"Your husband wants you back. He'll especially want the child."

His deep voice amplified Sigrid's earlier threat. I could get away from her, but I wasn't so sure I could escape William.

Tears jammed my throat. I'd heard tales of murders as I'd moved from port to port. I had prayed for the lost souls, including my own. Now I implored the ocean to save me.

"Go on. Run. But Sigrid and I will be waiting for you on the dock. It won't take long to ship you back to Vienna."

I hurried my awkward frame across the deck and headed through the portal. Unshed tears rose, quickly filling my eyes. But I refused to let one spill. I kept my chin up and put one foot in front of the other until I'd reached my room. I locked the door. My hand over my mouth, I sank down on my bunk. The past I'd been running from was determined to ensnare me again.

Heavy footsteps sounded in the hallway. The person paused outside my door. A knuckle wrapped against the door three times. I sat still, barely breathing. Finally, the person moved on, only to enter room 112.

I rose and crossed to my bag, then pulled out the kitchen knife I'd carried since Vienna. Many times, I'd nearly tossed it into a river or the ocean, but the waters always rose as if to warn me I needed to keep it. When I was in Lisbon, I'd visited a blacksmith in a small shop on a darkened alley. I'd paid well to have it sharpened so that it could slice through a single sheet of paper.

Seven months of running had changed something inside me. I hid out of necessity but not fear. I was not Naida. I had escaped Alfred, Europe, and Port of Spain. And soon I'd be in New York.

If my past was destined to follow me, I wouldn't accept it lightly. I would die fighting now.

I would remain free.

And this child would never be sent back to Alfred.

CHAPTER TWENTY-NINE

Gertrude

Friday, April 24, 1942, 9:30 a.m.
Less than four hours until the** Oceanus **is torpedoed

When the morning bell announced breakfast, I heard William and Sigrid leave their cabin. I sat on my bunk fully dressed, the knife gripped in my fist. I'd spent most of the night awake and wondering how I could slip away.

The steward knocked on my door several times. He always came when the breakfast bell rang as guests ambled to the dining room. This was his chance to clean the rooms. Each day, I assured him that I didn't need towels, nor did my room require cleaning.

"Mrs. Werner? It's Steward Thomas."

This time I crossed to the door, slipped the knife into my pocket, and opened it. "Good morning," I said.

The young sailor's startled gaze rose to mine.

"Would you change my bed linens today?" I asked.

"Of course."

Down the hallway, I saw that William and Sigrid's door was open. Another steward appeared, carrying their soiled sheets, which he shoved into a cloth bag.

In the hallway, I walked toward the toilet and past William and Sigrid's room. As I closed the lavatory door partway, the second steward turned away from their room, then closed and locked the door behind him. He moved to the next room.

I quickly left the toilet. As the other steward cleaned my room, I walked back toward his cart, where his keys dangled from a small hook by a stack of towels.

My heart raced as I stared at the numbered silver keys dangling and daring me. As I drew closer, I saw that each key was marked with its corresponding room number. With careful, quiet steps, I hurried to the cart and snatched the keys carefully in my fingers, holding them tight. I had only a short time before the stewards realized the keys were gone.

I fumbled through the collection until I found room number 112. With a trembling hand, I inserted the key into the lock and twisted. The handle gave way, and I pushed the door open. I gently closed it behind me. In my room, the steward thumped about and sounded rushed and ready to be done with his task.

William and Sigrid's room held the heavy scent of William's aftershave. Normally, the fragrance would be considered pleasant, but it curdled in my belly.

I rushed to the closet and found several suits hanging in precise order. They were dark and still held a sharp crease. Beside them were several silk dresses. My hands trembled as I searched the pockets, where I found a lighter, several German coins, and the ticket stub for this trip.

On a small dressing table, William's collection of aftershaves, razors, and tie clips were lined in a neat row. Beside them were elaborate perfume bottles, powders, and lipsticks.

In the top dresser drawer were socks, ties, and clean shirts. I carefully slid my hand under the garments, searching for papers or anything else that would tell me more about William.

The bottom drawer was filled with Sigrid's silk undergarments. Under a red satin slip, my fingers grazed a beaded purse. I opened it, and inside was a set of identity papers that belonged not to him but to Sigrid.

Sigrid. If I could believe anything she'd said to me, Alfred had found her and jailed her in a prison cell and sent her family to a camp. She'd been forced to find me. And now I had her papers.

The ocean rolled past the porthole, splashing water against the ship. I closed and replaced the purse and pocketed the papers.

I crossed to a small desk and opened the file on top. Inside the folder were photographs. They were all of me. In several, I was entering my uncle's bookshop in Vienna. I was walking along the river. Or exiting a shop. They dated back to shortly after I'd met Alfred. Had he had someone watching me all along?

I closed the folder and carefully stacked the photos and placed them back where I'd found them. As I turned, I noticed three books on the nightstand by the bunk. I crossed. The first two were from the United States but the last was English. It was a rare copy of *The Tempest*. I thumbed through the pages, and out fluttered a small card. It read, DR. ATTICUS BROOKS, NORFOLK, VIRGINIA.

Of course, the two had crossed paths on the ship, but it was unsettling to know she had his card. I didn't want to believe Dr. Brooks was helping them, but I couldn't trust anyone. My mouth went dry as I replaced the books and tucked the card into my pocket.

As I closed the door, I heard the steward near my open door. I hurried toward the cart and hooked the keys on the peg seconds before he exited my room.

"All finished?" I asked.

"Yes," he said.

"Thank you."

I closed and locked my door behind me. I sat on my bunk. My face was warm and flushed as I stared at the card and Sigrid's identity papers. She was older than me, but the picture appeared to have been taken several years ago. We had a similar look, and the differences could be explained away by the round face of pregnancy.

My stomach cramped, and for several seconds the discomfort grabbed my full attention. I breathed deeply as I'd seen many Viennese midwives instruct women in their time.

Once the spasm had subsided, I lay back on the bunk. This cabin was my prison. We were so close to New York. The *Oceanus* was cutting through the water at full speed as if it could skate across dangerous waters and skirt past the U-boats.

There had to be some place on this ship where I could hide as we neared land. If I could reach Chief Mate Riggs, I might have a chance.

I'd become good at blending into crowds and staying out of sight. I just needed to do it on board long enough to lose sight of William and Sigrid.

CHAPTER THIRTY

Tula

Monday, June 15, 2026, 11:30 a.m.

When I made it to dry land, I rushed off the dock. I needed to get across the bridge and into Currituck and pick up cleaning supplies for Kaitlin. The drive took longer than I'd imagined, and as the minutes ticked away, my anxiety rose. I'd promised Kaitlin I'd get these supplies, and I didn't want to let her down.

I rolled my shoulders, smoothing out knotted muscles. Being on the water and seeing the *Oceanus* had been more draining than I'd imagined. I'd spent seven years blocking it and the loss of my mother from my mind. And yet I couldn't shake the idea that it had been patiently and silently waiting for my return.

Inhaling, I crossed the bridge. This time I didn't feel a rush of panic. The ocean and the sound connected by endless inlets, waterways, and rivers weren't going anywhere. The water was beautiful. Ugly. Wild. Untamable. It wasn't looking for forgiveness.

The lapping waters of the sound whispered a question: *Ah, so you accept me on my terms now?*

That was the logical me.

And most days I could cling to reason.

But in the middle of the night, or when I lowered my guard, I wasn't rational. I was filled with anger, fear, and anxiety. Beautiful memories could instantly morph into fury.

I looked forward to being on the mainland, where the ground was solid. The constant strain that hummed when I was on the barrier island eased.

When I realized I'd overshot the store, I pulled into a lot, turned around, and backtracked. I found the supply store and parked. Bells rang over my head as I pushed through the front door.

No one was at the front desk. I crossed and rang the counter bell.

Seconds later, Lynn appeared. "Back for the rest of your order?"

I pulled a crumpled piece of paper from my pocket. I ran down the list for her.

"Got it all boxed up. Wait here."

She vanished into a back room and then appeared seconds later with two cardboard boxes loaded with supplies. "Here you go."

"Great." I reached for the first box.

The woman studied me over half-glasses. "You need to settle the bill?"

"Bill? I thought Kaitlin had an account."

"She's behind."

"How much?"

She laid the statement on the counter. Kaitlin was a grand in the hole. "Can I give this to her, and she can pay you with her card?"

"Her card was maxed as of last week. That's why she took a partial order the other day." She tugged the supplies back. "When you get the money, I'll have this for you."

I was not hiking back across the bridge empty handed. Kaitlin could settle with me when I saw her. I pulled out my credit card and watched as she swiped it. My phone dinged with a text alerting me to the charge.

Lynn handed me a printed receipt.

I folded it in half, creasing the edge. "Thanks."

"Thank you. See you in a month?"

"Sure." I swiped a box off the counter, and Lynn helped me load the other box into my car. Behind the wheel, I turned on the AC, headed back toward the water. I dialed Kaitlin's number.

"Hey," she said. "You survived the dive."

"And now heading back from the mainland. I picked up your supplies like I promised."

"And Lynn let you have them?"

"After she swiped my credit card."

"Sorry about that."

"What's going on? I thought you had more work than you know what to do with?"

"I do. The price of all the supplies has doubled, but I haven't raised my rates."

"This is bigger than rising prices."

She sighed. "It cost me a fortune to set up the surf shop. And that business has been slow."

"How slow?" I crested the bridge and saw the ocean in the distance.

"If we can make it to the surf competitions in August and pick up just a few more students, we might see our way clear."

"And if you don't?"

"It'll work itself out."

"That's where the money is going, isn't it? You've been traveling to surf."

"I racked up a few bills over the winter in Australia. I've been trying to pay them off. I'm moving money around like a juggler. I owe a few vendors."

"How many?"

"Three or four."

"How much?"

"Ten thousand, give or take."

The number was large for a business with a low overhead. "All that went to surfing?"

"Basically."

"How late are these invoices?"

"Sixty to ninety days." She shoved out a sigh. "I'm not a numbers person."

"Neither am I, but I'm an expert at fooling myself. And I've grown skilled at spotting people who do the same."

"What's that mean?"

I slowed as a light up ahead turned red. I didn't want to have this conversation on the phone. "I'll be at your house in ten minutes. Where are you?"

"I'm in Hatteras."

The barrier island town was sixty miles south of her surf shop. "Why?"

"Trying to scramble up some surf business. I might hold a clinic down here for the tourists."

A horn honked behind me, and I realized the light had turned green. I punched the gas.

"Look, I got to go," Kaitlin said. "About to pitch to a resort general manager."

Before I could say anything else, she hung up. I drove the last few miles and took a left toward the beach road. I parked outside the closed surf shop, punched the security code in the back door, and hauled the boxes of supplies to the back room storage closet.

Back in my car, I drove north toward Southern Shores. I admired Kaitlin for chasing her dream. Dreams came with rewards. But they also exacted a toll. My mother had chased hers, and it had cost her.

But not living life also came with a million different invisible sacrifices.

By the time I pushed through the front door of the flattop house, my body was covered in salty sweat. I stripped and jumped in the shower. The cool water felt good on my skin, and it was nice to wash my flat hair.

Out of the shower, I toweled off and changed into clean shorts and a T-shirt. I made a peanut butter sandwich, grabbed the manuscript, and then retreated to the living room couch. I spent an hour on the manuscript.

My phone rang. I recognized the number. "This is Tula?"

"This is Sharon Morrison. I'm with Morrison's Auction House. You left me a voicemail message."

"That's right. Thank you for your call. I have a houseful of furniture."

"Doug tells me you're closing the Brooks house."

"I am."

"I'd love to see what you have."

"Great. What time works for you?"

"Very early Wednesday."

"Perfect." We agreed on the time, and I thanked her again.

I looked around the house. I liked the old place and wanted to see it and its contents properly handled. I owed Dr. and Mr. Brooks that much.

CHAPTER THIRTY-ONE

Gertrude

Friday, April 24, 1942, 12:00 noon
Less than two hours until the Oceanus _is torpedoed_

I stood before the mirror and stared at the face that had no traces of the girl who'd once laughed so easily. I unpinned my hair and ran my fingers through the natural curls, just as Sigrid did. She clearly enjoyed the attention of men.

Alfred had said my curls looked too wild for a proper woman. So, I'd pinned my hair up. It remained in a twist for most of my marriage. I only let it down when Alfred and I were alone. He liked fisting his fingers in the strands as he'd pulled my face toward his. _"You have possessed me."_

I felt for the knife in my pocket. Everyone on the _Oceanus_ knew Gertrude Werner was pregnant, but once I reached the crowded docks of New York City, I would become invisible again. I'd been practicing the name "Sigrid Stein" so it would roll off my tongue easily. Sigrid and I were two Central European women with accents that sounded much the same. Our dialect differences were only noticeable in Vienna.

If I could get off the ship, find Chief Mate Riggs, and make it to the dock, I might make it past immigration. First, I had to outsmart William.

A knock at my door startled me. I quickly secured my hair and tucked Sigrid's papers away.

"Yes?"

"It's Dr. Brooks. I came to check on you."

I unlocked the door to find Dr. Brooks standing there with a plate of food in hand. "I didn't see you at dinner or breakfast."

"I was tired."

"I thought you might be hungry."

My stomach grumbled. "That's very kind of you, Dr. Brooks."

"Is everything all right?"

It took no effort to say, "As I said, I'm tired."

His eyes narrowed a fraction as he assessed my quickly pinned hair. "You look worried."

Why did Sigrid have his business card? Was he prepared to buy the rare volume? "I'm always worried. Who isn't?"

His head tilted as if he was solving a puzzle. "What's worrying you?"

Being close to him altered something inside me, the way salt changes water. "The U-boats. The baby. The war. There is plenty to worry about."

"I don't think that's what's troubling you. You've proven you're very resilient and willing to take chances, otherwise you wouldn't be here now." His steadfast gaze was hard to read.

"I'm not as strong as you think." I'd played this game with Alfred. I was always careful never to show him what I was thinking.

"I disagree." He shook his head slowly. "Reading people is what I do best. Listening to the stories they tell is how I make my way in the world."

I took the plate. "You inject too much into a simple woman's expression. I have simple goals and wish only to reach the United States."

He looked left and then right. "Is someone bothering you?"

I'd encountered plenty of trouble during the last seven months. My best defense was to avoid, deflect, and hide. "Why would someone bother me? I'm no one."

"I noticed the way some watch you in the dining room. Some have asked about you."

I could feel the color draining from my face. "Who?"

"William. And Sigrid."

The ship rolled, catching the crest of a wave. "They stare at me?"

"Why are they interested in you?"

"I don't know." My denial tripped over my lips as a weak whisper. "Perhaps because I am Austrian. Kindred spirit of sorts."

He shook his head. "They know you, don't they?"

And if I admitted the truth, then what? Would he save me, or would he use the information against me? "They might."

"From where?"

I rubbed my thumb against the side of the stoneware plate. "Austria, I suppose."

"Or Vienna." He spoke the word without a hint of a question. "How would a US industrialist in Vienna and his actress lover know you?"

"I don't know. And I don't care. Austria is the past. And I can't keep moving forward if I dare look back."

Dr. Brooks's eyes sharpened in a way I hadn't seen before.

His silence soaked under my skin and dug into my bones. "When we dock in the morning, I'll knock on your door and escort you to the immigration offices."

Would he? If he did deliver me to immigration, I could produce Sigrid's papers. But the credentials wouldn't matter if I didn't escape this ship.

"Chief Mate Riggs has made the same offer."

"He's a good young man. But he doesn't understand people like William and Sigrid. I do. We'll dock in New York late tomorrow morning. Wait for me. Stay in your room. I'll bring you a plate tonight and in the morning."

"You don't have to take care of me."

"I want to." He touched his index finger to his forehead in a salute. "The least I can do is get you safely into the United States."

"Why would you help me?"

"Do you still have the coin I gave you?"

"Yes."

"Good. It'll bring you luck."

He wasn't a remarkable-looking man, but when he met my gaze, I noted the slight hardening of his jaw. I now glimpsed a darker man accustomed to the shadows. That man was cunning and clever.

"Thank you, Dr. Brooks."

And then his expression softened. "Maybe one day we'll meet after the war, and you can tell me your entire story."

"It's very dull," I said.

"I doubt that very much."

CHAPTER THIRTY-TWO

Gertrude

Friday, April 24, 1942, 1:00 p.m.
Minutes until the Oceanus *is torpedoed*

I was eating the last of the breakfast Dr. Brooks had left for me. Several times I heard heavy footsteps outside my door, and I suspected they were William's. Whoever was there paused and seemed to lean close as if listening. I could feel eyes staring at me through the wood.

The baby kicked hard in my belly, forcing me to stand. I walked to the porthole, pressing my hand to the base of my back. My stomach had grown agitated over the last couple of days. The child wasn't due for another seven weeks, and I wasn't sure if this was normal or not. If I'd had my mother or another woman I could talk to, I might find out, but my mother was long passed, and I didn't dare try to contact anyone.

As I stood at the porthole, waves rolled high around the ship. They rose and toppled as the vessel cut through the water.

Several passengers had finished lunch; I could hear them moving down the corridor, and then doors closing and silence. I turned from the porthole. How many times in Vienna had I seen others lost and afraid, clinging to hope? Keep moving.

As I crossed the room, I felt a large jolt. It caused me to miss a step, and I nearly fell forward. I reached for the bunk to steady my pear-shaped body. The ship often rocked, but I'd never felt an abrupt jolt like this. I stood still, listening for signs of distress. Seconds passed. A hush stretched.

Assured the vessel was fine, I turned toward my bunk to rest. I was again mid-step when a siren blared and echoed down the empty hallway.

Dr. Brooks had warned me to heed any alarm. And Dr. Brooks had told me to get familiar with my life jacket. I hadn't done that. For the first time, I reached for my flotation device, then slipped it on over my big belly. I let out the straps several inches before I could fasten the side ties.

The alarm's painful shriek was unnerving. Excited voices in the passageway blended with hurried footsteps. The ship was in trouble.

I grabbed Sigrid's and my identity papers and tucked both in an oilcloth sack beside *A Farewell to Arms* and my few remaining loose diamonds. I checked the knife in my pocket and, despite my better judgment, grabbed the coin Dr. Brooks had given me.

If the ship hadn't been struck, the precaution might be for naught. I tucked the pouch inside my bodice.

This couldn't be the end of my life. I had come so far.

In the hallway, a growing tide of passengers dashed into their rooms and then hurried out likely with life jackets and whatever items they could quickly shove inside their pockets.

Realizing I couldn't stay in my room any longer, I opened my door to the chaos and stepped into the fray. I kept my head ducked, praying William and Sigrid cared more about their own survival than me. Several people wrestling with suitcases bumped into me, jostling me sideways and forward. None looked back or offered an apology. It was a sea of panic.

I maneuvered through the current of people and climbed the stairs. An explosion blasted from somewhere in the boiler room, and the ship tipped hard to the left. Passengers screamed, and the ones ready to hurry down the stairs toward me hesitated. Did they have time to reach their life jackets, or should they stay on deck?

I gripped the banister and continued up the stairs. As I reached the top, my stomach cramped so violently, I doubled over. Two men and a woman pushed past me. I breathed deeply. The noise around me faded as I focused on calming my body. "Not now. Not now."

Finally, the cramping eased, and I stood upright. I climbed to the top level and stepped out of the portal. I looked around and saw that so many had gathered on the deck. Artillery shells roared from the top deck as the sailors stationed at the large guns fired toward the rolling sea. Another woman bumped into me. I would have pitched forward onto the deck if strong arms hadn't grabbed ahold of my arm.

When I looked up, William grinned. "Careful. It's dangerous up here."

I tried to jerk away, but he held tight. "Let go of me."

"Not yet, Frau Gruber. First, we must get you to a lifeboat."

My hand slid to the knife in my pocket. I gripped the handle.

The deck sloped left. The gears designed to lower the lifeboats on that side had been partly destroyed. William tightened his grip on my arm and pulled me toward the lifeboats sailors were now uncovering. Other passengers were gathering around, and several crew members forced them back so that they wouldn't rush the first lifeboat. People clamored and pushed.

William yanked me forward through the crowd toward the front. "She's pregnant. She should be first on the boat."

I faced him. And in a swift impulse, I jammed the knife into his side. The blade met with resistance as the tip grazed a rib. He looked at me, astonished.

"The kitten has claws," he growled.

I released the handle, leaving the blade in his midsection. He yanked it clear, his fingers now red with dark blood.

Several people paused and looked in my direction, but no one noticed William. Some stepped aside for me. When I reached the lifeboat, a crewman lifted me and set me in the boat. William swayed, but he stepped forward ready to follow. Then he was blocked.

"Women first," Chief Mate Riggs said.

"I need to stay with her. I can help her," William insisted.

"Mrs. Werner, do you need his help immediately?" Chief Mate Riggs asked.

"No," I said.

"Then sir, you won't board yet." The sailor's hand dropped to the service weapon on his hip. "Back away."

William glared. His fingers gripped the knife at his side. He jerked his coat forward, hiding the blood bloom on his white shirt. "No need to worry, Gertrude. I'll find you."

Anger tightened his voice, and I knew I would suffer if we saw each other again.

"Don't worry about him," Chief Mate Riggs said. "Stay in the boat, and I'll take care of the rest."

I nodded toward Chief Mate Riggs. "Thank you."

There was no sign of Sigrid or Dr. Brooks as more women were helped into the lifeboat. In the chaos, the lifeboat still had several empty seats as it lowered. It carried only ten women and a young sailor, who looked as terrified as the passengers. The metal cables suspending the small vessel jerked. The gears turned and lowered the vessel. The sailor signaled for the mariner on deck to keep lowering the boat. I recognized Mrs. DuPont huddled at the opposite end of the lifeboat.

We were halfway down the tall ship when the *Oceanus* rocked again. The lifeboat banged against the ship, and I pitched sideways. The hard, wet metal of the hull brushed my shoulder. I peered down a narrow gap between the boat and the ocean as we dangled above the choppy waters.

Just as quickly, the ship tilted deeper, and the lifeboat shifted violently. The women around me screamed. I pressed my hand against the life vest and felt the metal coin under the fabric. I looked up toward the overcast skies, determined not to ask for help from a being who had tricked me so well before.

The cable on the mechanisms above us shifted, and we fell a couple of feet quickly toward the ocean. We hit the water hard. My hand went to my belly, and I leaned forward as another cramp tightened my midsection. Women screamed. Some wept softly.

A hand rested on my shoulder. Mrs. DuPont now appeared at my side. She was oddly calm as her chin rose in defiance. When she met my gaze, I saw a confidence I wouldn't have expected of her. "Chin up, Gertrude. We'll be fine. Your baby will wait until we are safely ashore."

I nodded, silent, as the spasm eased. "The baby is coming."

"Is this your first?" she asked.

"Yes."

"Good, the first ones take longer." Her gaze was determined, as if her order would make it so. "First things first. The sailors need to get us away from the ship. Once we're clear, then we can figure out the rest."

Cold ocean air washed over my face, chilling my flushed cheeks. I nodded.

Mrs. DuPont shifted closer to me. "How often does your belly cramp?"

Breathing deeply, I willed my body to hang on. "Every couple of minutes."

"That's not the kind of answer I want to hear," Mrs. DuPont said gently. "Tell your impatient little miss or mister to hold tight."

I gripped my belly as if I could stop it from expelling the child. "I'm not sure he'll listen."

Above us, the other two lifeboats were filling. I pictured William finding his way into one of the boats. I hoped I'd wounded him badly. At least my very impatient baby would be born soon. I could give the child to Mrs. DuPont. And if I was forced to return to Alfred, I would do it alone.

A wave smacked the lifeboat. I lurched forward and barely caught myself. Water splashed as the small vessel pitched back and forth. The sailor set the boat's motor in the water and cranked on it until it started. He steered the lifeboat away from the *Oceanus*.

I looked up toward the deck and saw Dr. Brooks standing close beside Sigrid. They were speaking intently, and then he looked in my direction. Their intense gazes floated down to me.

The *Oceanus* suddenly listed badly farther to the left, and the couple's terrified expressions came into focus. The lights on the deck flickered as if the generator struggled against rushing salt water. The guns kept firing rounds. Crew members loaded more passengers into the boats.

The U-boat wasn't in view, and it could be anywhere now, circling, ready to finish off its prey. We'd been warned so many times about their relentless hunting. But each day the ship had crossed more miles and as we had come within a day's sailing of New York City, I'd begun to think we'd escaped the underwater dangers. I remembered the map Chief Mate Riggs had shown me, and I pictured the jagged coast of North Carolina. How far away was it?

Another explosion inside the *Oceanus* rocked the interior. Through the shattered portholes, smoke billowed. Above, passengers screamed and shouted. More freshly fired lifeboat engines pulled hard against the sinking ship's undercurrent.

Mrs. DuPont took my hands in hers and rubbed them until they warmed. "See how lucky we are?"

"Lucky?"

"We're alive, my dear," Mrs. DuPont said. "And we have hope. The rest we'll tackle one step at a time. How is the baby?"

"My belly is calm for now."

"Good."

Another lifeboat slapped against the water. More people shrieked. Black smoke billowed from the guns' barrels as they fired more shells at a spot on the horizon.

"Gertrude!"

A breeze carried my name, and when I looked up, Sigrid was in the third lifeboat. Sitting up tall, she scanned the boats, searching for me. Rising and falling waves gave us some cover, but still I ducked and turned my face away from her.

"Gertrude!" Sigrid's voice skimmed over the rolling waves.

A chill skidded over my nerves. I thought about her alliance with William and then pictured her huddled close to Dr. Brooks on the deck.

"Why is that woman calling out to you?" Mrs. DuPont asked. "She appears worried."

"She's not my friend," I said. "She remembers me from Vienna."

Mrs. DuPont absorbed my stricken features and then looked again toward Sigrid's imposing frame. "She'll have to go through me first."

CHAPTER THIRTY-THREE

Tula

Tuesday, June 16, 2026, 12:00 noon

I arrived in the small island town of Manteo and followed directions to Mr. Green's, a ranch-style house located on a wooded lot at the eastern edge of Roanoke Island. I parked behind an older van and grabbed my backpack. A blue hydrangea blossomed, and neat gardens were filled with azaleas that had lost their spring blooms. A dog barked in the backyard, enclosed with a white picket fence. I climbed three brick steps and rang the bell.

I listened for the sounds of footsteps. When I heard nothing, I rang the bell again, when a door inside the house closed. The front door opened to a man with a thick shock of white hair and a deeply tanned face.

He studied me closely as if the past now stood on his doorstep. "Tula?"

"Yes. Mr. Green."

He pushed open the door. "Yes. Please come inside."

"Thank you for seeing me."

"Of course. I'm so glad Doug reached out."

Inside, sunlight streamed in from a large sliding glass door, brightening a small space with a large stone fireplace, a well-worn couch, and a dining table covered in books.

"I made coffee," he said.

"That would be amazing."

He vanished into a galley kitchen. Mugs clinked. The walls were covered with dozens of framed pictures of Manteo, views of the sound and the ocean. Some images were black and white and captured the area before the recent explosion of vacation homes and businesses. There were also dozens of local and regional awards on shelves and coffee tables.

Mr. Green appeared with a tray, awkwardly sporting two mugs, a bowl of sugar, and a small pitcher of cream. He set the tray on the large table in a small spot not covered with books or papers. "I wanted to clean up, but there's no place to put anything. As you can see, I've saved everything."

"No problem." When he motioned toward a chair, I took a seat.

I sat and accepted a cup of coffee. I poured in cream. As I looked at him, I realized I'd seen him the day I'd seen Dr. Brooks walking away. "You met Mom for coffee at the mall café?"

"I did. I think you were shopping." He settled slowly, as if his bones ached. He took the second cup.

I fingered the sea glass and coin. "I thought it was odd she'd given me money to shop."

"I really liked your mother. She was a free spirit. Made me long for the days when I traveled."

"How did you meet Mom?"

"Well, you know she was born in Norfolk, and she came down here often to dive and surf."

"She never talked much about living in the States. We never visited until seven years ago." I shook my head. "She was always so open and friendly with customers on our dive boats. She told stories of all our dive spots and the wrecks, but never here. I'm not even sure why she decided to dive the *Oceanus*."

"It was personal. Like I said, your great-grandmother, Margaret, was on the *Oceanus*."

I sat back, ready to ask the question that had been chewing on me. "Why wouldn't she tell me?"

"I don't know. She avoided talk of her parents. I just knew enough local history to know she was connected to the *Oceanus*. After your great-grandmother survived the wreck, she settled in Norfolk in 1942. She took a job with a bookshop."

"There's no mention of a Margaret on the ship's manifest."

"Your mother didn't have many details about Margaret. She died of cancer in 1978."

"We know she was pregnant on the *Oceanus*, or I wouldn't be here."

"Her married name was Riggs."

"There was a Chief Mate Riggs on the *Oceanus*."

"Kevin Riggs. He worked as a merchant marine for nearly fifty years. A great guy. He missed the hell out of Margaret after she died. They never had children of their own, but he adored her son."

"My mother never talked about her father. I don't even know his name."

"Eric Riggs. He married a local girl in Norfolk—Cassidy—and he was at sea a lot."

"Our last name is Cassidy. Mom must have taken her mother's name as her surname. Why?"

"Your mother said she cared for her mother while she was ill. Her dad was at sea when her mother died, and Mariah was angry he hadn't been there to help. By the time he was stateside, Mariah was gone. It was a shame. Eric would have been here if he could have."

I was talking about a stranger rather than my mother. "Mom never talked about any of this."

"She never liked to look back."

I shifted my focus back to the *Oceanus* so I could process what I'd just learned. "In the manuscript, the author focuses on Gertrude Werner and Sigrid Stein. Are either of those names familiar?"

"I know they were listed on the manifest, but other than that, I'm not familiar with them."

I thought about the pictures I'd found of the woman with Dr. Brooks. I had no idea who she really was. I opened my phone and showed him the pictures I'd snapped of the black-and-white photos. "I found these pictures in the house."

He adjusted his glasses and took the phone. "She's not familiar to me."

"It was taken in the 1940s. Maybe it was a younger version of my great-grandmother."

He shook his head and handed the phone back. "Maybe."

"None of the images capture a clear view of her face." A woman running from a violent husband would always have lived in fear. I added, "Have you heard the name Alfred Gruber?"

"No."

"According to the manuscript, Alfred was Gertrude Werner's husband. Though Gertrude's real name wasn't Gertrude. It was Naida. She changed her name when she fled Austria. I believe Alfred put a bounty on her head."

"I don't know about that." He sipped his coffee.

"Do you have pictures of Margaret?"

"I might be able to dig one up. If I find it, I'll text it to you."

"Thank you."

"Your mother sure did love the water. She said she couldn't imagine a life without it."

Bitterness tightened my throat. "Sometimes I think she picked it over me."

He sat back and pulled off his glasses. He seemed to wrestle with his words before he asked, "Did you know your mother was sick?"

All my images were of a tanned, fit, and energetic woman. "She wasn't sick. She was in top form."

"She had cancer. It was a brain tumor. It was a matter of time before the cancer caused dementia. She shouldn't have been diving that last day, but I'm sure she didn't want to die in bed like her mother, and she sure didn't want you to see her wither."

A dull headache pulsed behind my right eye. "She never told me anything about this. She never looked sick. She didn't see doctors. She hated doctors."

"A Greek doctor made the diagnosis when you were in Athens."

We'd been in Greece the year before she vanished. She'd had a bad headache that wouldn't let her go. "She'd taken the bus into Athens and left me behind at the boat with Nathan and her customers. I'd been annoyed because I wanted to see Athens. She said I had to stay and cover the boat. When she'd returned the next day, she'd seemed okay. Happy. Her headache was gone."

"The doctor put her on painkillers to manage her symptoms until she got stateside to see a specialist."

"She never saw a doctor here." I shook my head, searching for signs Mom had been ill. She'd seemed a little tired that last day, but nothing else. "She told you this?"

"I don't think it was her intention. But her morning medication was wearing off. She became pale. I got her a glass of water, and she took a pill. I saw the bottle. I told her my wife had died of cancer and had taken a similar painkiller."

Betrayal and hurt burned. "I wish she'd told me."

"It's natural for a parent to protect a child."

Memories of her skimming along the hull of the *Oceanus* flooded. She looked so free, at peace. "She left me."

"She knew the end was coming fast, so she reached out to Dr. Brooks and asked him to look out for you."

I thought about the old man walking away from Mom's table as she'd been speaking to Mr. Green. "Dr. Brooks. I've heard he was really old."

"A hundred and eighteen when he passed."

I shook my head, still marveling at the age. "We never spoke, but he moved like his entire body ached."

"His last few years were tough. He was ready to close out this life."

Wishes and curses—two sides of the same coin? "He set up the trust for you after your mother died."

"Why? And why would she reach out to him?" I sat back.

"He must have crossed paths with Margaret on the *Oceanus*. When you endure a torpedo attack with someone, it tends to create a bond."

"But Mom was a granddaughter."

"Dr. Brooks was known for his loyalty. You worked for his great-nephew's law firm, didn't you?"

I thought back to how I'd gotten the job. A recruiter from the firm had found me working in a coffee shop and had given me her card. She'd said the practice was looking for bright interns. I'd thought it was a con. But Dave had encouraged me to take the appointment. They'd hired me on the spot.

"His great-nephew sent me back down here to clean out his house."

"Maybe it was Dr. Brooks's way of telling you the truth."

His expression softened.

The sea glass and coin felt cool against the hollow of my neck. I'd never questioned why she'd given me money for a gift that day. But now, I realized she was trying to keep me away from Dr. Brooks and Mr. Green while they talked. She'd vanished the next day.

I opened my phone and pulled up the picture I'd taken of Mom and me that last day. She was wearing her dive suit, but there was no sign of the necklace. I'd assumed it was tucked inside the suit. She'd already left it behind.

"She wasn't perfect," he said. "None of us are. But she wanted the best for you. In her way, she tried to provide it for you."

CHAPTER THIRTY-FOUR

TULA

Tuesday, June 16, 2026, 3:30 p.m.

The sun was high in the sky as I drove north to the flattop house. Heavy traffic slowed the trip, and when I pulled into the driveway, I was exhausted.

Tomorrow the auctioneer would arrive, and we'd discuss the sale of Dr. Brooks's furniture. Unraveling the house's story had led me to my mother's truth. "Why didn't you tell me, Mom?"

The question was becoming as repetitive as it was annoying. I unlocked the front door, flipped on the light, and stepped into the living room that now smelled faintly of pine cleaner.

I made my way back to the office and grabbed a box of files and sifted through the papers. Maybe Dr. Brooks had a few more answers for me about Mom.

This box was filled with articles about more shipwrecks off the Outer Banks. I'd never met Dr. Brooks, but I'd heard over and over that he was precise and careful. And yet he'd saved maritime articles that dated back decades. If he was the Dr. Brooks in the manuscript,

I could only suppose surviving the *Oceanus'* wreck had connected him not only to my great-grandmother but also to anyone else who'd endured a sinking ship.

It took three hours before I'd sifted through all the old papers and shredded them. Several times the machine jammed with too much paper. I dragged the bags of chopped-up paper out to the recycling bin.

"Was this job another way to take care of me?" I asked.

I grabbed a broom and swept out the office. I hauled the desk to the side and pulled up the small area rug. Dust kicked up, and I was coughing when I noticed what looked like the seam of a small door in the floor. I set the broom aside, knelt down, and rapped my knuckles against the floor. The space underneath sounded hollow. Was this a door? I pushed on it, and when it didn't budge, I stomped on it. It creaked.

From the kitchen I found a dull old butter knife and returned to the office. I ran the edge along the joint, digging out what looked like years' worth of dirt. The floorboard began to loosen. I tunneled deeper until the edges had freed.

I pried open the wood until I could get my fingers under one end. When the lid popped off, I set it aside. I grabbed my phone and turned on the flashlight and searched the space.

Inside was a small box. Feeling a bit like Pandora, I remembered all my mother's cautions about finding trouble in the past. Was it best to leave history alone?

Maybe.

Carefully, I opened the lid.

Inside were old documents: passports, travel visas, and maps. There was also a set of tarot cards bound with twine that reminded me of the ones Dr. Brooks had used to entertain the *Oceanus* passengers.

The cards were well worn and had a slight greasy feel, as if they'd been handled countless times.

I shifted my focus to the documents. The four passports were from four different countries: the United States, Great Britain, France, and Austria. The credentials dated back to the 1930s, and they all had stamps from dozens of countries. However, the black-and-white identity photos were all of a younger version of Dr. Brooks.

The ordinary man who was easily overlooked and could blend in with anyone had traveled under multiple identities. "Dr. Brooks, you were a spy."

I searched the entire opening. I was about to declare it empty when I felt a small envelope tucked in the corner. I immediately recognized my mother's handwriting. The letter had been posted from Greece two months before we'd returned to the States.

My heartbeat pulsed in my head as I shut off the flashlight on my phone. I removed the letter from the envelope. Mom's handwriting, which had always been so precise and clear, looked shaky. I blinked back tears. As I read the letter, I grew sadder and angrier.

I texted Nathan.

Me: Can I come over? Interesting find at the flattop house.
Nathan: What?
Me: I need to show you.
Nathan: I'll be home in an hour.

I arrived at Nathan's rented condo forty-five minutes later and was relieved to see his truck was already parked out front. I hurried to his unit and knocked on the door.

Footsteps sounded, and seconds later the door opened to Nathan. His hair was wet and slicked back, and the soft scent of fresh soap drifted around him. His gaze skimmed over me. Appreciation flashed as quickly as it vanished.

My own flare of desire left me feeling helpless. "Hey."

"Come on inside." He stepped aside. "I've been out shooting B-roll today."

Now very aware of the salty sweat coating my skin, I said, "I should've showered before I came. I've been cleaning the Brooks house."

"Can I get you something to drink? I've got water and soda."

"A soda would be amazing."

"Done."

I followed him into the small galley kitchen. The appliances and countertops were as clean as I'd left them days ago. It looked like he'd barely lived here.

He popped the tops off the sodas and handed me one. I took a long sip before I reached into my purse and pulled out a large envelope filled with the documents I'd found. I laid them out on the countertop.

He set his untouched soda aside, wiped his hands on his shirt, and reached for the first: an Austrian passport. He carefully thumbed through the pages. "That's Atticus Brooks."

"They're all identity papers for Dr. Atticus Brooks. Different names but the same photograph. They were hidden under the floorboards of his office."

"Wow. Good for him. Looks like he was more dangerous than most realized."

I gulped soda, recognizing I'd drunk almost half. "Yeah. I guess he was one of those guys who secretly made a difference."

Nathan watched me take another sip. "You're going after that soda. Everything all right?"

"I also saw Mr. Green today. The reporter who wrote about Mom several times before she vanished." Heat rose in my cheeks.

He leaned against the counter, folding muscled arms across his chest. "And?"

"He said Mom was sick when she dove that last time. She was dying."

A muscle pulsed in his jaw. "Did he give specifics?"

"This reporter said it was cancer that would cause dementia. I can't picture Mom dying in a hospital hooked up to machines." I swallowed. "Did you know she was sick?"

"I knew she got headaches. When I asked her, she said it was allergies." He sighed. "But there were days that she seemed slow. And she took pills, which I assumed were for the allergies."

"You never told me."

"Every time I asked her, she'd insisted she was fine. You remember how your mom was. She hated anyone fussing over her."

"But I was her daughter. And she never said a word to me."

"I'm not surprised. She wanted to protect you. She wasn't the cookie-baking kind of mother, but she loved you very much."

I dug in my purse and removed the letter I'd found. "My mother wrote to Dr. Brooks about two months before she came back to the Outer Banks." My hand shook a little as I held out the envelope postmarked Athens, Greece. "She told him we were coming to the Outer Banks. She didn't know who else to reach out to. She said her father had always told her to call Dr. Atticus Brooks if she ever needed help."

A frown furrowed Nathan's forehead.

Frustration chewed at me. "The reporter said Mom took care of her mother while she was dying. Then she changed her name to Cassidy and left. She asked Dr. Brooks to look out for me. Why didn't she tell me anything about my past? It's one thing to protect me, but another to hide such key information."

"She was trying to protect you."

"She didn't."

"If your mother's illness was terminal, she made the only choice she could."

"But why not tell me?" My tone sharpened. Under all my anger and frustration was a deep sadness. My mother hadn't trusted me with the truth.

"Could you see your mother hooked up to machines and bedridden?"

"No. It would've been torture." And I'd never have wished that fate on her. I swiped away a tear. "Even if you'd been on the boat that day, she'd have found a way not to surface."

Anguish deepened the lines on his face. He stepped forward and pulled me into his arms. The embrace was the intimate connection of two people who'd shared the same loss. I leaned into him.

He was stable, solid, and in this moment my safe harbor from turbulent emotions. The past melted away, like the sun slipping below the horizon. I'd felt this once before, when I'd married Dave. I'd thought I'd found my sanctuary. But living Dave's life had grown oppressive.

I never wanted to resent Nathan. I pulled free. "I'm sorry. I'm getting weird."

He studied my face and traced my jaw with his calloused finger. His voice was raspy when he spoke. "Not weird at all."

Even as his gaze softened, I was mentally putting space between us. "Thanks for hearing me out. I just needed to talk to someone who knew her." I reached for my purse.

He stood back, confused. "You don't have to go. We can talk more."

I realized I cared for Nathan deeply. "No, I'm out of words. Maybe tomorrow."

"I'm always here for you, Tula."

But once this storm in my life had passed, would I want him here for me? "Thanks."

CHAPTER THIRTY-FIVE

Tula

Tuesday, June 16, 2026, 7:30 p.m.

I drove to Kaitlin's surf shop and was relieved to see the light on in the second-story apartment. I climbed the back staircase and knocked on the door before I fished my keys from my purse and unlocked the dead bolt. "Kaitlin! It's Tula."

She emerged from her kitchen. The shoulders of her purple T-shirt were damp from her loose wet hair. Cutoff jean shorts hugged her tanned, muscular thighs. She was carrying a beer. "Hey, I'm sorry you had to pay that bill for me yesterday. I thought they'd give me more time."

I kicked off my flip-flops and dropped my purse on a small table. I crossed straight to the refrigerator and plucked out a juice, then plopped on the couch as I twisted off the top. I'd forgotten about the money. "I know you're good for it."

She moved toward me, her expression a blend of worry and curiosity. "It might take a while."

I drank. "How did the sales pitch go?"

She cradled her beer. "Okay. They've committed to two Saturdays in July. If it goes well, they'll evaluate."

"That's good, right?"

"It's a start."

"Great."

"Why do you look like you lost your best friend?" she asked. "It's the money, isn't it?"

I pressed the juice to my temple. "It's not a lot of money."

"At the rate I'm going, I'll be ninety before I pay off my bills."

Having money, not having money. It seemed simple right now. "Can you take on more cleaning gigs?"

"I can." She shook her head. "But I don't want to. I have a dream to chase."

"Okay."

"I thought if I pursued what I loved, my life would fall into place. I thought I could be as free as you and your mother were."

How many of Mom's clients had envied our free life? How many people thought our lives were all fun and adventure?

"Our life had problems. Plenty of times it was hard. Never enough money, slipping out before the rent was due, bumming rides when the car broke down." Not enough money for medical care to catch a cancer earlier. Since Mom had died, I'd pushed the bitterness deep, stamping on it until it was so small, I could almost forget about it. But it was always there, waiting.

"Did your mother ever want a more conventional life?"

"No. Never. I asked her plenty of times—could we find a house and just stay put for a while?"

"What did she say?"

"She brushed me off. She'd been on her own since she was young and didn't know how to stay in one place."

"Sounds sad."

"I guess it was. She didn't have a conventional home and didn't know how to make one."

"What about her parents?"

"Her dad was gone a lot, and then her mother died of cancer." A restless spirit, many had said. A few times I'd called Mom "selfish" in private. But in public I'd always defend her. For better or worse, we were a team. We looked out for each other. Now, I could see others—I—had paid the price for her choices.

"You could have had my life. Stuck in the same place. Scrubbing toilets and pushing brooms. And now here I am, about to take on more cleaning gigs because my dream is too expensive."

I didn't have the mental space to hear her complain about a life I'd craved. Not glamorous. Few really were. But it was stable. And now she was endangering it with selfish choices that mirrored my mother's. "You have friends. A community."

"This place feels so small sometimes."

"You sound like Mom."

"What's that mean?"

I gulped more juice. "Every time we put down roots, Mom started to get restless. She complained about it feeling small. Didn't matter what I wanted. Always her."

"I'm not selfish, okay. I just want to live a bigger life."

"Bigger is not better." My patience was shredded. "We need to walk away from this conversation, Kaitlin."

Kaitlin shook her head. "Nope. We aren't doing that. I want to know why you showed up here tonight and decided you could dump your anger on me."

Waves of frustration were poised to knock me over. I'd come here to talk to her about my mother, but the more she complained about her life, the more I heard my mother. Mom was never satisfied. "You remind me of Mom. She was always on the verge of bankruptcy because she couldn't stop chasing the next adventure."

Kaitlin shook her head. "Is that why you quit? Did you decide, 'Better to live small than risk the price'?"

The honesty hurt. Mentally, I raised fists, ready to fight. "I didn't quit! I changed directions. I've lived a good, stable life."

She set the beer on the counter so hard, liquid splashed her hand. "You're divorced. You hate your job. And you don't have a home. Doesn't sound like it's working out for you."

The fight drained from me. She was right. I'd lived the last seven years trying not to be my mother. I'd married, taken an office job, embraced routines, and lived Dave's dreams.

When I didn't respond, Kaitlin added, "I remember she didn't listen to you." She hesitated, not voicing what I'd feared. That Mom knew she wasn't coming back.

"My mother . . . she didn't. She wasn't trying to hurt me. She just only knew one way to live her life."

"I get that. I do. And even though I was pissed at her for years for putting you in that position, I still admire her. Because she *lived* her life, you know."

"Unlike me, is that it?"

"Your words." Kaitlin picked up her beer. "Why did you come back? Why are you here?"

"Good question." I grabbed my purse and shoved my feet into the flip-flops.

"Running again?"

"Best of luck. I really hope you make all this work. The surfing is something special."

"Where are you going?"

"Back to the house in Southern Shores. The auctioneer will be there tomorrow. I want to get the house on the market as soon as possible. And get on with my life."

"In a cubicle?"

"What do you care?" I shouted. "It's my choice."

Her jaw hardened. "I'll pay you back."

"Okay. Pay me back when you can. The office job pays well, and I don't need the money."

"What's going on with you?"

Everything. Nothing felt right. I was drowning. "Overwhelmed. Disappointed in myself."

Instead of sympathy, I saw steely resolve. "What are you going to do about it?"

No pity party or soft landing from Kaitlin. It was up to me. "I'm calling Nathan. Time to dive the *Oceanus*."

Kaitlin blinked. "I wasn't quite expecting that. You don't have to do anything that extreme. Dive in a pool, walk along the beach, swim in the surf. You don't have to go to DEFCON ten."

Living in a military town had taught me a few things. "One."

"One, what?"

"One is the highest level. Five is the lowest."

She shook her head. "You get my point."

The muscles in my chest constricted. But I couldn't express my feelings out loud. And as Mom used to say, *Once you speak words, their power grows.*

"I get it. And I'm diving that damn wreck."

CHAPTER
THIRTY-SIX

Tula

Tuesday, June 16, 2026, 8:00 p.m.

Me: I want to dive the Oceanus.

I'd texted Nathan right after I'd left Kaitlin's and climbed into my car. If I'd given myself five more minutes, I'd have found an excuse not to dive. He responded almost immediately.

Nathan: Where are you now?
Me: At Kaitlin's.
Nathan: Come back to my place.

Seeing him again tonight wouldn't solve anything. Too much emotion churning in me. OK.

I tossed the phone into my lap and gripped the wheel. I nosed my car south back toward his condo. When I spotted his truck parked out front, I almost kept going. I didn't need to justify myself to anyone.

But I needed to prove something to myself.

I parked next to his truck and grabbed my purse. The walk to his front door felt so long compared to an hour ago. After hesitating for what felt like years, I rang his bell.

When he opened the door, he was wearing the same T-shirt and shorts, and his feet were bare. His dark hair was dry, and the thick strands, now curling at the nape of his neck, swept over his forehead. My mouth was sand-dry.

"Is your hair ever tamed?" I asked.

"Not often. It's kind of a trademark."

"I envy that freedom."

He cocked a brow. "Why envy it? Live it."

My body tensed with fear. "Right."

"You really are serious. You're still going to dive, right?"

Doubts tugged at me, trying to pull me back. "Yes."

"You don't have to prove anything to anyone. I think the dive would be good for you, but you don't have to."

"I have something to prove to myself."

"What?"

"That I haven't lost who I was."

"Fair enough."

He stepped aside and motioned for me to come in. My soda still sat on the counter next to his. This time, I noticed his shoes were lined up by the front door, his rain slicker was hung on a peg, and his dive equipment was arranged in a neat row against a wall.

"Still a stickler for routine?" I asked.

He closed the door. "Can't help it. Only way to keep your sanity when you're on the road."

"I've been landlocked for seven years. No issues with finding anything in all that time. Then I move here, and I'm convinced the Brooks house is hiding things from me."

He chuckled. "I have no patience for searching for lost anything. I need to know where all my stuff is, or I can't sleep."

"Yeah." I picked up the soda. It was warmer.

His eyes narrowed. "Why the sudden change of heart?"

I took a gulp and set the can down. "Kaitlin and I had a fight."

"Want to talk about it?"

"I don't."

"You sound like your mother."

"Shut up."

He laughed. "Is diving about Kaitlin or your mother?"

This dive wasn't about Kaitlin or Mom. For the first time ever, it was about me. "Me. It's about me. I can't ignore the ocean any longer. It won't allow it."

Anyone else would have found the comment odd, but he understood. The ocean ran in his veins. "Let's work our way up to the *Oceanus*."

"What does that mean?" All this buildup and then nothing. "I have thousands of diving hours."

"Skills grow stale over seven years. We can start in a pool."

"A pool. You're kidding me? Should I wear water wings?"

Even white teeth flashed. "There's a pool attached to this complex. We can do it now."

I looked out the sliding glass doors to the round pool, not even long enough to swim laps. "It's a bathtub. And the sun will set soon."

He chuckled. "Security lights come on. Visibility is great. Show me the water doesn't scare you. Then we'll talk about the *Oceanus*."

I ran my hand over my head. "I don't have a suit."

"Are you wearing underwear?"

Heat warmed my cheeks. "Yes."

"Covers like a bikini, right?"

"Yeah, I guess."

"Grab a towel from the bathroom."

I moved into the bathroom, closed the door, and pulled off my T-shirt and shorts. The black bra and panties at least matched, but they did little to hide the extra pounds. I wrapped a towel around my middle. "Shit."

Nathan was waiting in the living room, dive equipment now surrounding him. His gaze slid quickly over me, but it was unreadable, just like it had been all those times when we'd dived in Greece. I couldn't look at him without admiring his form.

Without a word, he grabbed the larger tank and a buoyancy compensator. "Carry your own stuff."

I hefted the smaller tank, a mask, and the BC. He opened the sliding door and walked toward the pool. Ignoring the water, I checked the tanks and the mouthpiece. Full tank. Free flow of air.

"Good, you remember the basics," he said.

Always check your equipment. How many times had Mom said that? I slid off the towel, settled the mask on my head, and pulled the tanks onto my back. I tested the mouthpiece again. The cool burst of oxygen rolled into my lungs.

"All good?" he asked.

My upper lip was sweating, and my stomach rolled. "Sure."

Suited up, he jumped into the water. He moved like a fish, his muscular arms pulling him to the middle. He motioned me to enter.

I settled the mask over my eyes and walked to the edge. I jumped into the water. The cold impact knocked my mask sideways and flooded it. I shoved back panic as pool water stung my eyes. I cleared my mask and put the mouthpiece between my lips. I breathed in more oxygen.

When I met Nathan's gaze, he was watching me closely, as if deciding how much rust had accumulated on my skills.

"Go on, dunk your head," he said.

I drew in two deep breaths and then tipped backward, letting the water flow over my body and face. The water rushed over me, encasing my skin in coolness. I pulled on the mouthpiece. Air filled my lungs.

The water slowly warmed, and the wetness caressed my skin. *See, it's not so bad,* it whispered.

The tension always tightening my neck and back slackened. I rolled face down into the water and stared at the plaster pool bottom. I kicked my feet and glided toward the deep end.

Come on in.

I angled my head down and kicked my feet. My fingertips skimmed the bottom. I rolled on my back and looked up toward the late-evening sky, now obscured by a watery haze. I floated along the pool bottom's rough surface. The water winked. I was weightless, and the world shifted from three dimensions to four. I swam to the shallow end and then back to the deep. My hair drifted around my face like an inky halo.

I didn't have on flippers, but the pool water offered little resistance. A pool wasn't the ocean, just like a minnow wasn't a shark. But still it felt like home.

I looked behind me and saw Nathan. His mask magnified his eyes as he watched me closely. He gave me a thumbs-up and swam toward me. As he reached for me, I thought he was brushing away my hair.

Instead, he yanked off my mask.

The flood of water cut through the tranquility. And for a second I was pissed and confused. Then I adjusted the mask and blew air outward to clear the water.

I faced him and raised my middle finger.

His eyes danced with laughter.

We swam in the pool for fifteen minutes before he motioned me upward.

We surfaced in the shallow end. I stood, pushed up my mask, and pulled the mouthpiece free.

"How was it?" he asked.

"Good. Think I'm ready for the *Oceanus*?"

He shook his head. "We'll try an ocean dive tomorrow. One step at a time."

"Fair enough."

❧

Inside his house, I toweled off and stripped off my wet underwear. I wrung them out and draped each piece on the shower rods. The dive hadn't been a challenge, but it was a first step. I'd let too much time pass since my last dive.

I wiggled into my T-shirt and shorts. When I returned to the living room, Nathan was leaning against the kitchen counter, a glass of water in his hand.

"I'm so sorry I wasn't there that last day. If I had been, I might have spotted red flags before the dive."

"And then what? You'd have saved Mom, and she would've died slowly in a hospital. She ended it on her terms." I didn't like her choice, but she'd lived life her way.

He set the glass down and laid his hands on my shoulders. His fingers felt warm and soothing against my skin.

I looked up at him. He'd hugged me earlier, but this felt different. He'd never touched me in such a sexual way. If there had ever been any physical contact between us, it had always been professional. A hand to guide me, an adjustment to my tanks, or a fist bump. I'd soaked up every moment like that, thinking it was a kind of tenderness.

But this touch wasn't cursory. It was intimate. I wasn't sure if I'd ever appreciated the pure excitement of such a simple gesture. Now I did.

And I wanted him as much as the seventeen-year-old version of me had.

Rising on my toes, I leaned toward him and gently kissed him on the lips. He tasted of salt. At first, he didn't lean into the kiss, and he stared, studying me. The eye-to-eye contact was intense. I feared I'd misread the situation. I'd always assumed he hadn't wanted me before because of my age. But maybe he just didn't want me. Maybe I wasn't his type.

And then his hands slid to my waist, and he pulled me closer. The strength of his hands was sexy. I was breathless.

"Are you going to kiss me back?" I whispered.

Instead of answering, he pressed his lips to mine. A groan rumbled in his chest as his hand slid up under my T-shirt. Since I wasn't wearing a bra or panties, his fingers easily grazed over my nipple. My knees nearly buckled.

"That the kind of kiss you want?" he whispered.

"I'm not sure. Try again."

He backed me up to the wall and planted a hand on either side of my head. "I want more than a kiss."

"Me too."

He leaned in and brushed his lips over my jaw and then down to the nape of my neck. His reluctance, if he'd had any, evaporated. My nerve endings tingled. And that hand found its way under the waistband of my pants. His kiss deepened and time melted.

Finally, he paused, his lips close to mine. "My bedroom?"

"Yes."

He kissed me again and pulled me down the narrow, carpeted hallway. I barely noticed the trek toward the bedroom. I'd dreamed about him more times than I could count when we'd worked together. He had been the fantasy. The dream guy who would make my world just perfect.

And then that world had shattered, and I was gone. But this moment wasn't going anywhere. He was here now. And I wasn't a kid. I knew what it felt like to talk myself into liking a guy. I didn't need any persuading with Nathan. I pulled off my T-shirt. My nipples hardened as the cool air brushed over the sensitive skin.

Nathan yanked off his shirt. God, he looked amazing. I hesitated a fraction before pulling off my pants. I wasn't the skinny bikini-clad kid I'd been in my teens. I had curves, and not all of them were welcome.

When he took me in his arms, I forgot about everything but this moment. As I'd dreamed, he lowered me to the bed, and I scooted up to the pillows. I'd never felt so unrestrained or so alive.

He smoothed his hands over my skin. "So pretty."

"You're the stunning one."

He kissed my breasts and my belly. The sensations overwhelmed my nervous system, now humming with desire I hadn't had in a long time. I'd been in limbo, encased in glass ever since the wreck. I didn't realize how frozen I'd become.

Nathan rose off me and leaned over the side of the bed. Cool air hit my warm skin. I reached for him, tracing my finger down his muscled back as he grabbed a condom from his wallet. As he slid it on, his hands trembled a little, and I was so charmed. Dave's hands had never trembled for me.

I rubbed my hands up and down his leg, anticipating and so ready. "You aren't nervous, are you?"

A nervous chuckle rumbled in his chest. "Maybe."

"You were a huge fantasy for me for a long time."

"Yeah."

Faint worries whispered. Fantasies were all well and good, but they often didn't live up to the hype.

When he had settled between my legs, he slowly slid into me, and I was pretty sure my out-of-balance life had finally tilted back in the right direction. It might still not be totally centered, but it was better. And this night, this dream, lived up to the hype.

CHAPTER THIRTY-SEVEN

GERTRUDE

Friday, April 24, 1942, 3:15 p.m.
Two hours after the Oceanus *was torpedoed*

The lifeboat rocked back and forth, farther away from the ship, which now listed badly to the left. In total, ten lifeboats had launched, and from what I'd heard from those on our boat, over a hundred people had survived the attack.

My belly squeezed again tightly, and I could barely breathe as the pain rocketed through my body. Mrs. DuPont had given me her hand, and I squeezed it with all my strength.

"That's thirty seconds," Mrs. DuPont said, checking the slim watch on her wrist. "Has your water broken?"

My skirts were wet, but I'd thought it was from the ocean water that had washed over the side of the lifeboat when we'd crested a wave.

"I can't tell," I said.

"I know, dear, we're all wet." She lifted her head and looked around, scanning the other boats. "Everyone in this boat, I want you to have a sharp eye out for that doctor. We're going to need him."

Several of the ladies rose and scanned the rolling seas. As soon as one boat appeared, it dipped quickly behind a wave, giving no one time to scan the occupants.

Finally, one young woman pointed. "I see him over there! His boat is about a hundred yards from us."

Mrs. DuPont stood up. Her gaze followed the girl's outstretched arm and pointed finger. Several times the shifting boat nearly sent her toppling forward, but she was stronger than she'd appeared and braced her legs against a woman sitting behind her.

She removed a red handkerchief from her pocket and began to wave it. "Hello!"

The other women began waving their arms and shouting Dr. Brooks's name. Several other ladies grabbed anything with color and began waving these items as well. The ocean's roar made it hard to hear, but finally the gestures and sounds caught someone's attention in his boat. I wasn't sure if Dr. Brooks noticed us, until the boat motored toward us.

I also wasn't sure how long it took for them to join our vessel, but by the time they did, my need to push was overwhelming. I'd attended the birth of a neighbor's daughter with my mother. She didn't have a doctor, but my mother had been so calm. The midwife was on her way, but the baby refused to wait. Mother and the housekeeper had delivered the infant while I watched.

I'd thought I'd understood the mother-to-be's plight, but I'd had no idea. All the good-wishing and soothing were blocked by agony. So many times, Alfred had spoken of the moment we would welcome our child into the world. Greta for a girl. Roland for a boy. But each time he'd mentioned a child, I'd stiffen with terror. The first time I was pregnant, I was terrified. And then the child had slipped away. I'd sworn I'd never get pregnant again and bring a baby into the prison of my marriage. And now I was doing just that.

Boats bumped against each other, and ours tipped slightly as one of the ladies left and a man arrived. I looked up and saw Dr. Brooks's face looming over mine. His expression was relieved and curious. Sigrid had been beside him and climbed onto the boat and took a seat. Her sharp blue eyes lingered on me.

"Thank heavens you made it, Dr. Brooks," Mrs. DuPont said. "I've never delivered a baby."

I tried to push up and move away from him, but the movement nearly split me in two.

"Steady, Frau Werner," Dr. Brooks said. "Now's not the time for moving. We must deliver this baby now, okay?"

I stared into his eyes and then looked at Sigrid. I couldn't decide if I was more afraid of them now or of giving birth. "I can't have this baby now."

"You have no choice," he said. "Ladies, I need blankets or coats."

One woman with a blanket wrapped around her shoulders draped it over my legs. Another reached for the first aid box each lifeboat was equipped with and handed it to Dr. Brooks.

Dr. Brooks laid his hands on my legs. "You must raise your knees, and your undergarments must be removed."

The idea of him touching me now in such a way reminded me of Alfred.

"That's a lady's job," Mrs. DuPont said. She shouldered him aside. She arranged the wool blanket over my midsection and legs before she reached up under my skirt for the knit undergarments. "Lift up a little, my dear."

Gritting my teeth, I lifted my bottom, and she slid off my thick cotton underwear. Another contraction racked my body with such intensity I lost my breath. "It's coming."

Mrs. DuPont sat behind me and helped me sit up. Another lady held up another blanket so my body would be shielded from everyone else's view. I couldn't look at Dr. Brooks. I closed my eyes and imagined Alfred at my side, staring at me with those intense gray eyes that always searched for flaws and reasons to punish.

A contraction overwhelmed my body, and I pushed hard this time. A scream escaped past my gritted teeth.

Push harder. I could hear Alfred's voice as clear as day. *I want my son.*

My body tightened, resisting the baby's release. I felt as if I were being torn in two. I didn't want to see the baby I was certain I couldn't love or condemn to life with his father.

"Don't fight it," Mrs. DuPont said. "Let the babe come. He needs to take that first breath."

But there should be no babe. My body should never have held on to this one. I'd been traveling for seven months, hiding in ports, avoiding police and the army, and going without food. My body should've let him go. But he'd held on tight, refusing to let go. Was his presence a miracle or a curse for us both?

Give me my son, Alfred whispered.

The lifeboat rolled and pitched over a wave. Sea spray misted my face, now damp with sweat and exertion.

He's a child of the ocean, the water whispered back. *Alfred will never have him.*

The ocean's whispered words felt like a gentle brush against my forehead. The lifeboat rolled over a tall wave and then crashed down. Tears rolled down my cheeks as I looked up toward the cloudy sky.

"You're safe," Dr. Brooks said.

I looked past him to Sigrid, who watched me closely.

"I am not. I am not."

CHAPTER THIRTY-EIGHT

Tula

Wednesday, June 17, 2026, 7:00 a.m.

Mornings were awkward. And I'd never done them well.

Before I opened my eyes, I listened to Nathan breathe quietly beside me. Last night had been great. Too great. And if I'd learned anything, good things always ended.

He rolled onto his back. "Stay."

"It's a busy day. I'm meeting the auctioneer at the house."

He faced me. His dark hair was messy from my fingers clutching fistfuls when things had really gotten rolling. His crooked smile made me sorry good things didn't last. "Do you need help?"

"No, I've got it."

"You need open water practice before we can dive the *Oceanus*."

"When do you think we can dive the wreck?"

He traced a strand of hair from my eyes. "If all goes well, a few days."

It would be easy to be with Nathan. "Great."

I raised the coverlet and swung my leg over the side of the bed. Carefully, I picked up my pants and shirt. As I pulled them both on, he rose and walked toward me, unmindful that he was naked. He cupped my face in his hands and gently kissed me on the lips. "I have two charters today, and I won't be back until after sunset." It would take him time to chat up his clients, unload his tanks, and clean the boat. He wouldn't be back here until close to nine.

"I'll catch up with you soon. The rest of the week is going to be crazy."

He laid his hands on my shoulders. "Sounds like you're trying to avoid me. Is it the dive or me?"

"Both, I think. I might need a few days to process."

"I thought what happened was pretty great."

"It was. Just unexpected."

"I get it." The patience in his voice made him so much more appealing. It would have been easier if he weren't such a nice guy.

"Last night was great. But . . ."

"You think it's all going to go sideways."

"I'm worried that I'm attaching to you out of fear. I did that with Dave, and it wasn't good for him or me."

"I'm not asking you to live my life."

"I know."

"Do you?"

"This really is a me thing. I don't trust myself not to grab the first anchor when life gets difficult."

He pulled me into a hug, and despite myself, I relaxed into his arms. He smelled of sunshine and his own musk. After he'd moved away seven years ago, he'd left one of his shirts behind. I'd slept in it for at least a year. "We can figure this out," he said.

I wasn't so sure. "Okay. For now, I just need a little time."

"I'll text you for our next dive date."

"Terrific." Either way, I was going to dive the *Oceanus*, and there was no other diver I trusted more than Nathan. I pulled out of his embrace, kissed him again, and then left.

When I slid into my car, I found him standing in his doorway, wearing shorts but shirtless. He looked a little sad, as if he faced another problem he couldn't fix.

I started the engine and backed out of my spot. The wheels were rolling, but I felt a little like I was on autopilot. At a stoplight, I leaned against my steering wheel, wondering why I'd let our relationship go to such a different level. Any other guy, and I would've appreciated the night and left with no lingering emotional strands. But Nathan was kind, and I'd always known I could rely on him. He'd never ask me to live a life that wasn't mine. And yet, I feared loving him more than I feared the ocean now.

A horn honked, and I looked in the mirror and saw an SUV behind me. I pressed the accelerator and drove back to the flattop house.

When I walked through the front door, light from the morning sun leaked through the shutters facing the ocean.

I showered and took time to dry my hair and apply a little makeup. I set up the percolator. I leaned against the countertop, my head in my hands as it gurgled. When the coffee was finally ready, I poured a large cup and made a peanut butter sandwich. I was halfway through the coffee and sandwich when my phone dinged with a text from Kaitlin.

Kaitlin: What's up?
Me: Just gearing up for the day.
Kaitlin: I'm sorry. I didn't mean for it to get like that last night. I really will pay you back.
Me: It's really not about the money.
Kaitlin: It is for me.

I sighed and sat down in the living room. I get it. Hard to need help.

Kaitlin: I'm the solid one. The practical one.
Me: I know. And I love you for that.
Kaitlin: The surf shop is going to work.

Me: And I'll get back to diving. Life is short. Do what we love, right?

A truck rumbled into the driveway, and I looked out to see **Morrison's Auction House** on its front door panel.

Me: Got to go. Time to sell some furniture.
Kaitlin: See you soon.
Me: Definitely.

I slid the phone into my back pocket, walked to the front door, and opened it to a woman in her early sixties. She had dark brown hair and bright red lipstick.

Her expression radiated curiosity when she saw me. "Tula?"

"Yes."

"I've been doing a lot of research on this house since you contacted me. I have to say, I'm excited to see what you have."

"Please come inside. I have coffee."

"No, thank you." She grinned. "I've already had a few too many cups."

"I'm often guilty of the same." I motioned her inside.

She entered, and immediately her gaze scanned the room. I could almost hear a calculator adding up the prices for a house full of mid-century modern furniture. Clearly fascinated, she appeared to be holding back her need to explore. "May I look around?"

"Of course."

Sharon scanned the stack of books in the living room and then moved to an upholstered solid-wood chair. "Do you know much about this style of furniture?"

"Mid-century modern. I've been reading up on it."

"What about the house?"

"I know a little about it. Not much as far as construction."

She walked toward a solid-walnut sideboard. "These homes were built by Frank Stick. He was an artist and developer who optioned the land in Southern Shores in the late 1940s. He oversaw drawing the plotlines, the installation of roads, and the building of the first houses. They were designed to look like cottages he'd seen in Florida. This house was one of the first he'd built."

"I don't see many Florida influences in the house. But the theme of the art is very nautical."

"I did some research. I found a picture of Mr. Stick and Dr. Brooks." She reached into her large purse and pulled out an eight-by-ten image.

Curious to see Dr. Brooks, I crossed to her. The black-and-white picture was of two men standing in front of this house shortly after it had been constructed. The builder was a tall, thin man with a vivid grin. Dr. Brooks's face was in profile, but I noted his expression was neutral. Beyond the passports I'd found in the floor, I hadn't seen any good pictures of Dr. Brooks except the ones with the mystery woman.

"Hard to find pictures of Dr. Brooks," she said. "I was curious about him, but there's not much written about him."

"I think he was very private." I reached for my phone and opened to the images of Dr. Brooks and the brunette. "Do you know who she might be?"

Ms. Morrison studied the picture, enlarging the woman's face. "I've never seen her before. You should check at the history center in Manteo."

"I will." I accepted the phone back and tucked it into my pocket.

"He was more involved in the community toward the end of his life. But for many years he kept to himself. I hear he wasn't down here a lot."

Dr. Brooks had come and gone like the tide. He'd drifted into Gertrude's life and into mine. "That's what I could gather."

She crossed to a stack of boxes. "What are these?"

"His books."

"I'll take these two," she said.

"Great."

"Why is the family selling?"

"His great-nephew is ready to let the property go."

"So, this will go on the market soon?"

"I assume so. My job is to clean out the house and get it ready to sell. I don't know what Mr. Brooks's plans are."

"It's a shame. I'd have kept this place intact. I'd have sold the furniture with the house. There's a market for this period."

"I agree. I like the house just as it is. But selling is not my call. Would you like the grand tour?"

"Yes, I sure would."

We walked from room to room, cataloguing the contents. When we entered Dr. Brooks's office, I stared at the simple cherry desk and chair. Mr. Brooks had said I could keep whatever I wanted from the house, and originally, I'd had no plans to keep anything. The desk was tempting, but I'd have no use for it wherever I was going. I sensed I was going to be traveling light. But I'd keep all the photographs.

"I think this house is ready for more people," I said. I wasn't sure what had made me the authority, but the house felt lonely. It needed life, activity.

"I'll take everything you want to sell."

"Seriously?"

"I can sell it all. Mid-century modern is hot now, and anything to do with Frank Stick is very collectable. I already have buyers for the house."

"Great. I'll put you in contact with Mr. Brooks."

"I can have my movers here next Monday."

And just like that, my life here was ending again. "Can you send me a contract?"

"Of course, I'll email it to you as soon as I get to the office."

"Terrific."

Ms. Morrison's wide smile was infectious. "I'm so glad you called. I'll take very good care of Dr. Brooks's estate."

I'd never met the guy, but he'd looked out for me. He'd given me a place to land when I was lost. And I'd do the same for him. "Thank you."

CHAPTER THIRTY-NINE

Gertrude

Friday, April 24, 1942, 8:15 p.m.
Seven hours after the Oceanus **was torpedoed**

The sun had long set, and the air had turned colder. Everyone in the lifeboat was huddled several feet from me, but they kept their gazes averted as if to give me as much privacy as possible. I lay against blankets and stared up at the night sky as the boat rocked over the rolling waves.

"You're doing very well, Frau Werner," Dr. Brooks said.

His soft expression hid so much, and I didn't trust his gentle tones. He was like the ocean, as calm as it could be dangerous.

I'd been running for so long, but I was again held prisoner in a life I didn't want. And if I survived childbirth, getting away from Dr. Brooks, Sigrid, and William with an infant would be doubly difficult. There'd been no sign of Chief Mate Riggs, and even if he did appear, even he couldn't swim against these strong tides.

"Don't look so distressed, Gertrude," Sigrid said. "You're young and strong. I know your baby's father would be pleased."

Not his child. This child belongs to the ocean.

The boat rolled over a wave, spraying water on my face. Sigrid wiped it off. My fears were silenced when another contraction racked my body. The strain was ripping me in two. Mrs. DuPont, who'd been sitting beside me, took my hand and allowed me to squeeze. My grip was strong, and I didn't care if I was hurting her.

The urge to push overwhelmed every cell in my body. Dr. Brooks laid his hand on my calves and slid his hands up my legs. I cringed and tried to draw my legs closed.

"You must let the baby come, Gertrude," Dr. Brooks said. "I want to see your baby safely into this world."

I shook my head. "I won't let him have this baby."

"He won't be a problem for you anymore," Dr. Brooks said.

"Can you be sure?"

"I am very sure." His steady gaze reminded me of an unruffled still lake. Inviting. Calm. But what was under the surface?

My body convulsed again with another spasm, and I could barely inhale. I was bare before this stranger, and even with the pain, my humiliation was real.

Dr. Brooks pushed up my skirt higher and pressed my legs apart. "It's going to be fine," he said softly. "I can see your baby's head. A few more pushes, and the pain will be over."

The waves rolled under me, coaxing me to relax and push.

Sigrid moved behind me, next to Mrs. DuPont. She steadied my shoulder with strong hands. "We must do this now. You must bear down."

I had no choice but to comply, no matter how hard I resisted. So, I bore down and pushed. My body screamed. A moan rumbled in my throat. My body felt as if it were splitting.

"Breathe," Dr. Brooks said. "Breathe."

I pulled salt air into my nose and huffed it out through my mouth. I repeated it over and over. The pain built. I was convinced that I was dying.

"One more big push and the shoulders will pass," Sigrid said.

Gritting my teeth, I bore down so hard I could feel the veins in my neck bulge. And then I felt the child leave my body. There was a rush of relief. My breathing grew rapid, and I was suddenly anxious to see the child.

I looked over my bent knees and watched Dr. Brooks holding my child face down. He was patting the child's back. The baby remained silent. Its small body was so still and small. It wasn't breathing.

Dr. Brooks turned the baby on its side and cleaned out its mouth. Another flip and smack on the bottom, and the baby let out a loud wail.

My sense of relief was sharp. Tears that I'd refused to shed for years welled in my eyes. I'd spent my pregnancy dreading this moment. I'd sworn I didn't want this child. I'd believed it was a curse, a tangible reminder of my foolish choices. And yet the child was here, and I wanted to hold it in my arms.

Dr. Brooks tied off the cord and wrapped the baby in a blanket. Sigrid moved beside me and accepted the child from Dr. Brooks. "Next, the afterbirth."

"Give me my child," I said.

"Not just yet," Dr. Brooks said. He kneaded my belly with his fist. The discomfort was as intense as the birth. But whatever was yet to come rushed out of me.

Sweat—or was it seawater?—plastered my hair to my head. "I want my child."

"Not just yet," he said.

He tied off the cord and cut it with a knife from the boat's first aid kit. He wrapped the afterbirth in another blanket and tossed it over the side of the boat. The ocean swallowed it up.

Slowly, he pulled my skirt down and lowered my legs. He nodded to Sigrid, who clung to the child for what felt like an endless beat as the boat swayed with the sea.

And then the infant's wails echoed in the night, tearing at my heart. The women and the sailor, who'd been so quiet, cheered. Finally, Sigrid, with all the others watching her, laid the child in my arms.

If all the others on the boat were to describe this moment, they'd call it touching and heartwarming. But I knew the truth. The presence of Dr. Brooks and Sigrid around my child and me was a dark and ominous threat as dangerous as any U-boat.

The baby stopped fussing and nestled into the blanket and my arms. I studied the small face. It was round like mine, but I could see hints of Alfred in the curve of its brow. There was a tuft of dark hair on the baby's head. Alfred now had the perfect weapon to break me.

"It's a boy," Dr. Brooks said.

"Congratulations," Sigrid said. "The child looks healthy and sound."

I understood the implication simmering under her words.

A boy. An heir. My husband would move heaven and earth for his son. I imagined Sigrid bargaining for a higher bounty on the boy.

"You're safe," Dr. Brooks said.

"How can I trust you?" I asked.

He glanced toward Sigrid. "I'll always protect you."

CHAPTER FORTY

TULA

Friday, June 19, 2026, 10:00 a.m.

Nathan and I had practiced diving yesterday. The first dive was close to the Nags Head shore, and that first dip was far more unsettling than the steady waters of the pool.

The second dive in the afternoon was farther out to sea. No wrecks to explore, but we swam past sandbars, fish, and shells. Each time, the ocean was on its best behavior. But it was a mischievous child waiting for its chance to throw a wave.

And today, we were diving to the *Oceanus* with several of Nathan's other clients. Nervous chatter swirled among the divers. They were excited and ready to jump.

"All right, folks," Nathan said. "Let's do this."

I'd hoped today would be different. My skills had come back to me on the practice dives, and my muscle memory had jumped to life. Intellectually I knew I could do this. Fourth time is the charm, right? But fear still hummed like a low growl.

I waited as the other divers took large steps into the water. One by one, they vanished under the surface. Finally, it was just Nathan and me on the boat. While he kept a keen eye on the others, he remained by my side.

We hadn't spoken about the other night or the future. Our arrangement had been professional and all business.

"Jump or dive, Tula," he said.

I'd played the water game when I was a kid. And Nathan and I had often repeated the phrase when we were diving on one of Mom's tours.

Either way, I had to decide. "You mean 'Jump or run,' right?"

"You've got this," he said.

You know me. Stop being so afraid, the water teased.

I didn't, but I settled my mask on my face, making sure the connection was tight. I inched to the edge of the dive platform, and before I could think too much, I leaped into the water. The cold waters swirled around me, the small waves buoying me up and giving me a moment to collect my thoughts.

I checked the straps on my tanks and checked my regulator. The waters remained calm and beckoned me forward.

I will behave. I promise.

Nathan watched me closely as he stood perched on the edge of the platform. He tossed me a thumbs-up, and I held up mine. He slid into the water as if he were strolling down the beach. As my heart slammed my chest, I found my bearings and then tipped forward and dove below the surface.

Under the water, he was at my side again. He studied me, searching for a sign that I should be pulled out of the water. But I was dealing with the water. We were getting reacquainted.

I followed him deeper, breathing slowly and swimming toward the wreck, masked by darkness. Nathan had told me over and over to return to the boat if I had any issues. The boat's hull rocked gently on the surface.

Kicking my flippers hard, I pushed deeper, farther away from the sun and air. Schools of silver fish with black stripes swam around me. A tiger shark drifted past, casting side-eye in my direction.

I again looked back up, catching faint hints of light, now as distant as the sun and stars.

If I continued down, my ascent would have to be slow and steady. No panicking and swimming wildly back to the boat. Spooked or not, I'd have to stay in control or risk the bends.

Shifting my focus back to the ocean floor, I kicked. The other divers moved easily, without fear. I followed. And just like that, after seven years of nightmares and old regrets, the *Oceanus* came into view.

Just like Bob's video, she lay on her side, her belly gashed with the fatal wound. Her metal hull was covered in barnacles, now a feeding ground for thousands of tiny fish. The death of this ship and the people aboard had created a new life for these creatures.

My mother would have been pleased that this underwater haven was thriving. She'd always felt more connected to the underwater world than she had to life on the surface or even me.

Welcome.

The whisper drifted around me like a current. I closed my eyes and savored the buoyancy I hadn't enjoyed in years. On land, my limbs always felt heavy and uncertain. But this felt right. Yes, the danger still existed, but it was forgotten in the wake of a glorious peace.

I swam closer to the *Oceanus*. And as the distance narrowed, fragments of the debris field—broken plates, bits of metal, a bottle— came into view.

My fingers skimmed over a remarkably intact dinner plate. Once, divers had collected these trinkets and displayed them in dive shops, on mantels, or in museums. But scavenging was now illegal. I was fine with that. What the sea had taken, it deserved to keep.

My gloved fingers skimmed the ship's metal surface, rough with barnacles. I thought about Dr. Brooks, the DuPonts, Gertrude Kevin Riggs, Captain Stoddard, and even Sigrid and William. They'd all set to sea on her, hopeful for a new life in the United States. And they'd all felt the jolt of the torpedo and experienced the solid ship under their feet rock and then tilt.

I thought once I was here, I'd feel closer to Mom, but I couldn't feel her. If she was here, the ocean had completely absorbed her.

Swimming along the wreck's starboard side, I passed portholes coated in sea salt, algae, and muck, as if the *Oceanus* had drawn a curtain closed on the past.

As I moved toward the bow, I swam by the gash in the side. For years this submerged hull had sailed through my nightmares. It had instilled fear in me and kept me away from the ocean.

But now, I could see it was nothing more than a lifeless artifact. It wasn't good or evil. It was metal and bone that had no power over me.

I lost track of time as I moved around the large guns and toward the center section. Disinterested fish swam past me, sliding in front but always out of reach.

This is for you, Mom. I hope you're at peace.

A tap on my shoulder, and I turned to see Nathan. He was motioning his thumb topside. Time to go. Time to leave the *Oceanus* behind.

I nodded. As I turned, my necklace floated and tapped me under the chin. The sea glass had been with me every day since I'd bought it in that little shop. It was my final, almost-birthday gift from Mom. And the coin had joined it days later.

The current tugged at the coin and glass. It would have floated toward the wreck if not tethered by the cord around my neck.

Do you want it?

The ocean tugged.

I unfastened the cord and let the crystal and coin dangle. The undercurrents strengthened and churned around them. It was the last I had of my mother. The last tether.

My fingers opened, and the crystal and coin slid free, floating around my open palm before the duo fell like a creature finally free from captivity. The stream caught it. Fish circled around the pair in quick tight loops.

The water dragged the crystal willingly toward the gash in the *Oceanus'* side. It vanished into the darkness.

I hesitated another moment before making my way slowly to the surface.

CHAPTER
FORTY-ONE

Tula

Friday, June 19, 2026, 11:00 a.m.

Once Nathan and I had returned to the boat, I was breathless. I pulled off my mask and shrugged off my tanks. Neither of us spoke as the other divers chatted about what they'd seen. He piloted the boat along the shore, and soon we were docked in the harbor. After the other divers had left, I lingered.

"You okay?" he asked.

I stared at the still, calm waters under the vivid blue sky. "I am."

"Your mom would have been proud."

I shook my head. "If she were here, she'd ask what took me so long."

His smile didn't dim the concern in his gaze. "You've jumped a big hurdle. What next?"

"Good question." I could no longer see myself back in the cubicle. Like it or not, I was bound to the ocean. "I might stay here for a while. Kaitlin will rent me a room."

"I'll be here for the summer."

He let the statement trail. No promises or big asks about the future.

"I was anchored to my mother. I was anchored to Dave. I don't want to be tied anymore because I'm too afraid to take care of myself."

He frowned. "I'm not asking you to do that."

I sighed. "I know. But you're the kind of person I could become attached to very quickly."

A brow raised. "And that's bad?"

"Not bad. I just need to figure me out a little. I need to know I can handle life without a prop."

"I know you can, but you need to see it for yourself." He lowered his tanks to the deck. "You aren't really like your mother. She was always impatient, unapproachable at times. Often, she jumped before she thought. You were always more careful. And that's a good thing."

"Maybe too cautious," I said.

"We can't fight our nature."

I closed my eyes. "I've read the manuscript. My employer said I could keep it. You can have a copy of it and use it for your film."

"You're sure?"

"Yes. I've made my peace with the *Oceanus*. And Mom. But I don't know who died with the wreck and who survived. I need to get to the historical center in Manteo and see if they have a survivors list. I'm hoping the list will tie up a lot of loose ends."

"Want me to come?"

"No. Thank you. I need to see this through myself."

"Fair enough." He leaned toward me and gently kissed me on the lips. The warm, soft touch made me want him more. "Meet me for burgers at Arthur's later?"

Dinner I could commit to. "Sounds good."

I dried off and changed out of my suit and into shorts and a T-shirt. I left Nathan on the dock and hurried to my car. By this time of day, folks generally were off the beach and shopping or hunting for an early dinner spot in Manteo.

The Outer Banks History Center was located near Festival Park, which overlooked Albemarle Sound. The center's one-story building was nestled in a cluster of trees.

The air was hot and humid, and by the time I reached the front door, sweat dampened my neck and upper lip. Inside the air was cool and the lighting low. I crossed to the central desk, where a woman was studying a computer. She looked up as I reached the desk.

"Can I help you?"

"I was hoping to find out more about the *Oceanus* shipwreck. The ship was sunk by a U-boat torpedo in April 1942."

She looked at the clock. "Do you have an appointment?"

"No. Do I need one?"

"Usually, yes." She studied my damp hair and the faint line of the dive mask still on my face. "What do you need?"

"I found an old manuscript that details the ship's last voyage. But the story kind of stops. I was hoping there was a list of survivors." I decided to play the mom card. "My mother died diving that wreck seven years ago."

"Mariah Cassidy?"

"That's right."

She studied me a beat. "I remember that accident. You're Tula Cassidy."

Hearing my name reminded me again of small-town living. "That's right."

"I thought you'd moved to Norfolk."

"I did. And now I'm back for the summer. I'm cleaning out Atticus Brooks's house in Southern Shores."

"Ah, Dr. Brooks was very generous to us. We wanted to dedicate a room to him, but he refused."

"He was very private."

"Makes sense you'd be curious about the wreck."

I hated looking back, but I couldn't go forward until I understood the past better.

"I think Atticus Brooks wrote the manuscript, but there's no name on the pages." I removed my phone from my pocket and pulled up the black-and-white images. "This is Dr. Brooks and a mystery woman, around 1946. I'd also like to figure out who she is."

She pulled glasses from the top of her head to her nose and looked closely at the phone screen. "Let me search the database."

"What do you know about Dr. Brooks?" I asked.

"A scholar, benefactor, kept to himself. Made several generous donations, not only to us but to ocean-related foundations. Everyone knew of him, but no one really knew him."

She typed, pressed keys, and then leaned forward. "I have a list."

"Seriously?"

She pressed another button, and a printer on the desk behind her came alive.

"That was easy," I added.

"We try to stay organized." She leaned forward. "What does the manuscript cover?"

"A handful of people who were on the ship at the time it sank."

"And it's definitely nonfiction?" she asked.

"I think. It doesn't feel made up."

"The best fiction books don't."

"If you think of anything, call me," I said. "I'll give you my number."

"Of course. Can you text me those pictures of Dr. Brooks? I'd like to add them to the database, and I might be able to figure out who the woman is."

When she gave me her number, I texted the pictures, along with my name and number. As I scanned the printed list, I searched Margaret's name but didn't find it. "My great-grandmother was on the *Oceanus*. But I don't see her name on any list."

"What was her full name?"

"Margaret Riggs. There was a Chief Mate Kevin Riggs on the *Oceanus*. I think she married him. I do know Margaret and her husband lived in Norfolk."

"Maybe the chief mate told her stories that she recounted as her own," she said.

"I have no idea."

"Let me see what I can find."

"Thank you," I told her.

"If you want to find a permanent home for the manuscript, send it to us. We'd love to have it."

"Once I've copied it, I'll give it to you."

"Excellent. So glad you stopped by today, Tula."

I left the center and slid into my hot car, fired up the engine, and switched on the air-conditioning. I studied the list of names. It was on US Navy stationery, and the typeface was from an old typewriter. I scanned the list. Among the living were Dr. Brooks and Sigrid Stein. The DuPonts had survived, as had Margaret's husband, Chief Mate Riggs. Captain Stoddard was listed among the dead. William was listed among the dead. There was no mention of Gertrude Werner or her baby.

Gertrude had taken Sigrid's identity papers. Maybe she'd entered the country under her name. But what happened to Sigrid? And Alfred? As much as I didn't like either of them, I wanted to know their fate. I had many pieces of this puzzle in place, but the picture wasn't complete.

CHAPTER FORTY-TWO

Gertrude

Saturday, April 25, 1942, 4:00 a.m.
Eight hours after the Oceanus *was torpedoed*

I woke with a start and slowly realized it was early morning. For a moment, I was aware only of my aching body and the cold, wet wood pressing into my back. And then, just as quickly, I realized my stomach was as empty as my arms. I sat up, searched the women in the boat. The other women were dozing, all huddled in coats and blankets. Dr. Brooks sat against the side of the boat, his arms crossed over his chest and his eyes closed. The other lifeboat had drifted away from our tiny vessel and bobbed in the distance.

Sigrid sat beside me, gently rocking the baby.

"Give me my child," I said.

She carefully lowered the infant into my arms. "He's perfect. He reminds me so much of my daughter."

The warmth of the baby's small body against my arms eased some of the fear gripping me.

"I think he'll be hungry," Sigrid said. "Do you know how to feed him?"

I had a general sense, but I'd never had anyone show me.

Her face was barely visible in the moonlight, but I could see the seawater had washed off her makeup, revealing freckles splashed over her nose. "I can help you, if you'll allow me."

"You can't have him," I said.

"I don't need him now. That torpedo has erased me and my past. Once we are saved, I'll make up a new story."

"What about your family?"

"I will return and save them." Such confidence.

The baby turned his mouth toward my breast and rubbed his lips. Not finding what he sensed must be there, he began to fuss.

Sigrid rose. "Unbutton your blouse."

Heat warmed my cheeks. The idea of baring my breast in public was unsettling.

"Everyone is asleep. And you're the only one who can feed him now."

Now. As if there would be others later. I unfastened my buttons, exposing a silk camisole. My breasts were tight and my nipples hard.

Sigrid unknotted a scarf from around her shoulders and draped it over my breast and the baby. "Put the nipple in his mouth."

I wrestled my breast free and held the baby closer. The child rooted but didn't seem to attach. He began to fuss.

Sigrid removed her gloves. "May I?"

Before I could answer, she'd adjusted my breast so my nipple landed directly in the baby's mouth. He latched on to me and began to suck hard. The sensation was both shocking and comforting.

Sigrid sat beside me. "You and the baby will get used to each other. It takes time."

I studied the baby. He fisted his tiny hands and kneaded them into my breast.

"See, he knows," Sigrid said gently.

The purity in his face was as touching as it was tragic. I was almost as innocent when I'd married his father. I'd believed in fairy tales and happy endings. Now, somehow, my son and I would have to make our own ending.

"You told William about me."

She sighed. "I did. I needed to maintain his trust."

I hadn't expected her loyalty, but the betrayal stung. "You and he wanted to force me back to Vienna."

"He won't be doing that now."

"Where is he?" I scanned the calm, rolling waters as if I expected him to rise like a leviathan.

"The *Oceanus* owns him now."

"What does that mean?" When I saw him last on the deck, he'd been furious and bleeding.

She shook her head. "He's dead. He can't hurt anyone."

I thought about the knife in my hand as I'd plunged it into his side. Had I done more damage than I'd realized? "He was on the deck with me."

She shook her head slowly. "The final report will simply list him among the dead. How he died doesn't matter."

But I would carry the memory of his death. "You can still betray me."

"I don't need to. Dr. Brooks offered a different solution."

"What?"

"He has connections. He'll help me return, and if I help him, he'll find my family."

"Help him?"

"A man like him is always searching for a good contact."

I looked over at Dr. Brooks. His eyes were closed, but the slight tension in his jaw suggested he was listening and paying very close attention.

The baby continued to nurse and soon seemed to have gotten his fill. I removed my nipple from his relaxed lips and refastened my blouse. In the distance, another lifeboat bobbed on the horizon.

As I searched the vessel, I noticed someone stand up and wave their hands.

The currents carried us close, but never near enough for the boats to join. As if sensing the shift in my attention, Dr. Brooks opened his eyes.

When he stood, the other ladies on the boat roused. They looked around, hope brightening their tight expressions.

"We must try to stay close to them," Dr. Brooks said.

"As long as the engine holds, we can," the sailor said.

"And if the engine fails, we'll row," Dr. Brooks said. "I don't intend to spend another night bobbing and weaving, and we have a woman in need of medical attention."

The sailor straightened his shoulders. "We're in the shipping lanes. And there could still be U-boats."

"They wouldn't shoot a life raft," Dr. Brooks said. "We carry no bounty that's of value to them now."

"That doesn't mean they won't."

Dr. Brooks ignored the comment. "The radio operator got off a Mayday, correct?"

"Yes, sir."

Dr. Brooks removed his jacket and rolled up his shirtsleeves. "The engine?"

The sailor yanked on the pull cord. The engine sputtered, sounded as if it would catch, and then faded to silence. He pulled again. And again. "Out of gas," the sailor said.

"Then we row. We will be easier to find if there are several boats together."

The soldier nodded. "Yes, sir."

The men each settled on either side of the lifeboat, forcing two women to shift their positions, and took the oars in hand.

"Frau Werner, are you in immediate need of assistance?" Dr Brooks wasn't looking in my direction, but I suspected he was very aware of me. To underestimate Dr. Brooks would have been foolish.

"I'm well enough."

"Good."

The tension on the boat eased. The two men dug the oars into the waters, which parted for us, and the vessel moved easily toward the other lifeboat.

CHAPTER FORTY-THREE

TULA

Thursday, July 2, 2026, 9:00 a.m.

The next couple of weeks were hectic. I coordinated with the auction house about the picking up and selling of the furniture. I duplicated the manuscript and gave one copy to Nathan and kept one for myself. I donated the original to the historical center.

The movers came yesterday and cleared out the furniture, leaving me with a mattress and bedding. The auction was on Saturday, and I instructed the Morrisons to send the final check to Mr. Brooks in Norfolk.

I'd dived with Nathan as often as I could and had become a kind of assistant on his dives. The nervous first-timers and I got along great. When Kaitlin's summer help texted and said they'd be a few weeks late, I also kept cleaning houses with her. She was a long way from paying me back, but her surf camps were filling up, and she'd sent me a few small Venmo payments.

I also did some internet research with the history center's help. I'd been curious about Alfred Gruber's fate. It took a few days, but the librarian had reported back that she'd found an Alfred Gruber, born in Vienna in 1910. He'd died in April 1942, when a boat he'd been traveling on the Danube River had unexpectedly sunk. He'd drowned. Still no word on the mystery woman pictured with Dr. Brooks.

Though Mr. Brooks had said I didn't need to send him updates, I had sent weekly reports. Seven years at the firm had left me with a begrudging respect for documentation. He'd never responded to my reports until last night. He'd emailed back that he'd be at the house sometime today.

So, I'd awoken early and mopped the floors and wiped down the kitchen and bathrooms again. I wanted the Southern Shores house to be spotless. Seemed fitting that I give Dr. Brooks's home the best send-off I could. Once the house sold, Kaitlin had said I could sleep in her spare room again. Nathan had offered me the spare room in his condo. I'd already decided I wasn't staying here. Like my mother, I loved the beauty, but I was dreaming of far-off places I'd never seen.

Nathan had told me last night he was leaving the Outer Banks in early August. He was going to Florida to head up a diving expedition. He didn't ask me to come, and I hadn't offered. I really liked him, but I still feared I would let his life become mine.

The front doorbell rang, and as I crossed the center room, my footsteps echoed. I opened the door to find Nathan on my doorstep. His hair was damp, and he wore the same gray T-shirt, board shorts, and flip-flops I'd seen him in so many times. I was beginning to wonder if he owned any other clothes.

"Hey, what are you doing here? I thought you had a lesson."

"He canceled. Rescheduled for tomorrow."

"So, a rare morning off."

He ran long fingers through his hair. The morning light caught hints of silver that made him look even more attractive. "It almost never happens."

I stepped into a hug. He wrapped his arms around me. He felt so good. Too good.

"I finished the manuscript," he said.

"Kind of a big loose end, isn't it? Baby born on the high seas, and then nothing."

"Did you find out more about your great-grandmother, Margaret?"

"No pictures. Nothing in the newspaper databases, not even an obit. The only time she's mentioned is in Kevin Riggs's death notice. She's referred to as 'his late wife, Margaret.'"

"I'd like to know where everyone ended up."

"The history center has no leads so far, but they promised to keep digging."

He stepped inside and looked around the empty room that smelled faintly of pine and window cleaner. "This place is something. I got to hand it to Dr. Brooks. He picked a great location."

"He'd lived close to Margaret and Kevin in Norfolk. Do you think the proximity of this house to the *Oceanus* was an accident? It was his vacation house, but what are the chances?"

"I think he knew exactly what he was doing." He drew in a breath. "I wanted to let you know, I'm leaving for Florida sooner than expected," Nathan said.

We hadn't slept together since the first time. I'd worried about muddying the waters, and he'd been patient about my reservations. But we dove often, ate dinner at Arthur's, and took long walks on the beach. I'd enjoyed getting to know him and hearing stories of his life. The idea of not seeing him again was more deflating than I'd imagined. I didn't need him to stay, but I would miss *him* terribly. "When?"

"Two weeks."

"So soon."

"Yeah. I need to be down there before hurricane season kicks up. They made me an offer I couldn't refuse."

"I get it. You got to go where the money is."

He laid his hands on my shoulders. He hadn't said the l-word, but I could see it churning in his eyes when he looked at me over burgers or across the dive boat. Maybe he was afraid the words would send me running. Maybe they would.

He brushed a hair strand off my forehead. "I know you well enough now to realize you're never going to ask for anything. But I'm doing the asking, okay?"

"Okay?" The underlying question couldn't be hard to guess.

"Will you come with me? You're an excellent diver, and you have enough skills to get a job anywhere. So, if you came with me to Florida, you could still be doing your own thing. It's not like we'd be inseparable." And before I could answer: "I am not your anchor. You're unbound and free-floating."

Before I could reply, there was another knock at the door. Nathan muttered a curse.

"Hold that thought," I said.

My footsteps echoed in the empty house as I crossed to the door. When I opened it, I found Mr. Brooks standing on the front steps. He looked so much like his great-uncle that it was hard not to mistake the two for each other. He wore khakis, a white pullover, a blazer, and loafers. Casual but still kind of formal. "Mr. Brooks. Please come in."

"As I said in my email, I'm here on vacation for a week. Made sense to stop by and see the house. Your detailed reports have been very interesting."

In the last report, I'd included a PDF of the manuscript pages, as well as the images of Dr. Brooks in front of the house with Frank Stick and the mystery brunette. "I hope they were helpful."

"Fascinating. The detailed inventory list of furniture and what they sold for at auction was thorough." He reached into his pocket and removed an envelope. "I'd like you to have this."

My gaze drifted to the slim envelope. "What's this?"

"It's from the sale of the furniture."

"Does the number work for you? I thought the auction house did a great job of getting top dollar." I knew the number because I'd been on site the day of the sale and reviewed all the receipts.

"It's acceptable. And I'd like you to have it."

"It's too generous for me to accept."

"The estate doesn't need it. And my great-uncle would rather you have it."

"He's already done so much for me. He set up the fund for me, and I'm pretty sure he helped me get the job at your firm."

"We were lucky to have you."

"I can't take this money."

"Yes, you can."

He spoke with such certainty I didn't argue. "This is very generous. Thank you." I sensed Nathan behind me. "I'm sorry, I didn't introduce you two. Mr. Brooks, this is Nathan Rogan. We dove the *Oceanus* together a few weeks ago."

Nathan crossed and extended his hand. "It's a pleasure to meet you, Mr. Brooks. I had the pleasure of reading your great-uncle's manuscript, and it was fascinating."

Mr. Brooks accepted Nathan's hand. "Pleasure is mine. I read the copy Tula sent me. Never a more documented wreck, I think. Nan always said you had an excellent eye for detail, Tula."

Nan hadn't always loved that attention to detail. She'd scrawled "compulsive" on my last job review. "Hopefully I didn't overwhelm you."

"Not at all." He looked around the house. "You've done an amazing job. The house feels alive again."

"It was always alive. Just a little dormant. Can I give you the grand tour?"

"Sure."

I walked both men through the house and each clean room. I felt a sense of satisfaction that I was leaving it in good shape.

"Whoever buys the house will have a gem," I said. "The sunrise views in the morning are amazing."

"You're right about that. I had a lot of happy memories in this house."

"You were here as a kid?" I asked.

"I was here often." He walked into his great-uncle's office and looked toward the hiding space in the floor, the cleaned seams now clearly visible. For a moment, he said nothing. "Excellent work."

"Thank you."

"The house has already sold," he said. "Word of mouth, so I never needed an agent."

"I can be out today, if I need to be."

"Beginning of August is fine."

"In the manuscript, your great-uncle delivered a baby on the lifeboat. Did that really happen?"

"I don't know. My great-uncle never told me much about the wreck."

"He was a medical doctor?"

Mr. Brooks shook his head. "He had several PhDs and was well read. I assume he'd read about delivering babies in a book."

"He sounded like he was confident in the manuscript." I hesitated. "Do you think Dr. Brooks wrote it?"

"I don't know."

"Do you think he had anything to do with William's demise?"

Mr. Brooks looked amused. "I'm an attorney. I could never answer a question like that."

"The manuscript just ended. There was no accounting of the passengers. I was especially interested in Gertrude and Sigrid."

"I can't help you with that," Mr. Brooks said.

"My great-grandmother Margaret was on the *Oceanus*. I didn't see Margaret's name on the ship's passenger list."

"I'm glad you mentioned that. I almost forgot. I found a picture of Margaret in my great-uncle's files." He reached into his breast pocket and pulled out an envelope and handed it to me.

I opened the envelope and pulled out the single photo. It appeared to have been taken in the late 1940s. It was of a woman, a man, and a little boy. I recognized the woman immediately.

"That's Margaret and Kevin Riggs and their son," Mr. Brooks said.

"She's the woman in the pictures with Dr. Brooks. They were standing in front of this house."

"She must have visited my great-uncle several times."

"Must have."

He drew in a breath and turned toward the front door. "I'll leave you both now. I just wanted to give you the check and picture, see the house one last time, and offer my thanks again. Are you coming back to the firm in September?"

"I've drafted an email. I'm sending it to Nan in the morning, right after I call her. I won't be coming back."

His smile showed no hint of surprise. "I thought as much. Something about the ocean that's hard to resist. I can never stay away too long."

"I might have argued that point a few months ago, but you're right. I'll always be close to it."

"I'm glad to hear it. Good luck to you both."

He left, and I watched him slide behind the wheel of a dark Mercedes. "He reminds me so much of the Dr. Brooks in the manuscript."

"Me too. I guess genetics are sometimes powerful."

I'd started to replace the picture in the envelope when I felt something else inside. I reached in and pulled out a coin.

"That looks like the coin your mom and you wore."

I turned the coin over and over in my hand. "It has the same nicks and rough edges." The last time I'd seen my coin, it was floating toward ocean silt next to the wreck. There was no way it could be the same one.

"Why would he give that to you?"

"I don't know." I smoothed my finger over familiar ridges. "I wonder where he got this one."

"You left yours behind at the *Oceanus*, right?"

"I did."

"How many coins are there like that in the world?"

"There can't be many."

"Are you going to keep it?"

I'd given mine back to the ocean. And now here it was again. "Yes, I suppose."

He took my hand. "Come with me to Florida. We don't have to make it formal. We can keep it casual, but I hate the idea of leaving you."

The coin felt warm in my hand. "If I ever get to be an anchor . . ."

"You won't." He pulled me into his arms and kissed me.

I kissed him back, falling into scents of sea and sun. I didn't know what life with Nathan would bring, but I wanted to find out. For the first time in a long time, I was home.

EPILOGUE

GERTRUDE

Friday, May 1, 1942
The lost pages

I dressed carefully in a skirt and blouse that one of the ladies in the Norfolk hospital had donated to me. I still had my oilcloth sack containing Sigrid's papers, the book from Chief Mate Riggs, my gems, and the coin. And of course, my son was with me now. The baby was perfect, and though he'd been made in a shattering moment of violence, he was all mine. Somehow the two of us would find our way in this country.

A knock on the door, and I looked up to see Dr. Brooks. He looked as he always did, unruffled and perfectly at ease. "Gertrude, it's good to see you up."

I held my breath. I hadn't seen him since I'd been transferred to the hospital. "Dr. Brooks."

"I won't stay long. Just wanted to see how you're faring. How's the baby?"

"Very well."

"What did you name him?"

"Eric. After my uncle."

"Excellent name. I'm certain you two will be just fine. You're a survivor."

I'd never seen myself as strong, but that would have to change.

"Did Sigrid return to Austria? It's very dangerous there now."

"All I can say is that she's traveling." He met my gaze. "She'll be fine. She's also a survivor."

"And William?"

"There was an accident on the ship as he was fleeing. He fell and broke his neck. Unfortunately, he died."

I pictured him bleeding out. Had that loss of blood caused him to fall?

As if reading my thoughts, Dr. Brooks said, "He got into a fight with another man at one of the lifeboats. He stumbled back. Tragically, he landed very hard."

"Did you see him die?"

"I did." He moved to a stack of cards on the table. Many of the sailors of the USS *Roper*, which had rescued us, had sent notes. There were also flowers from the DuPonts. "He's in the past now."

It all sounded good. But questions lingered. "I saw you and Sigrid on the deck of the *Oceanus*."

"I suppose you did. But that doesn't matter now. As I said, she's traveling across the Atlantic." He faced me. "I also received word that Alfred Gruber was killed four days ago. A boating accident on the Danube River. Took days to recover his body."

Fear and relief collided. Could Alfred really be dead? "How do you know that?"

He looked amused. "I still have many contacts. I put out feelers and heard about the tragedy."

"I never mentioned his name."

"Sigrid did."

My knees became so weak I sat on the edge of my bed. "You're certain of all this?"

"Very."

I suspected if I pressed for more details, he'd be polite and charming and, in the end, tell me nothing. "Thank you."

"Of course. Happy to help." Determined footsteps sounded in the hallway. "That would be Mr. Riggs. He's been worried about you."

"Me?"

"You seem to have that kind of effect, I think. Good luck to you, Gertrude."

I reached for the pouch and handed him Sigrid's identity papers. "I'll choose a new name."

He nodded but didn't accept the papers. "You keep them."

"Can you suggest a name that sounds as if it belongs in the United States?"

"I like the name Margaret."

It sounded different from all the other identities I'd used in the last year. "I like it."

"Good luck, Margaret."

He was gone before I could say another word, and seconds later, Mr. Riggs entered the room with a small bouquet of flowers that looked as if he'd picked them from the garden outside my hospital window.

ABOUT THE AUTHOR

Photo © 2017 Studio FBJ

A Southerner by birth, Mary Ellen Taylor has a love for her home state of Virginia that is evident in her contemporary women's fiction. When she's not writing, she spends time baking, hiking, and cycling.